Richard Whately Cooke-Taylor

The Factory System

and the factory acts

Richard Whately Cooke-Taylor

The Factory System
and the factory acts

ISBN/EAN: 9783337396800

Printed in Europe, USA, Canada, Australia, Japan

Cover: Foto ©Andreas Hilbeck / pixelio.de

More available books at **www.hansebooks.com**

THE

FACTORY SYSTEM

AND

THE FACTORY ACTS

BY

R. W. COOKE-TAYLOR, F.S.S.; F.R. HIST. S.

H.M. INSPECTOR OF FACTORIES

AUTHOR OF "INTRODUCTION TO A HISTORY OF THE FACTORY
SYSTEM;" "THE MODERN FACTORY SYSTEM"

Methuen & Co.

36, ESSEX STREET, STRAND, LONDON

1894

PREFACE

HALF-A-CENTURY ago the Factory System meant to the minds of most people a new and portentous phenomenon in industry against which unusual precautions had to be taken lest it should issue in a degenerated race of operative labourers; Factory Acts meant the partial and peculiar body of laws specially devised to avert this catastrophe. At the present day both these significations are completely obsolete. So far from the Factory System being regarded now as likely to degenerate labourers, it is that persistently recommended by some of the best friends of labour as a happy means of escape from other modes of industry; and the Factory Acts are so little partial in their operation, that it is difficult for anyone, not an expert, to say what is, and what is not (within the compass of productive industry) excluded from their wide-spreading influence. These great changes seem to require some explanation. The fundamental explanation resides, of course, in

> " The age and body of the time
> Its form and pressure : "

which have welded out those malleable materials into this new mass; but a popular statement of how it all has come about, and to what extent actually proceeded, should not be out of place either in view of the manifold interests concerned. This is the purpose of the following pages.

CONTENTS

CHAPTER I.

THE FACTORY SYSTEM

CHAPTER II.

THE FACTORY CONTROVERSY

CHAPTER III.

THE FACTORY ACTS

(1802 TO 1833)

CHAPTER I.

THE FACTORY SYSTEM.

FACTORY—ANCIENT FACTORIES—EARLY ENGLISH FACTORIES —THE DOMESTIC SYSTEM—SPINNING MACHINERY—THE FIRST MODERN FACTORY.

FACTORY.—The word Factory is one that has altered much in meaning, and is still in process of alteration. Its early signification was that of a trading establishment; usually in a distant country; with which were associated in idea the settlements and surroundings appertaining, and it is primarily defined in this sense even yet in most dictionaries and works on industrial technology. But a quite different signification came to be attached to it later. In this new one it implied a place of *production* not *sale*; an establishment where something was made, or manufactured, and—more specially—made or manufactured for profit, and (commonly) on a large scale; which is also its legal meaning and that with which we have here to deal.

At what time precisely this transformation occurred is uncertain. Dr. Aikin, in a *History of Manchester*, published in 1793, uses the words "mill" and "factory" indiscriminately; Mr. Baines, in his well-known *History of the Cotton Manufacture*, refers—as late as 1835—to the use of the latter term in its present sense as still a modern innovation; Ure's *Dictionary of Arts and Manufactures* does not possess

B

any article on the word; in Dod's *Dictionary of Manu-factures, etc.* (1876) no allusion to an altered meaning is made, and in the last edition (1880) of McCulloch's *Commercial Dictionary* it is merely described as an abbreviation of *Manufactory*. The nearest approach to a definite date that the present writer has been able to find is in French's *Life and Times of Samuel Crompton* (Manchester, 1862), where it is stated that in the year 1792, "the word 'factory' occurs *almost for the first time* in the rate-books of the township" (Bolton)—a sufficiently unsatisfactory one it must be allowed.[1]

What is at all events certain is, that at the commencement of the present century, namely as early as 1802, this term was interpreted in a modern sense by the English legislature. In that year the first Factory Act (42 Geo. III., c. 73) was passed; being entitled "An Act for the Preservation of the Health and Morals of Apprentices employed in Cotton and other Mills, and in Cotton and other Factories;" where the words *mill* and *factory* are used as complementary or exchangeable terms, but are nowhere defined, while the older signification of the latter is obviously abandoned. In a succeeding statute (3 & 4 Will. IV., c. 103); in which the area of restrictive legislation was considerably enlarged; they are again found coupled together, descriptive of places where certain productive operations are performed, and still with no separate meanings attached to them; and it was not in fine until a much later one (7 & 8 Vic., c. 15) that this deficiency was at length made good and the title "factory"

---

[1] For an extended analysis of the terms Factory, Factory System, Mill, Manufacture, etc., see my *Introduction to a History of The Factory System*; Chap. I. (R. Bentley and Son, 1886).

for the first time fixed by law. The seventy-third section of the last named Act recites as follows :—"the word 'factory' . . . shall be taken to mean all buildings and premises situated within any part of the United Kingdom of Great Britain and Ireland wherein or within the close or curtilage of which steam, water, or any other mechanical power shall be used to move or work any machinery employed in preparing, manufacturing, or finishing, or in any process incidental to the manufacture of cotton, wool, hair, silk, flax, hemp, jute or tow, either separately or mixed together, or mixed with any other material ;" the expression "mill" not being used herein at all, except in connection with "mill gearing," between which and *machinery* some nice distinctions are drawn, which do not concern us now. At this time, then, a factory meant simply any place devoted to spinning or weaving certain fabrics by power, that is it pretty nearly fulfilled what was until quite recently the popular conception of the term.

Scarcely was it settled in that signification however when another new development occurred. The circumstances that led to that new development, and the changes which resulted from it, are of cardinal importance in the history of English factory legislation. They will form the substance of some future chapters. It will suffice to say of them at present, that the general result was greatly to expand the notion of what constituted a factory beyond the characteristics here indicated, to a point that has not even yet been very clearly defined or ascertained.

ANCIENT FACTORIES.—The modern conception of a factory, then, is of a place of production, where labour is congregated and divided within an establishment of definite bounds, sometimes with and sometimes without the aid of exterior motive power. Congregated labour is in this view the very body, as divided labour is the spirit of any factory system not of the wholly automatic kind,[1] and in this con- nection it will be of interest to enquire to what extent fac- tories and the Factory System were known, and were availed of, in ancient times : from which we have so much more to learn on social and industrial matters than we are often willing to allow. Unfortunately, the information that is accessible on these points is extremely scanty. The writers of antiquity —those especially of the Classical age, with whose works we are the most familiar,—had an inveterate scorn of trade and industry, things which they considered as in their nature mean and sordid, and beneath the dignity of history. Aristotle would allow the title citizen only to those who needed not to earn a livelihood by labour (*Politics*, iii. 3), and held the highest industrial duty of a freeman to consist in making proper use of his slaves ; Cicero regarded commerce as tolerable only when carried on upon a large scale and for the benefit of the State ; while the Emperor Augustus actually pronounced the sentence of *death* against the senator Ovinius for having stooped to direct a manufactory.[2]   Such writers have left, accordingly, scarcely any trustworthy accounts of these matters, and we have to seek information upon them among the chance allusions of poets and travellers, in the sacred books of a few old nations, and, more hopefully of late, from the great results of modern antiquarian and anthropological research. With these aids we are able to throw a little light at length

[1] See page 28.

[2] Blanqui's *History of Political Economy in Europe* ; p. 49 (Bell and Sons, 1880).

on this neglected branch of enquiry. We know now for certain that a system of production by means of organised labour not only did exist among very ancient races, but was a device familiar to times so remote as to long precede the dawn of history, to be, in fact, a recognised feature of the early Stone age, in the very infancy of mankind. Sir Charles Lyell (*Antiquity of Man*) was the first writer to direct attention to a "manufactory" of stone implements near Bern in Switzerland; and since then many have been discovered elsewhere, in France, in the United States, and largely of late years in Ireland. In a little book, "Who are the Irish?" (Bogue and Co., 1880) we read, for example, not alone of "primeval diggings," whence flint was procured for industrial purposes in remote ages, but it is added, "vast manufactories were there established." Their existence has become in fact a scientific commonplace. That great factories were a feature of the labour system of ancient Egypt seems likewise certain. How else, to begin with, could all the linen, linen yarn, and other commodities so largely exported have been produced there? Domestic industry might suffice, indeed, for the supply of native needs, but not for such a foreign trade. Moreover, most writers who have expressed themselves on the subject at all have come to that conclusion. Treating of "recent discoveries in Egyptian antiquities" fifty years ago, Dr. Cooke Taylor bears the following testimony; "we find from them," he says, "that the Pharaohs had very large spinning establishments, such as we should in the present day call factories, so that there was not only enough of yarn left for home consumption in the valley of the Nile, but also for exportation" (*Silk, Cotton, and Woollen Manufacture*). Mr. James (*History of The Worsted Manufacture*, p. 5), is no less explicit. "The Egyptians," he says,

" resembled ourselves in this, that they possessed large *weaving* establishments, and supplied with their products foreign lands;" and Mr. Warden (*Linen Trade Ancient and Modern*) offers even a description of such places, to the effect that they were "of a kindred nature to the hand-loom weaving shops, not yet extinct in this country" (Scotland). Lastly, M. Maspéro, one of the latest and most accomplished writers on Egyptian archæology, actually locates. some of them, and even traces their descent to the present day. Writing of the reign of Rameses II. (*i.e.* the fourteenth century B.C.), " Apu," he says, "is celebrated for its spinning mills,"—adding in a note: "The spinning mills of Ekhurem (Apu) still exist; their chief manufacture is a material with little blue and white checks, of which the fellah women make their outer garments" (*Ancient Egypt and Assyria*; p. 74).

The evidence from ancient Babylonia is equally con-vincing, but space will not admit of its being given. It shall suffice to quote the observation of Bonomi (*Nineveh and its Palaces*), that Semiramis is "stated by many writers of antiquity to have founded large weaving establishments along the banks of the Tigris and Euphrates." It must be allowed, however, that this testimony would have been more satisfactory had the author furnished the names of the "many writers" referred to.

Of the great dye-houses, and glass and metal works of Phœnicia; the (possibly) great silk and porcelain factories of ancient China; of the woollen manufactures—so renowned —of Lydia, Phrygia, and Persia; the carpet manufacture of old Carthage, we must not pause to treat;[1] we know, indeed,

[1] This branch of the general subject is dealt with at some length in my *Introduction to a History of the Factory System*; Chap. ii.

extremely little of them, nor is the subject very closely related to our theme. Instead, we may proceed at once to the next great civilization of the ancient world, to Rome in the plenitude of her power. There is no doubt that the Factory System was largely availed of both in ancient Italy and her colonies. Not to go beyond our own experience for an example, we are aware that the Romans established a great woollen factory for clothing their troops at Winchester, and immense potteries in many parts of the country. They had also a " Fabrica," or vast military forge, at Bath. Mr. Scrivenor (*History of the Iron Trade*) gives the following very graphic account of it. "The *fabrica* . . . . . was a large college of armourers, where the varied weapons used by the Roman soldiers were manufactured. The business of this society, and the laws which regulated it, are developed by the Theodosian and Justinian codes. It there appears that towards the commencement of the second century the army smiths were created into companies, each governed by its own president or head, denominated the *primicerius*. That the employment of these bodies was to make arms for the use of the legion or legions to which it was attached, at public forges or shops, called fabricæ, erected in the camps, cities, towns, or military stations; that these arms when forged were to be delivered to an officer appointed to receive them, who laid them up in arsenals for public service; that to prevent any abuse in this important branch of military economy, and to ensure its proper and methodical management, no person was permitted to forge arms for the imperial service unless he were previously admitted a member of the society of the Fabri; that to secure the continuance of their labours after they had been instructed

in the art a certain yearly stipend was settled on each
armourer, who (as well as his offspring) was prohibited from
leaving the employ till he had attained the office of *primicerius*, and, finally, that none might quit his business
without detection, a mark or *stigma* was impressed upon the
arm of each as soon as he became a member of the
Fabrica." But it was not in her colonies only that Rome
availed herself of the Factory System. We learn from
Blanqui[1] that, about this time, Italy itself "was full of
manufactories . . . . where paid workmen shared
with slaves consigned to the rudest tasks, the fatigues,
though not the profits of manufacture : "—from which we
are not to infer, however, that there were free operative
labourers as well as slaves there, but rather many free
overseers, who were requisite to keep the slaves in order,
and who had no closer interest in the work.

These two descriptions of the interior economy of Roman
factories, brought thus together, are very interesting. We
view herein the actual operation of two archaic forms of
the organization of labour which, in one mode or other, have
prevailed from an immensely remote past, and may
quite possibly prevail again. The collegiate or *guild*
system would not, of course, be always necessarily in the
service of the State, nor the servile organization always outside it ; on the contrary, the opposite of this was more commonly the case. But whatever their civil circumstances and
prospects they are types of extraordinary persistency in
the industrial history of mankind, beside which the devices
of to-day directed towards the same end can but be considered immature, experimental, and exceptional, and are
probably temporary at the best.

[1] Page 54.

EARLY ENGLISH FACTORIES.—When the Romans retired from Britain, the great works they had established for the manufacture of textile fabrics, of metal, and of earthenware were closed, and for eight or nine hundred years there were no factories The nearest approaches to such places remaining were the workmen's quarters attached to religious houses, to the castles of the more powerful nobles, and the king. In these, but especially in the first named, whatsoever industry was left other than of the purely isolated kind was to be found, but it was agglomerated not combined industry : the operatives worked under no general labour system, and the produce was for use, not profit. Gradually, after the conquest by the Normans, other developments tended to arise. First, the early Norman sovereigns brought many skilled workmen over in their trains : who were forthwith endowed with certain privileges, settled in selected districts, and given the opportunity of starting on an independent career ; and next, industrious foreigners came over occasionally of their own accord ; whether induced to do so by political or topographical causes, or by the mere love of change and hope of gain. In the reign of Henry I., in particular, a considerable colony of Flemish weavers ; driven across the sea owing to inundations in their own country settled here ; and were established by him chiefly on his northern and western frontiers, where they acted as a protection against the incursions of the Scotch and Welsh. Under the Plantagenets, and while our kings were often abroad, these workmen colonies increased in prosperity, and at about this time we begin to read of " factories of a rude kind " set up in various parts of the country.[1] Such factories were probably

[1] *Romance of Trade ;* p. 103.

fulling mills; and it is in connection with one of them that Manchester makes a first appearance in industrial history with "a fulling mill on the banks of the Irt" (1301); Halifax and Bradford (in Yorkshire) being each noted as in possession of another at about the same period. In the neighbourhood of these, other buildings would often gather in time, where the cloth—still spun and woven at home—might be dyed, and subjected to other processes, or where possibly all processes of manufacture might occasionally be . accumulated in a single establishment; and in such a one, accommodating a congeries of free workmen in the service of a capitalist employer, we have the germ of the modern Factory System.

A great advance was made in the reign of Edward III. Edward had married a Flemish princess, Philippa of Hainault, and it is to that union—indeed to the queen's own personal interest and efforts it is said—that England owes the re-establishment of her woollen manufacture on a large scale.[1] Thenceforth progress was uninterrupted, uninterrupted even by those terrible scourges the Black Death, and Wars of the Roses; or, at the worst, only temporarily interrupted to start afresh with redoubled vigour. By the time the Tudors were firmly seated on the throne undoubted evidence is found of the existence of large textile factories, not inconsiderable even in comparison with many of the present day. The most notable (in the reign of Henry VII.) was that of John Winchcombe, Wynchcomb, or Whitcomb, commonly called "Jack of Newbury," but, whose real name was John Smallwood—Winchcombe being the Gloucestershire village whence he

---

[1] The story is told with much quaintness of detail by Fuller ; *Church History*, Book iii.

originated, and Newbury the town in Berkshire where his works were situate. Fuller writes of him (*Worthies of England*), "He was the most considerable clothier without fancy and fiction England ever beheld. . . . His looms were his lands, whereof he kept one hundred in his house, each managed by a man and a boy," . . . . a house that would "now make sixteen clothiers' houses, whose wealth would amount to six hundred of their estates." From another account we gain a still more imposing idea of this establishment, namely from Thomas Deloney's metrical romance "Jack of Newbury," published in London in 1596.[1] We read in it of *two hundred looms within one room*, of "one hundred carders," "two hundred spinners," one hundred and fifty children employed as wool pickers ; fifty shearers, eighty "rowers," forty dyers, and twenty fullers ; in all over one thousand persons occupied in manufacture ! This is a very large number for even a modern woollen factory of the most extensive kind. The names of three other factory masters belonging to this era have come down to history, Cuthbert of Kendal, Hodgkins of Halifax, and Martin Brian, or Byron, of Manchester. "Each of these," says Anderson (*History of Commerce*, vol. ii.), "kept a great number of servants at work—carders, spinners, weavers, dyers, shearers, etc."; and there were no doubt others whose names have not been preserved. About the same time metal factories began to be established also, principally for the manufacture of iron. Iron and iron products had been little made in England from the departure of the Romans till the reign of Edward III., when some evidence of a native manufacture is given in an Act of

[1] Quoted at some length in *The Modern Factory System* ; p. 50 (Kegan, Paul and Co., 1891).

Parliament, passed in 1354, forbidding their export; while over a hundred years later (1483) another Act, prohibiting the importation of a great variety of metal goods, seems to show that this industry had spread. But by that time the great Sussex iron manufacture had arisen. Mr. Smiles' *Industrial Biography* (chap. ii.) gives a graphic and very interesting account of this industry: and how considerable it really was one may further learn from the statement of Simon Sturtevant, a German metallurgist who (in his *Treatise De Metallica*) estimated the number of iron mills in England and Wales in 1612 at eight hundred, of which, he says, "there are foure hundred milnes in Surry, Kent, and Sussex alone." Wood was the fuel exclusively used; the establishments were owned by private capitalists; and the organization of labour was of the nature of the modern factory system.

The material prosperity thus indicated continued to grow under the Stuarts, and throughout the civil wars, in spite of the political complications of the time; and it received a powerful stimulus from successive immigrations of Protestant refugees, driven out of the Netherlands and France respectively by the infatuated policy of the rulers of those countries. These immigrants introduced a great variety of new industries, which rapidly took root. A further stimulus to enterprise was the founding of British colonies, which now began on a pretty extensive scale. Hitherto English manufacturers had had to depend on a home demand mostly; or their products were sold to a few foreign merchants at local fairs; henceforth there were illimitable possibilities before them. The Factory System continued to spread under such circumstances, and great efforts were made to cope with the increased opportunites thus originated. Sir George Nicholls (*History of The English Poor Law*) mentions that in the reign of William III. several of the clothiers of Norwich "employed as many as five hundred hands;" which he evidently thought an unprecedented number. The industrial genius of the country, in short, was thoroughly aroused, and was preparing for the further great changes in store.

THE DOMESTIC SYSTEM.—But in the meanwhile another mode of industry had taken root in our congenial soil, rivalling for a while this nascent Factory System, sometimes even successfully. It has come to be called the Domestic System: by which is meant not merely family labour for purposes of domestic utility, nor what is now designated "home work," but an organized system of production for sale and profit, responding to no impulse but its own, and dominated by no other productive organization. Family industry may exist, of course, in every industrious home circle; and when this is hired out on the same economic basis as factory labour will correspond economically with it; but an independent manufacture, spontaneously developed, untrammelled by tradition, custom, or law; producing commodities for an open market; this is by no means the same thing.

The origin of the Domestic System dates in England from the decay of the municipal and feudal constitutions of society, the first the legacy of the Roman, the second of Norman dominion. It is not implied in this statement that either of those systems was extinct when it had its rise; they are not extinct yet; what is meant is, that as they ceased to closely overshadow the whole national life, certain movements began below the surface of society, which by degrees made themselves manifest above, resulting in changed currents of thought and action among the people. The present was one of these. It was, like the early factory system, much indebted to constant immigrations of foreigners, who were in turn much indebted to the peculiar circumstances and institutions of this country for the welcome they received. The bye-laws of guilds, corporations, and trade fraternities of various kinds ; which had succeeded the imperial organizations of ancient Rome; had become at length so oppressive and pernicious as to draw from Lord Bacon their denunciation as' " fraternities in evil," and already in Henry VII.'s reign an Act of Parliament (19 Henry VII.) had been passed restraining them from promulgating further rules; while the disuse of walled towns, proceeding conterminously, gave industry an opportunity of spreading out into the country that it had not enjoyed before. Foreign artizans ; and their English brethren ; " began therefore to settle in such towns less than heretofore, and more in their vicinities, or even to seek voluntarily, as they had formerly been compelled to accept (p. 9) for their locations wild and unfrequented districts, where a patch of land could be had for the asking (or without it), and the means of livelihood thus to some extent secured."[1] The cutlery trade of Sheffield, the woollen trade of Yorkshire, the miscellaneous trades of Birmingham, and the great cotton trade of Lancashire, were founded under such conditions. All of these were handicraft industries at first and followed the method of domestic labour. The unit was the family; not the corporate society, whether self-composed or superimposed. The labour supplied was free; that is civilly free; it was not slave labour. The master manufacturer was also

[1] *The Modern Factory System ; p. 57.*

workman ; he was the owner of his instruments of production, the arbiter of his own industrial life. Occasionally
the circle would be widened by the admission of strangers ;
but they were admitted as members of the household—
domestic workers with the rest. Very divergent opinions
have been expressed respecting the social advantages of this
mode of industry. On the one hand it has been lauded to
the skies as the very perfection of industrial arrangement ;
on the other very severely criticised by very capable
observers.[1] One hundred—or even fifty—years ago there
seemed an almost unanimous opinion in its favour, and
against the Factory System : on the sentimental side at least ;
to-day the tide of opinion is ebbing in precisely the opposite
direction, and the cry is all to shut up home industries and
force the workers into factories. Into this controversy we
cannot enter here, it will be more to the purpose to illustrate
the actual working of this Domestic System, to which end
two typical descriptions of it will be cited, one from textile
manufacture ; in which beyond all others the points of contrast with the factory system are usually held to be best
defined ; the other from the cutlery industry, next to textile
perhaps the most famous of British manufactures. Mr.
William Radcliffe,[2] describing his own experiences of
a manufacturing district of Lancashire just before the coming
change, expresses himself on this subject as follows :—" In the
year 1770 the land in our township was occupied by
between fifty to sixty farmers ; rents to the best of my
recollection did not exceed ten shillings per statute acre ;
and out of these fifty or sixty farmers there were only six or

---

[1] See in particular the caustic remarks of Mr. Carroll D. Wright :
Report of The Factory System of the United States (Washington, 1884).
[2] *Origin of Power Loom Weaving;* pp. 59, 60 (Stockport, 1828).

seven who raised their rents directly from the produce of
their farms ; all the rest got their rents partly in some branch
of trade, such as spinning or weaving woollen, linen, or cotton.
The cottagers were employed entirely in this manner except
for a few weeks in the harvest. Being one of these cottagers,
and intimately acquainted with all the rest, as well as every
farmer, I am better able to relate particularly how the change
from the old system of hand labour to the new one of
machinery operated in raising the price of land. Cottage
rents at that time, with a convenient loom shop and a small
garden attached, were from one and a half to two guineas
per annum. The father of a family would earn from eight
shillings to half-a-guinea at his loom ; and his sons, if he
had one, two, or three alongside of him, six or eight shillings
per week ; but the great sheet anchor of all cottages and
small farms was the labour attached to the hand-wheel ; and
when it is considered that it required six or eight hands to
prepare and spin yarn of any of the three materials I have
mentioned, sufficient for the consumption of one weaver,
this shows clearly the inexhaustible source there was for
labour for every person from the age of seven to eighty
years (who retained their sight and could move their hands),
to earn their bread, say from one to three shillings per week,
without going to the parish." In this extract we notice the
shadow of one of the great changes that was approaching,
the employment namely of more efficient labour-saving
machinery. In the next to be made, we shall perceive the
development of a still more fundamental one, the increasingly
dominant position accorded to realised wealth as an agent
in production.

Sheffield had been famous for its cutlery as early at all
events as the time of Chaucer (who alludes to it), but

previous to the commencement of last century had "discovered in the manufacture"—says Dr. Aikin[1]— "more of industry than ingenuity." The workmen "dared not exert their abilities in labour for fear of being overstocked with goods . . . their trade was inconsiderable, confined, and precarious." But, "in 1751, the river Don was made navigable to within three miles of the town . . . . a stage waggon was set up . . . . master manufacturers began to visit London in search of orders with success, and several factors established a correspondence with various parts of the Continent." The proceedings of these *factors* were noteworthy. "The common arrangement between masters and workmen during the early and comparatively unfluctuating periods of the cutlery manufacture was, that the former found shop-room, tools, every description of materials, and, of course, such capital as was necessary to carry on the business, paying the latter for work done generally by the piece. During this state of things almost all dealings in the raw material and finished articles were conducted between the master manufacturer and those who visited the town for the purpose of buying his wares, or with the merchant, to whom consignment was made for exportation. Later years, however, witnessed the springing up . of a large and influential class of monied or speculative individuals, who, under the denomination of factors, took advantage of the fluctuation of the markets to collect goods and merchandise at a cheap rate, never purchasing at the regular prices when they could avoid it. These enterprising dealers presently obtained large influence in the foreign markets, and, catching the full spirit of modern competition,

[1] *A Description of the Country from Thirty to Forty Miles round Manchester* (1795).

they soon distanced the tradesmen of the old school." "The latter, indeed "—he continues—" frequently became, through necessity, first satellites, and then victims to the new system." This is a very interesting description of a form of domestic industry differing in several particulars from that before mentioned, as well as a concise summary of results flowing from the more fundamental economic influence last alluded to, which was the origin of many others hereafter to be named. At present, our attention is most required to the particular phase of change which first attracted the attention of the legislature, the development and application, namely, of labour-saving machinery in production.

SPINNING MACHINERY.—In the description of the domestic industry of Lancashire just quoted, it was shown how it required in Radcliffe's time "six or eight hands to prepare and spin yarn . . . . sufficient for the consumption of one weaver." So long as English manufacture was principally for the home trade this disproportion was comparatively unimportant, producers could adapt themselves without much difficulty to the wants of consumers, or if they failed to do so the latter must wait. The disproportion itself was to the advantage of spinners, who were a very deserving class of the community, and whose extra opportunities in this direction enabled them to bear with some success the decreasing gains from agriculture. But when England became a great Colonial power, distancing all competitors in commerce and commercial enterprise, such was the case no longer. The demand for her fabrics (and all other products of manufacture) became overwhelming, and every known expedient was resorted to for increasing them. It was under these circumstances that certain ingenious men set themselves the task of trying if yarn (the demand for which we have seen was especially great) might not be spun by machinery. The movement seems to have attained importance first in Birmingham; where Lewis Paul and John Wyatt took out a joint patent for this purpose in 1738,[1] and where it is quite possible the process of rolling metal wire, which might be seen in operation any day in the neighbourhood, furnished them with the first hint. After several unsuccessful endeavours to make their invention profitable they abandoned it. Nevertheless, the enterprise was not unfruitful. The idea spread. In 1761 the Society of Arts is found offering prizes of £50 and £25 respectively for the best and second best "inventions of a machine that will spin six threads of wool, flax, hemp, or cotton at one time, and that will require but one person to work and attend it;" and the records of that Society show that several machines were submitted in response to this appeal, though apparently without result. But in the meanwhile a poor hand-loom weaver of Blackburn, James Hargreaves, had—quite independently it would seem—devised an instrument of just this kind for his own use, and was applying it with success. And just about the same time another poor workman, one Thomas Highs, or Hayes, of Leigh, Lancashire, had, in conjunction with a local clock-maker, produced still another, which came under the notice of a Bolton barber, one Richard Arkwright; with important consequences, as we shall see; while eventually, Samuel Crompton, likewise of Bolton, by uniting the

---

[1] John Kay, of Bury, had taken out a patent for spinning worsted before this, namely, in 1730; and there is mention of a much earlier one than either (1678), in the joint names of Richard Dereham and Richard Haines, of which, however, nothing further is known.

principles of these two in one (called on that account
" The Mule ") brought spinning appliances to so
high a degree of excellence that the old type of
labour became obsolete and an entirely new era was inaugurated in this department of manufacture.   How, presently, these cardinal inventions were supplemented by
others, equally important to the end in view ; and how,
ultimately, the Rev. Mr. Cartwright, a clergyman of the
Church of England, succeeded in constructing a mechanical
loom which accomplished for weaving what had,been already
done for spinning would occupy more space to tell than we
have at command now ; as likewise it would to record other
great inventions of this time applicable to other branches of
industry, and the application to all of them at length of a
completely new motor (steam) destined to start them on a
career of unexampled prosperity.   It will answer our
purpose best to take this prodigious advance in textile
manufacture as a type of what was going on throughout all
industry, and to concentrate attention for the present on that.

THE FIRST FACTORY.—It has been generally assumed
that with the perfecting of the mechanical appliances for
spinning, and the application to them of external motive
power, the modern Factory System came into existence,
and that this was largely the work of Richard Arkwright.
There is this much truth in the belief, that it was probably
the genius of Arkwright which first saw clearly the full
possibilities inherent in the new machinery, and it was undoubtedly his untiring energy and ability that brought them
earliest to a full fruition.   But he was not the inventor of the
spinning machinery (the " water frame ") with which his name
is most closely associated, nor was he by any means the first

to apply mechanical power successfully in textile manufacture. Arkwright's first regular factory (at Nottingham) was driven by horse-power; and the idea of the machinery employed there was borrowed (or purloined) from Highs. It was not until 1770 that he occupied a small water mill (at Wirksworth, in Derbyshire), nor until the year after that he formed his celebrated partnership with Need and Strutt of Derby, which resulted in the building of the well-known Cromford works. Now, fully half a century before this time, a textile factory, answering in every respect to even the most modern definition of that term, had been in full operation in England. Further, it was not in connection with any of those staples (wool, flax, or cotton) upon which the inventors of spinning machinery had hitherto exercised their ingenuity that it had its origin, but with quite another fibre. It was a silk mill; begun in Derby in 1715, and at work there shortly afterwards. The story of its establishment forms one of the strangest and most romantic episodes of industrial history, rich as that history has ever been in such.

It is known that the process of "throwing" silk (a process analogous to, but not the same as spinning) was practised in England as early as 1562, when the *throwsters* of London were united into a fellowship, to be afterwards incorporated by Charter in 1629. Half a century later we learn that "the said Company of silk throwsters employs above forty thousand men, women and children" (13 & 14 Chas. II., c. 15); and this astonishing prosperity seems to have ·continued till towards the end of the seventeenth century, at which time unusually large quantities of thrown silk (or "organzine") began to make their appearance on the English market, sent from abroad, and offered at prices much below what this commodity could be produced for here. The supply, it was noticed, came mostly from Italy ; and it was soon rumoured that " something like in appearance to the machinery of a great water-mill (*i.e.* water-driven corn mill) was used to perform the delicate operation of unwinding the cocoons, and that, thus assisted, it was possible for human labour to produce almost any required quantity of organzine."[1] A practical silk throwster, one John Lombe, who had been in business in London, determined to personally investigate the truth of these reports ; he went over to Italy in disguise, and managed to get engaged at one of the factories supplying the mysterious filament. His adventures there were of a truly astonishing kind.[2] He not only found that the above report was true, but managed to obtain drawings of all parts of the machinery, to transmit them home in safety, and eventually to follow them himself. With these in his possession, and in conjunction with his brother, afterwards Sir Thomas Lombe, a factory similar to the Italian one was erected on the banks of the Derwent, which presently produced organzine equal in quantity and quality to all needs. "This amazingly grand structure," as Anderson (*History of Commerce* ; vol. iii., p. 91) calls it, "was propelled by mills which work three capital engines," and contained "twenty-six thousand, five hundred and eighty-six wheels, and ninety-seven thousand, seven hundred and forty-six movements, which work seventy-three thousand, seven hundred and twenty-six yards of organzine silk thread every time the water wheel goes round, being thrice in one minute, and three hundred and eighteen millions, five hundred and four

---

[1] *Introduction to a History of the Factory System* ; p. 358.

[2] The story is told very graphically in Knight's *Old England*, Book vii. ; chap. 2 ; where also a picture of Lombe's factory may be seen.

thousand, nine hundred and sixty yards in one day and night. . . . . One water wheel gives motion to all the other movements, of which any one may be stopped separately without obstructing the rest;" and "one fire engine conveys warm air to every individual part of this vast machine, containing in all its buildings half a quarter of a mile in length." Other details, from a little work of not much pretension *All about Derby*, by Mr. Edward Bradbury (Simpkin and Marshall, 1884), may with advantage be compared with these.

This edifice was almost without doubt the first English factory in the modern sense. It was the first, that is, where the motive power was supplied from outside, where operations of manufacture hitherto performed by human hands, were performed by inanimate machinery thus set in motion, and where independent workpeople, congregated in one building, were occupied in production about this machinery. It was something very different, for instance, from the great textile factories that had preceded it, either here or in more ancient times. Congregated and divided labour was employed in them also, but the operations of manufacture were not performed by machinery, nor was the motive power supplied from outside. The motive power and machinery alike were for the most part embodied in sentient human creatures. It was different again from the early English iron works, in Sussex and elsewhere, to which allusion has been made ; and still more different from the great metal factories and potteries of the period of the Roman occupation. In the former of these water-power was sometimes used also ; to move the great tilt hammers, and for other purposes ; but such establishments were wide open spaces, where the workers were much scattered, never collected altogether in a single building. Water-power may have been employed about the latter likewise,[1] but we have seen from the instance of the *Fabrica* at Bath how different was the organization of labour. In those old times the worker was tied to his work ; by the unequivocal compulsion of law or usage ; as he was, or is, or may be to this day in countries where political despotism prevails, or trades are divided into castes, or occupations are hereditary. But under the modern factory system in this country the contrary of all that was from the first the case. The workers under this system were personally free ; they were bound neither by law nor custom to any particular factory nor kind of manufacture, but at liberty to transfer their labour wheresoever, to whomsover, and as often as they would ; whereby quite different relations were established between them and their employers ; involving quite different considerations, and, at length, formal regulations ; the regulations namely which came to be, and are continuing to be, embodied in our ever-expanding Factory Acts.

[1] Water-driven corn mills were introduced into Britain by the Romans, and there are some symptoms that they were also used about mines.

CHAPTER II.

THE FACTORY CONTROVERSY.

PHILOSOPHY OF THE FACTORY SYSTEM—PHILOSOPHY OF
FACTORY LEGISLATION—THE FIRST REFORMERS—PARISH
APPRENTICES—THE FACTORY AGITATION : ROBERT PEEL
AND ROBERT OWEN—RICHARD OASTLER—LORD ASHLEY—
OTHER) LEADERS — PROGRESS OF THE CONTROVERSY —
SUMMARY.

PHILOSOPHY OF THE FACTORY SYSTEM.—At the conclusion of the last chapter an attempt was made to indicate
certain characteristics of the modern Factory System distinguishing it from others which have preceded, or may
have preceded it in more or less ancient times. That
attempt leads naturally to the question what actually is this
System ?—a more difficult one to answer than might
appear at first sight. The Factory System—says Dr. Ure [1]
—" designates the combined operation of many orders of
workpeople, adult and young, in tending with assiduous skill
a series of productive machines, continually impelled by a
central power." But this definition fails in two directions.
On the one hand it fails by including machinery and a
central motive power among necessary characteristics of the
Factory System, whereas they are only characteristic of the
modern form of it ; and, on the other hand, it fails to in-

[1] *Philosophy of Manufactures ;* pp. 13, 14.

clude, or even to indicate, many classes of works now generally recognised as being within the meaning of this expression. It includes, "such organizations as cotton, flax, silk, and wool mills, and also certain engineering works ;" but it excludes "those in which the mechanisms do not form a connective series, and are not dependent on one prime mover," . . . such as "iron-works, dye-works, soap-works, brass-foundries," etc. "Some authors, indeed" — Dr. Ure continues—"have comprehended under the title *factory* all extensive establishments wherein a number of people co-operate towards a common purpose of art, and would therefore rank breweries, distilleries, as well as the workshops of carpenters, turners, coopers, etc., under the Factory System. But I conceive that this title in its strictest sense involves the idea of a vast automaton, composed of various mechanical and intellectual organs, acting in un-interrupted concert for the production of a common object ; all of them being subordinated to a self-regulating moving force." "If," he concludes, "the marshalling of human beings in systematic order for any technical enterprise, were allowed to constitute a factory, this term might embrace every department of civil and military engineering—a latitude of application quite inadmissible." It is not easy to follow this reasoning. There are few manufacturing establishments where machinery in a "connective series" plays a more important part than in the modern brewery and distillery, and where the proportion of manual to machine labour is distinctly less. Here, if anywhere, it is that the idea of a "vast automaton" is most nearly realized, and that it is possible for the organism to go on performing its productive functions under the impulse of "a self-regulating motive force" with the least human supervision.

Moreover, this definition is certainly too recondite for ordinary use. "An automaton composed of various mechanical and intellectual organs, acting in uninterrupted concert," is a definition of the Factory System which, even if technically correct, would be of little practical usefulness, and the technical correctness of which is extremely doubtful.[1] Nor is there much danger, one would say, that the expressions "factory" and "factory system" should ever be so expanded in meaning as to embrace civil and military engineering. It is surely one of the essentials to the proper conception of either that their purpose is production always; while the eventual purpose of all military labour is of course destruction. Or even in those cases where works of civil and military engineering might be turned to productive use, as in the building of roads and bridges; in so far as these are instruments of production they may be classed as such but not as products of manufacture. They are in reality means of transport.[2] A more recent writer essaying to describe the Factory System under cover of defining the term factory, goes to an opposite extreme. "A factory," writes Mr. Carroll D. Wright (*Report on The Factory System of The United States*, 1884), "is an establishment where several workmen are collected for the purpose of obtaining greater and cheaper conveniences of labour than they could procure individually in their homes; for producing results by their combined efforts which they could not accomplish separately, and for

[1] See p. 3.

[2] That the above was not merely a rhetorical slip of Dr. Ure's is proved by his elaborating the same idea in another work of equal pretension, namely his *Cotton Manufacture of Great Britain* (C. Knight, 1836). "*War*," he there declares "was in reality the staple trade, the sole *factory system* of the ancient world." Vol. I. p. 3.

preventing the loss occasioned by carrying articles from place to place during the several processes necessary to complete their manufacture." Here, it will be noticed, machinery and mechanical moving power are entirely omitted, and attention is fixed on other means of abbreviating and facilitating human labour. And on the whole this is the truer conception, for in ultimate analysis the employment of machinery and exterior motive powers are but particular instances of this same effort to abbreviate labour. Only, in this case, too much stress seems to be laid on the purely *human*, apart from the mechanical element in production, which is so obvious a feature of the modern system. How would it be for instance, one may ask, if Dr. Ure's conception of an automaton factory were *completely* realized, but with the " many orders of workpeople " omitted ; if the machinery had but to be set going to turn out commodities (within certain limits of course) at pleasure ; would not a purely automatic place of production like this be a factory ? Something nearly approaching such a result has already been achieved in certain industries: as in the most modern form of corn-milling; while even in the old fashioned country corn-mill (the true precursor of the modern factory) the whole productive apparatus is often superintended by one man—and he not infrequently locks the door and goes home to dinner leaving the machinery to do its work alone. In the still more alien department of Distribution, again, we have automatons now disposing of goods, and taking payments in return, at our street corners.

The truth is that since the term factory was wrested from its elder meaning, and that new one substituted for it which has been noted, no sufficiently rigid analysis has been applied to the system of production which then assumed its name, and to the circumstances under which it did so. It is confounded with the increased employment of machine labour [1] (an extreme instance of which has just been cited), with mere capitalism—the industrial power vested in accumulated wealth—[2] or it has been fitted to any emergency that the wants of the moment suggested. But increased employment of machinery has affected agriculture just as much as it ever affected manufacture; and the almost limitless power permitted to capital in the hire of labour is but a particular instance of the reign of open competition distinguishing modern times. Both are features of the Industrial Revolution of the last two centuries, which affected the Factory System precisely as it affected other systems of industry, and not necessarily more. Dr. Ure seems to have been led into error by his nearness to these great events, and to have never really understood the organization he was nevertheless at such pains to describe. He took the Factory System for a *new thing*; the truth, of course, being very different. Such a system of labour is a quite usual phenomenon in *any* industrial community, ancient or modern, which has reached a certain stage of economic progress—the stage generally of an export trade or even of a very abounding native population —*the institutions of which permit it.* In other countries, India for example,[3] it never has prevailed, simply because their institutions would not permit it; were, in many instances, directed deliberately against it. Alter

[1] This is the mistake of Marx, Engels, and writers of that school, who seem incapable of distinguishing properly between machine industry and factory labour.

[2] See p. 16.

[3] On the organization of labour in India, see *Industrial Arts of India,*. by Sir George Bidwood; Part I. (Chapman and Hall, 1880).

them ; give capital and competition free scope ; and—the industrial spirit continuing—we hold that it certainly would follow. The exterior features might differ : for it would take upon itself the colour of surrounding things ; its interior economy would certainly vary, in harmony with these, but the thing itself would be there, so long at least as combined labour can produce more cheaply and efficiently than isolated labour can, which has hitherto in human affairs been generally the case.

This error vitiated many of the best intentioned arguments of the early factory reformers and was a stumbling-block in the path of the earlier Factory Acts. It produced uncertainty, and even contradiction, in dealing with the many problems presented to them, and popularised an altogether false notion of their actual sanctions and proper aim. And thus it came about that that most valuable and beneficent body of laws only approached the fulfilment of its mission by a circuitous and partial, instead of, as might have been, in a direct course, that so much still remains to be explained about them, and something even to be explained away.

PHILOSOPHY OF FACTORY LEGISLATION.—For factory legislation is not only a most important concomitant of the modern Factory System, but, regarded from its social side, is perhaps the most important concomitant of all. The interest attaching to mechanical improvements is no doubt great, and increased production of itself a highly desirable thing, yet it is doubtful, after all, if the greatest boon which the modern Factory System has conferred upon mankind resides so much in these material gains as in the revolt against the abuses connected with them which produced the Factory Acts. It is more than possible that when all those contrivances have been superseded by others—as they surely will be—those laws will remain the chief glory of their time. They are likely to do so for several reasons. First, because their value is by no means limited by the conditions under which they came into being, nor indeed by any conditions that can be yet foreseen. Secondly, on account of their remarkable success in a previously untried sphere of legislation ; but thirdly and chiefly, that they embody a great practical protest against the base belief, engendered of modern economic philosophy, that the concerns of human beings can ever be entrusted to motives of pure cupidity without shocking and degrading results. Against that shameful doctrine they set up a legal barrier, weak and partial at first, but gradually growing till it became a powerful instrument, which repeatedly encountered oppression in one of its most insidious forms and snatched from it its prey.

The philosophy of factory legislation is concerned with factories, nevertheless, in an almost exclusively historical category, the connection being to a large extent casual. It may seem strange at first sight to make this assertion, and some further explanation is necessary. The great industrial establishments of antiquity, we must remember, were not called factories ; hence the system of labour belonging to them was not called factory labour, nor the mode in which it was regulated factory regulation. But those places were factories nevertheless ; [1] and any law that was enforced for their conduct amounted in effect to factory law. Now, we know that in Rome, in Egypt, and generally in old times where the labour of production was performed by slaves, there were very strict laws for their protection ; as where this was

[1] See page 3.

not the case there were trade customs, or feudal or tribal obligations, typifying in such instances a like thing. But when the new producing establishments came into being and assumed the title factory slaves were not employed, nor therefore were such laws in operation, the guild organizations had died out, and the obligations of feudality become effete. [All citizens were supposed free and equal, while at the same time competition was allowed its utmost range, and great accumulations of capital were being formed by individuals, and used without question in the affairs of industry. This, too, was the epoch of the great mechanical inventions. Such circumstances threw obviously immense power into the hands of wealthy and enterprising men over their less wealthy and enterprising fellow-men.] They acquired the first command of those new and greatly efficient instruments of production, and could then practically (till a remedy was found) dictate terms to the less efficient human instruments.] " The various processes (of manufacture) which had heretofore been chiefly performed by hand under the master's own roof, began now to be executed in public *mills*, in which, in one or more buildings, as the case happened, the operatives worked up the materials belonging to the manufacturers under the supervision of overseers appointed by the employer."[1] Neither was this movement confined, of course, to such places ; it necessarily penetrated wherever labour could be employed for any productive purpose on the same footing. A description was lately quoted (p. 17) of what occurred coincidently in the cutlery manufacture ; where the industry was, and still is, to a large extent domestic and manual ; and the same process occurred, as is well known, in the stocking industry, the lace

[1] *Conflicts of Capital and Labour* ; p. 84.

industry, and others, and continues doing so to our own day ; it merely attained its evil notoriety first in them. The true philosophy of factory legislation becomes thus apparent, and its connection in a historical category only with any particular class of places denominated at any particular time factories. Its real nature is resolved into a protest against a method of economy which subordinated immediate human interests to the blind discretion of employers filled with the most pitiless of all passions, the pursuit of gain, that passion manifesting itself in unusually atrocious forms under the novel stimulus of the Factory System.

THE FIRST REFORMERS.—The new system of production had been upwards of half a century in operation before public attention was directed to it in any considerable degree. During that time it had spread from its first home in Derby over a wide area, principally in the midland counties, where it had been mostly confined to the manufacture of metal products and silk. But towards the end of this period the great inventions for the treatment of wool and cotton fibre (referred to in the last chapter) had been coming into use, and in 1787 were likewise applied to flax.[1] Almost immediately complaints began to be heard of abuses connected with factories, especially the cotton factories of Lancashire, and in 1795 a Committee was appointed at Manchester to report upon the whole subject. Before this Committee, on the 25th of January 1796, Dr. Perceval, an eminent local physician, brought up the following resolutions for approval, which were subsequently adopted. " 1st. It appears that the children, and others who work in the large cotton factories, are peculiarly disposed to be affected by the contagion of

[1] *Modern Factory System* : p. 72.

D

fever, and that when the infection is received it is rapidly propagated, not only amongst those who are crowded together in the same apartments, but in the families and neighbourhoods to which they belong. 2nd. The large factories are generally injurious to the constitutions of those employed in them, even when no particular diseases prevail, from the close confinement which is enjoined, from the debilitating effects of hot or impure air, and from the want of active exercises, which nature points out as essential in childhood and youth to invigorate the system, and to fit our species for the duties of mankind. 3rd. The untimely labour of the night, and the protracted labour of the day, with respect to children, not only tends to diminish future expectations as to the general term of life and industry by impairing the strength and destroying the vital stamina of the rising generation, but it too often gives encouragement to idleness, extravagance, and profligacy of the parents, who, contrary to the order of nature, subsist by the oppression of their offspring. 4th. It appears that the children employed in factories are generally debarred from all opportunities of education, and from moral or religious instruction. 5th. From the excellent regulations which subsist in several cotton factories, it appears that many of these evils may, in a considerable degree, be obviated ; and we are therefore warranted by experience, and are assured that we shall have the support of the liberal proprietors of these factories, in proposing an application for parliamentary aid (if other methods appear not likely to effect the purpose) to establish a general system of laws for the wise, humane, and equal government of all such works."

In the last paragraph of these justly celebrated resolutions the definite suggestion is made of a *code* of factory legislation, for the "equal government of all such works." In those words the principle of the earlier Factory Acts is stated in its simplicity and entirety. The proposal is for the amelioration of what was then assumed to be a novel evil, by means of legislative action specially adapted to that end. It did not occur to these early reformers to enquire too curiously into the origin and area of such evils ; it was enough for them that they existed in an offensive and dangerous form within the particular area in question. It is to be noted, too, that mention is made of several cotton factories wherein " excellent regulations subsist," a proof that factory reformers of the most genuine type, *i.e.* spontaneous reformers who were at the same time factory masters, flourished before even the earliest suggestion of anything of this kind. In this purely local connection then with evils assumed to be peculiar to a particular mode of dealing with a single staple of manufacture did that controversy originate, from which were to be deduced in time those wider generalizations and humaner conceptions of public duty that have done, and are doing, so much to ameliorate the modern worker's lot.

PARISH APPRENTICES.—One of the worst abuses of the Factory System in its early years arose in connection with the method of obtaining workers for the mills, especially juvenile workers. This furnished also the opportunity for a decisive step.

The first factories were water-mills ; often of necessity situated in remote places : situated in fact wherever power from running water could the most readily be obtained. To these places operatives had to be brought, occasionally from great distances and at considerable expense, and that this

outlay might the more readily be recouped it was usual to
bind them under a system of apprenticeship to serve for a
term of years. "The moral results of this practice were
sometimes very shocking. Removed from the constraint of
publicity, and, to a considerable extent even, of the common
law, the masters often treated those helpless people with
horrible inhumanity."[1] The system attained its maximum
degree of wickedness when children were sent from distant
country workhouses into the factory districts, nominally to be
taught a trade, but really to be disposed of at the discretion of
the employer. "Under the operation of the factory apprentice
system," writes "Alfred,"[2] "parish apprentices were sent
without remorse or enquiry, to be *used up* as the cheapest
raw material in the market;" and he thus describes the
ordinary procedure. "The mill-owners communicated with
the overseer of the poor, and when the demand and supply
had been arranged to the satisfaction of both the contracting
parties, a day was fixed for the examination of the little
children, to be inspected by the mill-owner or his agent.
Traffickers contracted with the overseers for removing their
juvenile victims to Manchester, or other towns. On their
arrival, if not previously assigned, they were deposited in dark
cellars, where the merchant dealing in them brought his
customers,"—and where—"the mill-owners, by the light of
lanterns being able to examine the children, their limbs and
stature having undergone the necessary scrutiny, the bargain
was struck, and these poor innocents were conveyed to the
mills." What followed is related by another writer. "The
custom," says Mr. Fielden (*Curse of the Factory System* ; p.
10), "was for the master to clothe his apprentices and to feed

[1] *The Modern Factory System* ; p. 87.
[2] *History of the Factory Movement*, by "Alfred" ; vol. i. ; chap 2.

and lodge them in an apprentice house near the factory ; overseers were appointed to see to the works, whose interest it was to work the children to the utmost, because their pay was in proportion to the quantity of work they could extract. Cruelty was, of course, the consequence ; and there is abundance of evidence on record, and preserved in the recollections of some who still live, to show that in many of the manufacturing districts, but particularly, I am afraid, in the guilty county (Lancashire) to which I belong, cruelties the most heart-rending were practised upon the unoffending and friendless creatures who were thus consigned to the charge of master manufacturers ; that they were harassed to the brink of death by excess of labour, that they were flogged, fettered, and tortured in the most exquisite refinement of cruelty ; that they were in many cases starved to the bone while flogged to their work, and that even in some instances they were driven to commit suicide to evade the cruelties of a world in which, though born to it so recently, their happiest moments had been passed in the garb and coercion of a workhouse." A most shocking revelation of this condition of things, written from personal experience, is contained in the well authenticated narrative of Robert Blincoe ; who was sent at the age of seven years from the St. Pancras workhouse to serve at a cotton mill near Nottingham, whence he was transferred to others afterwards. The statements in this record are simply *appalling*; and would be absolutely incredible were they not fully borne out by evidence from other sources. We will not burden these pages with them,[1] substituting instead some particulars from one of those cotton factories wherein " excellent regulations

[1] They are given in some detail in *Modern Factory System* ; pp. 189, 98.

prevailed," from what was, indeed, by pretty general consent reckoned the model factory of the time. This was the establishment at New Lanark in Scotland owned by Mr. David Dale, and the subject of a high encomium in the *Annual Register* for 1792. "Already in 1784" writes Mr. R. D. Owen (*Threading my Way*—p. 13 *et sub*), "the population of New Lanark was upwards of 1700, of whom several hundreds were orphan children; it was, I believe, the largest cotton-spinning establishment at that time in Great Britain, employing about a thousand workpeople." Just at the end of the century it passed into the hands of the celebrated Robert Owen; who gives some details of what he found there.[1] There were about five hundred children employed at that time, who "were received as early as six years old, the pauper authorities declining to send them at any later age." "It was found, or thought, necessary that these little creatures should work with the other people *from six in the morning till seven in the evening;* and it was only after this task was over that instruction began. The inevitable results followed. The poor children hated their slavery; many absconded: some were stunted and even dwarfed in stature; at thirteen or fifteen years old, when their apprenticeship expired, they commonly went off to Glasgow and Edinburgh, with no natural guardians, ignorant of the world beyond their village, and altogether admirably trained for swelling the mass of vice and misery in the towns." . . . . . "The condition of the families who had immigrated to the village was also very lamentable.

---

[1] The above statements are taken at second-hand from Mr. W. L. Sargant's book, *Robert Owen and his Social Philosophy* (Smith and Elder, 1860); but Mr. Sargant explains in a note to p. 32 that they are in turn copied verbatim from Owen's *Autobiography*, I. xxvi. 57, 61, 62, 276.

The people lived almost without control, in habits of vice, idleness, poverty, debt, and destitution . . . . Thieving was general . . . . Yet (says Owen) the workpeople were systematically opposed to every change which I proposed, and did whatever they could to frustrate my object." If such was the condition of things in a model factory and under the best of masters one may imagine what it must have been under others less scrupulous.

THE FACTORY AGITATION : ROBERT PEEL AND ROBERT OWEN.—To the honour of his class it was a master manufacturer, the first Sir Robert Peel, who earliest brought this matter effectively under the notice of Parliament. The measure of relief that he proposed was a small one ; as we' shall see more fully hereafter ; but it was a step in progress, and it definitely inaugurated the factory controversy in the legislature. In the meanwhile a popular agitation had been set in motion also, having its origin in those five resolutions passed at Manchester (p. 33), and gradually spreading, and increasing in volume as it spread, till it too became a powerful motive force. Among names which come earliest before us in connection with it is that of Robert Owen ; who, having devoted himself with unremitting ardour to the reform of abuses at his own works, commenced about the year 1812 the agitation of factory reform upon a large scale outside them. In 1813 he addressed a public letter to owners and managers, in which he broached his views, and in 1815 undertook, in concert with his son Mr. R. D. Owen, a journey through England and Scotland for the purpose of collecting full evidence , as to the position of affairs. "The facts we collected," writes the latter gentleman, "seemed to me terrible almost beyond belief. . . . In some large factories from one-fourth to one-fifth of the children were cripples or otherwise deformed, or permanently injured by excessive toil, sometimes by brutal abuse. The younger children seldom lasted out more than three or four years without severe illness, often ending in death" *(Threading My Way)*. Owen laid these facts before several influential members of Parliament with whom he had interviews about this time. He even prepared a remedial Bill of his own; an excellent and comprehensive measure[1] which would have ante-dated future factory legislation by at least a quarter of a century had it been adopted. Unfortunately it was far in advance of the opinion of those days and the opportunity was lost. He next sought to enter Parliament himself, and failed; after which his name gradually disappears from the Factory Controversy, to be succeeded by those of other workers in the same good cause, to whom a few words of notice are due.

RICHARD OASTLER.—There had by this time been formed at Manchester a small committee of friends of factory reform to watch the action of such poor and partial legislation as had now been obtained; the first of those "Short Time Committees" of which a good deal was heard afterwards. The members originally composing it were John Doherty, James Turner, Thomas Daniel and Philip Grant. Unfortunately their efforts up to about 1829-30 had not been very successful; they were disheartened, and had almost broken down for want of support. "At this critical moment," writes one of them,[2] "the atten-

[1] The full text of the Bill is to be found in "*A Supplementary Appendix to the first volume of The Life of Robert Owen; Written by Himself;* p. 21 (Effingham Wilson, 1858).

[2] *History of Factory Legislation*, by Philip Grant (Manchester, 1866).

tion of some humane men in Yorkshire was attracted to
the subject. Mr. John Wood, of Bradford, had for some
time been endeavouring by his own private influence to
bring about a better system in the woollen mills of the West
Riding; but, alas, the avarice of mankind, and the desire to
accumulate wealth was too great to be subdued by that
great and good man." He determined, therefore, to make a
more public protest, and take more decided action, and
began to look about for someone with energy and ability to
aid him in this enterprise. "He laid his case before a
philanthropic friend, Mr. Richard Oastler, of Fixby Hall,
Huddersfield, agent for the property of Thomas Thornhill
Esq., a large Yorkshire landowner. Mr. Wood was a
wealthy worsted manufacturer, and well acquainted with the
ins and outs of the factory question. He knew Oastler to
be a brilliant controversialist, for he had more than once
taken a stirring part in Yorkshire politics, on the Tory side.
He knew him to be a friend of liberty, for he was an eager
emancipationist, at a time, too, when to be a follower of
Wilberforce meant to be in strong opposition to most men of
his own set and party. To him he went then."[1] . . . The
rest of the story is well known. Oastler threw himself with
all the energy of a fervid and noble nature into the cause of
the factory children, nor ever ceased advocating it till
victory crowned his efforts and that cause was won. Misfor-
tune came to him afterwards, and he withdrew somewhat
from the arena of conflict, but the good work had been
initiated, and it failed not subsequently for other friends.

LORD ASHLEY.—With the appearance of Oastler as a
prominent figure in the factory controversy, a new epoch

[1] *Modern Factory System* ; p. 212.

in it may be said to have commenced.   Hitherto the agitation
had been mostly confined to Lancashire, and concerned
about cotton mills : henceforth for a while its principal seat
was Yorkshire, and worsted and woollen factories constituted
the places most under debate.   On November 22nd,
1830, at a representative meeting of Yorkshire manufacturers held at Bradford just cause of complaint was
acknowledged to exist ; and on April 24th 1832, a
memorable meeting was held at York,[1] which exercised a
strong influence on public opinion.   In the meanwhile a
Society, "The Metropolitan Society for the Improvement of Factory Children" had been formed in London ; of
which Mr. William Allen, a distinguished member of the
Society of Friends, was president, and the Duke of Sussex,
one of the King's brothers, a member ;—and others in other
parts of the country ; Mr. Michael Thomas Sadler had
taken up the cause with vigour in the House of Commons,
(in succession to Sir J. C. Hobhouse), and the Rev. G. S.
Bull, a clergyman of the Church of England, and the Rev. J.
R. Stevens, a dissenting minister, were powerful auxiliaries
outside.   Unluckily, in the general election of 1832 Sadler
lost his seat in Parliament, and died not long afterwards
(1835), to the lasting loss of the cause of factory reform.   A
notable piece of good fortune then befell it, just when it seemed
to need it most.   The political leadership of the movement,
thus vacant, was offered to Lord Ashley, already known to
fame as a young man of high promise and exceptionally
noble character ; and after a short hesitation on his part, was
eventually accepted.   The precise details of this most
interesting transaction are told best in his own words, trans-

---

[1] A very interesting account of this meeting, and what ensued on it, is
given by "Alfred"; vol. i., chap. x.

scribed from a personal memorandum found among his papers many years afterwards. They are quoted in Mr. Hodder's *Life of Lord Shaftesbury* (vol. i., p. 148.) "In the autumn and winter of 1832," it runs, "I read incidentally in *The Times* some extracts from the evidence taken before Mr. Sadler's Committee. I had heard nothing of the question previously, nor was I even aware that an enquiry had been instituted by the House of Commons. Either the question had made very little stir, or I had been unusually negligent in Parliamentary business. . . . . I was astonished and disgusted ; and knowing Sadler to be out of Parliament (for he had been defeated at Leeds) I wrote to him to offer my services in presenting petitions, or doing any other small work that the cause might require. I received no answer, and forgot the subject. The Houses met in the month of February, and on the second or third day I was addressed by the Rev. G. S. Bull, whom till then I had never seen or heard of. He was brought to me by Sir Andrew Agnew, and they both proposed to me to take up the question that Sadler had necessarily dropped. I can perfectly recollect my astonishment, and doubt, and terror, at the proposition. I forget the arguments for and against my intermeddling in the affair; so far, I recollect, that in vain I demanded time for consideration ; it was necessary, Bull replied, to make an instant resolution, as Morpeth would otherwise give notice of a Bill, which would defraud the operatives of their ten hours' measure by proposing one which would inflict eleven." The respite of a single day was allowed ; and Lord Ashley took the course thereafter which will long shed lustre on his name.

OTHER LEADERS.—This happy solution of the problem of leadership occurred just after the election of the first reformed Parliament, the names of at least four other members of which are also deserving of special mention in connection with the factory controversy. They are William Cobbett, Joseph Brotherton, Charles Hindley, and John Fielden. Two still more eminent ones, prominent on the same side at first, were afterwards transferred to the other: namely Daniel O'Connell and Sir Robert Peel. Under such auspices as these then, and with a growing feeling in its favour throughout the country, that controversy, waxing ever warmer, was presently lifted to an altogether higher level, and given a new scope and significance.

PROGRESS OF THE CONTROVERSY.—It was a subject of constant complaint, nevertheless, both among the more thoughtful supporters and opposers of factory legislation, that the arguments used commonly in favour of reform were so partial and illogical, covering but a small space of the whole wide field of industrial employment, or debating the question at issue on insufficient grounds. Very early in its course this defect was made powerful use of by the opponents of interference in a pamphlet, published in 1818,[1] criticising the Report of the first Committee of Enquiry, which had now been appointed, at the instance of Sir Robert Peel. It was pointed out in this pamphlet how that the conditions of labour in other factories; as, for instance, linen and woollen mills (which, nevertheless, would not be touched by the legislation then proposed); were as bad as, or worse than, in cotton factories (pp. 16, 17), and the same argu-

---

[1] *An Enquiry into the Principle and Tendency of the Bill now pending in Parliament for imposing certain Restrictions on Cotton Factory* (London, 1818).

ment remained a valid one, with a still wider application,
when all textile works were ultimately brought under supervision. It began to be asked; sometimes with bitter
sarcasm ; why only these places ?   How it was that factory
children alone were deserving of protection by the State [1]
—whilst other children, employed in places not so called,
yet subject to like influences, were neglected ?   Why mines
and collieries, where shocking barbarities were said to prevail,
were exempt ; and, at length, on what plea of justice agriculture, the poorest of all occupations, was entirely left out ?
It is known now how keenly Lord Ashley resented some of
these sarcasms;[2] which in the case of agricultural labour were
often aimed directly against himself, his lordship's family being
large landowners in a poor agricultural district, and he himself sitting for an agricultural borough (Dorchester).   Stung
to further action by them, and ever ready to undertake
good work, he submitted on August 4th, 1840, a resolution
to the House of Commons, one of the most important
ever : ubmitted to that tribunal in its long and useful history.
He moved :—" That an humble address be presented
to her Majesty, praying that her Majesty will be
graciously pleased to direct an enquiry to be made into the
employment of the children of the poorer classes in mines
and collieries, and in the various branches of trade and
manufacture in which numbers of children work together,

[1] Thus on February 25th, 1819, Lord Chancellor Eldon stated in the
House of Lords that " the offence of overworking children was one
indictable at Common Law." He "saw no reason why the master
cotton-spinners, manufacturers, and master chimney sweepers should
have different principles applied to them than were applied to other
trades."

[2] *Life of Lord Shaftesbury*, vol. i., p. 519. Compare Miss Martineau's
History of the Peace, vol. iv., pp. 206, 8.

not being included in the provisions of the Acts for regulating the employment of children and young persons in mills
and factories." In introducing this resolution his lordship
made use of the following words :—" I have long been
taunted with narrow and exclusive attention to the children
in the factories alone ; I have been told in language and
writing, that there were other cases fully as grievous, and
not less numerous ; that I was unjust and inconsiderate in
my denouncements of the one, and my omission of the
other. I have, however, long contemplated this effort
which I am now making ; I had long resolved that, so soon
as I could see the factory children, as it were, safe in harbour
I would undertake a new task."

Such was the origin of the first great commission of
enquiry into the industries of the country as affected by
changed methods of labour, commonly called the " First
Children's Employment Commission," from the date
of which it was clear that the old basis of factory legislation was shifting, and previous notions of its scope and
mission could no longer be considered adequate.

The Commission issued two Reports, the first dealing
exclusively with mines, the second with other trades and
manufactures. That concerned about mining was acted
upon at once ; but much further agitation had to occur, and
yet another Commission to investigate and report before
anything comprehensive was done respecting the other subjects of the enquiry. Of the details then brought to light we
shall have something to say hereafter ; for the present our
concern is with the earlier Report and its influence on legislation and the Factory Controversy. The second part of
this (Part II. *Trades and Manufactures* ; Parl. Pap., 1843,
XIII.) presented a series of recommendations of the most

exhaustive kind ; dealing not only with occupations in which machinery was used, but with many manual ones as well ; not merely with industries of the congregated class, but with many forms of isolated labour, and domestic manufacture. It was proved that in nearly all of these, abuses existed in no wise less, in some cases even greater, than what had been proved against factories—that is against textile factories as then defined by law. What was to be done ? Exponents and opponents of legislation had alike (with few exceptions) no doubt upon the matter. Those industries must be legislated for too. So argued opponents, that every branch of the new system of production might be subject to a like supervision, and none be more " free " than another ; so argued its exponents on the ever broadening ground that circumstances had compelled them to occupy in their constant endeavours to ameliorate the conditions of modern labour. What matter if such places were not really factories, they might easily be called so ; or might not the same, or similar laws be extended to them in any case, by whatsoever name they were called ? Nay, *must* they not after such disclosures ? Not only sentiment now, but sound reason, seemed on the innovator's side ; having gone so far they must to be consistent go farther or go back of what had been already done.

With this general consensus of public opinion in favour of legislation the Factory Controversy, as as originally understood, comes properly to a close. It was no longer a question of kind that the reformers of the next quarter of a century had to deal with but of degree ; it is scarcely a question either of kind or degree that reformers are concerned with now, but of application, of administration, and of the ultimate limit of

State interference—in the last resort—with all material labour.

SUMMARY.—The story of the Factory System has thus been traced, from the first application of the word " factory " in its modern sense to a time when a later signification of it had become nearly obsolete too. We have found this term neither fixed by law nor usage in any invariable meaning, but to have had, on the contrary, an extremely variable one, and to have been the occasion of much varied legislation accordingly. This variability it has communicated to the expression Factory System : a mode of labour into which the industrial revolution of modern times has introduced great changes. The Factory Acts are in this view the necessary counterpoise that seeks to restore equilibrium between the new ethical and economical ideals. On the historical point, we have quoted evidence of the existence of factory systems in very ancient times, and, in particular, under the great ancient civilizations of Rome and Egypt ; in connection with which matter the statement has been hazarded that it is a method of industry ever likely to present itself when existing economic circumstances are favourable. On the subject of the development of factory legislation, it has been shown that supervision was applied in the beginning only to very special industries, but afterwards more generally ; and in this development the *title* factory has remained while almost nothing else has done so, till at length an epoch has been reached when Factory Acts are called upon to deal with many kinds of labour and forms of industry other than are popularly associated with this name. The

process of the development is that of which we have next
to treat. To it the next three chapters will be given ; the last
being concerned with occupations still unincluded, or included
only in part, together with such other matter as may seem
proper then. In this way, it is hoped, the whole field of
investigation will best be covered, and some definite and
precise conceptions be conveyed. We have to relate, how
a new edifice for freedom's sake, though not at first in
freedom's name, was raised upon the ruins of elder systems
of productive industry as a refuge from cupidity and tyranny,
and to take the place of older barriers which "the wisdom
of our ancestors " had provided. And once again, as ever
heretofore, the cement to hold its parts in place was *law*.
Let it ever be remembered ; and the present is a notable
illustration of the truth ; that there is no liberty without law.
Anarchy there may be, the rule of the strongest, cruellest,
cleverest :—freedom never ! It is quite possible—it is even
probable—that the political slavery of ancient times was no
whit more heavy than the economic slavery under which
English labour groaned previous to the enactment of the
Factory Acts. From that slavery, by a long course of constitutional agitation, it has been gradually emancipated up to
the point that it has reached to-day ; and the process is not
over. Be it so. So long as the friends of progress arm themselves only with the same weapons as heretofore there is little
cause to fear what further developments are in store,
but there is good reason to distrust hasty and ill-considered
courses, which have seldom in the history of mankind been
successful in the end.

E

CHAPTER III.

THE FACTORY ACTS
(1802 TO 1833).

PREVIOUS LEGISLATIVE ENACTMENTS—THE FIRST FACTORY
ACT—FIRST PARLIAMENTARY ENQUIRY—RESULTING LEGISLA-
TION—THE FACTORY ACT, 1831—SADLER'S COMMITTEE—
THE FACTORY ACT, 1833.

PREVIOUS LEGISLATIVE ENACTMENTS.—Not until a very
recent time in the history of mankind did the belief prevail
that the relations of men to one another in respect to
industrial production should be less a matter for exterior
regulation than in regard to any other subject of contract.
On the contrary, this had been always held to be one of the
first and most obvious relations requiring careful public
supervision. In the great slave-holding countries of history,
for example, from ancient Egypt and Assyria, to Great Britain
in the last, and America in the present century, that obligation had been duly recognised, and in those where slavery
did not prevail, the still stronger and more permanent
compulsions of custom, tradition, caste, or voluntary association, had usually supplied the place of law.[1] In mediæval
Europe the form this supervision took commonly was that of

[1] See page 36.

guilds or trade societies, which supplied the necessary machinery and undertook the task of government. But in England the guilds were abolished (after being plundered) by Henry VIII., and thenceforward for a while no adequate supervision of labour was provided. The executive authority intermittently, and the local authority (in the persons mostly of magistrates at Quarter Sessions), stepped in for a while, but their intervention was partial and ineffectual.

It was under these circumstances—combined with others heretofore described [1]—that factory legislation became a necessity of existence among a free and self-respecting people. But for some such protection the battles of civil and religious liberty, that had made the course of English history glorious through many preceding centuries, had been fought in vain so far as a considerable and most respectable portion of the population was concerned ; a grinding economic despotism had grown up notwithstanding, and eaten its way into the heart of industry. To put a stop to this gross evil and injustice was—and is—the bounden duty of Government in any civilised community. There is, and can be, no more important and immediate one.

The Factory Acts were not, however, as has been said, the first attempt at State regulation of labour in this country. They were, indeed, far otherwise. From about the middle of the 14th to about the middle of the 18th century the statute book is crowded with enactments having reference to this subject, the most important of them (for our purpose) being the series known as the "Statutes of Labourers," which had their rise in the reign of Edward III. (1349), and were often renewed, amended, and re-enacted afterwards. But all of these were distinguished by a common

[1] *Ante,* chap. i.

purpose which is the exact opposite of the purpose of factory legislation; they belong to an era, and breathe the spirit of an epoch antecedent to the Industrial Revolution. Whilst it is the constant purpose of Factory Acts to shorten the working day, a common object of those laws was to lengthen it; or, as Mr. Jevons puts it, they dealt with the question of hours of work "not by way of limitation, but by imposition."[1] They were, in fact, Acts passed in the masters' interests, not the men's. Thus, the first of them provided, that "from the middle of the month of March to the middle of September, all artificers and labourers hired by time were to be and continue at their work at or before five o'clock in the morning, and continue at work and not depart until betwixt seven and eight of the clock at night,"— three hours being allowed for meals: namely one hour for breakfast, one and a half for dinner, and half an hour for "noon-meate." In winter the work-time was to be from five in the morning until dark, with the same intervals. A subsequent one (Statute of Apprentices, 1562), curtailed the above intervals by more than half an hour :—dinner was to last one hour, and the "afternoon sleep of half an hour" to be permissible "only between the middle of May and the middle of August;" . . . . so that (Mr. Jevons continues) "the legal day's work was to be twelve hours *at the least*;"—and the same spirit characterised them to the end. Another particular in which they differed from modern factory legislation was in the attempt to fix the rate of wages in a great variety of occupations. The proposal was to find a "reasonable wage;"—a desirable enterprise if it were only feasible, and one not without earnest and able advocates at the present day. But it was never, and could

[1] *The State in Relation to Labour*; p. 35 (Macmillan, 1882).

never be more than partially operative under the circumstances, and its constant evasion cast an air of unreality over the whole system. Further, these laws were enforced or not as the masters (who were their authors) pleased, but seldom or never at the discretion of the workers; and finally, to make "confusion worse confounded" did not in many cases apply at all. The Statute of Apprentices, for instance, was limited in operation to towns corporate, and industries already in existence; so that new ones springing up elsewhere, or afterwards, were left to shift for themselves, under the fostering care of the competitive principle and in full view of the other protected ones. The great cotton industry, among others, came thus into being, and many of the early arguments for factory legislation were based on that circumstance. Some of these have been partially discussed already (p. 32), and will be occasionally alluded to again; others may emerge hereafter. We proceed now to describe the very remarkable body of law which ensued on the disruption of this old industrial order, and with special relation at first to that fibre of manufacture.[1]

THE FIRST FACTORY ACT.—The first Factory Act ever passed by the British Parliament was called "The Factory Health and Morals Act, 1802" (42 George III., c. 73), and applied principally, though not exclusively, to apprentices in cotton and woollen mills. The preamble runs as follows:—

"Whereas it hath of late become a practice in cotton and woollen mills, and in cotton and woollen factories, to employ a great number of male and female apprentices, and other persons, in the same building, in consequence of which

---

[1] This part of the subject is very efficiently dealt with in another volume of the present series, *Trade Unionism New and Old*, by G. Howell, M.P.

certain regulations are become necessary to preserve the health and morals of such apprentices : be it therefore enacted . . . . that from and after the 2nd day of December, 1802, all such mills and factories within Great Britain and Ireland, wherein three or more apprentices, or twenty or more other persons, shall at any time be employed shall be subject to the several rules and regulations contained in this Act."

These regulations, briefly stated, were the following :—

1st. The first section enjoins the " master or mistress " of the factory to observe the law. 2nd. All rooms in a factory are to be lime-washed twice a year and duly ventilated (sec. ii.) 3rd. Every apprentice is to be supplied with two complete suits of clothing—one new suit every year—with suitable linen, stockings, hats and shoes (sec. iii.) 4th. The hours of work of apprentices are not to exceed twelve a day, nor commence before six in the morning, nor conclude before nine at night (sec. iv.) 5th. They are to be instructed every working day during the first four years of apprenticeship in reading, writing, and arithmetic " by some discreet and proper person," the time so occupied to be counted out of their hours of work (sec. vi.) 6th. Male and female apprentices are to be provided with separate sleeping apartments, and not more than two to sleep in one bed (sec. vii.) 7th. On Sunday they are to be instructed in the principles of the Christian religion ; they are to comply with various religious ordinances during their apprenticeship, and to go to church once a month at least (sec. viii.) 8th. Two visitors are to be appointed by the adjacent Justices of the Peace, one of whom must be himself a Justice and the other a member either of the Church of England or of the Church of Scotland, to enforce the provisions of the Act (sec. ix.)

9th. In case of infectious disorders prevailing, these visitors may require the employer to call in medical assistance (sec. x.) 10th. Copies of the regulations of the Act are to be affixed in conspicuous places (sec. xii.) 11th. A list of the factories situated in his district is to be kept by every Clerk of the Peace (sec. xiv.) Penalties are enacted for breaches of the law (secs. xi. to xiii.), and the method of recovering them (secs. xv. xvi.) is provided for."

This is a very interesting statute to students of factory legislation from several points of view. The primitive character of some of the clauses "show that the new industrial system had not yet emerged from that transitional phase when mills were built in unfrequented places, and it was necessary to provide for their working by lodging apprenticed workers sent from a distance," and one readily infers from it what were the chief industries of which complaint was at that time made. Its application was to cotton and woollen factories; therefore cotton and woollen factories were the establishments considered especially faulty. It imposed, we note, no limit of age on workers, nor required any proof of their fitness for employment.) The provisions about clothing, medical attendance, and religious teaching are strange to modern notions. "They clearly point to a time when the relations between employer and employed were closer and more intimate than they have since become, when something of paternal interest and authority lingered about the former, and the link that united these partners in production was not a purely mercenary one." [1] It was an important statute; "as being the first definitely in restraint of modern factory labour and in general opposition to the *laissez faire* policy in industry;" a genuine attempt, it would seem, to

[1] *Modern Factory System*; p. 282.

supply in some sort the place which the guilds had held formerly in trade organization. It must be particularly observed, however, that its special application was to apprenticed, not free labour; free that is of *civil* compulsion ; and that non-apprenticed children might still be taken into employment as formerly. In practice it proved inoperative. The duty cast on factory visitors was an invidious one ; for which no recompense was provided; and they generally failed to carry it out. Changed circumstances of industry, too, soon rendered it obsolete, and though remaining for a long time actually unrepealed[1] it was soon superseded by others.

FIRST PARLIAMENTARY ENQUIRY. The changed circumstances alluded to were principally the result of the new motive power which now began to be applied to production on a large scale. Hitherto factories of the modern type had been built in water-abounding districts, and often in remote localities, but the introduction of steam-power transferred them to populous places instead, whither coal could be carried more easily, and where an unfailing supply of labour might generally be obtained. One result of this was that children brought into such factories did not need to be apprenticed, and worked there accordingly without participating in the benefits of the first Factory Act. Sir Robert Peel brought this matter under the notice of the House of Commons on June 6th, 1815, proposing an amended measure which should apply to apprenticed and non-apprenticed children alike. "A bad practice had prevailed," he said, "of condemning children whose years and strength did not admit of it to the drudgery of occupations often severe, and

[1] It was not formally repealed till 1878 ; 41 Vic., c. 16; sec. 107 and Sch. VI.

sometimes unhealthy.   What he was disposed to recommend
was, that no children should be so employed under the age
of ten years, either as apprentices or otherwise, and the
duration of their labour should be limited to twelve hours
and a half per diem, including the time for education and
meals, which would leave ten hours for laborious employment." [1]   This proposal met with little opposition and the Bill
was brought in and read a first time.

Up to this stage factory legislation had excited but little
general interest and absolutely no alarm.   Nothing had been
said about the necessity of any public enquiry into the matter ;
a device destined to play a great part thereafter in its development.   Nor had Sir Robert Peel confined his attention to the
case of children employed only in cotton mills.   Nevertheless,
he is found the next year limiting the scope of his endeavours
in just those two directions, and inaugurating a new policy of
a distinctly retrograde kind.   What had occurred meanwhile ?
The answer is supplied by " Alfred " (*History of the Factory
Movement ;* vol. i., p. 44), and is valuable not alone as an
index to the character of this distinguished man, but for the
light it sheds on subsequent events.   " He was ever anxious "
(writes " Alfred " [2]) to conciliate his opponents, a desire very
creditable to his heart, but in the then existing state of parties
by no means favourable to the speedy success of the measure
of which he was the exponent. . . .   He was conscious
of the justness and practical utility of the cause he advocated,
and, like many other men of good intentions, gave to
opponents credit for openness of conviction and conscientious

---

[1] *Hansard* ; First Series, vol. xxxi. ; p. 624.

[2] It is, I believe, no longer a secret that the real name of the author so
long concealed under the above *nom de plume* is Mr. Samuel Kydd,
Barrister-at-Law.

candour not always well placed," . . . . and, in fine,
"to the anxiety of the first Sir Robert Peel to conciliate opposition, then comparatively powerless in numbers and influence, may be attributed"—this well informed writer thinks
—"the protracted struggle for factory legislation that ensued."

On the 3rd April, 1816, he came forward, accordingly, with
his new proposal, the appointment of a Committee of Enquiry,
"to take into consideration the state of the children employed
in the different manufactories of the United Kingdom, and
to report the same, together with their observations thereupon,
to the House :" it being generally understood that the Enquiry
should be practically confined to cotton mills. He was again
successful. But the committee thus originated was foredoomed
to failure from the first. "The disagreement of the witnesses
examined was distinct and irreconcilable, ... men
of the highest respectability gave evidence on the same
subject leading to opposite conclusions."[1] The fact was,
that a great many of those whose testimony was taken did
not believe in the practicability of any such legislation, whilst
others did not believe in its utility, and many more allowed
their judgments to be coloured by their supposed interests.
The proposals were at this stage novel, absurdly limited in
scope, and opposed to current economic belief; and any
arguments at all seemed fair under such circumstances to
use against them. It was generally felt that this committee had been appointed in vain, or, if it had proved
anything, had proved only a divergence of opinion wider
and more fundamental than had been before suspected.

RESULTING LEGISLATION.—Nevertheless, contradictory
as its conclusions were, the enquiry was not quite un-

[1] "Alfred," vol. i., p. 59.

fruitful. Those conclusions afforded material for further argument and investigation; and from about this time it is possible to distinguish two well-defined parties in the Factory Controversy, which did not exist before, the one strongly urging, the other as resolutely opposing, special legislation. Early in 1818 both were active in Parliament. On February 18th, Lord Stanley presented a petition from Manchester, condemning the evidence given before the committee of 1816, and praying "that if the House required further information upon the subject it would be pleased to appoint a Special Commission of its own members for the purpose of examining on the spot into the actual condition of persons employed in the various cotton and other manufactures." This was a reasonable, and, as the terms implied, a comprehensive proposal; but on the following day the first Sir Robert Peel brought the same subject forward from his narrower point of view. "In Manchester alone," he said, "about twenty thousand persons were employed in the cotton manufacture, and in the whole of England about three times that number. . . . . It was notorious that children of a very tender age were dragged from their beds some hours before daylight, and confined in the factories no less than fifteen hours; and it was also notoriously the opinion of the Faculty that no children of eight or nine years of age could bear that degree of hardship with impunity to their health and constitution. . . . . Those who were employers of the children, seeing them from day to day, were not so sensible of the injury that they sustained from this practice as strangers, who were strongly impressed by it. In fact, they were prevented from growing to their full size. In consequence, Manchester, which used to furnish

numerous recruits to the army, was now wholly unproductive in that respect." He concluded by moving "that
leave be given to bring in a Bill to amend and extend an
Act made in the forty-second year of his present majesty's
reign, for the preservation of the health and morals of
apprentices and others employed in cotton and other mills,
and cotton and other factories."

The measure thus heralded was brought in and read a first
time, and the second reading taken almost immediately. On
this occasion Sir Robert Peel gave the following explanation of
the changes that he proposed. "In the Bill brought in in
1815, the age at which children might be employed was
fixed at ten. He now proposed the age of nine years, and
that the powers of the Act should terminate when the child
reached the age of sixteen and could be considered a free
agent. He, therefore, now recommended that children
employed in cotton factories should from nine to sixteen
be under the protection of Parliament, and before nine
that they should not be admitted; that they should be
employed in working eleven hours, which, with one hour
and a half for meals, made on the whole twelve hours and a
half." The Bill was read a second time, and ultimately
passed the Commons. On May the 7th it was formally
brought before the House of Lords, was read a second
time on the 8th, and on June 5th both sides in the
debate agreed to postpone further consideration for that
session. In the next one, a new committee (not a
Special Commission as had been asked for) was appointed
to take further evidence.

This second committee need not detain us long. It
resembled in its main features that of 1816, but
enough evidence was tendered to it on the side of reformers

to make further action in regard to cotton mills
a necessity, and in 1819 a new law was passed to that end.
It enacted that after the 1st of January 1820 no child
should be employed in cotton-spinning under nine years of
age ; and no persons under sixteen years for more than
twelve hours a day, with one hour and a half out for meals.
Time lost by the scarcity or excess of water was to be made
up at the rate of not more than one hour extra work per day ;
ceilings and interior walls of cotton factories were to be
lime-washed twice a year ; an abstract of the Act to be hung
up in a conspicuous place ; and the Act itself was "to be
deemed and taken to be a public Act," and "be judicially
taken notice of as such by all judges, justices, and others,
without specially pleading the same."

Though retrograde in respect to the Act of 1802, this
statute, (entitled "The Factories Regulation Act,"[1])
embodied (within its limitation to cotton mills) some
important principles, and foreshadowed the lines upon
which further legislation was to proceed. Where the law
was faithfully observed a considerable improvement in the
condition of the operatives was perceptible, but unhappily
it was more generally ignored or evaded. The permission
to recover lost time was found in particular to give
facility to such evasions ; and the absence of any satisfactory provisions for inspection left the law altogether
inoperative in many places.

It was unfortunately the tendency of the next one
(60 Geo. III., c. 5) to exaggerate rather than minimise
these defects. The principal provisions of this statute
(which was passed mainly at the instance of employers)
"conceded to the owners of such cotton mills as had been

[1] 59 Geo. III., c. 66.

destroyed by fire, or damaged by some casualty (providing they were in possession of other factories in active operation at the time), the privilege of employing in the latter the hands thrown out of work in consequence of the accident "—and of appointing the meal-times at any period of the day that might best suit their convenience. And so the matter rested for a period of about six years. Factory legislation presents at this epoch the appearance of a body of almost worthless laws, openly violated in a great majority of instances, and so ill-conceived and partial in operation as almost to invite the contempt of that very small section of employers who were even nominally subject to them.

In 1825 Sir John Cam Hobhouse carried a fresh measure (6 Geo. IV., c. 63) designed to remedy some of these evils, but too weak in its machinery to do so effectually; supplemented by others (10 Geo. IV., c. 51 and 10 Geo. IV., c. 63), still with the same end in view. It is unnecessary to enter into detail concerning any of them, for they were all soon repealed, and none did more than touch the fringe of the real great issue, still involved in deep obscurity, concealed by insufficient knowledge and slowly perishing ideals. The first was remarkable, however, for containing a provision to shorten work on Saturday, a privilege incorporated into all subsequent ones, and which has since become an integral part of the industrial life of the nation.

THE FACTORY ACT OF 1831.—In the meanwhile that series of events had been occurring in the country briefly described in Chapter II. A number of just and able men had taken the cause of factory reform to heart, and were agitating it with unparalleled power and perseverance.

Many things had conspired to cast discredit on the laws a it then stood and to favour their designs. Its ridiculous limitation to one textile staple (cotton), the notorious disregard of its provisions even in that single manufacture, the evidence that had been taken both for and against interference ; and not less the evidence against than for ; all these had largely contributed to instruct the public mind. In 1831, Sir J. C. Hobhouse introduced a new Bill, to apply to the whole textile trade, reducing the hours of labour to eleven and a half a day ; but it was fiercely opposed and ultimately defeated. An Act was passed instead (1 & 2 Will. IV., c. 39) which, once more, and for the last time, applied exclusively to cotton factories. The provisions of this Act showed again both progress and retrogression. It commenced by repealing the four preceding ones ; it prohibited night work to all persons between nine and twenty-one years of age, fixing the time of labour for persons under eighteen at twelve hours per day and nine on Saturday, *i. e.*, sixty-nine hours per week ; but on the other hand the recovery of lost time was facilitated, and night work permitted to persons from sixteen years upwards. Owners of cotton mills, and their immediate relatives, were disqualified from adjudicating on factory cases. This was virtually—remarks Von Plener [1]—" the first Factory Act, which was, at least, to some extent, carried out, and which gave rise to still further agitation." . . . . Yet, ... ". despite the law, most factories worked thirteen hours ; and numerous cases of infringement were subsequently brought to light. Out of several (workers) of the legally determined age one only was dismissed the factory after twelve hours' work, the remainder having to do

[1] *English Factory Legislation*, p. 7.

overtime.   In many cases "—he adds "—the men were compelled to subscribe to a fund out of which the manufacturer
paid the fines incurred by him for breaking the law, which
seems to have been better observed in Scotland than in England,and in the latter kingdom more so in town than country."
It was clear that matters could not rest permanently here ;
and certain extrinsic influences contributed at this point to
give factory agitation an unexpected and most powerful
impulse, which presently thrust it to the very forefront of
political questions and started it on a career of assured
success.

This unlooked for assistance came to it from the peculiar
position of party politics at the time.   A section of the
democracy was calling loudly for the reform of Parliament,
and the Whig party had generally thrown in their lot with
it.   Against this combination the Tories mustered all their
strength.   It was an effective stroke of policy to play off
factory reform against parliamentary reform, the more so as
factory masters were at this time generally on the democratic or popular side.   Encouraged by so favourable a
conjuncture of affairs the operatives became more ambitious
in their demands.   They declared that nothing less than a
" Ten Hours Bill " would satisfy them now, and under the
brilliant leadership of Mr. M. T. Sadler; who had lately
entered the House of Commons ; and somewhat to the
dismay of their former champions there, no less than this
was the proposal with which they now confronted an alarmed
and bewildered legislature.   On the 16th of March 1832,
Sadler did actually introduce such a Bill ; in a speech
of remarkable ability, power, and comprehensive eloquence.
It was met, of course, with the strongest opposition ; even
sincere friends of factory reform regarding it in many

instances with unconcealed aversion. The most he could effect was to have the/whole subject remitted once again to the consideration of a Special Committee, but one over which he was himself invited to preside.

The appointment of this celebrated committee marks a distinct turning point in the history of the factory question. By means of the evidence produced before it the public was more generally enlightened as to the true position of things than it had yet had any opportunity of being, and even the legislature gained over to something like a proper appreciation of the task that lay before it. Unfortunately, just at the very crisis of the opportunity, Sadler lost his seat in Parliament, and was not again returned; but his place was quickly supplied by Lord Ashley. Under the leadership of that nobleman the contest was maintained with renewed vigour and with results that will occupy our attention soon. A small space must be allotted first to some record of that terrible body of facts which compelled prompter, and, as it turned out to be, far more efficient, action than had yet been attempted or imagined.

SADLER'S COMMITTEE.—A large number of influential gentlemen were nominated on the new committee. The evidence taken before previous ones had been principally confined to cotton factories; the most important evidence given before this was connected, therefore, with other staples. Eighty-nine witnesses in all were examined, and eleven thousand six hundred and eighteen questions asked and answered. From this prodigious mass of material we select two or three instances which may be considered fairly typical, letting the witnesses in every case

F

speak for themselves but abbreviating somewhat their remarks.

The first evidence to be cited comes from Scotland, where the law was said to have been best observed. It is that of an overlooker, James Paterson :—

"I reside at Dundee, am twenty-eight years of age, and my business is a mill-overseer. I have been acquainted with the mill system in Dundee and neighbourhood for a long time. At ten years of age I entered a mill. I worked in the carding-room, which was very dusty. There were fourteen hours' actual work, and fifteen hours a day confinement, including meals. I suffered from shortness, and stoppage at the breast, and was forced to leave in consequence. Other children were similarly affected. I had a brother who was at that work too and he was compelled to leave from bad health, and was laid up and died of consumption. The doctor said it was occasioned by being confined at that work. My brother died at eighteen years of age ; he had originally a good constitution.

*   *   *   *   *   *

"I worked at Mr. ——'s mill, of Duntruin ; there we worked as long as we could see in summer-time, and I could not say at what hour it was we stopped. There was nobody but the master and the master's son had a watch, and we did not know the time. The operatives were not permitted to have a watch. There was one man who had a watch. I believe it was a friend who gave it to him ; it was taken from him and given into the master's custody, because he had told the men the time of the day. There was no clock at that mill. There were a great many children in proportion to the number of adults, most of them were orphans. There were some of the orphan children from Edinburgh who had been in the mill, I believe, from four to five years. The children were incapable of performing their day's labour well towards the termination of the day; their fate was to be awoke by being beaten, and to be kept awake by the same method. They were guarded up to their bothies to take their meals, and were locked up in the bothies at night, and the master took the key away with him to his own bedroom; they were guarded to their work, and they were guarded back again; and they were guarded while they were taking their meat, and then they were locked up for rest. They were not allowed to go to a place of worship on the Sunday. There were twenty-five or twenty-six of us together. There was one bothy for the boys, but that did not hold them all, and there were some of them put into the other bothy along with the girls. The ages of the boys that were put into the girls' bothy might be, I should suppose, from ten to fourteen, the ages of the girls, perhaps, from twelve to eighteen.

"The children and young persons were sometimes successful in their attempts to escape from labour and confinement. I have gone after them on horseback and brought them back myself. Those brought back were taken into the mill, and got a severe beating with a strap; sometimes the master kicked them on the floor, and struck them with both his hands and his feet. Those who had made engagements for any length of time, when they ran away, the master, if he could not find them before they got home to their relations, if they had any, he sent after them and put them in gaol. I knew a woman put in gaol, and brought back after a twelvemonth, and worked for her meat; and she had to pay the expenses that were incurred.

"When the hands worked those long hours, the master came himself and roused them in the morning, and those that would not rise, I have seen him take a pail of water and throw it upon them to make them rise. One of the means taken to secure those children and young persons from running away was that their clothes, if they had any not in use, were kept locked up, so that if they ran away they could only run away with what was on their backs.

Let an ordinary factory operative speak next, the scene being this time laid in England. Joseph Habergam :—

"I reside at Northgate, Huddersfield, in Yorkshire. I was seven years of age when I began to work at Bradley Mill, near Huddersfield; the employment was worsted-spinning. The hours of labour at that mill were from five in the morning till eight at night, with an interval for rest and refreshment of thirty minutes, at noon; there was no time for rest and refreshment in the afternoon. We had to eat our meals as we could, standing or otherwise. I had fourteen and a half hours' actual labour when seven years of age; the wages I then received was two shillings and six-pence per week. I attended to what are called the throstle machines; this I did for two years and a half, and then I went to the steam looms for half a year. In that mill there were about fifty children, of about the same age as I was. These children were often sick and poorly. There were always, perhaps, half-a-dozen regularly that were ill because of excessive labour. We began to grow drowsy and sleepy

about three o'clock, and grew worse and worse, and it came
to be very bad towards six and seven. I had still to labour
on. There were three overlookers; there was a head overlooker, and then there was one man kept to grease the
machines, and then there was one kept on purpose to strap.
Strapping was the means by which the children were kept at
work. It was the main business of one of the overlookers
to strap the children up to this excessive labour—the same
as strapping an old restive horse that has fallen down and
will not get up. This was the practice day by day. The
children were not capable of performing the amount of
labour that was exacted from them without perpetual cruelty.
I had at that time, similarly occupied, a brother and sister.
I cannot say how old my sister was when she began to work
in the mill, but my brother John was seven. They were
often sick; my brother John died three years ago—he was
then sixteen years and eight months old. My mother and
the medical attendants were of opinion that my brother
died from working such long hours, and that it had been
brought about by the factory."

He discloses a scandalous form of cheating
which was only too common at this time.

"Out of the thirty minutes allowed for dinner, five
minutes and sometimes ten were occupied in cleaning the
spindles. On Saturday night we gave over at six o'clock,
after which time we used to be made to fettle the machines,
which took an hour and a half. Sometimes . . . .
the clock was a quarter of an hour too soon in the meal
time; we had just done fettling, and we had but half got
our dinners, when the overlooker put the clock forward to

one, and he rang the bell, and we were obliged to run
back to work." . . . .

"When trade was particularly brisk I was obliged to
work from five in the morning till half-past ten, sometimes
till eleven. On one occasion I worked all Friday, Friday
night, and Saturday."

Benjamin Gummersil :—

"I am now sixteen years of age. I have been employed
in pieceing at a worsted mill. The hours of labour were
from six in the morning to seven, and half-past seven and
eight at night ; half an hour was allowed at noon for dinner—
not any time was allowed for breakfast or 'drinking.' I
entered the mill at nine years of age ; my father was obliged
to send me to the mill in order to keep me. If we are higher
than the frames we have to bend our bodies and our legs—
so. [Here the witness showed the position in which he
worked.] I was a healthy and strong boy before I went to
the mill. I had worked about a year for those long hours
before I found my limbs begin to fail. The failing came
on with great pain in my legs and knees ; I felt very much
fatigued towards the end of those days—then the overlooker
beat me up to my work. I have been beaten till I was
black and blue in my face, and have had my ears torn. I
was beaten because I had mixed a few empty bobbins,
having not any place to put them into separate. (I was
generally beaten most at the end of the day, when I grew
tired and fatigued.) In the morning I felt stiff, very stark,
indeed ; I was beaten in the morning as well, but not so
much as towards the latter end of the day. I continued to
attend the mill after my limbs began to fail. After I became deformed, I did not get on so well with my work as I

could before. I got less in height. I cannot exactly say how tall I am now. I have fallen several inches in height. I had to stand thirteen or fourteen hours a day frequently, and was constantly engaged as I have described. [The witness, at the request of the Committee, exhibited his limbs, 'and they appeared to be exceedingly crooked.'] I was perfectly straight before I entered upon this labour. There were other boys deformed in the same way."

The next evidence shall be of a woman employed in a flax mill.

Elizabeth Bentley :—

'I am twenty-three years of age, and live at Leeds. I began to work at Mr. Busk's flax mill when I was six years old. I was then a little 'doffer.' In that mill we worked from five in the morning till nine at night when they were 'throng'; when they were not so 'throng,' the usual hours of labour were from six in the morning till seven at night. The time allowed for our meals was forty minutes at noon ; not any time was allowed for breakfast or 'drinking'; these we got as we could. When our work was bad, we had hardly any time to eat them at all; we were obliged to leave them or take them home. When we did not take our uneaten food home the overlooker took it and gave it to his pigs. I was kept constantly on my feet; there were so many frames, and they ran so quick, the labour was excessive, there was not time for anything. When the 'doffers' flagged a little, or were too late, they were strapped. Those who where last in 'doffing' were constantly strapped—girls as well as boys. I have seen the overlooker go to the top end of the room, where the little girls 'hug' the can to the 'backminsters'; he has taken a strap, and a whistle in his mouth, and sometimes he has got a chain and chained them, and strapped them all down the room.

"I worked in the card-room; it was so dusty that the dust got upon my lungs, and the work was so hard. I was middling strong when I went there, but the work was so bad and I got so bad in health, that when I pulled the baskets down, I pulled my bones out of their places. The basket I pulled was a very large one; that was full of weights, upheaped, and pulling the basket, pulled my shoulder out of its place, and my ribs have grown over it.

"I have had experience in wet spinning—it is very uncomfortable I have stood before the frames till I have been wet through to my skin; and in winter-time, when myself and others have gone home, our clothes have been frozen, and we have nearly caught our death from cold. We have stopped at home one or two days, just as we were situated in our health; had we stopped away any length of time we should have found it difficult to keep our situations.

"I am now in the poor-house at Hunslet."

A pathetic interest attaches to the last evidence to be quoted, which inspired no less a person than the Chairman of the committee with the theme of a mournful little poem " The Factory Girl's Last Day," to be found in his collected works.[1]

Gillett Sharpe examined.

The witness having detailed the results of excessive labour on members of his own family, was asked :—

[1] About half of it is quoted in *The Modern Factory System*, p. 226.

"Have you reason to think that any of the children lose their lives in consequence of this excessive degree of exertion ?—I have no doubt in my mind that such has been the case, and I may mention one instance of the kind. Four or five months back there was a girl of a poor man's that I was called to visit; it was poorly ; it had attended a mill, and I was obliged to relieve the father in the course of my office (assistant-overseer), in consequence of the bad health of the child. By-and-by it went back to its work again, and one day he came to me with tears in his eyes. I said, 'What is the matter, Thomas ?' He said, 'My little girl is dead.' I said, 'When did she die?' He said, 'In the night ; and what breaks my heart is this, she went to the mill in the morning, she was not able to do her work, and a little boy said he would assist her if she would give him a halfpenny on Saturday ; I said I would give him a penny,' but at night when the child went home, perhaps about a quarter of a mile, in going home she fell down several times on the road through exhaustion, till at length she reached her father's door with difficulty, and she never spoke audibly afterwards ; she died in the night."

THE FACTORY ACT, 1833.—Such is a fair sample of the evidence accumulated by Mr. Sadler's committee. Its Report, though wholly in favour of further immediate legislation for textile factories, did not immediately attain the end in view. Sadler was not present himself to reintroduce his Bill in the House of Commons, and when Lord Ashley did so next session he found himself anticipated by Lord Morpeth, whose object was to promote a compromise between the extreme pretensions of the advocates of a Ten Hours Bill and the more modified measure of factory reform favoured by himself and Sir J. C. Hobhouse. The Government was not satisfied with either scheme. It had in fact determined to take the initiative itself. Before doing so, however, it resolved on yet another enquiry; this time in the form of a Royal Commission; which should visit factory districts and whose members were to make themselves personally acquainted with the operatives' needs. A few exceptionally well qualified men were appointed, more evidence was taken, and again with the same result. The Commissioners, contrary to many anticipations both of friends and foes, reported strongly in favour of further legislation.

It rested with the Executive now to produce an alternative Bill to the other two, and no time was lost in doing so. The measure that emerged, and which rapidly became law, (3 & 4 Will. IV., c. 103), was by far the most important Factory Act yet placed upon the statute book. It formed the ground-work and model of all future factory legislation for at least a quarter of a century, and to a large extent remains a model still, both in this and other countries. Its principal provisions were the following. It enacted that from and after the first day of January 1834, " it shall not be lawful for any person to employ in any factory or mill, except in mills for the manufacture of silk, any child who shall not have completed his or her ninth year." That, "from and after the expiration of six months after the passing of this Act, it shall not be lawful for any person to employ, keep, or allow to remain in any factory or mill, for a longer time than forty-eight hours in any one week, nor for a longer time than nine hours in any one day, ... any child who shall not have completed his or her eleventh year of age, or after the expiration of eighteen

months from the passing of this Act any child who shall
not have completed his or her twelfth year of age, or after
the expiration of thirty months from the passing of this Act
any child who shall not have completed his or her thirteenth year of age,"—except in silk mills.   Daily attendance
at school for at least two hours was provided for; and two
whole and eight half-holidays in the year (besides Saturday).
Surgical certificates of age for young persons and children
were for the first time required ; and, for the efficient carrying
out of the law, four factory inspectors were appointed, to
whom very large powers (including in some instances a
penal jurisdiction concurrent with that of magistrates) were
confided.   No person under the age of eighteen (instead of
twenty-one) was to be employed at night; *i.e.* between the
hours of 8.30 p.m. and 5.30 a.m. ; and the terms
children and *young persons* were to mean thenceforth
persons between the ages of nine and thirteen, and thirteen
and eighteen respectively.   No mention is made of a
religious obligation on employers, as heretofore, nor of
any requirement for providing clothes for workers.   The
expressions *mill* and *factory* were not specially defined, but
an incidental interpretation of their statutory meaning is
afforded in section i., where the operation of the Act is
confined to textile industry.   Its relation to preceding enactments was settled by section xlviii., repealing 1 & 2 Will.
IV., c. 39, which had in its turn repealed 59 Geo. III.,
c. 66 ; 60 Geo. III., c. 5 ; 6 Geo. IV., c. 63, and
10 Geo. IV., cc. 51, 63; but not 42 Geo. III., c. 73
(the Apprentice Act), which therefore remained in force.
In a general sense the law applied to all textile manufactures
where motive power other than human was employed, and
to those alone, and to all persons (male and female) under

the age of eighteen years employed in them, and no others. Still more generally considered, it brought factories (as then defined) under a system of supervision by appointed government officers, and it was the first English statute to formally recognise compulsory education as a State concern. From a yet wider point of view, it reveals the growing tendency to substitute purely *economic* for moral or religious sanctions in this kind of legislation, and marks a long step forward towards the reinstatement of the normal working day, lost to British industry for several generations.

CHAPTER IV.

THE FACTORY ACTS
(1833 TO 1867).

THE FACTORY ACT OF 1833 IN OPERATION—THE RELAY
SYSTEM—AGE CERTIFICATES—RENEWAL OF AGITATION—
PROGRESS OF LEGISLATION—THE FACTORY ACT, 1844—
SOME SUBSEQUENT ENACTMENTS—SECOND CHILDREN'S
EMPLOYMENT COMMISSION—THE FACTORY ACT, 1864—THE
FACTORY ACT, 1867.

THE FACTORY ACT OF 1833 IN OPERATION.—The Factory
Act, 1833, viewed in its widest historical connection was an
attempt to establish a normal working day in a single
department of industry, textile manufacture. The way in
which it proposed to do this was the following:—"day"
was to commence at 5.30 a.m. and cease at 8.30 p.m.,
within which limit of fifteen hours a *young person* (aged
thirteen to eighteen) might not be employed beyond any
period of twelve hours, less one and a half for
meals ; and a *child* (aged nine to thirteen) beyond any
period of nine hours, under similar limitations. From
8.30 p.m. to 5.30 a.m. ; that is during " night ; " the employment of such persons was altogether prohibited. But al-
though this is the proper historical perspective in which this
Act should be regarded, it by no means follows that the

above intention was acknowledged by its originators. On the contrary, they seem to have considered the establishment of a normal working day, so far at least as adult labour was concerned, as an evil to be avoided at all hazards. In the first Report of the Central Board of the Royal Commission (June 28th, 1833) the following passage occurs, which puts this point beyond all question :—"The great evil of the Factory System as at present conducted"—say the Commissioners—"has appeared to us to be that it entails the necessity of continuing the labour of children to the utmost length of that of the adults. The only remedy for this evil, short of the limitation of the labour of adults, which would, in our opinion, *create an evil greater than that which is sought to be remedied*, appears to be the plan of working double sets of children." That is to say, in the opinion of these gentlemen, the establishment of a normal working day for adults seemed a greater evil than the excessive employment of child labour.

The "remedy" thus deliberately suggested to employers was the origin of the celebrated Relay System ; about which a great deal was heard for the next ten years or so, which is a well-established device in other forms of industry, but which secured for itself an extremely evil reputation in connection with this one.

THE RELAY SYSTEM.—To understand this rather complicated matter rightly, it is necessary to point out that the provisions of the Act of 1833 as regarded meal times and the hours of work of protected persons were very loosely drawn. Sec. vi. enacted : "That there shall be allowed in the course of every day not less than one and a half hours for meals to every such person restricted as hereinbefore provided;" so that apparently a child might be employed many hours without cessation—say from 5.30 a.m. to 1.30 p.m.— and another set come in at 1.30 and work till 8.30, the meal time being supposed to be given in either case either immediately before or after the period of work.) Or still more elaborate arrangements might be made. The law had left it optional with employers to fix the hours of work at any time within the legal fifteen provided children and young persons did not exceed their nine and twelve respectively. They could apparently, then, require any of these to begin, to end, or resume at any moment they thought fit; to the utter confusion of all exterior control, and the confounding of every attempt at systematic super-vision. After a little experience of those arrangements inspectors declared that the clauses restricting the employ-ment of protected persons were valueless so long as such anomalies were permitted to exist.

AGE CERTIFICATES.—Another point in which this statute was defective was in relation to the method of proving the alleged ages of persons seeking employment. There was no Registration Act in those days, and the certificate of any physician or surgeon, founded on personal examination only, was accepted as sufficient proof of age. It is unnecessary to dwell on the unsatisfactory nature of this test; even with the best intentions and under the worthiest inducements on the surgeon's part; but it is painful to note that parents, and too often employers also, were not above lending themselves sometimes to the shabbiest artifices to pass off immature children as within the stipulated age.[1] A further defect was the ridiculously inadequate time within which an

[1] *Modern Factory System* ; p. 369.

Information for an alleged breach of the law might be laid ;
namely fourteen days ; and another (as it unhappily proved)
that manufacturers were no longer prohibited (as under Sir
J. C. Hobhouse's Act) from sitting in judgment on factory
cases, and sometimes took unfair advantage of their position
when doing so.   Finally, there was a grave suspicion in the
minds of reformers that the Government of the day was not
very hearty in its approval of this portion of its own legislation, and looked upon its zealous enforcement with even
some impatience.[1]

RENEWAL OF AGITATION.—It will easily be gathered
from these statements what the principal difficulties were in
the way of the successful operation of the Factory Act of
1833.   There were the imperfections of the Act itself ; and
there was the opposition of the employers affected by it.
To these must be added considerable dissatisfaction with it
among the operatives.   This statute, the first really solid
contribution to factory legislation, had the singular result of
pleasing nobody.   With regard to the opposition of employers, it should not be all set down to mere selfishness,
as has been sometimes too hastily done.   Many of them were
thoroughly convinced (and it must be remembered that the
best economists of the day were with them) that all such
legislation was unsound ; whilst others were unable to re-
concile it with reason that the industries in which they were
engaged should be alone singled out for exceptional disqualifications.   Such as these considered it an absolute
duty to their class to evade or outwit a law thus partial in its
operation ; and however wrong such a conception of duty
was, it cannot be said to have been wholly without excuse.

[1] Compare *Life of Lord Shaftesbury* ; vol. i., p. 216 *et circa*.

under the circumstances. "Show us," they said in effect, "why we, and not others, have to submit to these impediments to money-making at the expense of our fellow-creatures, and afterwards we will join issue with you on the general subject." Until that was done, they believed their best policy to be to render the administration of the law ineffectual, and so possibly bring about its repeal, and this was the course they took. It is not so easy to account for the opposition of the workers. Still it is by no means impossible. The legislative results of the first reformed Parliament were the occasion of dissatisfaction to many other persons besides factory operatives. But, besides any general causes of complaint, there were in this case special ones as well, in connection with the fate that had overtaken their cherished project of a Ten Hours Bill. This had been completely thrust into the background as a sequel to the production of the Government measure, and when last brought to a division its principle rejected by the overwhelming majority of 238 to 93. Add to the above, that the Commission on whose report action was taken had from the first been viewed by them with dislike ; they were resolved not to be satisfied with anything that resulted from it, and were not so accordingly.

It was this inauspicious moment that was selected by the Administration for paltering with the new law by proposing to minimise its utility in a vital point. It will be remembered how certain clauses had been given more than two years to come into operation,[1] of which was the clause limiting the labour of children between nine and thirteen to nine hours a day. Shortly before the expiry of this period, then, Mr. Poulett Thompson, President of the

[1] " Thirty months from the passing of this Act."

G

Board of Trade, introduced a measure for the purpose of reducing the maximum age to twelve, thus prospectively depriving all children between that age and thirteen of the relief which had apparently been secured them. The reformers were up in arms at once. (It needed only such a stimulus to set light afresh to the smouldering fires of agitation, and, thus stimulated, they broke out with re-doubled violence.) The inefficiency of the law, and un-trustworthiness of ministers, furnished Oastler, Bull and others, with ample material for fresh diatribes; which were delivered with increasing bitterness from a still increasing number of platforms, and to an ever increasing number of converts. The demand for a Ten Hours Bill was renewed afresh and prosecuted with increased ardour.

The Government viewed this recrudescence of agitation with some alarm; as they well might. On Mr. Poulett Thompson's Bill coming to a division it escaped defeat by the narrow majority of *two*: and was of course with-drawn : and Mr. Charles Hindley was only prevented from introducing a somewhat novel proposal, imposing a ten hours limit on the use of machinery, by the urgent as-surances of Lord John Russell that the provisions of the late Act should be rigorously enforced in future. In the opinion of the agitators this pledge was not kept; and so dissatisfied were they at this time with the general position of affairs, and so infatuated, in particular, with their own scheme, that they could not be even induced to interest themselves in a very useful Bill which Mr. Fox Maule now brought forward, and that failed in consequence to become law : really on account of this lack of their support, but nominally of a small amendment which was carried against it in

Committee.[1] "The Bill, the whole Bill, and nothing but the Bill ;" such was the popular cry.

PROGRESS OF LEGISLATION.—These extreme pretensions, combined with certain political changes just then in progress,[2] had the effect of limiting for awhile further legislation for factories. The interval was far from being a barren one, however, in the history of industrial legislation generally. In 1840 Lord Ashley had procured the appointment of that celebrated first Commission on the Employments of the People, to which reference has been made (p. 45), one of whose first results was the passing of a much needed Mines Act (5 & 6 Vic., c. 69). In the following year (1843) this Commission published its second Report, destined to open up thereafter far wider fields of legislative activity than had yet been traversed or even conceived of in connection with labour regulation generally. In the meanwhile factory legislation itself had been taken in hand again. A Conservative administration under the second Sir Robert Peel was now in office, and understood to be sympathetically disposed towards any scheme of reform short of the obnoxious Ten Hours Bill. No such compromise making its appearance, the Government decided to bring in a measure of its own, and on the 7th of March 1843, such a one was introduced by Sir James Graham (Home Secretary). This Bill was marked from the first by novel features. It proposed to reduce the hours of

[1] The Government had proposed to exclude silk mills from the operation of the Act. Lord Ashley carried an amendment including these, and on this pretext the whole Bill was withdrawn.

[2] In the course of 1841 a Whig Ministry, in office since the passing of the Reform Bill, had resigned, and at the succeeding general election that party was defeated.

work of children to six and a half a day—to be taken either in the morning or afternoon, but not in both ; but the age at which they might commence to work at all was to be reduced from nine to eight years. During five days of the week these children were to receive three hours' instruction ; either in the forenoon or afternoon ; at a school approved by the Privy Council. The maximum age of male young persons was to remain at eighteen, but in the case of females to be extended to twenty-one ; and the hours of work of both these classes of workers were to be twelve on the first five days of the week (taken any time between 5:30 a.m. and 8.30 p.m.), and until 4.30 p.m. on Saturday. Some provision was made for the fencing of dangerous machinery in factories, hitherto much neglected ; and the recovery of lost time was confined to those of them using only water-power.

It will be generally allowed now, that, so far as it went, this was a carefully drawn and well thought-out measure, and that many of its proposals were excellent. In particular, one might have singled out beforehand the educational proposal as being specially deserving of commendation, yet, singular to say, it was on this hitherto unknown rock of offence that the whole structure was fated to suffer shipwreck. The Dissenters strongly objected to any State interference with elementary education, and, as they were on other points powerful supporters of the Bill though generally adverse to Ministers ; their opposition proved fatal. Within the remaining time at the disposal of Government during that session no terms of compromise could be arranged, and the measure was withdrawn.

It was reintroduced on the 6th of February 1844, the " religious difficulty " being compromised by the appointment of the Factory Inspector in place of the Privy Council as judge of the efficiency of schools Most of the other clauses remained the same as before with the striking exception that it was now proposed to extend the protection of the law to adult women !) The time for filing an Information for a breach of the Act was extended to two, and in some instances three, months after the commission of the offence, and minute precautions were directed against the notorious frauds which had hindered the due execution of the Act of 1833. But the ten hours men were still unsatisfied; and the Government were equally resolved not to give way. A series of manœuvres in Committee[1] resulted in the withdrawal of this Bill yet a second time, and its reproduction two months afterwards almost in the exact form that it has ultimately come down to us a completed statute. On this last occasion Lord Ashley, leading the opposition sustained a crushing defeat ; the numbers being for his amendment 159, against it 297; majority for the Bill 138.

THE FACTORY ACT, 1844.—The Factory Act of 1844 (7 Vic., c. 15) is an extremely important one in the history of factory legislation, and it is absolutely necessary for anyone desiring to familiarize himself with this subject to study it carefully. It was directed, in the first place, thoroughly and systematically, against the defects which hindered the due administration of former Acts, and originated an elaborate machinery for keeping them in check. Most interesting it is to compare its provisions with those of the first Factory Act, for the purpose of marking the changed tone that characterized

[1] A description of these will be found in *The Modern Factory System* ; pp. 386, 7.

the new legislation in regard to social sanctions, and scarcely less so to compare the debate that preceded its enactment with that which preceded the enactment of the Act of 1833, with economic sanctions in view. By this means the most readily can the advance made in the comprehension and formal treatment of certain important objects of such legislation be seen, while certain others will be noted as being relinquished. Its operation was exclusively confined to textile industry; the term factory being now for the first time specifically defined in that sense (p. 2); and to that province of it only where exterior motive power was employed in manufacture. Though not destined to be a final settlement of labour troubles even in that limited sphere, it was a statesmanlike and vigorous measure of reform, honourable alike to the motives, knowledge, and foresight of its promoters.

This Act reduced the hours of work for children between eight and thirteen (not *nine* and thirteen as formerly) to six and a half a day, either in the morning or afternoon, no child being allowed to work in both on the same day, except on alternate days, and then only for ten hours. Young persons and *women* (now included for the first time) were to have the same hours, *i.e.* not more than twelve for the first five days of the week (with one and a half out for meals), and nine on Saturday. These hours were to be reckoned consecutively from the period of commencement; half an hour at least being allowed for a meal before 1 p.m., and the whole meal time given between 7.30 a.m. and 7.30 p.m. Eight half-holidays, besides Christmas Day and Good Friday and the usual interval on Saturday (and of course Sunday), were to be allowed every year, notice of which was to be given beforehand. The regulations about recovering lost time were revised; and certificates of age were to be granted in future only by surgeons appointed for the purpose. Accidents causing death or bodily injury were to be reported to these surgeons, who were to investigate their cause and report the result to the inspector. Dangerous machinery was to be fenced. The factory was to be thoroughly washed with lime every fourteen months, or painted with oil once every seven years. An abstract of the law was required to be hung up in every factory ; and a Notice, on which were to be inscribed the name of the inspector, the time of commencing and ceasing work, and the name of some public clock by which the hours of labour were regulated. A Register was likewise to be kept ; in which were to be entered the names of all children and young persons employed, the dates of the lime-washing, and some other particulars. Certificates of school attendance were to be obtained in the case of children ; the employer being responsible for the school fees. Inspectors were deprived of their magisterial jurisdiction, but in some other particulars their powers were increased.

SOME SUBSEQUENT ENACTMENTS.—The next two years were years of great interest in the political and industrial world but not of special note in the history of factory legislation. A Print Works Act (8 and 9 Vic. c. 29) was passed, however, in 1845, containing requirements closely akin to those of the Factory Acts, and similar provision for administration. This statute was the earliest fruit of the second Report of the first Children's Employment Commission. It prohibited work by women and children between 10 p.m. and 6 a.m. but not by "young persons," and was otherwise faulty in respect to the regulations as to duration of labour, meal-times, school attendance, and sanitation. It was subsequently repealed and incorporated with other Acts, and is principally interesting now as being the first one of the series applied to a process other than strictly textile manufacture. Following it at intervals of some distance came the Bleach Works Act (23 & 24 Vic., c. 78), with its amending Acts (25 & 26 Vic., c. 8, 26 & 27 Vic., c. 38, and 27 & 28 Vic., c. 98); and the Lace Works Act (24 & 25 Vic., c. 117). These, like the above have been since incorporated in one general law.[1] In the meanwhile the agitation for a Ten Hours Bill had by no means ceased. Early in 1846 Lord Ashley again brought forward a measure cast in this mould, which, on his defeat at the General Election that year, was taken up by Mr. John Fielden, and ultimately pressed to a division, when the Government escaped defeat by the narrow majority of ten. The next year the Whigs were in office, and Lord John Russell Prime Minister. Mr. Fielden reintroduced the Bill, and its progress through Parliament was one continued triumph. The second reading was carried by a majority of over a hundred; the third reading by eighty-eight; while on the critical division in the House of Lords, the numbers voting were, fifty-three for, and only eleven peers against it. After this great success it received the royal assent forthwith and became law almost immediately (June 8th, 1847).

With the enactment of this law (10 Vic., c. 29) the long struggle for a Ten Hours Bill is generally held to have come to a close. It limited the hours of labour to sixty-three per week from the 1st of July 1847, and to fifty-eight per week, from the 1st of May 1848, which with the stoppage on Saturday afternoon was the equivalent of ten hours work per day. Great was the rejoicing in the manufacturing districts when its success was assured, but events showed this rejoic-

---

[1] Namely, in *The Factory and Workshop Act,* 1870 (33 & 34 Vic., c. 62) itself incorporated in *Factory and Workshop Act*, 1878 (41 Vic., c. 16).

ing to be premature. The Bill contained a fatal defect.
It did not provide exactly *when* the hardly-won ten hours
were to be worked ; between 5.30 a.m. and 8.30 p.m. ; so
that apparently they might be taken any time between those
limits.   The result was the immediate reintroduction of the
discredited Relay System, with all its opportunities for trickery
and evasion, and renewed discontent among the operatives.
Early in the session of 1850 Lord Ashley brought this
matter forward for debate.   He was met in a conciliatory
spirit by Sir George Grey, then Home Secretary, who proposed as a compromise to fix the period of employment for
protected persons from six in the morning till six in the
evening in summer, and from seven in the morning till seven
in the evening in winter (with one and a half hours out for
meals), and that all work should cease at two o'clock on
Saturday : the effect of which would be to slightly increase
the weekly working hours from fifty-eight to sixty, while
rendering the enforcement of the definite working day practically secure.) Lord Ashley was for accepting this proposal,
while Mr. Oastler and some others were against it.   The
contest was short and sharp ; the official suggestions
being assailed from very diverse quarters ; but eventually
a measure (13 & 14 Vic., c. 54) containing the above
provisions became law (August 5th, 1850).   It formed an
admirable and most successful sequel to the Acts of 1844
and 1847.   By it the ten hours dispute was finally set at
rest, and the normal working day really established throughout the whole range of industries affected.   Some anomalies
still remaining were remedied by two subsequent statutes ; 16
and 17 Vic., c. 104 and 19 & 20 Vic., c. 38 ; the former
dealing principally with the employment and education of
children, the latter with the fencing of mill-gearing and

machinery; and with these the elder series of Factory Acts, those specially confined to the textile and closely related industries, came to an end, for twenty years at least.

SECOND CHILDREN'S EMPLOYMENT COMMISSION.—Not so the general course of protective labour legislation, which, on the contrary, began from this time to spread from point to point in ever-widening circles of usefulness, thus gradually but certainly disclosing its real character and aims. The direction of this advance was along the usual lines. The disclosures made in the second Report of the first Children's Employment Commission had had, we have already observed, a marked effect on public opinion. Their immediate result was seen in the passing of a Print Works Act;[1] and subsequently, Bleaching and Dyeing Acts;[2] and, still more remotely connected with the conventional notion of factory labour, a Bakehouse Act (July, 1863). But the indisposition to push these investigations to their only logical conclusion and require a similar protection for all competitive industries was still very strong. The conception of a factory as necessarily a place of textile manufacture only, stood in the way, and it was also not unreasonably pleaded at first that the system of factory inspection was comparatively novel, nor had yet been particularly successful. But under the elaborate provisions of the Act of 1844, applied to the clearly defined hours of labour introduced by that of 1850, factory inspection presently became a recognised success, a source of increasing satisfaction to the operatives, and even at length to masters : who found no evil results flowing from it of the magnitude they had been led to expect, and many good results, the nature and quality of which they had not at first foreseen. Under these

[1] *Ante*, p. 87. [2] *Idem.*

circumstances, all the Government could plead for now in view of the ever increasing pressure put upon them both by facts and arguments, was more delay and fuller information before embarking again on the wide sea of industrial enterprise with further projects of reform. The weightiness of that plea, if not its abstract justice, was allowed by reformers, and yet another appeal to the arbitration of facts decided on. In 1861 a new Royal Commission was appointed to go fully over the whole ground again, being issued to three gentlemen, Hugh Seymour Tremenheere, Richard Dugard Granger and Edward Carleton Tufnell. "This second great Commission, whose members laboured," says Herr von Plener,[1] "from 1862 till 1866 with extraordinary diligence, and to an almost complete exhaustion of the subject, found a much easier field of action than did their predecessors in 1840 and following years. The decided improvement of the textile labourers in moral and material respects, and the continuous increase in production, notwithstanding the reduction in the hours of labour, had gradually convinced the manufacturers and the public at large that their originally violent opposition to the legal reduction of labour was fallacious and groundless, and that its further extension to other branches of industry would not be fraught with such ruinous consequences as had been generally supposed and predicted in 1843, the exaggerated description of which was the principal reason why no practical course was given to the recommendation of the first Children's Employment Commission—except in the case of mines—and of Print and Bleach Works, etc., as before explained." The result more than justified, as usual, the anticipations of those who were urging further legislation, the facts elicited being at

[1] *English Factory Legislation* ; p. 56.

least as bad as anything that had been proved against textile manufacture. In the trade of *letter-press printing* in London, for instance, certain houses where books and newspapers were printed, had acquired, we read, the name of "slaughter-houses," owing to the exceptional mortality prevailing there, especially amongst boys. "Similar excesses," writes Karl Marx,[1] "are practised in *book-binding*, where the victims are chiefly women, girls, and children." " A classical example of overwork," he continues, . . . "is afforded by *brick and tile-making*." . . . " Between May and September the work lasts from five in the morning till eight in the evening, and where the drying is done in the open air, it often lasts from four in the morning till nine in the evening. Work from five in the morning till seven in the evening is considered 'reduced' and 'moderate.' Both boys and girls of six, *and even of four years of age*, are employed. They work often longer than the adults." In a certain field at Mosley, *e.g.*, "a young woman, twenty-four years of age, was in the habit of making two thousand tiles a day with the assistance of two little girls who carried the clay for her and stacked the tiles. These girls carried daily ten tons up the slippery sides of the clay pits, from a depth of thirty feet, and then a distance of two hundred and ten feet." He cites the opinion of one of the Commissioners on the general subject of child labour in this occupation as follows : " It is impossible," this gentleman writes, "for a child to pass through the purgatory of a tile-field without great moral degradation . . . . the low language which they are accustomed to hear from their tenderest years, the filthy, indecent, and shameless habits, amidst which, unknowing and half wild, they grow up, make them

[1] *Capital* ; vol. ii., p. 466 (Swan Sonnenschein, 1887).

in after life lawless, abandoned, dissolute." One "frightful source of demoralization" was "the mode of living;"—but the details are painful, and not immediately pertinent, and may be omitted. In the industry of *straw-plaiting* about seven thousand children were employed. They commence to be employed, we learn, "generally in their fourth, often between their third and fourth year." "Education, of course, they get none." . . . "The straw cuts their mouths, with which they constantly moisten it, and their fingers." The space allowed for working was in one instance "$12\frac{2}{3}$, 17, $18\frac{1}{2}$, and below 22, cubic feet for each person," taken from actual measurement; the lowest of these numbers representing "less space than the half of what a child would occupy if packed in a box measuring 3 feet in each direction." In the occupations carried on in the "Black Country:" nail-making, chain-making and the like, many atrocious evils were disclosed; and also in the miscellaneous trades in and about Birmingham. Terrible dangers were found to characterise the Sheffield industries. But possibly the worst conditions of environment were found to belong to the manufacture of articles of *wearing apparel.* "The description of the workshops . . . surpasses the most loathsome phantasies of our romance writers." All the smaller classes of industries, indeed, were found—as might have been expected—in an even more pitiable condition than the larger classes, and places where machinery was not used than where it was. Thus : "Young people are worked to death at turning the looms in *silk-weaving* when it is not carried on by machinery." Where it was carried on by machinery they had, of course, the protection of the Factory Acts. The same remark applied, of course, to *hosiery* and *lace-making*. The Factory Act of 1861 regulated the making of lace so far as it was done by machinery, but lace-finishing is done "either in what are called ' Mistresses' Houses,' or by women in their own houses, with or without the help of their children." "The number of the work-women employed in these workrooms varies from twenty to forty in some, and from ten to twenty in others. The average age at which the children commence work is six years, but in many cases it is below five. The usual work-ing hours are from eight in the morning till eight in the evening, with one and a half hours for meals, which are taken at irregular intervals, and often in the foul workrooms. When business is brisk the labour frequently lasts from eight or even six o'clock in the morning till ten, eleven, or twelve o'clock at night." . . . It is not at all uncommon in Nottingham (writes a Commissioner) to find fourteen to twenty children huddled together in a small room, perhaps not more than twelve feet square, and employed for fifteen hours out of the twenty-four at work that of itself is exhausting from its weariness and monotony, and is besides carried on under every possible unwholesome condition." Yet, "when women and their children work at home . . . . the state of things is, if possible, *even worse!*" Another kind of lace was found to be made in "lace schools." "The rooms are generally the ordinary living rooms of small cottages, the chimney stopped up to keep out draughts, the inmates kept warm by their own animal heat alone, and this frequently in winter." In other cases "these so-called schoolrooms are like small store-rooms without fire-places. . . . The overcrowding in these dens and the consequent vitiation of the air are often extreme, and added to this is the injurious effect of drains, privies, decomposing substances, and other filth usual in the purlieus of the smaller cottages." As regards space in such instances: "In one lace school, eighteen girls and a mistress,—35 cubic feet to each person ; in another, where the smell was unbearable,—eighteen persons and 24½ cubic feet per head ;" and age : "In this industry are to be found employed *children of two and two and a half years* !"[1]

THE FACTORY ACT, 1864.—This Commission issued its Reports at intervals during the progress of the enquiry ; which was conducted on a pre-arranged plan. The first set of industries dealt with were such as had already been unfavourably reported on by the Commissioners of 1840, and included the manufacture of earthenware—"except bricks and tiles,"—of lucifer matches, of percussion caps, of cartridges, and the two "employments" of paper-staining and fustian-cutting. All of these were again strongly animadverted upon, and a Bill was brought in forthwith to afford them the protection recommended.

The Act that followed (27 & 28 Vic., c. 38) was passed on July 25th, 1864. It inflicted a death-blow on all current conceptions of the mission of factory legislation and may be even said to have commenced a new industrial era. The conventional notion of a factory, and of any scheme of factory legislation founded on employment there, was hereby utterly abandoned, and not merely several new processes, not only isolated as well as congregated labour, (as in the case of fustian-cutting), but even certain *employments* (as such) were assumed henceforward to be fit subjects for it. The last was in reality a conclusive step. If some employments were proper subjects for Factory Acts, with no other qualifica-

[1] This last statement may well appear incredible. It is necessary to state, therefore, that it is taken from the Chld. Empl. Comm., II. Rep., (1864) p. xxx.

tions for inclusion beyond the hardships endured in them, why not others, and every other, in a like way ? To such an enlargement of the possible category there was practically no limit, and the economical counterpoise to the Industrial Revolution seemed already on the very eve of fulfilment.

THE FACTORY ACT, 1867.—For a while, too, it looked as if no less than that consummation were actually contemplated by the legislature. When the full Reports of the second great Enquiry into the Employments of the people were published, it was found that the commissioners unanimously recommended the extension of the system of factory inspection to a number of occupations previously regarded as quite outside its sphere, and its modified application in others, hereafter to be dealt with ; which seemed practically to exhaust the whole field of material labour. Bills were prepared with all despatch, accordingly, and took formal shape next year. The first of these was The Factory Extension Act, 1867 (30 & 31 Vic., c. 103); the second The Workshop Regulation Act of the same year (30 & 31 Vic., c. 146). The former extended the principles and practice of preceding Factory Acts to the following industries, and places where industries were carried on, *specifically* in the first place, as follows :—

1. Any blast furnace or other furnace or premises in or on which the process of smelting or otherwise obtaining any metal from the ores is carried on (which furnace or premises are hereinafter referred to as a blast furnace) :

2. Any copper mill :

3. Any mill, forge, or other premises in or on which any process is carried on for converting iron into

malleable iron, steel, or tin plate, or for otherwise making or converting steel, (which mills, forges, and other premises are hereinafter referred to as iron mills) :

4. Iron foundries, copper foundries, brass foundries, and other premises or places in which the process of founding or casting any metal is carried on :

5. Any premises in which steam, water, or other mechanical power is used for moving machinery employed—
   - (a.) In the manufacture of machinery :
   - (b.) In the manufacture of any article of metal not being machinery :
   - (c.) In the manufacture of india-rubber or gutta-percha, or articles made wholly or partly of india-rubber or gutta-percha :

6. Any premises in which any of the following manufactures or processes are carried on ; namely,
   - (a.) Paper manufacture :
   - (b.) Glass manufacture :
   - (c.) Tobacco manufacture :
   - (d.) Letterpress printing :
   - (e.) Bookbinding :

and *generally* to,

7. Any premises, whether joining or separate, in the same occupation, situate in the same city, town, parish, or place, and constituting one trade establishment, in, on, or within the precincts of which fifty or more persons are, or have been during the preceding year, employed in any manufacturing process :

and,

Every part of a factory shall be deemed to be a factory, except such part, if any, as is used exclusively as a dwelling.

H

A very wide meaning was assigned to the expression
' manufacturing process" :—

" Manufacturing Process " shall mean any manual
labour exercised by way of trade or for purposes of gain in
or incidental to the making any article or part of an article,
or in or incidental to the altering, repairing, ornamenting,
finishing, or otherwise adapting for sale any article.—30 & 31
Vic., c. 103, s. 3.

Apparently it only remained now to include premises
where less than fifty persons were at work " in adapting for
sale " an *article* to cover every material industry.

A striking ahd exceptional characteristic of this very comprehensive statute lay in the numerous modifications which
it contained, chiefly in the direction of mitigating the
stringency of the normal working day. Ômitting purely
temporary exceptions, the following were the principal ones.
Boys above sixteen might be employed in printing-offices
on alternate days for fifteen hours a day, and in alternate
weeks at night. In bookbinding establishments, young
persons above fourteen, and women, might work fourteen
hours, and in paper mills and glass works the customary
hours, provided they did not exceed sixty altogether in a
week. Night work was permitted to *male* young persons in
blast furnaces, iron mills, paper mills, letterpress-printing
works, and works driven exclusively by water-power, provided they were not employed either on the preceding or
following day, and, in the case of blast furnaces, for not
more than six—in the case of paper mills—seven, nights
in one fortnight. A power was vested in the Secretary of
State of extending such modifications at pleasure, where, in
his opinion, " the customs or exigencies of certain trades "
required it, and also of sanctioning alterations in the usual

working hours (from six to six o'clock, to seven to seven, or to eight to eight), and in other matters of detail.   The Act was supplementary to, and not in place of, any preceding Act; it effected no change in the ages of protected persons, in the normal hours of labour, nor in the mode of administration that had been hitherto found effective. Its mission appeared to be to simply extend the protection of the State, found to be of use in certain industries and employments, to other ones, on the wholly unambiguous plea that they stood in equal need of it.

CHAPTER V.

THE FACTORY ACTS

(1867 to 1891).

THE WORKSHOP REGULATION ACT—THE FACTORY ACT, 1871
—THE FACTORY ACT, 1874—ADULT LABOUR—THE FACTORY
ACT, 1878—" SWEATING "—THE FACTORY ACT, 1891—
PRACTICAL RESULTS OF LEGISLATION.

THE WORKSHOP REGULATION ACT.—The Factory Act of
1867 extended the current system of factory inspection to a
great variety of new industries, but made no important
alterations in it, nor in the general practice of factory
legislation. But besides the occupations brought thus
under supervision a large number of similar ones which had
engaged the attention of the second Children's Employment
Commission remained untouched, such as domestic occupations, small handicrafts, and generally all those forms of
manual labour carried on in workplaces where less than
fifty persons were employed at once (see p. 97). After
prolonged consideration it was decided to subject these to
supervision also, but supervision of not quite the same kind,
and a supplementary statute (30 & 31 Vic., c. 146) was
devised and enacted for that purpose. The title given to
this one was The Workshop Regulation Act, the

term *workshop* being now introduced for the first time into
this series of laws.   Its purpose is stated with great distinct-
ness in the preamble : "Whereas by the Factory Extension
Act, 1867, provision is made, amongst other things, for
regulating the hours during which children, young persons
and women are permitted to labour in any manufacturing
process conducted in an establishment where fifty or more
persons are employed.   And whereas it is expedient to
extend protection so far as respects the regulation of the
hours of labour to children, young persons, and women working in smaller establishments. . . . Be it therefore enacted,"
etc. ; a series of provisions following, which resembled,
while they did not coincide with, the provisions of preceding
Factory Acts.   Thus, while protected persons might only
work the same aggregate number of hours per day in both,
a wider latitude was allowed to workshops than factories
in the selection of those hours, *i.e.* any period of the same
length between 6 a.m. and 8 p.m. for children ; and between 5 a.m. and 9 p.m. for women and young persons ;—
on ordinary week days, and until 4 p.m. on Saturday.
Other relaxations of the prevalent obligations in factories
followed.   Surgical certificates were not required for
children and young persons in workshops, nor was it
compulsory to keep a register of particulars.   The Half-
Time System of education, now thoroughly established in
factories, was supplanted here by a very inferior system
of ten hours schooling a week ; and many modifications
even of these maimed regulations were left to the discretion
of the Home Secretary for the time being.   But the
greatest novelty was the means by which it was proposed
to enforce this Act, namely, through "local authorities"
in the several districts where the workshops were situate.

Factory inspectors were only authorized to visit them, and report on their condition; the responsibility of actually putting the law in force was taken out of their hands. Another very important peculiarity resided in the definition of the term workshop, which, though in some respects more extensive in conception than that of the kindred term factory, contained a limitation of a highly important kind. Section iv. enacts : "Workshop shall mean any room or place whatever, whether in the open air or under cover, in which any handicraft is carried on by any child, young person, or woman, *and to which and over which the person by whom such child, young person, or woman is employed has the right of access and control* ;" so that a person might be employed at home, as an "out-worker" for instance, in the same industry and under still more unhealthy conditions than in a factory, without the employer having any responsibility in regard to that place or person. Lastly, the definition of "employed" was strictly confined to being "occupied in any handicraft" ; and this, taken in conjunction with the definition of *handicraft* itself, prescribed a special limitation in yet another direction of very great significance. Handicraft was defined to mean :—"any manual labour exercised by way of trade or for purposes of gain in or incidental to the altering, repairing, ornamenting, finishing, or otherwise adapting for sale any article"—which removed, therefore, from the purview of the law all workers except those engaged in the production of actual material wealth ; as *e.g.* such as are employed in distribution, transport, or in rendering any immaterial service, whether concerned about wealth creation or not.

The full importance of these peculiarities of The Workshop Act, and their effect on the future course of protective labour laws, will appear more fully in the sequel. For the moment it is more to the purpose to consider it and the Factory Extension Act analogically, and taken together, as the last results of a long series of efforts directed towards the same end—the amelioration of the modern worker's lot, and viewed in this way, and consequentially, it certainly does not appear that the high hopes entertained of their common purpose and powers were justified by events. It did not turn out, as some sanguine people anticipated, and even stated,[1] that the whole field of material industry was forthwith covered and the limit of this kind of legislation reached ; on the contrary, they mark a retrogression as well as an advance in the general development of events, and their analogy with preceding Acts is by no means always in their favour. True, a vastly wider area of industrial activity was brought thus within the cognizance of statute law, but that law was rendered less stringent in parts, and great and obvious gaps in the general scheme remained. The number of exceptions to the broad principle of the normal working day, for instance, either actually or potentially enacted (see p. 98), and the shifting about of the working hours permitted (in face of all precedents) in workshops, were in striking contrast with the admirably uniform regulations which had on those points dominated factory legislation since 1850 ; whilst the novel mode of administering this Act, however undeniable its inherent advantages, was at first a conspicuous failure. It soon became apparent that, whatever the intention of their framers, the dual Acts

[1] Von Plener, for instance, writes " that all work done for wages by young persons and women " was by means of these Acts, "placed under supervision and subject to distinct regulations" (*English Factory Legislation* ; p. 85). This is an astonishing exaggeration.

of 1867 were not destined to be a crowning effort of legislative wisdom.

THE FACTORY ACT, 1871.—The first objections came principally from employers—as ever heretofore. The limitation of working hours (even with the many modifications allowed) was said to be oppressive in many cases, and inimical to the interests of trade. The interaction of the two statutes too, administered side by side by dissimilar authorities and with conflicting provisions, was confusing . and annoying, and led to the strangest anomalies. On this point the inspectors spoke out with emphasis, and the work-people joined in the complaint. Presently new developments appeared. The objections of employers grew less as they became more familiar with the earlier statute, whilst the administration of the later one became more and more a " dead letter." The Factory Extension Act, like other Factory Acts, was found to be less alarming in experience than prospect, but the Workshop Act, owing to the appointed authorities either failing to carry it out or repudiating the obligation to do so, was generally ignored. An obvious deduction from these two sets of circumstances was the propriety of transferring its administration to the Factory department ; but first a rectification of preceding anomalies had to be made. This was done by the enactment (in 1870) of a short Act (33 & 34 Vic., c. 62) bringing printing, bleaching, and dyeing works up to the standard of the Factory Act of 1867. Then the way was clear. A Factory and Workshop Act—these terms now for the first time combined—passed the legislature in 1871, by which the enforcement of the Workshop Regulation Act was transferred, just as it stood, from the local bodies to the inspectors of factories, to be administered by them alongside their other duties.

At this point in the narrative it seems proper to pause, for the purpose of taking a survey of the path traversed since the Factory controversy entered on that new and wider phase typified by the changed significance of the distinguishing term, and with a view to what is to follow. The early conception of a modern factory, it will be remembered, was of a place (p. 3) where industry was "congregated and divided within an establishment of definite bounds:" the establishments thus designated being further limited by law to such as were "devoted to spinning or weaving certain fabrics by power." The Act of 1844 mentioned these included fabrics by name. Under the Factory Act of 1864, a complete alteration of this signification occurred, and several new industries were incorporated: comprising not only manufactures but "employments," and not only congregated labour but petty industries. The Factory Act of 1867 added greatly to this list. Under the Workshop Regulation Act an attempt was made, or appeared to be made, to practically complete it; but it was considered that the vast number of new occupations which would thus be brought in, and the obscure places where many of them were carried on, would render State inspection a task of great difficulty, and a new system was inaugurated of placing them partly under local, partly under imperial control. This new system, it may be noted, was in complete harmony with the spirit of the time; as since revealed in the success of such legislation, for instance, as the Education Acts; but it failed owing to inherent defects in the law itself. It was incontinently abandoned; and the multifarious duties judged but four years previously to be quite beyond the power and scope of the Factory Department to undertake, were transferred to it nevertheless, to be dealt with as best they might. It is clear enough now, it was probably clear then, that such a proceeding could be only tentative and experimental, and events have proved this to be the case. But it is extremely interesting to contemplate that change of front as part of a general advance made good by this time in the conception of the rightful sphere of State interference with labour. Workshops as well as factories, then, were fit subjects of factory legislation (still so called), and it was even possible to put them under the control of government inspectors without offence. But this term factory had been repeatedly expanded: from very narrow limits indeed, to the very indefinite ones we have instanced. Was the same fate in store for workshops? Or would the qualifying definitions introduced in the latter case, and still retained, oppose an efficient barrier against that inclusion of nearly all branches of industry which was supposed to be in contemplation? Should they be allowed to do so? Was there any longer any need, in fact, for the dual titles at all? Why not the same regulations for both places? Nay, would it be possible to stop even here? Why only material industry?—and was the inspection of the future to be a centralised or localised function, or local and central combined? Such was the pass the controversy, once so narrow, had come to, and in this condition of uncertainty and of vague possibilities was left by the legislation of 1871.

THE FACTORY ACT, 1874.—In the meanwhile an agitation had been going forward in the country, little concerned indeed with these speculations, and applying only to a particular class of works, but very closely related to the history and fabric of factory legislation. A demand had been made in certain quarters for specially limiting the time of women's work in textile factories, and subjecting those of them who were mothers to exceptional disqualifications on that account. With regard to the first of these proposals, it was nominally advocated in the interests of women themselves; with regard to the second, nominally in the interest of their offspring. In the latter case, as no action ensued then it is unnecessary to say anything more about it. The other agitation is deserving of careful consideration from several points of view. What was the meaning of this sudden demand for further limiting women's industry, and why was it confined to textile factories? There is little doubt now that it originated in the desire for a general shortening of the working-day in that industry: for male and female operatives alike: that women were, in fact, the stalking-horse behind which this larger demand was but partially concealed. But why in this particular class of works alone; were there not other employments—even among those subject to law—where women were notoriously exposed to greater hardships and worked longer hours; and many more, far worse, still untouched by factory law at all? The attempt to answer these questions will bring us face to face with a new determining influence in the history of the Factory Acts, and lead us eventually towards a long postponed discussion, as to who were in truth the proper objects of that form of legislation at all.

The textile operatives, besides being the first to benefit by factory laws, had by this time become a well-organised body outside their sphere, they had evolved a powerful and well disciplined trade union to represent their interests. Other representative trades had done the like before, several to an even greater degree, whilst many more still remained unorganised and unregulated either from without or from within. Now, the best organised, as the building and engineering trades, had early set about obtaining a reduction of working hours, extra-judicially and by the mere force of combination, so that at the passing of the Factory Extension Act it came about that legal hours were sometimes in excess of customary ones among the industries brought under its control. This was naturally displeasing to the already favoured textile trades ; especially after their disappointment as to the ten hours day ;[1] and they set about obtaining a further reduction too, only they availed themselves of different machinery for the purpose : they agitated under the shadow of an Act of Parliament, an instrument with which they had been long familiar and to which they already owed much. The artifice was of course a perfectly legitimate one, and turned out a great success. They obtained their shorter day, whilst trades that had not agitated and were not organised continued as before. This was an object lesson of extreme importance to all branches of industry, but what is specially interesting in the present connection are mainly two things—the official sanction thus given to the contention that the regulation of all labour in textile factories is involved in the regulation of certain kinds there, and the spectacle of the modern trade society relying (like the mediæval guild) on State aid for the accomplishment of its ends. Hitherto, agitators for factory reform had been mostly philanthropic persons, generally outside the sphere

[1] Chap. iv.

of interests affected, or, when the operatives themselves had joined in any number, it was commonly in response to their highly-pitched appeals; the new agitation marked the entrance on the scene of the trade association in place of the beneficent outsider, of a sectional, no longer national, impulse of action—with consequences to the Factory System the Factory Acts which are far as yet from being all foreseen.

The immediate consequence was the complete success of the agitation, as shown in the passing of the Factory Act of 1874 (37 & 38 Vic., c. 44), which took half-an-hour a day off textile factories alone, leaving all others still subject to the settlement of 1850. Some other changes were the raising of the age at which a *child* might work as a *young person* (*i.e.* for a full day) from thirteen to fourteen years (but a child of thirteen who had the requisite educational qualification might be employed as if fourteen), and certain alterations respecting their attendance at school, with a view to making the schooling more efficient. The surgical certificate of age was changed now to a certificate of fitness; and the exceptional privileges allowed to silk factories were abolished. These were valuable, if partial, gains. By far the greatest interest that attaches to this Act resides not in them, but in the debates—in Parliament and elsewhere—by which it was preceded, and in which, almost for the first time, the relation of adult labour to factory legislation was discussed in a comprehensive, though characteristically indirect manner. As the point is of extreme interest in view of some recent developments it will be desirable to deal with it at some length.

ADULT LABOUR.—The form in which adult labour first became directly subject to the provisions of the Factory

Acts was by the inclusion of women under them in 1844 (see p. 86). It is curious to notice in looking back to the debates of that year how little interest this proposal excited at the time. It appears to have been an entirely spontaneous one on the part of Sir Robert Peel's administration, which was then in power. "No section of the operatives "—writes the late Mr. Henderson [1]—"had ever proposed to impose this exceptional restriction upon the work of adult women, and it was stated during the debates in Parliament that not a single petition had been presented in favour of it." The fight had hitherto ranged round the *subjects* of legislation : the particular industries that were to be included : and it had been tacitly assumed that only juvenile labour should be protected. Suddenly this tremendously revolutionary change is made, and passes almost without comment. Then for a while the former process goes on. First one new industry, and then another, is swept within the legislative circle, which is continually widened to receive them, and at length (in 1867) something like an attempt to comprehend all is made—though we notice at this stage the impulse, hitherto triumphant, waxing somewhat faint in the effort (as shown in the varying provisions of the statutes of that year). And now arises, a proposal to further limit women's work in a very special direction, and forthwith, after a silence of nearly thirty years, the primal question is brought forward of the propriety of legislating for it at all. What does it all mean? Many explanations are forthcoming. "Manufacturers and employers "—says Mr. Henderson—" no

[1] *Great Industries of Great Britain*—"Industrial Legislation," by James Henderson, one of H.M. Superintending Inspectors of Factories, vol. iii., p. 34 (Cassell and Co.).

doubt looked with some indifference upon the proposal
to include adult women from the fact that practically a
restriction on the hours of work upon children and young
persons in a textile factory is a restriction upon all who are
employed," . . . . for "the conditions of labour in
a factory are such that one section of the workpeople
cannot be profitably employed without the other, and a
limitation upon one section proves a restriction on the
whole." This is the argument which found successful
expression in the Act of 1874. Again, "It is probable that
the source of much of the agitation which has recently
arisen over this question about the restriction of the hours
of work of adult women, may be traced to the fact that in
subsequent extensions of the factory regulations to miscellaneous trades and occupations, this special feature of
factory labour was lost sight of. When the hours of work
in occupations in which adult women were mainly or
exclusively employed came to be limited, a sharpness was
given to the contrast between the restrictions imposed upon
them and the freedom enjoyed by adult men, which did not
previously exist" (*idem*). Another explanation is that as
women had been directly legislated for by the Mines Act of
1842, it became a kind of necessity to include them in the
Factory Act of 1844; that precedent being considered
sufficient justification. It is to be remarked also that the
popular demand for a ten hours' working day, like the
modern demand for eight hours, or the abortive demand
for a restriction on machinery—which had some powerful
adherents just at this time (p. 82),—was a demand for the
restriction of male and female labour, adult and young alike.

But the real reason why the discussion of this particular
feature of factory legislation came so prominently to the

front just then can scarcely with justice be relegated to any
of these causes but is found in quite another set of circumstances, which are the following.   During the quarter
of a century that had elapsed since 1844 a highly
respectable party had arisen in this country demanding for
women equal powers and privileges with men, all laws and
institutions notwithstanding.   Now, equal privileges implied
equal responsibilities, and this party—which greatly valued
itself on its logical position—fixed on the Factory Acts as
an obvious case in point where equal responsibilities or
equal privileges (according as they were regarded) were not
entrusted to both sexes.   A man might work as long as
he liked, or could be made; a woman only (in certain
occupations) as long as the law considered just and right.
Where was the sanction for this difference of treatment;
had it ever been fairly shown to exist?   Was not a woman
of thirty (say) as good a judge of her own requirements as
(say) a man of thirty?   If not, why not?   The discussion
proceeded with vigour and, at length almost with acrimony :
the women's advocates demanding—not the protection of
their industry from unequal competition by the inclusion of
men's, and the wider extension of factory law to other
occupations (as to-day), but their complete withdrawal
from women :—the abrogation, in short, for both alike, of
those legislative tendencies which were obviously gaining
ground on every side.   This was allying themselves with
the " high and dry" school of economics, and it may be ques-
tioned if the general cause of women's advancement has not
suffered therefrom.   Moreover, it was a hopeless enterprise
in view of the steady flow of popular sentiment the other way.
Professor Fawcett was the most distinguished mouthpiece
of this party in the House of Commons, Mr. Mundella and

Sir Richard Cross (Home Secretary) were conspicuous on the other side. Throughout the debate no direct representative of the interests of adult men appeared; while the case of industries neither self-organised nor under protection by the State was quite overlooked. The result was that only one half the problem of adult labour ever came under discussion at all ; and it is awaiting full discussion still ; that the reactionaries gained some apparent concessions, which were but the prelude to an almost general rout.

Meanwhile it is becoming increasingly clear that official opinion has for some time relinquished the distinctively *non possumus* position formerly taken up in regard to men's labour, and that a full discussion of the problem cannot much longer be postponed. The enactments in successive Factory Acts on the subject of fencing machinery point inevitably to that conclusion. The first took no notice of danger from such a source at all. That of 1844 applied only to machinery "near to which children or young persons are liable to pass or be employed." A subsequent one (19 & 20 Vic., c. 38, sec. iv.) included, for the first time, "women ; " the latest (41 Vic., c. 16, sec. v., amended by 54 & 55 Vic., c. 75, sec. vi.) omits all qualifications as to persons, and makes the requirement absolute. Two other Factory Acts (though this is anticipating), passed in 1883 and 1889 respectively, are even more pertinent on this head. The first (46 & 47 Vic., c. 53) is concerned principally with sanitary evils arising in the manufacture of white lead, and enacts an extremely stringent code of regulations for persons so employed. The second (52 & 53 Vic., c. 62) is of similar import in regard to cotton factories ; the object being in this instance to check excessive moisture in weaving-sheds. In neither of these is any distinction made

I

between the requirements incumbent on male and female workers, adult and young. Both are the products of agitation by men. All the while too women are forming trade unions likewise, and, led by a new school of advisers, bringing their corporate influence to bear on the factory controversy, no longer on the side of exclusion only, but inclusion. How long, under such circumstances, sex distinctions will be preserved in factory legislation, and by what arguments ultimately justified, is a matter that belongs not to this but future history, and with the decision of which the whole position as to adult labour is inevitably bound up.

THE FACTORY ACT, 1878.—It will be easily understood after this summary that the various motives of legislation which had now been enunciated, the numerous Acts that had been passed, and the complicated and divergent provisions appertaining to them, had introduced great confusion into the administration of factory law. There had grown up, not merely a very general uncertainty as to the proper objects to be dealt with, but renewed uncertainty as to its subjects likewise. All sorts of occupations, accordingly :— wandering trades, the business of transport, shop labour, even at length domestic service, began to agitate for the application of a Factory Act (so called) to them, and, on the other hand, a reverse movement against supervision, on the usual plea that it injuriously affected trade, claimed some attention. To assimilate those dissimilar provisions, and consider these contending claims, a time-honoured device was resorted to. A Royal Commission was appointed to take the whole matter into consideration. This Commission was issued to several distinguished gentlemen, most of whom are still living. They laboured with much assiduity, and accumulated a great quantity of valuable material, the result being given in a Report, published in 1876, and their principal recommendations embodied afterwards in an Act of Parliament (41 Vic., c. 16) often called the Factory Consolidation Act, but whose proper title is The Factory and Workshop Act, 1878.

This is the Factory Act now in force (succeeding modifications of the law will be explained hereafter). Its primary purpose was to "consolidate and amend" existing Acts, so as "to remove discrepancies prevailing amongst them and render their administration more even and secure." But a secondary object was to "relieve minor industries from the pressure of legislation and secure more independence for adult labour—" the Commissioners yielding on this point to the great mass of strenuous and well-organized evidence that was submitted to them. With this double object in view a new nomenclature for Factories and Workshops was introduced.

The Act deals with five classes of works : [1]

Textile Factories,
Non-Textile Factories,
Workshops,
Workshops in which neither children nor young persons are employed,
Domestic Workshops.

A "factory" is a place in which machinery is moved by the aid of steam, water, or other mechanical power, and factories are divided into two classes, Textile Factories and Non-Textile Factories, "these expressions being now first

[1] Abbreviated from *The Factory and Workshop Act*, 1878, by Alexander Redgrave, C.B.—Introduction (Shaw and Sons, 1885).

used in an Act of Parliament." The old legal term "which was originally defined to mean a place in which cotton, wool, etc., was operated upon by the aid of steam or water-power; is retained for both, but as the regulations differ in some factories from those in others it has been necessary to use distinctive terms for the two classes."

The definition of a Textile Factory remains the same as under former Acts, and the regulations affecting them continue the same as before as to hours of work and meals, and education of children, lime-washing, holidays, etc., etc. In one or two particulars (however) the precise enactments of the old Factory Acts have been varied and made applicable to all factories, which variations will be noticed in their place.

The term "Non-Textile Factory" applies to the occupations enumerated in the Acts of 1864 and 1867, whether using power or not, and includes in addition all unnamed occupations in which mechanical power is used. This definition "releases from the special factory regulations all those occupations which were (constituted) factories under the Factory Act, 1867, by reason of fifty persons being employed, and in which mechanical power is not used."

All the unnamed occupations in which power is not used, except those specially named in the Acts of 1864 and 1867. are defined to be Workshops.

In these the hours of work and meals, and education, are as strictly provided for as in Factories, but unless circumstances satisfy the Secretary of State that they are required, registers and certificates of fitness are not compulsory.

The next class of works, to which fewer regulations apply, are the workshops in which none but women above the age of eighteen are employed.

In these workshops the actual number of hours of work and of meals must be the same as in Non-Textile Factories, but with more elasticity of arrangement.

The last class of works is designated "Domestic Workshop." These are Workshops carried on in a private house, room, or place in which the only persons employed are members of the same family dwelling there.

In these the number of hours of work and meals for children and young persons must be the same as in Non-Textile Factories, but with more elasticity of arrangement; the education of children is the same. The employment of women themselves in Domestic Workshops is unrestricted.

But the Act exempts from the regulations in respect to Domestic Workshops, and leaves altogether free from control certain occupations of a light character when carried on in a dwelling-house by the family dwelling therein, viz. :—

Straw-plait Making,
Pillow-lace Making,
Glove Making,

and others of a like nature to which a Secretary of State might extend this exemption.

It also exempts from the regulations as to hours of labour and meals, Flax Scutch Mills in which women only are employed intermittently, and for not more than six months in the year.

It further exempts any handicraft which is exercised in a dwelling-house by the family dwelling there, at irregular intervals, and does not furnish the whole or principal means of living to the family: that is, practically, what is known as "home work;" and,

Finally, workshops in which men only are employed are entirely beyond its purview.

"SWEATING."—The Factory Consolidation Act was a great boon to those who had the duty of administering the law and it removed several long-standing anomalies. Where it failed to give general satisfaction was in those carefully-devised provisions for shielding adult labour from intrusion, which was also where it conflicted most with the needs and spirit of the time. Neither of themselves, nor in their relation to the development of any just and comprehensive scheme of protective labour legislation, were these successful. It will be remembered how the second Children's Employment Commission had reported very strongly on the evils pervading "domestic" industries [1] (p. 93), and that it was the obvious intention of the Workshop Regulation Act to accord a protection to these similar to what had been extended to the numerous works legislated for by the Factory Act of 1867. But defects in that Act itself (pp. 101, 2), and the unwillingness of local authorities to fulfil, in many cases, their obligations under it, had prevented this consummation. By now excepting altogether adult labour in domestic workshops from supervision the new Act took a long step backward in the same direction, and this action, combined with the old difficulty of the legal signification of the term workshop, went far towards placing a large class of helpless persons (equally the victims of competition with any employed in factories, and not organized for their own protection as factory operatives were), outside the pale of State concern. The natural result of this proceeding was a strong

[1] By these "domestic industries" must not be understood, of course, the Domestic System of industry ; on the contrary they were mostly occupations which had passed from under the influence of that more archaic type of production and were exposed to the full force of competition, like factory labour. Hence the necessity of affording them the same protection.

reaction against both the intentions of this statute and their faulty mode of fulfilment ; an agitation was forthwith set on foot to bring such persons within the sphere of factory legislation too, and proceeding, as it is the nature of strong reactions to do, somewhat to extremes, enthusiastic reformers were soon found to propose not merely the wholesale extension of factory legislation to homes, but the utter abolition of home industry, and the forcing all persons working there out of them and into factories !

A term which seemed to carry much weight in this discussion was the term "sweating." It is not a new one, and has been used with very varying meanings at various times. Mr. Howell (*Conflicts of Capital and Labour*) uses it in connection with the Spitalfield Acts (passed in the reign of George III.) ; leaving its meaning however unexplained.[1] In " Alton Locke," the letters of " Parson Lot," and the literature of that day, a rather more precise signification is assigned it :[2] and now a whole host of new ones appeared, circling for a while round the notion that a " sweater " was a middleman, or agent, intermediate between the wholesale producer and retailer. Upon this functionary a great deal of honest indignation was for a while expended ; till presently it was found that "sweating" is only "the undue advantage which is taken of labour in general," that " labour is liable to be sweated under any and every system

[1] See also *Modern Factory System* ; p. 279.

[2] The system so vigorously exposed in these publications was that according to which money was advanced to workmen, generally beyond what they could possibly repay, who were thus kept in perpetual bondage by the weight of undischarged debt. But the horrible condition of their work-rooms, and the resulting danger to the public are also properly stigmatised. As at the present time, it was tailors' work rooms which incurred the heaviest condemnation.

of employment ; " is " a condition of industry under which workers are practically compelled to work at starvation wages for excessive hours and under insanitary conditions ; " [1]—with which discoveries its special economic significance may be said to have been disposed of. The time was ripe now for further action, and a Committee of the House of Lords having undertaken to investigate the matter, this was very thoroughly done, and a number of useful suggestions embodied in a subsequent Report. From the date when that Report appeared, and utterly dispelled the illusion that there was anything exceptional to investigate, ·the last shred of pretence that modern factory legislation is concerned more with concentrated than isolated labour, or with one form or fibre of manufacture than another, ceased, it must be supposed, to operate, and its proper relation to industrial history was at length established. By devious paths, and through many involutions of form and phrase, it had forced its way to this recognition, till now it stood confessed (whether actually or potentially operative) the requisite economic counterpoise to the enormous evils of unlimited competition which inevitably accompany its splendid triumphs.

THE FACTORY ACT, 1891.—It now became the duty of the Executive to embody these conclusions in a statute, and much care and thought was expended on the task.

---

[1] These quotations are from the writings of Mr. Schloss who has done much to arouse public opinion on this matter. The conclusion of the House of Lords' Committee, may be compared with them. Sweat-ing, we are informed, is, " taking advantage of the necessities of the poorer and more helpless classes of workers," Vol. V., p. 171. It is " Grinding the faces of the poor,"—the still more compendious definition of Mr. Arnold White.

The Home Secretary (Mr. Matthews) prepared a Bill for the purpose, which was considered clause by clause by a Grand Committee of the House of Commons, three competing Bills introduced into Parliament during the same session (1890) being withdrawn in its favour. This Bill when it emerged from the ordeal to which it was thus subjected was found to be a good deal altered, the spirit of compromise (which is the characteristic spirit of all committees) having decidedly left its mark upon it. The result is contained in The Factory and Workshop Act, 1891 (54 & 55 Vic., c. 75), which abounds with novel features. This Act is divided into seven distinct parts, as follows :—Sections 1 to 5 inclusive deal with *Sanitary Provisions*; 6 to 7 with *Safety*; 8 to 12, *Special Rules and Requirements*; 13 to 15, *Period of Employment*; 16, *Holidays*; 17 to 21 with *Conditions of Employment* ; and sections 22 to 41 are headed *Miscellaneous*. The first part is the most characteristic. It hands over again to local authorities the sanitary inspection of workshops (which had been in the charge of the factory inspectors since 1871), reserving, however, to the latter the enforcement of the current law (Factory Act, 1878) as regards hours of labour and schooling. Where a local authority becomes aware of the presence of any person in a workshop to whom the protective clauses of the Act apply the duty is cast upon it of reporting that circumstance to the factory inspector ; and on the other hand, where a factory inspector receives notice of the opening of a new workshop it devolves on him to forward that notice to the local authority. Thus a dual control is re-established, somewhat in the same spirit, though not after the same fashion, as under the Workshop Regulation Act. Provision is made (which was not the case before)

for the contingency of these authorities not availing themselves of their powers; in which dilemma the Secretary of
State may authorise factory inspectors to take steps
for enforcing the law at their expense, and it is to
be particularly observed that workshops include under
this Act those "conducted on the system of not employing
any child, young person, or woman therein," *i.e.* workshops
where adult men only are at work.   Under the categories
Safety, and *Special Rules*, the requirements for fencing
machinery are made more stringent; the Secretary of State
(*i.e.* Home Secretary) is invested with large discretionary
powers as to dangerous and unhealthy incidents of employment; and a new provision is enacted for providing means
of escape from fire—the enforcement of which is likewise
in the hands of the local authority (in London of the County
Council).   *Period of Employment*, and *Holidays*, contain
nothing of very great importance; but under the heading
Conditions of Employment two considerable additions to previous legislation are made.   The first is the prohibition on
employers to employ women within four weeks after confinement; the second the raising the minimum age at which
a child may be set to work from ten to eleven (after 1st of
January, 1893).   These two provisions were inserted in
accordance with resolutions passed at a labour conference
held in Berlin, at the instance of the Emperor of Germany,
in 1890.   Among the *Miscellaneous* sections the most novel
and important are the 24th and 27th.   The first, known as
the "Particulars Clause," lays the obligation on all occupiers of factories where payment is by the piece "to supply
weavers in cotton, worsted, woollen, linen, or jute; and
winders, weavers, and reelers in cotton; with particulars of
the manufacture sufficient to enable them to ascertain the

rate of wages at which they are entitled to be paid;" the second requires lists of *outworkers* to be kept by every occupier and "contractor," where so ordered by a Secretary of State: "the same to be open to the inspection of any inspector of factories or officer of a sanitary authority." The purpose of these novel additions to the previously unfamiliar course of factory legislation are too apparent to need description. They are sufficiently portentous, however, to merit something more than casual attention. What they seem to forecast are great changes both in the incidence and administration of factory law; a wider scope of action and wider sphere of duty for it; a more implicit and comprehensive usefulness, in short, than it had before any pretension of attaining to.

PRACTICAL RESULTS OF LEGISLATION.—The above are possible implications from the last formal addition to factory law; the actual results achieved by it thus far are deserving of particular statement too. The area of its supervision has been enormously extended. The age of half-time workers has been raised from eight years, at which it first stood, to eleven at which it stands to-day. The age of full time workers has been raised—in general—from thirteen to fourteen; but a child of thirteen who has passed a certain educational standard fixed by the Education Department from time to time (at present s. iv. but presently to be raised to v.) is entitled to work "full time."[1]   In the same

---

[1] See p. 109. By the Factory Act, 1874, a certificate of a standard of proficiency was required only in textile factories, and by the Elementary Education Acts, 1876, a similar standard was required in regard to non-textile factories and workshops. This was applicable only to England and Wales. The Act of 1878 (sec. 26), makes the obligation general.

connection, a certificate of having reached a certain stage
of educational proficiency (variously represented in different
school districts by s. ii., iii., or iv.) is now required before
a child can be legally set to work at all (Elementary
Education Act, 1880); while commensurately with this
advance in technical requirements the whole tone and
quality of teaching considered "efficient" in qualifying for
employment has been raised.   These ameliorations apply
both to factories and workshops.   Of like equal application
are the general provisions respecting sanitation ; except in
those cases where workshops have been lately removed
from under the immediate care of the factory inspectors and
placed in the first instance under that of the local authorities, where the dual system prevails (p. 121).   The hours
of labour originally fixed at nine for children, and fifteen for
grown persons, and with no proper intervals secured for
meals, have been by gradual instalments reduced to six and
a half and ten per day, in textile factories, for the first five
days of the week, and six on Saturday, = fifiy-six and a half
per week, and ten and a half per day in non-textile factories
and workshops, with seven and a half on Saturday, = sixty
per week for women and young persons :—particular exceptions being made in favour of certain classes of workshops
of the domestic kind, and the hours of child labour remaining practically the same throughout.   Women have
been brought directly under legislation since 1844 ; men
more directly than formerly (by the inclusion among places
to be inspected of workshops where only male adults are
employed) since 1891.   The proof of age requisite for children and young persons in factories, and formerly furnished
in an unsatisfactory manner, is supplied now in the most
satisfactory way po: ' ~ production of a certificate of

birth or "other satisfactory proof" of age.   The protection of dangerous machinery—which was not a requirement of the first Factory Act—is ensured by a series of provisions of continually increasing stringency up to a very high degree of precautionary care.   Dangers incident to employ-ment in unhealthy trades are far more closely supervised and provided for.   Eight half-holidays and two whole holidays in the year ; in addition to Christmas Day, Good Friday, and the weekly half-holiday ; are secured to all protected workers. Truck is forbidden.   The staff of factory inspectors has been very considerably increased, and of late an entirely new departure made in he appointment of female in-spectors, to co-operate with the others, hitherto confined to one sex, and that the one least affected by legislation. These elaborate laws have reacted on the philanthropic spirit that first stimulated them into being ; stimulat-ing it in turn to wider and more various efforts in similar directions.   Their success has inspired other attempts formed on the same model.   A higher conception of the purpose of law has been thus diffused, and a readier acquiescence with it secured.   Nor are even these, in ultimate analysis, the only gains.   Who shall tell the rasher experiments they may not have superseded, the possible catastrophes averted, in the sympathetic and ameliorative influences that they have brought to bear on the solution of the greatest problem of our time.

CHAPTER VI.

CONCLUDING CHAPTER.

COGNATE INDUSTRIES — CHIMNEY SWEEPS — MINES AND QUARRIES—ALKALI WORKS — EXPLOSIVES — BAKEHOUSES— CANAL BOATS — LAUNDRIES — SHOPS — PROTECTION OF CHILDREN'S ACT—TRUCK—UNREGULATED OCCUPATIONS— AGRICULTURE—TRANSPORT—BUILDING—DOMESTIC SERVICE — HOME WORK — LITERARY AND ARTISTIC INDUSTRY — FUTURE OF THE FACTORY SYSTEM—FUTURE OF FACTORY LEGISLATION.

COGNATE INDUSTRIES.—We have now passed in review the course of English factory legislation from its crude beginning in 1802 to the precise provisions and wide-spreading applications of the present day. But besides the laws dealing thus with factories and workshops, as therein defined, several of a cognate kind are found on the statute book, some more, some less closely related to them, some affiliated, and some not; some merely tracing their origin to the same source, in the democratic and sympathetic tendency of modern thought acting as a corrective to the purely economic conception of the purpose of industry; some taking very various shapes; some confessedly imitating in their provisions the above.

CHIMNEY SWEEPS.—The earliest of these; belonging to the last category but one; are the curious series of enactments relating to the somewhat obscure calling of chimney-sweeping. From about the middle of last century the public conscience seems to have been considerably stirred on this subject, and in 1760 a letter appeared in the *Public Advertiser* drawing attention to the hardships endured by child sweepers, and suggesting, in particular, that they should not be allowed to go about their business without proper covering. [1] In 1773, a committee of philanthropic persons was formed in London to endeavour by voluntary action to procure some alleviation of their position ; and eleven years later, Mr. Jonas Hanway, then a member of the House of Commons, published a pamphlet about them, under the rather ponderous title " *A Sentimental History of Chimney Sweepers in London and Westminster, shewing the Necessity of putting them under Regulation to prevent the grossest Inhumanity to the Climbing Boys.*" Voluntary action being found, as in so many similar cases, of little value, an Act of Parliament was passed in 1788 (28 Geo. III., c. 48) forbidding master sweeps to keep more than six apprentices, or take them under eight years of age :—which was all the relief (says Lord Shaftesbury's biographer) "that could be wrung from Parliament for nearly fifty years." Attempts made subsequently to obtain further legislation failed ; and in 1807 the whole subject was referred to a Select Committee of the House of Commons for investigation, which took abundant evidence, after the familiar manner of such bodies. The report of this Committee (remarks the above authority) "is a record of sickening horrors." "It reveals how children of a suitable size were stolen for the purpose, sold by their parents, inveigled from workhouses, or apprenticed by Poor Law Guardians, and

[1] Life of Lord Shaftesbury ; vol. i., p. 295.

forced up narrow chimneys by cruel blows, by pricking the
soles of the feet, or by applying wisps of lighted straw."
These atrocities, and many more which were brought
to light, excited much indignation. They formed the
subject of a well-known article by Sydney. Smith in the
Edinburgh Review, and another attempt was made to
extend the utility of the Act of 1788. But the Bill
was thrown out by the House of Lords; and it was
not till 1834 that any efficient protection was afforded
at length to the little victims. By an Act passed in that
year (4 and 5 Will. IV., c. 35) it was made a misdemeanour
to send a child *up a chimney on fire*;[1] and in two subsequent
ones (3 and 4 Vic., c. 84, and 27 and 28 Vic., c. 37) a
reasonable amount of security was at length procured for
them, the process being much aided by the invention of a
machine that practically supplanted human labour in
sweeping. Nevertheless, further legislation was undertaken
in 1862, and there is at the present time (1893) a Bill
before Parliament dealing once again with the subject.

MINES and QUARRIES. — The position of mines and
quarries in this connection is a peculiar one. The relation of
the extractive[2] to the manufacturing industries has been always
one of the moot points in protective labour legislation, which
displays accordingly some uncertainty in dealing with these
places. Mining is a process of industry conducted
on a system similar to the Factory System: that is to
say it is performed by a body of congregated labourers.

[1] Life of Lord Shaftesbury, vol. 1, p. 296.

[2] M. de Laveleye points out how "the manufacturing industries
receive from the extractive and agriculture their raw material, and give
them the final form demanded by consumption."—*Elements of Political
Economy* (Chapman and Hall, 1884.)

assembled for the purpose, within a place of definite bounds. But mines are not included under the Factory Acts, "because they appertain to the soil, which is not one of the materials of wealth, but one of its sources, the source in fact from which all the materials spring;"[1] they are provided for by special enactments. This is not, however, the case with quarries. They are included, (41 Vic., c. 16 ; sec. 93, and Sch. iv., Part ii.), and are classed as factories or workshops according to the usual method of creating that distinction, namely as to whether manual power only, or other motive power as well is made use of about them. A similar classification is reserved for " Pit Banks ;" that is "any place above ground adjacent to a shaft of a mine in which place the employment of women is not regulated by any of the Mines Acts." These are either Non-Textile Factories or Workshops. Points of resemblance and distinction in cognate processes of production are here very close indeed ; and the exceeding difficulty of a precise classification of industries is well exemplified by the example.

The special legislation affecting labour in Mines has been already mentioned. The first Mines Act was passed in 1842 ; and in 1850 and 1855 respectively two supplementary ones, 13 and 14 Vic., c. 100, and 18 and 19 Vic., c. 108. These applied exclusively to coal mines. In 1860, and again in 1872, new and far more comprehensive legislation was initiated, embracing in the first instance iron— and in the last all metalliferous mines. Under it, elaborate codes of regulations are provided, inferior only to the regulations of Factory Acts in respect to the younger age at which a child is permitted to work underground, and

Introduction to a History of the Factory System ; p. 31.

K

the less stringent quality of the educational requirements while doing so,[1] but displaying much care and forethought in other ways.

ALKALI WORKS.—The manufacture of chemicals is another instance of a cognate process of industry which stands in a peculiar relation to the Factory Acts. Dr. Ure (*Philosophy of Manufactures*, p. 2) distinguishes between a chemical and mechanical manufacture in these terms :—" A mechanical manufacture, being commonly occupied with one substance

[1] The following citations from a recent Report of a Committee of Enquiry to the Vice-President of the Council on Education will place this matter, which may seem to need explanation, in a clear light :—

6. In factories and workshops the number of hours constituting half-time employment is strictly defined by statute ; it is also defined as regards the employment of children between twelve and thirteen *above ground* in connection with coal mines : but *elsewhere* there is no definition of half-time employment, and no restriction as to the number of hours of employment beyond what is employed in half-time attendance at school.

9. In coal-mines the hours of the employment of children between twelve and thirteen *above ground* are regulated by statute so as practically to limit them to half-time, whereas *below ground* the hours of employment are not subject to similar regulations, and if the children have reached the standard for total exemption they are subject to no restriction except the limits of ten hours a day and fifty-four hours a week. The practical result of this is stated to be that in districts where the standard of total exemption is low, employment underground commences at twelve and above ground at thirteen (Labour Commission, Group A., 3, 100—3, 110.) In the case of metalliferous mines the contrast is still more marked, as the employment of children above ground is in this case regulated by the Factory Acts.

10. While in the Factory Acts the provision of half-time education is an essential condition of all half-time employment, the Mines Regulation Acts contain no provisions as to the education of those children whose employment is allowed.

which it conducts through metamorphoses in regular succession, may be made nearly automatic ; whereas a chemical manufacture depends on the play of delicate affinities between two or more substances." Accordingly, legislation in regard to such places, grouped under the general term Alkali Works, is somewhat complicated. Three special statutes regulate their conduct in the chemical connection, and are concerned with details of manufacture, and especially with the exhalation of noxious gases, while for all general labour purposes they are not merely affiliated to, or cognate with, the Factory Acts but actually under their control. Only, there is this further peculiarity : that as Alkali Works they are within the jurisdiction of the Board of Trade, but as factories of the Home Office.

EXPLOSIVES.—Places where explosive substances are manufactured are in much the same position, with a special and a general set of rules of which the usual Factory Act regulations forms one ; but in this case both sets are administered by Home Office officials.

BAKEHOUSES.—Legislation for bakehouses has pursued a somewhat erratic course. They were brought under inspection for the first time by The Bakehouse Act, 1863 (26 and 27 Vic., c. 40) ; the duty of supervision being then assigned to local authorities ; and were specially excepted from both the Factory and Workshop Acts of 1867. In the Factory Act of 1878 they were, on the contrary, specially included (Sec. 93, and Sched. 4, Part II.) ; being defined in the extensive terms, "any places in which are baked bread, biscuits, or confectionery, from the baking or selling of which a profit is derived." The Factory Act of

1883 introduced next a novel distinction (not known to any of the other subjects of factory legislation) between retail and wholesale bakeries ; the sanitary inspection of the former (but not latter) being re-transferred to local authorities, while for other purposes of inspection they were continued as before. By the Factory Act of 1891 their sanitary supervision is left in the same hands, where they are not " Factory Bakehouses," *i.e.* employing foreign motive power, in which latter case they come under the above designation. Where the labour is still all manual they are (whether wholesale or retail) in the position now common to workshops, that is local authorities are responsible for their sanitary condition in the first instance, but the factory inspectors are charged with the enforcement of the other provisions of the law where they apply.

CANAL BOATS.—An Act affecting life in canal boats was passed in 1884, but is very remotely connected with factory legislation, being affiliated rather to the Public Health and Education Acts. It is pleasant to learn, however, from a recent Report, that it has been very successful in its object. Its enforcement is committed to the Board of Trade.

LAUNDRIES.—Laundries occupy an anomalous position in the general scheme of philanthropic legislation which has issued in these and kindred laws. Great efforts were made to include them in the Factory Act of 1878, but the opposition was too strong. The technical difficulty was as to whether the process performed in such places could be construed to be a " manufacturing process," *i.e.* " altering, adapting, or finishing any article *for sale* ;" but the plea was also advanced of the exceptionally *domestic* character of the occupation, and the hardship to women in particular of any statutory curtailment of working hours. With regard to the first contention, the difficulty is one common to a large proportion of the subjects of factory legislation;[1] and with regard to the second, it is a plea more often heard now on the opposite side of the argument—as a reason rather for restriction, and they have, accordingly, found admission at length into the statute of 1891, though in a qualified way. The present position is the following. Steam laundries (a continually expanding feature in this industry) are factories if the goods made up there are provided for sale ; otherwise they are not ; while laundries attached to manufacturing establishments are either factories or workshops on the usual grounds. But laundries where the work is all manual and the articles provided for *use* not sale, are amenable to factory law only in respect to their sanitary conditions, and then only where a Secretary of State is pleased to make a special order on the subject (54 & 55 Vic., c. 75, sec. i.).

SHOPS.—Of all cognate occupations to those carried on in factories or workshops that carried on in establishments where goods are offered for sale seems to be in the least satisfactory condition, whether judged by the constant agitation that is kept up about it, by the provision that has at length been made for it, or by the actual results achieved. This is the more strange considering the unusual amount of public attention that has been attracted to the subject, and the length of time during which it has

---

[1] Most *Non-Textile Factories* and all *Workshops*.

been a matter of debate. It is notable, too, in connection with the original commercial signification of the term factory, which meant, we know, less a place of production than exchange (p. 1). The excuse that shops are not manufacturing establishments does not (as in the last instance) suffice to account for their exceptional position, for the sole purpose of shops is *sale*, and *manufacture* in the popular sense has been given up as a sanction for factory legislation since 1864. Is it then that the labour carried on in them is not material industry ; such as the Workshop Act, for instance, requires (p. 102) ; or productive, such as in the more general sense the genius of factory legislation is concerned about (Chap. II.)? It is clearly both. In the view of the most orthodox school of economists the operation of production is not completed until the produced commodity is in the hands of the consumer (*Principles of Political Economy*, by John Stuart Mill, vol. i. ; etc.[1]); and there is no doubt at all events about the material character of the transaction. Or, parting from these more technical conceptions, and taking a popular view: are the incidents of shop work of a kind to call for exterior regulation, like those of the many places now called factories,—is labour exposed there to the ordeal of unlimited competition, and the other influences distinctive of the modern industrial revolution ? It is so certainly. It is even exposed to those influences in a special degree; the conditions of shop labour having been often shown to be as hard in certain particulars as they were

[1] In his recent very interesting book, *The Unseen Foundations of Society*, the Duke of Argyll insists on this point with characteristic vigour. "Distribution," he says, "is not a separate and co-equal work with that which is called Production. Distribution is merely one of the provinces of Production " (p. 457).

ever shown to be in factories and workshops.[1] Are the assumed objects of legislation the same? The very same,—women, children, and young persons in the first instance; men later. Any special difficulties of inspection? None whatever; shops are open to the view, and can always be approached with ease while work is going on in them; factories and workshops are more difficult of access. Are they not included, then, in factory legislation? No; every effort to so include them has failed, and they are regulated at present by a law which, though cognate with, is not even affiliated to factory law, and has but a poor resemblance to it. The history of this anomaly is of sufficient interest to be pursued at some length.

As early as 1821 mention is made of an appeal emanating from shop assistants against "immoderately long hours of business;" and already in 1842 an association, "The Metropolitan Drapers' Association," was formed for agitating the subject. This, the first of a long series of others, was an association for voluntary action. Several attempts were made thereafter to bring the matters at issue before Parliament, and at length in 1873 Sir John Lubbock introduced a Bill into the House of Commons proposing to extend certain provisions of the current Factory Acts to shops. Though these Acts had already made great progress this Bill met with but scant encouragement, factory reform being just then in the midst of that strong individualist reaction which was so ably worked by the "women's rights" party. The debate served, however, to give point and consistency to the campaign outside, which was now proceeding vigorously: principally under the auspices of

[1] See *Death and Disease behind the Counter*, by Thomas Sutherst (Kegan, Paul and Co., 1884), where ample details are given.

the Early Closing Association and Shop Assistants' Labour League, the former of these societies favouring exclusively voluntary action, the latter seeking legislation. In 1883 Lord Stanhope introduced a Bill on the subject into the House of Lords. Its purport, like that of Sir John Lubbock's, was to place shops under the Factory Act, but it was imperfectly drawn, and, after a very sympathetic debate, was not proceeded with. The next effort was made again in the House of Commons. In 1886 a Shop Bill was introduced which dealt exclusively with young persons, (*i.e.*, "of the age of thirteen and under the age of eighteen "): who were not to work "for a longer period than twelve hours in any one day : "—*shop* being defined (sec. vi.) to "include retail and wholesale shops, and warehouses, in which assistants are employed for hire," but not refreshment houses of any kind. This measure was referred to a Select Committee, and presently resulted in an Act of Parliament, the first on this subject ever actually passed (49 & 50 Vic., c. 55). In this statute some remarkable alterations of current procedure occur. It applied only to young persons ; which in this case means *any* persons under the age of eighteen ; who were not to be employed in or about a shop for a longer period than seventy-four hours a week, including meal times, the definition of *shop* now embracing "markets, stalls," and "licensed public-houses and refreshment rooms of any kind." Thus the novel principle of a weekly, instead of daily, criterion of work was legalised, a child of any age might apparently be employed for seventy-four hours at a stretch, and women, contrary to the analogy of all cognate legislation, and to the principal object which reformers had in view, were shut out from the benefits of the law. This Act failed of effect owing to the absence of any proper provision for its enforcement, and remained inoperative up to 1892, when an amending Act was carried giving powers to local authorities to put it in operation. This has now been done to some extent. From a Parliamentary Return issued in the early part of 1893 we learn the upshot. It appears that seventy-one inspectors have been appointed in England and Wales. Fifty-six of these have been appointed by Town Councils, five by the London County Council, and ten by other County Councils. In Scotland eighteen Town Councils and one County Council have made appointments. No appointments have been made in Ireland. The latest accessible information concerning results is found in the annual report of the London County Council (June, 1893). In the metropolis :—" By the end of March 1893, a number of complaints had been received and investigated, but only in twenty-three cases had infringements of the Act been committed. In four of these, legal proceedings were taken and penalties imposed, and in the remainder the offenders were cautioned. More than one-tthird of the infringements were at the premises of hairdressers " !

PROTECTION OF CHILDREN'S ACT.—A recent statute whose intentions are of an undoubtedly cognate kind with those which from the first distinguished factory legislation, and which is in one respect very closely affiliated to it, is the *Act for the Prevention of Cruelty to, and Protection of, Children* (52 and 53 Vic., c. 44). The particular respect in which this affiliation occurs is in relation to public performances in which children bear a part. This development of the agency of factory legislation is of so unusual a kind, and opens up such wide vistas of possibilities that it demands something more than a passing notice. The section that makes the two Acts related is the third, dealing with the conditions under which children *over seven years of age* are permitted to perform "in premises licensed according to law for public entertainments, or in any circus or other place of public amusement." To such children a license may be granted by "a petty sessional court, or, in Scotland, the school board," authorising the performance on proof to the satisfaction of the authorities "that proper provision has been made to secure the health and kind treatment of any children proposed to be employed;" and "a Secretary of State may assign to any inspector appointed, or to be appointed, under section sixty-seven of the Factory and Workshop Act, 1878, specially, and in addition to any other usual duties, the duty of seeing whether the restrictions and conditions of any license under this section are duly complied with"—which duties have been assigned to them accordingly. Now, this is a very distinct departure from any previously assumed purpose of factory legislation which, as we have often said, has ever hitherto been held to be exclusively concerned about material products, and is, indeed, very rigidly defined in those terms. The question arises, therefore, is it an aberration only, or the beginning of a new departure?—a most important question in view of future eventualities. In any endeavour to provide a satisfactory answer two tendencies in particular would have to be taken into account. One, the changes now taking place in economic philosophy; which in the long run moulds popular conceptions of economic duties; the other, that tendency in factory legislation and in such imitations of it as last described, to generally ignore scientific precision in dealing with practical issues—and these two we may discuss. With regard to the first, there is no doubt that old categories of economic terms, as *productive* and *unproductive*, *material* and *immaterial*, *service* and *commodity*, are falling into disrepute, and labour, in whatever form and to whatever end, is coming to be regarded as essentially the same force under different manifestations, having the same obligations attached to it, and being entitled to the same privileges. From this standpoint then vast and novel extensions of the sphere of factory legislation might seem imminent. "The labour of clerks and salesmen is productive labour as much as that of the artisan," says Mr. F. A. Walker (*Political Economy*, p. 81); and why not also that of the teacher then,—the artist—author,—as well as the young actor? On the other hand, we have seen how little factory legislation from the first has been influenced by abstractions, but rather by the comparative pressure exercised on public opinion by competitive industry; and placing these two sets of considerations side by side a probable conclusion may be inferred. It is this; that in the extent to which those influences affect intellectual as well as physical pursuits there is likely to be an advance along this line; supposing always that some entirely new system of apportioning and regulating human labour is not meanwhile devised, that some more efficient organisation from within does not supersede the necessity of outside constraint.

TRUCK—An instance of legislation not of a cognate kind with factory legislation, and yet affiliated to it, is found in the Truck Acts (42 Will. IV., c. 37, and 50 and 51 Vic., c. 46). The object of these Acts is "to prohibit the payment in certain trades of wages in goods, or otherwise than in the current coin of the realm;" a purpose of legislation which dates back to the reign of George II. By the thirteenth section of the current Act it becomes the duty of the Inspectors of Factories and Mines respectively to enforce the provisions of this law as concerns those places. We have thus legislation not of a strictly cognate kind affiliated to factory legislation, and of a cognate kind (in the case of shops) not affiliated but in operation alongside it; we have a mixed jurisdiction in the instances of mines and chemical works; and lastly, " immaterial products," introduced within its elastic boundaries by The Protection of Children's Act, and with apparently small right to be there. The moral of all these vagaries is clear, and is that which has been preached throughout this volume. The principle of factory legislation is so far from being conterminous with the Factory System that it is related to it in an almost purely historical connection (p. 31). Neither derivatively, nor scientifically, nor historically, is a factory anything more nor less than it may at any moment be legally defined to be, nor has factory law any other meaning than a law to protect the industrially weak against the industrially strong —if its utility be eventually allowed to end even there. Conceived of, and first enacted, at a great crisis, and during a period of unparalleled changes in industrial methods, the Factory Acts have slipped into the position formerly filled by other regulations instituted with a like purpose, and whether further extensions of them; already contemplated or not yet thought of, are to come ; and if they are to come, whether by actual expansion, by lateral extension, or parallel action; whether the title thus acquired is to remain distinctive still of the whole aggregated mass of · laws, or not; these are matters of comparatively small account.

Before passing from the subject of Truck it should be noted that legislation is here concerned with adult male—equally with juvenile and female labour, and also that the Acts are only of partial operation, applying that is, "in certain trades."

UNREGULATED OCCUPATIONS.—It might well seem after this long list of instances that we had pretty well-nigh exhausted all possible subjects of factory and kindred legislation, but such is very far from being the case. It is so far, indeed, from being so that possibly as much labour still remains unregulated in this country as has ever yet been brought under any special form of State control. Passing by the learned professions, and all departments of the Public Service—the latter of which are, however, so controlled ; omitting even the difficult and as yet unsolved problem of the position to be ultimately assigned to immaterial products (to which a few words will be devoted afterwards), numerous important industries, more or less engaged about wealth production still are left much in the way that factory industries are, to which nevertheless no cognate system of supervision applies.

AGRICULTURE.—The most notable of these industries is the oldest and most important of all—Agriculture. The statutory definition of a workshop—"Any place whatever, *whether in the open air or under cover*, in which any handicraft is carried on,"—might, by a not very strained construction, have been understood as covering this employment, but it has not been so construed, and was not so meant. Agriculture formed, however, one of the subjects of enquiry of that most exhaustive of all public enquiries, the second Children's Employment Commission, and from the period of the publication of its Report, attempts, more or less sincere, were made from time to time to secure for it benefits similar to those conferred by the Factory Acts. The powerful opposition of the land-owning class, united — it must in justice be said — to the peculiar difficulties of the case, prevented for a long while any practical result. "The labourer in the fields," the present writer has said elsewhere, "is both naturally and historically, as well as economically and actually, a person occupying a very different position in the body-politic from the labourer in the factory or the forge. . . . 'The kindly fruits of the earth,' which are his especial care, are such as are only to be enjoyed in 'due time'; they are not the products of merely mechanical appliances set in motion by an unintelligent force acting with undeviating regularity" [1]—nor capable, it should be added, of practically indefinite increase on the same area of cultivation. At length a veritable statute, *The Agricultural Children's Act*, 1873 (36 & 37 Vic., c. 67) did indeed appear, but so mutilated in its parts, and of such poor construction, as to be quite useless. The principal provisions of this Act were the following: — No child under eight years of age was to be employed in any kind of agricultural work, "except by his parent on land of his own occupation." Between that age and ten years, not to be employed unless 250 attendances had been made at school within twelve months next preceding, or 150 between ten and twelve years; but a child who had passed standard IV. of the Education Code was to be exempt from all

[1] Article in *Fraser's Magazine* for May, 1876, "The Agricultural Children's Act."

restrictions. A parent is defined as " the parent, guardian, or person who is liable to maintain or has the actual custody or control over any child." No provision is made for enforcing the Act, nor even putting it in operation. But any Court of Summary Jurisdiction is invested with the power of suspending it. It is clear that such a statute was of no practical usefulness ; it never was enforced ; and to this hour there is no law dealing with agricultural labour in the manner that manufacturing labour is dealt with by the Factory and kindred Acts.[1]

TRANSPORT.—Agriculture is a directly productive process, and its exclusion from all similar legislation to factory legislation may be attributed to the inherent difficulties presented together with the different way in which it was affected by the results of the Industrial Revolution. While the social result of this latter influence on manufacture has been to immensely increase competitive production and accumulate labour in narrow areas, its result in agriculture was all the reverse — to greatly diminish intensive cultivation and drive the labourers from the land. Similarly, while the economic effect of machinery applied in manufacture is continually to increase productiveness, its effect in agriculture is almost certainly to drain the land of its fertility in an ever ascending scale.[2]

[1] The Agricultural Gangs Act (1867) is no exception, for it deals with the labour question in a quite different manner. Moreover, it is now practically obsolete.

[2] This is a fact, both practically and economically susceptible of proof, which might well engage the attention of the Royal Commission on Agriculture.

An industry which pertains to both, and much beside, is that of Transport. This is also unregulated in the precise sense of factory legislation, though not so wholly unregulated as agriculture. In certain departments the State has stepped in, as *e.g.* through the Canal Boats Act and Merchant Shipping Acts ; and there was an Act passed in 1893 relating to hours of work on railways. But its position in view of any general form of control is indeterminate and equivocal. In some instances local bodies are charged with supervision, and in others the Board of Trade, but not a like supervision in any instance.[1]

BUILDING.—A curious example of an unregulated industry is afforded by building. Builders are subject to the regulations of the Factory Acts when they prepare materials on their own premises, but not when they put them together outside them. This is quite in consonance with the legal conception of a factory as a definite "place," or area, but it is scarcely in accord with the general tendency of protective labour legislation. Reasoning *a priori* it might seem that this amongst all other occupations was one to call for closest supervision ; and certain well-known facts as to speculative building have the effect of emphasising rather than correcting

---

[1] A typical example of overwork in this department of labour is supplied by a case lately tried before a Metropolitan magistrate, wherein a London carman was charged with leaving his vehicle unattended while he went into a coffee-house to get some breakfast. He had been working at that time already *twenty-four* hours, and went on forthwith for another *fourteen*. It is melancholy to have to add, that owing to this summons having been taken out against him he was dismissed from his employment.

that presumption. Here is a distinct case of manufacture in its strictest sense ; namely of providing or adapting an article for sale ; the persons employed about the production being operative labourers engaged for a competitive wage. The mystery is deepened if we compare this process with some others that are included. A house in course of construction does not come under the supervision of factory officials, but a ship in course of construction does ; and also a quarry from which the stone for building is hewn. What is the explanation ? It probably resides in the very pertinent consideration of expediency. No compelling cause, we may suppose, has been shown, for extending the principle of the Factory Acts in this direction. The building trades are strongly organized, and may be held to have secured efficient protection for their workmen outside the law ; and if this surmise be correct the mystery is not only explained, but the explanation agrees with previous conceptions, just such being the considerations we have found most influential in the long run throughout the whole course of events portrayed.

A department of building deserving of separate notice is that concerned about the provision of works of utility as aids to industry: the production of roads, railways, docks, etc. This is the department which gives the single pretence of reason to Dr. Ure's unfortunate *dictum* about military engineering being a last resort of the Factory System (p. 27). Such works are either directly instruments of production ; when constructed directly for that purpose ; or indirectly so, when more nearly related to Transport ; and whatever we have to say of them in either capacity has now been said. The one case in which they are not, and cannot be, in any way related to manufacture ("producing an article for sale ")

L

is when they are provided by the servants of the State for exclusively military purposes. It has undoubtedly the appearance of an anomaly, however, that civilian labourers employed in this way—navvies—are under no special public supervision.

DOMESTIC SERVICE.—The great occupation of domestic service is wholly unregulated by any law similar to the Factory Acts. This also presents the appearance of an anomaly when we reflect how shockingly some servants—people for the most part of the kind and class for which this legislation is in other cases provided—are overworked : women and young persons in lodging houses, for example, and in hotels, and refreshment rooms. Yet it would certainly seem a somewhat extravagant straining of even the elastic term factory labour to expand it so as to include domestic service. Not that such action would be quite unprecedented. Ever since 1864, when certain selected employments were so designated, and still more since 1867, when their number was greatly increased, the way has been open. Its actual consummation has been even approached already. It is an open question if a woman making pastry in a hotel might not with propriety claim the protection of the Factory and Workshop Act, 1878 (41 Vic., c. xvi. sec. 93 and sch. iv., part ii.) ; and all persons living in the house with their employers and giving assist· ance, now in one direction, now in another, are little distinguishable from servants, or at all events it is not easy to know where to draw the line. Apprentices are in some sort, and have always been, in this position. Yet it was apprenticed labour which was first legislated for. Nor has the class in question been itself inarticulate on the matter. At Trades Union Congresses held at Liverpool and Dundee respectively, the subject was mooted, and very lately a Bill was prepared to be laid before Parliament in which redress of grievances was sought for one particularly hardly used class of domestic servants—barmaids. The whole subject is full of difficulty; of increasing difficulty too in view of changes (possibly not remote) which would bring the full force of the Industrial Revolution to bear in this arena, which as yet it has been slow to enter. In such an event, readjustments unfailingly characteristic of its presence elsewhere, should be expected. "Servants will become more of the nature of temporary helpers in the home; like shop attendants; their duties more definite, and their interest in the general concerns of the household more remote. It is even possible to anticipate a time when they will cease to live in their masters' houses, or to work in them beyond a stipulated time each day :"[1] a practice not uncommon in new countries now. Should that time come, might they not fairly claim to be treated as those same shop assistants will probably then be, and as the statutory objects of factory legislation now are ; and would it not be difficult to resist the claim ? Possibly so ; but that time is not yet. In the meanwhile their labour is on a different plane, it seems to us, from that of the factory and workshop (as either legally or popularly understood), which is the immediately important matter. " A servant enters your employment under ordinary circumstances to *wait upon you*, not to perform any specific act, and the contract between you is distinctly made on that basis. Moreover, there is an unwritten code of custom in domestic service which has all the force of law, and is, indeed, enforced by it in extreme instances—which is no

[1] *Modern Factory System* ; p. 455.

longer the case in industrial employment." Further-
more, and this is an important point, "this class of persons is
not (on the whole) in the condition that calls for interference ; they are not helpless nor the subjects-of economic
tyranny, but, on the contrary, have very much the control
of the market themselves, the demand for them (for capable
ones) being perennially in excess of the supply." They have
also, it may be noted, the protection of the Common Law in
the last resort, and of a special statute (*The Master and
Servants Act*); "and it is ever to be remembered that
Common Law in this country has constantly and beneficently
interfered between masters and servants in the domestic
sphere while it has resolutely held aloof from interference
in the industrial." [1] When these facts are borne in mind the
presupposed anomaly will not perhaps appear so great, even
if it does not wholly disappear.

HOME WORK.—The definition of a "workshop," as
a place "to and over which the employer of the
persons there has the right of access or control" was
deliberately framed to except a large body of industry from
supervision, and it has had that effect accordingly. But
besides this general exception, there are special exceptions in the Factory Acts applicable to other
descriptions of workshops, as well as numerous
modifications of the primary law (p. 101), whose
purpose is principally to limit the requirement of a
normal working day. There is also a particular exemption
(sec. xcviii.) for "The exercise in a private house or private
room, by the family dwelling therein, or by any of them, of
manual labour for the purposes of gain . . . . where

[1] *Modern Factory System* ; p. 454.

the labour is exercised at irregular intervals, and does not furnish the whole or principal means of living to such family;" and the following occupations are mentioned by name (sec. xcvii.) as specially excepted, viz., straw plaiting, pillow-lace making, and glove making. Lastly, there is the exemption (from all but sanitary provisions) of adult male labourers; whether working as above or even in workshops away from home; provided no regularly protected people work with them.

Here then is a vast and very various body of employment not under the cognizance of factory inspecting officials, though in all respects: except in respect to the place where it occurs: of a like kind to that which is, once isolated equally with congregated labour is allowed to be a proper subject of legislation. It will also be seen that this body of labour may conveniently be divided into two parts: that furnished exclusively by adult males, and by all other persons. The former, too, need not necessarily be labour at home, but as it is in this form that it has come most prominently forward of late it seems convenient to view it exclusively in that connection now. At the present time, for example, steps are being taken in one great branch of manufacturing industry—the boot and shoe trade—to utterly abolish home work by men,[1] and confine them to factory labour, or, at all events to workshop labour away from home; and that provision of the last Factory Act (p. 123) requiring lists of outworkers to be kept in establishments of this and some similar kinds, implies at least an intention of the State to countenance such action.

[1] At the instance, of course, of the Trade Unions, not of factory law.

Once again then, and indirectly as before, the inevitable question, that must sooner or later be answered somehow, of the proper attitude of the modern factory reformer towards the labourer of full years and masculine gender comes up for discussion. " Nothing "—says a recent writer in the *Daily Chronicle*[1]—" is more curious than the sort of respect which has been paid to the liberty of this unfortunate subject, the circuitous route by which protective measures have found their way round to him, thanks to the presence of women and children in the workshop." But at length he emerges on the scene alone ; ferreted out from his grim surroundings and disencumbered of every fiction as to his identity ; what is to be done with him ? Well-organised industries appear inclined to give the answer by taking the matter into their own hands, and forcing him under the Factory System ; but what of the ill-organised ones ; what of those not organised at all ; and what of the man's own option ? On the one hand, would it not seem a monstrous inversion of justice to withhold protection from a person who obviously needs it most as the revelations of the " Sweating Committee " have amply shown him to do ; on the other, an incomparable invasion of individual rights to prescribe to a man that he shall not work for his living in his own house if he think fit ?

The difficulty loses little of its acuteness when it is transferred to the case of women and children similarly situated. Is it proper that the home work of these when they result in products offered for sale on the principle of open competition should remain unregulated ? Is it fair to them—and others ? But could it in decency be hindered ? It is true that such

[1] The article appeared some time in the middle of September, I have ost the exact reference.

labour is defined in the Factory Acts as being "exercised at irregular intervals, and " (of a kind which) "does not furnish the whole or principal means of living to such family;" but who is to ensure this, or any part of it? Under the old guild organisation of industry all that was perhaps possible; is it so now? Now, it is no part of the present writer's duty to offer a solution of these, or any other, legislative problems here. Still it may be well to point out that no Factory, or other kindred Act, has yet proposed to interfere with the responsibility of a worker over his own industry, but only with the responsibility of one person over another. In this respect they differ from the ordinances of trade unions, etc., which have that end in view. The question of the home work, either of men or women, concerns factory legislation then on the above basis only. There must be an employer, otherwise it does not apply. May not the absent clue be found to reside somewhere about this fact? But what a splendid testimony it is in any case to the success of such legislation that it should now be tracking out the criminous employer in this, his last place of refuge, striving in spite of all obstacles to bring him too under the yoke of humane and beneficent law, like all the rest.

LITERARY AND ARTISTIC INDUSTRY.—A large field of human effort, both industrial and otherwise, remains under the above headings still unaccounted for. Of the first kind, are the labours of designers, draughtsmen, mechanicians —when applied to manufacture,—clerks in commercial houses, banks, lawyers' offices, and the like. Of the second, are the

---

[1] The subject will be found discussed at considerable length in my book, *The Modern Factory System*, pp. 328, 421.

labours of teachers, writers for the press, and copyists;
authors, artists, actors—and a host of others. Some of
these labourers are already provided for under separate
codes of regulations; as teachers in public schools; others
have secured some share of protection under the Factory
(and allied) Acts, as juvenile actors (p. 137), assistants to
photographers,[1] etc.; tradition and custom afford a measure
of protection to some more; as clerks in banks; and exterior organization may provide help for a few others
where that organization has been successfully undertaken.
Still a large number of such-like occupations remain quite
unregulated, as is the case with agriculture and domestic
service. In such instances as law-copying, for example,
and type-writing, no protection at all is afforded; and that
notwithstanding that it may in these instances be specially
needful—the keenest form of competition being rampant
there; notwithstanding, too, that letter-press printing
is a very carefully supervised industry under the
Factory Acts, and that the profession of the law affords in
its upper branches one of the most perfect modern instances of the old guild ideal. It may well appear
strange, too, in this connection that a well-ventilated
workshop where young labour is employed in some
healthy physical occupation is strictly required to be
whitewashed every *fourteen months*, while a lawyer's office,
where other young labour is employed, is apparently
under no obligation of cleanliness at all. This, with
some other seeming anomalies, the anomaly for instance,
that allows of a young person working at a lesser age
under ground in a mine than above ground, or that

---

[1] Photographic studios where pictures are provided for sale are
classed as Non-Textile Factories or Workshops.

requires a health certificate from one inside a textile factory, but not working outside in a rope-walk ; or that calls a great establishment where hundreds of garments are turned out by hand per week a work-shop, but a single room in a dwelling-house where a little book-binding is carried on a factory ; are mainly faults of classification, or they have some historical, technical, or other good reason for existence.   They are in no case irremediable.   The Factory. Acts do not profess to be a complete and final expression of the intentions of the legislature towards labour, even of the material, and still less of the immaterial kind.   It is their justifiable boast, on the contrary, that they continue elastic and receptive, responsive to any new impulses of proved justice and humanity that call to them for help. Whether it will be ever possible to so extend their basis as to comprehend under one measure the enormously wide field of human interests we have now passed in review is doubtful, it is certain at all events that they have still other triumphs before them, even if their ultimate form be very different from at present and the distinctive name pass away.

FUTURE OF THE FACTORY SYSTEM.—The certainty above referred to, and the obviously transitory conditions of modern industry, tend naturally to raise the speculative enquiry as to the probable future of the Factory System, a speculation of high practical, as well as deep philosophical interest.   In entering upon it for an exceedingly brief space it is well to recall the very peculiar constituents of that phase of this organization which has been primarily dealt with here. " The Modern Factory System," it has been justly said (*Modern Factory System* ; p. 317), "is a complex of many factors, several of them quite new to history. A congregated mode of industry, in which, nevertheless, the individual is the unit ; a free industry, and under the strictest economical bondage; an industry, served by the most perfect labour-saving appliances ever known, yet in which (without the strong compulsion of the law) the labour rendered is longer, closer, and more unintermittent than ever known before. . . . Had machine industry been applied to the Factory System in any other epoch or any other country ; had it lacked the impetus conferred on it by the invention of the steam-engine, had our social organization and theory of political economy been other than what it was ; the story of its development would certainly have been different." Accepting this view as substantially correct, three formative influences appear as chiefly responsible for the present characteristic form of this method of production. There is the increased use of superior mechanical appliances ; there is the application to them of a new motive power ; and there is the nature of the environment within which those energies are displayed. A complex of the three yields the distinctive lineaments of the Modern Factory System. Now it is immediately perceptible that none of these features are final. The mechanical improvements may go on improving, in fact are continually doing so. The motive power may be super-seded by others, has indeed to some extent been already, in the use of the gas-engine, the oil-engine, and finally of the electric dynamo. The political and economical standing of the operatives has changed, and is changing; for the evils of unlimited competition have been checked, labour has found a voice, and is learning how to make it heard. Let us suppose, then, machinery improved still further, to the extent namely of the automatic factory before imagined ;[1] manual labour would be reduced so much that it would be practically confined to only the making of these machines themselves, to the winding them up, like a clock, the feeding and setting them in motion. In face of such facts the social no less than mechanical side of the labour problem would have to be radically revised, and, in particular, according to the political-economical quality of the environment. According as to whom the machinery of production belonged to would the character of the future Factory System be probably determined. Or supposing machinery remaining not much different and the steam-engine got rid of in production, as the water-mill and wind-mill pretty nearly are. There would no longer be any need of a great central motor mechanism for each building, or pile of buildings : of the costly engine-house, boiler-sheds, the towering chimney, crowded coal-bunks, stokers, or stoking apparatus ; all that we are accustomed to associate with the great factory of the modern type. Motive power might be as easily distributable over wide areas as gas for lighting is, or electric power ; as susceptible of domestic management as in the oil-engine—and something of this kind seems approaching. What would the new type of factory that ensued be like ? Certainly not like an exaggerated edition of the old one. Concentration of labour would under such conditions be probably found to have passed its limit of usefulness ; the factories would be smaller, if indeed there would be any factories left at all, and each house not its own centre of production, a production as easily performed as cooking is now. Or should associated labour be still found most efficient, it might at least be expected to take a different form, the form of association in groups rather

[1] p. 28.

than in the mass. Applying the terms of Agriculture, the extensive system of production would have given place to the intensive, and great estates to small holdings.

But how does such a forecast coincide with the well-known fact that the factory system of the last hundred years is still spreading, and operatives themselves agitating to be placed compulsorily under its protection? Better than might at first sight appear. When, a century or so ago, that system developed the characteristic features we have now fully described, it was a new thing, disturbing by its entrance on the scene old industrial ideals, and supplanting what remained of more ancient and familiar forms of labour. To the quality of novelty, always a potent obstacle to change in uninstructed minds, it added the quality of utter recklessness in dealing with the human agents of production, availing itself without scruple of unlimited competition as the supreme economic law. Into this arena a new order has been introduced by compulsion based on other laws, of even greater consideration in the social sphere, the laws of justice and morality. Into this arena, but not into that earlier one. Accordingly, while the awful force of competition (awful both for good and ill) has spread there too, it has not been mitigated in the same way, but claims a still increasing crop of victims ; and a like instinct of self preservation which prompted workers to cling to the old ways before (organised after their own fashion) impels them now to seek asylum in the new. So it will be, we hold, when newer ways shall come ; as come they will ; for unorganized and unprotected labour is powerless to help itself in view of other concentrated forces it must face, and that lesson once learnt, and the power of easy transference assumed, will surely in the long run go where conditions of employment are the least exacting.

FUTURE OF FACTORY LEGISLATION.—And what is likely to
be the attitude of factory legislation towards industrial production carried on in some such way? It would probably
be the same as now ; so long as there were any need for it at
all ; such legislation shaping itself to combat economical
deficiences in the producing method, as from the first (however blindly) it did, and is doing. It is possible, of course,
that there would be no need for it. It is conceivable that
some far more comprehensive scheme of social reconstruc-
tion would ere then be operative, rendering all special
interference in this field of enterprise unnecessary. Capital
and labour would no longer require to be separately organized,
and nice adjustments made between them ; they would naturally coalesce. Or if none of these things should come about
and modern methods remain? In that case there would
remain also this beneficent body of laws, which, under the
(often inappropriate) name of Factory Acts is gradually over-
spreading all material industry, to raise it from a new serfdom
by means most in harmony with the spirit of the age. " For
just as the modern Factory System was but a novel incident
in the history of labour, so is factory legislation but a new
protest against the old forces of selfishness and cupidity, and
a new method, suitable to modern institutions and ideas, of
holding them in check " (*Modern Factory System* ; p. 468).
It is likely that central administration would in that event
avail itself more and more of local aid, in the exceedingly
detailed and complex duties devolving on it ; it is even possible
that Trade Union organization might be advantageously
utilized in some respects, as was the case with the mediæval
Guilds. What at all event seems certain is, that the principle
of a methodical supervision of industry once established,
or let us say recovered, will not again be parted with by

a free people.   With which certainty in prospect we may
go cheerfully on our way, confident that the labour problems of the present hour, which sometimes look so
threatening, are not incapable of just and rational solution
after all, but will yield, like those of any former age, to
intelligent and honest effort persistently directed towards
that end.

APPENDIX.

APPENDIX

REQUIREMENTS OF THE FACTORY ACTS

ABSTRACTS.

There are ten Abstracts of the law relating to the several classes of factories and workshops, *viz.* for Textile Factories ; Non-Textile Factories ; Print, Bleach, and Dye Works ; Workshops ; Domestic Factoriesand Workshops ; "Women's" Workshops ; Factory Bakehouses ; Wholesale Bakehouses (workshops), and Retail Bakehouses (workshops) ; and White Lead Works. A few requirements are common to all of these ; a few are common to several ; while in many particulars they vary.

NOTICE OF OCCUPYING A FACTORY OR WORKSHOP.

A requirement common to all is that of giving notice of first occupying a factory or workshop ; which is required to be in writing, and served on an inspector within one month, that is either the inspector of the district : whose name will be found at any other factory or workshop already inspected : or addressed to the Home Office, London. This notice should state "the place where it is situate, the address to which he (the occupier) desires his letters to be addressed,

M

the nature of the work, the nature and amount of the moving power therein (if any), and the name of the firm under which the business of the factory or workshop is to be carried on." If this notice is not sent within the stipulated time the person commencing business is liable to a fine of £5.

Affixing Papers.

Another requirement common to all is that of affixing the proper Abstract and Notices ; namely, in the first instance, notice of the names and addresses of inspectors and certifying surgeons ·(see below) appointed to that factory district ; of the periods of employments and time allowed for meals ; of some public clock by which those times are regulated ; of the mode of school attendance (where children are employed) ; but some of the latter particulars are not applicable in domestic factories and workshops, and where women only are at work. It has become usual for the factory inspector to supply these papers in the first instance (after receiving information of the opening of a new place of work), but it is not obligatory on him to do so, whilst it is obligatory on the occupier to have them always affixed, the penalty for default being anything up to £2.

Besides the above there are a number of other Notices, referring to exceptions, modifications, and enlargements of the general law (a list of which will be given hereafter), and which are alike required to be procured and affixed by the occupier before acting on them, and which must be kept so affixed, and renewed when necessary at his expense ; under penalty of the advantages derived, or the obligations imposed, in them being construed to his disadvantage if not thus kept, and the ordinary process of the law set in motion to punish him accordingly.

THE FACTORY REGISTER.

In all *factories* a Register is bound to be kept "in the prescribed form, and with the prescribed particulars." This requirement does not apply to workshops, except to those (at present none) in which certificates of fitness (see below) are required for any persons employed there. The prescribed particulars are the following. Particulars of the name, location, and nature of the manufacture; of the name of the employer; of the clock by which the hours of labour are regulated; and of the nature and amount of the moving power. Particulars of the holidays (see below) given each year; and of the period when the factory was limewashed or painted (see Sanitation). A list of children attending school, with certificates of their age and fitness for employment; and of young persons over the school age and under eighteen. All the entries in this book are to be made by the employer, except those made by the certifying surgeon, and one entry on the first page by the inspector. The fine for not keeping this book as required is a penalty not exceeding £2.

EMPLOYMENT OF CHILDREN.

The occupier of any factory or workshop taking a child into employment is bound to satisfy himself of the child's age, the child's health, and a certain educational proficiency; and is responsible to the law if under any circumstances he should employ him under the legal age or without the other necessary qualifications. At present it is illegal to employ one under eleven years of age; and at fourteen a child becomes a young person. The proper way of obtaining proof of age is by procuring a certificate of birth, but should this be unattainable the declaration of the child's parent before a magistrate may be accepted as sufficient evidence. The certificate of educational proficiency required, varies in different localities according to the local bye-laws of the district, and may be sometimes remitted for a certificate of attendance; and it is necessary for the employer to familiarize himself with these laws and see that neither in this nor any other particular he is imposed upon. It can never be too strongly pointed out that in all matters relating to employment under the Factory Acts the *employer* is responsible for whatever breaches of the law occur; except in the two unusual instances of its being shown to the satisfaction of an inspector that an agent has disobeyed his master's instructions and really committed the offence, or of himself being willing to prosecute that agent on the same plea. The employer is also bound to procure, besides the certificates of age and proficiency, a certificate of the child's physical fitness for employment (see Register). This is granted, or not, upon personal examination, by a medical man appointed for the purpose (called Certifying Surgeon), either at the factory or his own residence, and must be obtained within seven days of the first employment of the child, unless the factory be over three miles from the surgeon's residence when the period is extended to thirteen days. Where the total number of children and young persons at the same place is less than five the examination may be at the surgeon's house and the fee for each certificate is sixpence, but where more than that number are employed together it must be at the factory, when, either a rate of payment is agreed upon by the occupier and surgeon together, or appeal can be made to a scale of fees incorporated in the Act of Parliament. If even after all these precautions an inspector thinks a child not capable of work he can require him to be examined again, and unless the examination be satisfactory he will be disqualified; and under no circumstances can a child work full time in a factory or workshop under thirteen years of age.

EDUCATION.

Children once admitted into a factory or workshop are employed there in connection with either of two systems of instruction at school, either on the "half-time" or "alternate day" system.   The parent is liable if the child does not attend regularly, and the employer is liable if he fail to obtain from the schoolmaster weekly certificates of such attendance, and to keep them for two months, and exhibit them within that time to an inspector if required.   He is also liable to punishment if he sets a child to work during a current week before all deficiencies of attendance for the previous week have been made up.   But a child is excused from attending school on every Saturday, and on any school or factory holiday or half holiday ; and "on every day on which he is certified by the teacher of the school to have been prevented from attending by sickness or other unavoidable cause," or "where there is not within the distance of two miles, measured according to the nearest road from the residence of the child, a *recognized efficient school* which the child can attend."

EMPLOYMENT OF YOUNG PERSONS.

A *young person* is a person of the age of fourteen and under eighteen, but a child of thirteen who has passed Standard IV. of the Educational Code may be employed as if he were such a one.   In taking a young person into employment for the first time, or in passing it from the category of children to that of young persons, the preliminaries are the same as in first employing a child, with the exceptions that no certficate of proficiency is required at fourteen, nor of fitness after sixteen.   Up to eighteen its name has to be registered all the same ; but the Roman numerals XVI. are then inserted in the column provided for the purpose in the book : and when either a child or young person ceases to be employed the word Left should be written in that same column opposite the name.   No attendance at school is required from young persons ; nor any certificate of previous attendance, or proficiency.

WOMEN.

A *woman* is a female person above the age of eighteen. It is not necessary to register the names of women either in factories or workshops, nor are any certificates required in connection with their employment.   Their standing is in other respects, both in factories and workshops, the same as that of young persons : except when adult women work exclusively together, when there are different arrangements for the hours of labour.   A woman may not be knowingly employed for four weeks after childbirth.

HOURS OF LABOUR.

The hours of labour vary in the various classes of establish-ments.   In *Textile* factories the limits are from 6 a.m. to 6 p.m., or 7 a.m., to 7 p.m., with two hours out for rest and meals ; on every working day except Saturday ; and on Satur-day to 1 p.m. or 2 p.m. respectively, with one hour's interval = 56½ a week.   In *Non-textile* factories, the same hours (ordinarily) for beginning and ending, with 1½ hours out for meals, and till 2 p.m. on Saturday = 60 hours per week.   In Print, Bleach, and Dye Works, the same as Non-textile factories.   In Workshops (except Domestic and "Women's' workshops) the same. In Domestic Workshops, from 6 a.m. to 9 p.m., with 4½ hours out for meals, for women and young persons; and the same hours as in other factories and workshops for children. For " Women's " Workshops, that is to say places where no person under the age of eighteen is employed, a specified period of twelve hours, taken between six in the morning and ten in the evening at their own option, with 1½ out for meals; and of eight on Saturday, to terminate not later than 4 p.m., less half an hour for meal time. For Factory Bakehouses the same as Non-Textile factories: and for Wholesale and Retail bakehouses the same as Workshops (with some modifications).

All these regulations apply only to protected persons; the labour of adult men being unregulated.

The occupiers of the work-places, or their agents, are alone responsible for the hours of labour not being exceeded in them, whether with or without the consent of any person employed there; and appropriate penalties are provided in all cases for proved breaches of the law.

SANITATION.

The requirements of the Factory Acts in regard to Sanitation are very numerous and partly contained in other statutes. In general, all factories and workshops are bound to be kept in a cleanly state and free from any noxious effluvia, or other nuisance. They must not be overcrowded; and must be ventilated "so as to render harmless, as far as practicable, any gases, dust, etc., that may be generated in the course of the manufacturing process." With respect to *overcrowding*, it has been decided that 250 cubic feet of air for each worker is a reasonable allowance during ordinary work hours, and 400 when working overtime (see Overtime);

and, except in cases where *special exceptions* have been granted, all inside walls of rooms, and all ceilings, and all passages and staircases (unless painted with oil or varnished within seven years) are bound to be lime-washed once at least within every period of fourteen months. A considerable number of places are however exempted from this last requirement—for information as to which it is desirable to apply to the inspector of the district whose name is (or should be) written on the Abstract at the entrance of the workplace. In some places, as Lead Works, Bakehouses, etc., there are further exceptional requirements, which it is most important to become familiar with ; and in the case of Cotton Cloth Factories there is a special Act of Parliament dealing with humidity in Weaving Sheds. The place of this Act on the Statute Book is 52 & 53 Vic., Chap. 62.

HOLIDAYS.

No child, young person, or woman may work in any factory or workshop on Sunday (except male young persons employed in day and night shifts in blast furnaces and paper mills, and Jews). They must not be employed on Christmas Day or Good Friday (or the next Bank Holiday) ; besides which eight half-holidays or four whole ones must be given in the course of the year, half of them being between the 15th of March and 1st of October. Notice of the holidays proposed to be given must be affixed in January. But these last-named holidays are not compulsory in Domestic Workshops.

INSPECTION.

Employers must afford facilities of inspection to all officers furnished by a Secretary of State with a warrant for inspecting their places of work. Such officers have a right to call for the production of all registers, certificates, etc., required to be kept in conformity with the Factory Act, and to examine and copy them at their option. They may take a Medical Officer of Health, or other sanitary officer, with them into a factory or workshop, or a constable, where obstruction is anticipated. An inspector may " enter, inspect, and examine at all reasonable times by day and night a factory and a workshop, and every part thereof, when he has reasonable cause to believe that any person is employed therein " . . . . and "examine either alone or in the presence of any other person, as he thinks fit, with respect to matters under this Act, every person whom he finds in a factory or workshop . . . . and . . . . require such person to be so examined, and to sign a declaration of the truth of the matters respecting which he is so examined." He has certain powers in schools as well ; and finally may " exercise such other powers as may be necessary for carry ing this Act into effect." The penalty for obstructing an inspector in the discharge of his duty is one of the heaviest under the Factory Act. It is a fine not exceeding £5 if the offence is committed in the daytime, or not exceeding £20 at night. The fine for wilfully signing or making a false Declaration is one not exceeding £20, or imprisonment not exceeding three months, with or without hard labour. A factory inspector may also enforce the provisions of the Truck Act in factories and workshops.

SAFETY.

Some onerous requirements are made in regard to safety Every fly-wheel of an engine in a factory, *whether in the engine-house or not*, and every other dangerous part of it, and every hoist or teagle, is to be securely fenced.   Every wheel race not otherwise secured must be fenced close to the edge. All parts of the *mill-gearing*, and all dangerous parts of the *machinery*, must either be fenced or be of such a construction, or in such a position as not to need it.   The expression mill-gearing is defined.   It "comprehends every shaft, whether upright, oblique, or horizontal, and every wheel, drum, or pulley, by which the motion of the first moving power is communicated to any machine appertaining to a manufacturing process," while the term *machine* "includes any driving strap or band," in addition to the ordinary meaning.   No child, young person, nor woman may clean any mill-gearing in motion; nor a child any machinery in motion; nor any of them work "between the fixed and traversing parts of a self-acting machine" under the like condition.   Every fatal accident that occurs, and every accident from machinery moved by power, or from a vat or pan containing hot liquid, or from explosion, or from escape of gas, steam, or metal "which prevents the injured person from returning to his work and doing five hours' work on any day during the next three days" after, must be reported to the inspector and certifying surgeon.   But an accident of the kind requiring to be notified under the Explosives Act 1875 need not be so reported.

OUTWORKERS.

"The occupier of every factory and workshop (including any workshop conducted on the system of not employing any child, young person, or woman therein) and every contractor employed by any such occupier in the business of the factory or workshop shall, if so required by the Secretary of State by an Order made in accordance with Section sixty-five of the principal Act, and subject to any exceptions mentioned in the Order, keep in the prescribed form and with the prescribed particulars lists showing the names of all persons directly employed by him, either as workman or contractor, in the business of the factory or workshop, outside the factory or workshop, and the places where they are employed, and every such list shall be open to inspection by any inspector under the principal Act or by any officer of a sanitary authority."

In compliance with this requirement an Order, dated 20th November 1892, has been issued requiring such lists to be kept in the following industries :—The manufacture of articles of Wearing Apparel ; the manufacture of Electro Plate ; Cabinet and Furniture making and Upholstery work ; the manufacture of Files.

OVERTIME.

Overtime is allowed in certain classes of employment : allowed to be worked that is by young persons and women. It is in no case allowed to children ; and men are subject to no labour restrictions at all (see Hours of Labour). An idea of the processes in which it is allowed may be gathered from the subsequent list (see Special Exceptions) ; but it is usually wiser to apply to an inspector for information in each specific case. The mode in which the privilege may be availed of is the following. No protected person can be legally employed overtime unless there is a special exception from the general law to that effect, nor until seven days' notice has been given to an inspector of an employer's intention to avail himself of this exception. The appropriate Forms must then be procured (Nos. 12 and 21), displayed on the workroom walls while the overtime is worked, and a

Register of Overtime (No 40) kept in the prescribed way. This Register is a book, similar to a cheque book, and the counterfoil and body should be duly filled up with a statement of the quantity of overtime worked on each occasion. It contains forty-eight notices, and when used a notice should be torn off and posted every evening before eight o'clock. This notice is addressed on the back, and need not be prepaid. The number 48 is the number of times that it is legal to work overtime in any period of one year.

Special Rules.

In addition to all of these, the Secretary of State (Home Secretary) may make further special rules for the conduct of any industry or process as seems to him desirable; and such are made from time to time.

Special Exceptions.

The special exceptions and other Forms are contained on the following list. They can be procured direct from publishers in London, Dublin, and Edinburgh; and some other large towns; or may be ordered through any stationer. They should be procured in duplicate, and one copy served on the district inspector.

ABSTRACTS OF FACTORY ACTS.

No.			PRICE	POSTAGE
1.	For	Textile Factories	3d.	1d.
2.	,,	Non-Textile Factories	3d.	1d.
2A.	,,	White-Lead Works	3d.	1d.
3.	,,	Print-works, Dye-works, and Bleach-works	3d.	1d.

No.		PRICE	POSTAGE
4.	For Workshops · · · · · ·	3*d*.	1*d*.
4B.	,, Factory Bakehouses; and Wholesale and Retail Bakehouses · · · ·	3*d*.	1*d*.
5.	,, Domestic Factories and Workshops · ·	3*d*.	1*d*.
6.	,, "Women's" Workshops · · · ·	3*d*.	1*d*.

₊ *The above Abstracts are also printed in Welsh, and can be forwarded at the same prices.*

NOTICES AND REGISTERS.

7.	Places forbidden for Work · · · · ·	1*d*.	½*d*.
8.	,, ,, Meals · · · · ·	1*d*.	½*d*.
9.	Period of Employment, 8 a.m.—8 p.m. · ·	1*d*.	½*d*.
9A.	,, ,, 9 a.m.—9 p.m. — Straw Hats and Bonnets Factories	1*d*.	½*d*.
9B.	,, ,, 8 a.m.—8 p.m.—Special exception — Print-works, Bleach-works and Dye-works · · · ·	1*d*.	½*d*.
9C.	,, ,, 9 a.m.—9 p.m.—Special exception—Fish Curing ·	1*d*.	½*d*.
9D.	,, ,, 9 a.m.—9 p.m.—Special exception—Retail Drapers, Manchester and Salford, and to Bookbinding Factories in Metropolis	1*d*.	½*d*.
10.	Lace Factories, Overtime, Males above 16 · ·	1*d*.	½*d*.
11.	Bakehouses, Special period of employment for Males above 16 · · · · · ·	1*d*.	½*d*.
12.	Record of Overtime · · · · · ·	1*d*.	½*d*.
13.	Substitution of another Day for Saturday · ·	1*d*.	½*d*.
14.	Overtime.—To 4.30 p.m. on Saturdays.—Turkey Red Dyeing · · · · · · ·	1*d*.	½*d*.
15.	Five Hours' Spell in certain Textile Factories ·	1*d*.	½*d*.
16.	Different Holidays to different Sets · · ·	1*d*.	½*d*.
17.	Jew Occupier.—Overtime.—Holidays · · ·	1*d*.	½*d*.
18.	,, and Work-people.—Sunday Employment · · · · · · · ·	1*d*.	½*d*.

No.		PRICE	POSTAGE
19.	Different Meal Hours to different sets · · ·	1*d*.	½*d*.
20.	Employment, &c., during Meal Hours · · ·	1*d*.	½*d*.
21.	Overtime.—Additional 2 Hours · · ·	1*d*.	½*d*.
22.	,, 30 Minutes.—Incomplete Process ·	1*d*.	½*d*.
23.	,, for Prevention of Damage.—Turkey Red Dyeing.—Open-air Bleaching	1*d*.	½*d*.
24.	,, Additional 2 Hours. — Perishable Articles · · · ·	1*d*.	½*d*.
25.	Water Mills.—Lost Time · · · · ·	1*d*.	½*d*.
26.	Night-work.—Male Young Persons · · ·	1*d*.	½*d*.
27.	,, Printing Newspapers · · ·	1*d*.	½*d*.
28.	Glass Works.—Male Young Persons.—Accustomed Hours · · · · · · ·	1*d*.	½*d*.
29.	Workshop in which neither Children nor Young Persons are employed · · · ·	1*d*.	½*d*.
30.	Period of Employment.—8 Hours on Saturday ·	1*d*.	½*d*.
31.	Notice of Alteration of Period of Employment ·	1*d*.	½*d*.
32.	,, ,, Meal Times · ·	1*d*.	½*d*.
33.	,, ,, Employment of Children ·	1*d*.	½*d*.
34.	Notice of Holidays · · · · · ·	1*d*.	½*d*.
35.	Notice of Beginning to Occupy a Factory or Workshop · · · · · · ·	1*d*.	½*d*.
37.	Register of Children and Young Persons, Holidays, Limewashing, &c.—small size · · ·	3*d*.	1*d*.
	Register of Children and Young Persons, Holidays, Limewashing, &c.—250 Names · · ·	6*d*.	2*d*.
	Register of Children and Young Persons, Holidays, Limewashing, &c.—500 Names · · ·	9*d*.	2½*d*.
37A.	Register of Young Persons, Holidays, Limewashing, &c.—60 Names · · · ·	4*d*.	1*d*.
	Register of Young Persons, Holidays, Limewashing, &c.—250 Names · · · ·	6*d*.	2*d*.
	Register of Young Persons, Holidays, Limewashing, &c.—500 Names · · · ·	9*d*.	2½*d*.
37B.	Register of Children, Holidays, Limewashing, &c. —60 Names · · · · · ·	4*d*.	1*d*.

COTTON CLOTH FACTORIES ACT, 1889.

INDEX

A

N

B

C

D

H

I

J

K

L

P

Q

R

S

Waterlow & Sons Limited, London and Dunstable.

A CATALOGUE OF BOOKS
PUBLISHED BY METHUEN
AND COMPANY: LONDON
36 ESSEX STREET
W.C.

CONTENTS

FEBRUARY 1908

A CATALOGUE OF
MESSRS. METHUEN'S
PUBLICATIONS

Colonial Editions are published of all Messrs. METHUEN's Novels issued at a price above 2s. 6d., and similar editions are published of some works of General Literature. These are marked in the Catalogue. Colonial editions are only for circulation in the British Colonies and India.

I.P.L. represents Illustrated Pocket Library.

PART I.—GENERAL LITERATURE

Abbott (J. H. M.). Author of 'Tommy Cornstalk.' AN OUTLANDER IN ENGLAND: BEING SOME IMPRESSIONS OF AN AUSTRALIAN ABROAD. *Second Edition. Cr. 8vo. 6s.*
A Colonial Edition is also published.

Acates (M. J.). See Junior School Books.

Adams (Frank). JACK SPRATT. With 24 Coloured Pictures. *Super Royal 16mo. 2s.*

Adeney (W. F.), M.A. See Bennett and Adeney.

Æschylus. See Classical Translations.

Æsop. See I.P.L.

Ainsworth (W. Harrison). See I.P.L.

Alderson (J. P.). MR. ASQUITH. With Portraits and Illustrations. *Demy 8vo. 7s. 6d. net.*

Aldis (Janet). MADAME GEOFFRIN, HER SALON, AND HER TIMES. With many Portraits and Illustrations. *Second Edition. Demy 8vo. 10s. 6d. net.*
A Colonial Edition is also published.

Alexander (William), D.D., Archbishop of Armagh. THOUGHTS AND COUNSELS OF MANY YEARS. *Demy 16mo. 2s. 6d.*

Aiken (Henry). THE NATIONAL SPORTS OF GREAT BRITAIN. With descriptions in English and French. With 51 Coloured Plates. *Royal Folio. Five Guineas net.* The Plates can be had separately in a Portfolio. *£3, 3s. net.*
See also I.P.L.

Allen (C. C.) See Textbooks of Technology.

Allen (Jessie). See Little Books on Art.

Allen (J. Romilly), F.S.A. See Antiquary's Books.

Almack (E.). See Little Books on Art.

Amherst (Lady). A SKETCH OF EGYPTIAN HISTORY FROM THE EARLIEST TIMES TO THE PRESENT DAY. With many Illustrations. *Demy 8vo. 7s. 6d. net.*

Anderson (F. M.). THE STORY OF THE BRITISH EMPIRE FOR CHILDREN. With many Illustrations. *Cr. 8vo. 2s.*

Anderson (J. G.), B.A., Examiner to London University, NOUVELLE GRAMMAIRE FRANÇAISE. *Cr. 8vo. 2s.*
EXERCICES DE GRAMMAIRE FRANÇAISE. *Cr. 8vo. 1s. 6d.*

Andrewes (Bishop). PRECES PRIVATAE. Edited, with Notes, by F. E. BRIGHTMAN, M.A., of Pusey House, Oxford. *Cr. 8vo. 6s.*

Anglo-Australian. AFTER-GLOW MEMORIES. *Cr. 8vo. 6s.*
A Colonial Edition is also published.

Anon. FELISSA; OR, THE LIFE AND OPINIONS OF A KITTEN OF SENTIMENT. With 12 Coloured Plates. *Post 16mo. 2s. 6d. net.*

Aristotle. THE NICOMACHEAN ETHICS. Edited, with an Introduction and Notes, by JOHN BURNET, M.A., Professor of Greek at St. Andrews. *Cheaper issue. Demy 8vo. 10s. 6d. net.*

Atkins (H. G.). See Oxford Biographies.

Atkinson (C. M.). JEREMY BENTHAM. *Demy 8vo. 5s. net.*

Atkinson (T. D.). A SHORT HISTORY OF ENGLISH ARCHITECTURE. With over 200 Illustrations. *Second Edition. Fcap. 8vo. 3s. 6d. net.*
A GLOSSARY OF TERMS USED IN ENGLISH ARCHITECTURE. Illustrated. *Second Ed. Fcap. 8vo. 3s. 6d. net.*

Auden (T.), M.A., F.S.A. See Ancient Cities.

Aurelius (Marcus) and Epictetus. WORDS OF THE ANCIENT WISE: Thoughts from. Edited by W. H. D. ROUSE, M.A., Litt.D. *Fcap. 8vo. 3s. 6d. net.* See also Standard Library.

Austen (Jane). See Little Library and Standard Library.

Bacon (Francis). See Little Library and Standard Library.

Baden-Powell (R. S. S.), Major-General. THE DOWNFALL OF PREMPEH. A Diary of Life in Ashanti 1895. Illustrated. *Third Edition. Large Cr. 8vo. 6s.*
A Colonial Edition is also published.

THE MATABELE CAMPAIGN, 1896. With nearly 100 Illustrations. *Fourth Edition. Large Cr. 8vo. 6s.*
A Colonial Edition is also published.

Bailey (J. C.), M.A. See Cowper.

Baker (W. G.), M.A. See Junior Examination Series.

Baker (Julian L.), F.I.C., F.C.S. See Books on Business.

Balfour (Graham). THE LIFE OF ROBERT LOUIS STEVENSON. *Fourth Edition, Revised. Cr. 8vo. 6s.*
A Colonial Edition is also published.

Ballard (A.), B.A., LL.B. See Antiquary's Books.

Bally (S. E.). See Commercial Series.

Banks (Elizabeth L.). THE AUTOBIOGRAPHY OF A 'NEWSPAPER GIRL.' *Second Edition. Cr. 8vo. 6s.*
A Colonial Edition is also published.

Barham (R. H.). See Little Library.

Baring (The Hon. Maurice). WITH THE RUSSIANS IN MANCHURIA. *Third Edition. Demy 8vo. 7s. 6d. net.*
A Colonial Edition is also published.

A YEAR IN RUSSIA. *Second Edition. Demy 8vo. 7s. 6d.*

Baring-Gould (S.). THE LIFE OF NAPOLEON BONAPARTE. With over 150 Illustrations in the Text, and a Photogravure Frontispiece. *Royal 8vo. 10s. 6d. net.*

THE TRAGEDY OF THE CÆSARS. With numerous Illustrations from Busts, Gems, Cameos, etc. *Sixth Edition. Royal 8vo. 10s. 6d. net.*

A BOOK OF FAIRY TALES. With numerous Illustrations by A. J. GASKIN. *Third Edition. Cr. 8vo. Buckram. 6s.*

OLD ENGLISH FAIRY TALES. With numerous Illustrations by F. D. BEDFORD. *Third Edition. Cr. 8vo. Buckram. 6s.*

THE VICAR OF MORWENSTOW. Revised Edition. With a Portrait. *Third Edition. Cr. 8vo. 3s. 6d.*

A BOOK OF DARTMOOR: A Descriptive and Historical Sketch. With Plans and numerous Illustrations. *Second Edition. Cr. 8vo. 6s.*

A BOOK OF DEVON. Illustrated. *Second Edition. Cr. 8vo. 6s.*

A BOOK OF CORNWALL. Illustrated. *Second Edition. Cr. 8vo. 6s.*

A BOOK OF NORTH WALES. Illustrated. *Cr. 8vo. 6s.*

A BOOK OF SOUTH WALES. Illustrated. *Cr. 8vo. 6s.*

A BOOK OF BRITTANY. Illustrated. *Cr. 8vo. 6s.*

A BOOK OF THE RIVIERA. Illustrated. *Cr. 8vo. 6s.*
A Colonial Edition is also published.

A BOOK OF THE RHINE: From Cleve to Mainz. Illustrated. *Second Edition. Crown 8vo. 6s.*
A Colonial Edition is also published.

A BOOK OF THE PYRENEES. With 24 Illustrations. *Crown 8vo. 6s.*
A Colonial Edition is also published.

A BOOK OF GHOSTS. With 8 Illustrations by D. MURRAY SMITH. *Second Edition. Cr. 8vo. 6s.*

OLD COUNTRY LIFE. With 67 Illustrations. *Fifth Edition. Large Cr. 8vo. 6s.*

A GARLAND OF COUNTRY SONG: English Folk Songs with their Traditional Melodies. Collected and arranged by S. BARING-GOULD and H. F. SHEPPARD. *Demy 4to. 6s.*

SONGS OF THE WEST: Folk Songs of Devon and Cornwall. Collected from the Mouths of the People. By S. BARING-GOULD, M.A., and H. FLEETWOOD SHEPPARD, M.A. New and Revised Edition, under the musical editorship of CECIL J. SHARP, Principal of the Hampstead Conservatoire. *Large Imperial 8vo. 5s. net.*

A BOOK OF NURSERY SONGS AND RHYMES. Edited by S. BARING-GOULD, and Illustrated by the Birmingham Art School. *A New Edition. Long Cr. 8vo. 2s. 6d. net.*

STRANGE SURVIVALS AND SUPERSTITIONS. *Third Edition. Cr. 8vo. 2s. 6d. net.*

YORKSHIRE ODDITIES AND STRANGE EVENTS. *New and Revised Edition. Cr. 8vo. 2s. 6d. net.*
See also Little Guides.

Barker (Aldred F.). See Textbooks of Technology.

Barker (E.), M.A. (Late) Fellow of Merton College, Oxford. THE POLITICAL THOUGHT OF PLATO AND ARISTOTLE. *Demy 8vo. 10s. 6d. net.*

Barnes (W. E.), D.D. See Churchman's Bible.

Barnett (Mrs. P. A.). See Little Library.

Baron (R. R. N.), M.A. FRENCH PROSE COMPOSITION. *Second Edition. Cr. 8vo. 2s. 6d. Key, 3s. net.*
See also Junior School Books.

Barron (H. M.), M.A., Wadham College, Oxford. TEXTS FOR SERMONS. With a Preface by Canon SCOTT HOLLAND. *Cr. 8vo. 3s. 6d.*

Bartholomew (J. G.), F.R.S.E. See C. G. Robertson.

Bastable (C. F.), M.A. THE COMMERCE OF NATIONS. *Fourth Ed. Cr. 8vo. 2s. 6d.*

Bastian (H. Charlton), M.D., F.R.S. THE EVOLUTION OF LIFE. Illustrated. *Demy 8vo. 7s. 6d. net.*

Batson (Mrs. Stephen). A CONCISE HANDBOOK OF GARDEN FLOWERS. *Fcap. 8vo. 3s. 6d.*

Batten (Loring W.), Ph.D., S.T.D. THE HEBREW PROPHET. *Cr. 8vo. 3s. 6d. net.*

Bayley (R. Child). THE COMPLETE PHOTOGRAPHER. With over 100 Illustrations. *Second Ed.* With Note on Direct Colour Process. *Demy 8vo. 10s. 6d. net.*

Beard (W. S.). EASY EXERCISES IN ALGEBRA. *Cr. 8vo. 1s. 6d.* See Junior Examination Series and Beginner's Books.

Beckford (Peter). THOUGHTS ON HUNTING. Edited by J. OTHO PAGET, and Illustrated by G. H. JALLAND. *Second Edition. Demy 8vo. 6s.*

Beckford (William). See Little Library.

Beeching (H. C.), M.A., Canon of Westminster. See Library of Devotion.

Begbie (Harold). MASTER WORKERS. Illustrated. *Demy 8vo. 7s. 6d. net.*

Behmen (Jacob). DIALOGUES ON THE SUPERSENSUAL LIFE. Edited by BERNARD HOLLAND. *Fcap. 8vo. 3s. 6d.*

Bell (Mrs. A.). THE SKIRTS OF THE GREAT CITY. *Second Ed. Cr. 8vo. 6s.*

Belloc (Hilaire), M.P. PARIS. With Maps and Illustrations. *Second Edition, Revised. Cr. 8vo. 6s.*

HILLS AND THE SEA. *Second Edition. Crown 8vo. 6s.*

Bellot (H. H. L.), M.A. THE INNER AND MIDDLE TEMPLE. With numerous Illustrations. *Crown 8vo. 6s. net.*

Bennett (W. H.), M.A. A PRIMER OF THE BIBLE. *Fourth Ed. Cr. 8vo. 2s. 6d.*

Bennett (W. H.) and Adeney (W. F.). A BIBLICAL INTRODUCTION. *Fourth Edition. Cr. 8vo. 7s. 6d.*

Benson (Archbishop) GOD'S BOARD: Communion Addresses. *Second Edition. Fcap. 8vo. 3s. 6d. net.*

Benson (A. C.), M.A. See Oxford Biographies.

Benson (R. M.). THE WAY OF HOLINESS: a Devotional Commentary on the 119th Psalm. *Cr. 8vo. 5s.*

Bernard (E. R.), M.A., Canon of Salisbury. THE ENGLISH SUNDAY. *Fcap. 8vo. 1s. 6d.*

Bertouch (Baroness de). THE LIFE OF FATHER IGNATIUS. Illustrated. *Demy 8vo. 10s. 6d. net.*

Beruete (A. de). See Classics of Art.

Betham-Edwards (M.). HOME LIFE IN FRANCE. Illustrated. *Fourth and Cheaper Edition. Crown 8vo. 6s.*
A Colonial Edition is also published.

Bethune-Baker (J. F.), M.A. See Handbooks of Theology.

Bidez (M.). See Byzantine Texts.

Biggs (C. R. D.), D.D. See Churchman's Bible.

Bindley (T. Herbert), B.D. THE OECUMENICAL DOCUMENTS OF THE FAITH. With Introductions and Notes. *Second Edition. Cr. 8vo. 6s. net.*

Binns (H. B.). THE LIFE OF WALT WHITMAN. Illustrated. *Demy 8vo. 10s. 6d. net.*
A Colonial Edition is also published.

Binyon (Lawrence). THE DEATH OF ADAM, AND OTHER POEMS. *Cr. 8vo. 3s. 6d. net.*
See also W. Blake.

Birnstingl (Ethel). See Little Books on Art.

Blair (Robert). See I.P.L.

Blake (William). THE LETTERS OF WILLIAM BLAKE, TOGETHER WITH A LIFE BY FREDERICK TATHAM. Edited

from the Original Manuscripts, with an Introduction and Notes, by ARCHIBALD G. B. RUSSELL. With 12 Illustrations. *Demy 8vo. 7s. 6d. net.*

ILLUSTRATIONS OF THE BOOK OF JOB. With a General Introduction by LAWRENCE BINYON. *Quarto. 21s. net.*
See also I.P.L. and Little Library.

Blaxland (B.), M.A. See Library of Devotion.

Bloom (J. Harvey), M.A. SHAKESPEARE'S GARDEN. Illustrated. *Fcap. 8vo. 3s. 6d. ; leather, 4s. 6d. net.*
See also Antiquary's Books

Blouet (Henri). See Beginner's Books.

Boardman (T. H.), M.A. See Textbooks of Science.

Bodley (J. E. C.), Author of 'France.' THE CORONATION OF EDWARD VII. *Demy 8vo. 21s. net.* By Command of the King.

Body (George), D.D. THE SOUL'S PILGRIMAGE: Devotional Readings from his writings. Selected by J. H. BURN, B.D., F.R.S.E. *Demy 16mo. 2s. 6d.*

Bona (Cardinal). See Library of Devotion.

Boon (F. C.). See Commercial Series.

Borrow (George). See Little Library.

Bos (J. Ritzema). AGRICULTURAL ZOOLOGY. Translated by J. R. AINSWORTH DAVIS, M.A. With 155 Illustrations. *Cr. 8vo. Third Edition. 3s. 6d.*

Botting (C. G.), B.A. EASY GREEK EXERCISES. *Cr. 8vo. 2s.* See also Junior Examination Series.

Boulting (W.) TASSO AND HIS TIMES. With 24 Illustrations. *Demy 8vo. 10s. 6d. net.*

Boulton (E. S.), M.A. GEOMETRY ON MODERN LINES. *Cr. 8vo. 2s.*

Boulton (William B.). THOMAS GAINSBOROUGH With 40 Illustrations. *Second Ed. Demy 8vo. 7s. 6d. net.*

SIR JOSHUA REYNOLDS, P.R.A. With 49 Illustrations. *Demy 8vo. 7s. 6d. net.*

Bowden (E. M.). THE IMITATION OF BUDDHA: Being Quotations from Buddhist Literature for each Day in the Year. *Fifth Edition. Cr. 16mo. 2s. 6d.*

Boyd-Carpenter (Margaret). THE CHILD IN ART. Illustrated. *Second Edition. Large Crown 8vo. 6s.*

Boyle (W.). CHRISTMAS AT THE ZOO. With Verses by W. BOYLE and 24 Coloured Pictures by H. B. NEILSON. *Super Royal 16mo. 2s.*

Brabant (F. G.), M.A. See Little Guides.

Bradley (A. G.) ROUND ABOUT WILTSHIRE. With 30 Illustrations of which 14 are in colour by T. C. GOTCH. *Second Ed. Cr. 8vo. 6s.*

Bradley (J. W.). See Little Books on Art.

Braid (James) and Others. GREAT GOLFERS IN THE MAKING. By Thirty-Four Famous Players. Edited, with an Introduction, by HENRY LEACH. With 34 Portraits. *Second Ed. Demy 8vo. 7s. 6d. net.*
A Colonial Edition is also published.

Brailsford (H. N.). MACEDONIA: ITS RACES AND ITS FUTURE. Illustrated. *Demy 8vo.* 12s. 6d. net.

Brodrick (Mary) and Morton (Anderson). A CONCISE HANDBOOK OF EGYPTIAN ARCHÆOLOGY. Illustrated. *Cr. 8vo.* 3s. 6d.

Brooks (E. E.), B.Sc. See Textbooks of Technology.

Brooks (E. W.). See Byzantine Texts.

Brown (P. H.), LL.D., Fraser Professor of Ancient (Scottish) History at the University of Edinburgh. SCOTLAND IN THE TIME OF QUEEN MARY. *Demy 8vo.* 7s. 6d. net.

Brown (S. E.), M.A., Camb., B.A., B.Sc., London ; Senior Science Master at Uppingham School. A PRACTICAL CHEMISTRY NOTE-BOOK FOR MATRICULATION AND ARMY CANDIDATES: EASIER EXPERIMENTS ON THE COMMONER SUBSTANCES. *Cr. 4to.* 1s. 6d. net.

Browne (Sir Thomas). See Standard Library.

Brownell (C. L.). THE HEART OF JAPAN. Illustrated. *Third Edition. Cr. 8vo.* 6s.; *also Demy 8vo.* 6d.

Browning (Robert). See Little Library.

Buckland (Francis T.). CURIOSITIES OF NATURAL HISTORY. Illustrated by H. B. NEILSON. *Cr. 8vo.* 3s. 6d.

Buckton (A. M.) THE BURDEN OF ENGELA: a Ballad-Epic. *Second Edition. Cr. 8vo.* 3s. 6d. net.
KINGS IN BABYLON. A Drama. *Crown 8vo.* 1s. net.
EAGER HEART: A Mystery Play. *Sixth Edition. Cr. 8vo.* 1s. net.

Budge (E. A. Wallis). THE GODS OF THE EGYPTIANS. With over 100 Coloured Plates and many Illustrations. *Two Volumes. Royal 8vo.* £3, 3s. net.

Buist (H. Massac). THE MOTOR YEAR BOOK AND AUTOMOBILISTS' ANNUAL FOR 1906. *Demy 8vo.* 7s. 6d. net.

Bull (Paul), Army Chaplain. GOD AND OUR SOLDIERS. *Second Edition. Cr. 8vo.* 6s.

Bulley (Miss). See Lady Dilke.

Bunyan (John). THE PILGRIM'S PROGRESS. Edited, with an Introduction, by C. H. FIRTH, M.A. With 39 Illustrations by R. ANNING BELL. *Cr. 8vo.* 6s.
See also Library of Devotion and Standard Library.

Burch (G. J.), M.A., F.R.S. A MANUAL OF ELECTRICAL SCIENCE. Illustrated. *Cr. 8vo.* 3s.

Burgess (Gelett). GOOPS AND HOW TO BE THEM. Illustrated. *Small 4to.* 6s.

Burke (Edmund). See Standard Library.

Burn (A. E.), D.D., Rector of Handsworth and Prebendary of Lichfield.
See Handbooks of Theology.

Burn (J. H.), B.D. THE CHURCHMAN'S TREASURY OF SONG. Selected and Edited by. *Fcap 8vo.* 3s. 6d. net. See also Library of Devotion.

Burnand (Sir F. C.). RECORDS AND REMINISCENCES. With a Portrait by H. v. HERKOMER. *Cr. 8vo. Fourth and Cheaper Edition.* 6s.
A Colonial Edition is also published.

Burns (Robert), THE POEMS OF. Edited by ANDREW LANG and W. A. CRAIGIE. With Portrait. *Third Edition. Demy 8vo, gilt top.* 6s.

Burnside (W. F.), M.A. OLD TESTAMENT HISTORY FOR USE IN SCHOOLS. *Third Edition. Cr. 8vo.* 3s. 6d.

Burton (Alfred). See I.P.L.

Bussell (F. W.), D.D., Fellow and Vice Principal of Brasenose College, Oxford. CHRISTIAN THEOLOGY AND SOCIAL PROGRESS: The Bampton Lectures for 1905. *Demy 8vo* 10s. 6d. net.

Butler (Joseph). See Standard Library.

Caldecott (Alfred), D.D. See Handbooks of Theology.

Calderwood (D. S.), Headmaster of the Normal School, Edinburgh. TEST CARDS IN EUCLID AND ALGEBRA. In three packets of 40, with Answers. 1s. each. Or in three Books, price 2d., 2d., and 3d.

Cambridge (Ada) [Mrs. Cross]. THIRTY YEARS IN AUSTRALIA. *Demy 8vo.* 7s. 6d.

Canning (George). See Little Library.

Capey (E. F. H.). See Oxford Biographies.

Careless (John). See I.P.L.

Carlyle (Thomas). THE FRENCH REVOLUTION. Edited by C. R. L. FLETCHER, Fellow of Magdalen College, Oxford. *Three Volumes. Cr. 8vo.* 18s.
THE LIFE AND LETTERS OF OLIVER CROMWELL. With an Introduction by C. H. FIRTH, M.A., and Notes and Appendices by Mrs. S. C. LOMAS. *Three Volumes. Demy 8vo.* 18s. net.

Carlyle (R. M. and A. J.), M.A. See Leaders of Religion.

Channer (C. C.) and Roberts (M. E.). LACEMAKING IN THE MIDLANDS, PAST AND PRESENT. With 16 full-page Illustrations. *Cr. 8vo.* 2s. 6d.

Chapman (S. J.). See Books on Business.

Chatterton (Thomas). See Standard Library.

Chesterfield (Lord), THE LETTERS OF, TO HIS SON. Edited, with an Introduction by C. STRACHEY, and Notes by A. CALTHROP. *Two Volumes. Cr. 8vo.* 12s.

Chesterton (G. K.). CHARLES DICKENS. With two Portraits in photogravure. *Fifth Edition. Demy 8vo.* 7s. 6d. net.
A Colonial Edition is also published.

Childe (Charles P.), B.A., F.R.C.S. THE CONTROL OF A SCOURGE : OR, How CANCER IS CURABLE. *Demy 8vo.* 7s. 6d. net.

Christian (F. W.). THE CAROLINE ISLANDS. With many Illustrations and Maps. *Demy 8vo.* 12s. 6d. net.

Cicero. See Classical Translations.

Clarke (F. A.), M.A. See Leaders of Religion.

Clausen (George), A.R.A., R.W.S. AIMS AND IDEALS IN ART : Eight Lectures delivered to the Students of the Royal Academy of Arts. With 32 Illustrations. *Second Edition. Large Post 8vo.* 5s. net.
SIX LECTURES ON PAINTING. *First Series.* With 19 Illustrations. *Third Edition, Large Post 8vo.* 3s. 6d. net.

Cleather (A. L.). See Wagner.

Clinch (G.). See Little Guides.

Clough (W. T.). See Junior School Books and Textbooks of Science.

Clouston (T. S.), M.D., C.C.D., F.R.S.E., Lecturer on Mental Diseases in the University of Edinburgh. THE HYGIENE OF MIND. With 10 Illustrations. *Fourth Edition. Demy 8vo.* 7s. 6d. net.

Coast (W. G.), B.A. EXAMINATION PAPERS IN VERGIL. *Cr. 8vo.* 2s.

Cobb (W. F.), M.A. THE BOOK OF PSALMS : with a Commentary. *Demy 8vo.* 10s. 6d. net.

Coleridge (S. T.). POEMS OF. Selected and Arranged by ARTHUR SYMONS. With a photogravure Frontispiece. *Fcap. 8vo.* 2s. 6d. net.

Collingwood (W. G.), M.A. THE LIFE OF JOHN RUSKIN. With Portraits. *Sixth Edition. Cr. 8vo.* 2s. 6d. net.

Collins (W. E.), M.A. See Churchman's Library.

Colonna. HYPNEROTOMACHIA POLIPHILI UBI HUMANA OMNIA NON NISI SOMNIUM ESSE DOCET ATQUE OBITER PLURIMA SCITU SANE QUAM DIGNA COMMEMORAT. An edition limited to 350 copies on handmade paper. *Folio.* £3, 3s. net.

Combe (William). See I.P.L.

Conrad (Joseph). THE MIRROR OF THE SEA: Memories and Impressions. *Third Edition. Cr. 8vo.* 6s.

Cook (A. M.), M.A., and Marchant (C. E.), M.A. PASSAGES FOR UNSEEN TRANSLATION. Selected from Greek and Latin Literature. *Fourth Ed. Cr. 8vo.* 3s. 6d.
LATIN PASSAGES FOR UNSEEN TRANSLATION. *Third Ed. Cr. 8vo.* 1s. 6d.

Cooke-Taylor (R. W.). THE FACTORY SYSTEM. *Cr. 8vo.* 2s. 6d.

Corelli (Marie). THE PASSING OF THE GREAT QUEEN. *Second Ed. Fcap. 4to.* 1s.
A CHRISTMAS GREETING. *Cr. 4to.* 1s.

Corkran (Alice). See Little Books on Art.

Cotes (Everard). SIGNS AND PORTENTS IN THE FAR EAST. With 24 Illustrations. *Second Edition. Demy 8vo.* 7s. 6d. net.

Cotes (Rosemary). DANTE'S GARDEN. With a Frontispiece. *Second Edition. Fcap. 8vo.* 2s. 6d.; *leather*, 3s. 6d. net.
BIBLE FLOWERS. With a Frontispiece and Plan. *Fcap. 8vo.* 2s. 6d. net.

Cowley (Abraham). See Little Library.

Cowper (William), THE POEMS OF. Edited with an Introduction and Notes by J. C. BAILEY, M.A. Illustrated, including two unpublished designs by WILLIAM BLAKE. *Demy 8vo.* 10s. 6d. net.

Cox (J. Charles), LL.D., F.S.A. See Little Guides, The Antiquary's Books, and Ancient Cities.

Cox (Harold), B.A., M.P. LAND NATIONALISATION AND LAND TAXATION. *Second Edition revised. Cr. 8vo.* 3s. 6d. net.

Crabbe (George). See Little Library.

Craigie (W. A.). A PRIMER OF BURNS. *Cr. 8vo.* 2s. 6d.

Craik (Mrs.). See Little Library.

Crane (Capt. C. P.). See Little Guides.

Crane (Walter). AN ARTIST'S REMINISCENCES. *Second Edition.*

Crashaw (Richard). See Little Library.

Crawford (F. G.). See Mary C. Danson.

Crofts (T. R. N.), M.A. See Simplified French Texts.

Cross (J. A.), M.A. THE FAITH OF THE BIBLE. *Fcap. 8vo.* 2s. 6d. net.

Cruikshank (G.). THE LOVING BALLAD OF LORD BATEMAN. With 11 Plates. *Cr. 16mo.* 1s. 6d. net.

Crump (B.). See Wagner.

Cunliffe (Sir F. H. E.), Fellow of All Souls' College, Oxford. THE HISTORY OF THE BOER WAR. With many Illustrations, Plans, and Portraits. *In 2 vols. Quarto.* 15s. each.

Cunynghame (H. H.), C.B. See Connoisseur's Library.

Cutts (E. L.), D.D. See Leaders of Religion.

Daniell (G. W.), M.A. See Leaders of Religion.

Danson (Mary C.) and Crawford (F. G.). FATHERS IN THE FAITH. *Fcap. 8vo.* 1s. 6d.

Dante. LA COMMEDIA DI DANTE. The Italian Text edited by PAGET TOYNBEE, M.A., D.Litt. *Cr. 8vo.* 6s.
THE PURGATORIO OF DANTE. Translated into Spenserian Prose by C. GORDON WRIGHT. With the Italian text. *Fcap. 8vo.* 2s. 6d. net.
See also Paget Toynbee, Little Library, Standard Library, and Warren-Vernon.

Darley (George). See Little Library.

D'Arcy (R. F.), M.A. A NEW TRIGONOMETRY FOR BEGINNERS. With numerous diagrams. *Cr. 8vo.* 2s. 6d.

Davenport (Cyril). See Connoisseur's Library and Little Books on Art.

Davey (Richard). THE PAGEANT OF LONDON. With 40 Illustrations in Colour by JOHN FULLEYLOVE, R.I. *In Two Volumes. Demy 8vo.* 15s. net.

Davis (H. W. C.), M.A., Fellow and Tutor of Balliol College, Author of 'Charlemagne.' ENGLAND UNDER THE NORMANS AND ANGEVINS: 1066-1272. With Maps and Illustrations. *Demy 8vo.* 10s. 6d. net.

Dawson (Nelson). See Connoisseur's Library.

Fisher (G. W.), M.A. ANNALS OF SHREWSBURY SCHOOL. Illustrated. *Demy 8vo. 10s. 6d.*

FitzGerald (Edward). THE RUBÁIYÁT OF OMAR KHAYYÁM. Printed from the Fifth and last Edition. With a Commentary by Mrs. STEPHEN BATSON, and a Biography of Omar by E. D. Ross. *Cr. 8vo. 6s.* See also Miniature Library.

FitzGerald (H. P.). A CONCISE HANDBOOK OF CLIMBERS, TWINERS, AND WALL SHRUBS. Illustrated. *Fcap. 8vo. 3s. 6d. net.*

Fitzpatrick (S. A. O.). See Ancient Cities.

Flecker (W. H.), M.A., D.C.L., Headmaster of the Dean Close School, Cheltenham. THE STUDENT'S PRAYER BOOK. THE TEXT OF MORNING AND EVENING PRAYER AND LITANY. With an Introduction and Notes. *Cr. 8vo. 2s. 6d.*

Flux (A. W.), M.A., William Dow Professor of Political Economy in M'Gill University, Montreal. ECONOMIC PRINCIPLES. *Demy 8vo. 7s. 6d. net.*

Fortescue (Mrs. G.). See Little Books on Art.

Fraser (David). A MODERN CAMPAIGN; OR, WAR AND WIRELESS TELEGRAPHY IN THE FAR EAST. Illustrated. *Cr. 8vo. 6s.* A Colonial Edition is also published.

Fraser (J. F.). ROUND THE WORLD ON A WHEEL. With 100 Illustrations. *Fifth Edition. Cr. 8vo. 6s.*

French (W.), M.A. See Textbooks of Science.

Freudenreich (Ed. von). DAIRY BACTERIOLOGY. A Short Manual for the Use of Students. Translated by J. R. AINSWORTH DAVIS, M.A. *Second Edition. Revised. Cr. 8vo. 2s. 6d.*

Fulford (H. W.), M.A. See Churchman's Bible.

Gallaher (D.) and Stead (W. J.). THE COMPLETE RUGBY FOOTBALLER, ON THE NEW ZEALAND SYSTEM. With an Account of the Tour of the New Zealanders in England. With 35 Illustrations. *Second Ed. Demy 8vo. 7s. 6d. net.*

Gallichan (W. M.). See Little Guides.

Gambado (Geoffrey, Esq.). See I.P.L.

Gaskell (Mrs.). See Little Library and Standard Library.

Gasquet, the Right Rev. Abbot, O.S.B. See Antiquary's Books.

George (H. B.), M.A., Fellow of New College, Oxford. BATTLES OF ENGLISH HISTORY. With numerous Plans. *Fourth Edition.* Revised, with a new Chapter including the South African War. *Cr. 8vo. 3s. 6d.*

A HISTORICAL GEOGRAPHY OF THE BRITISH EMPIRE. *Second Edition. Cr. 8vo. 3s. 6d.*

Gibbins (H. de B.), Litt.D., M.A. INDUSTRY IN ENGLAND : HISTORICAL OUTLINES. With 5 Maps. *Fifth Edition. Demy 8vo. 10s. 6d.*

THE INDUSTRIAL HISTORY OF ENGLAND. *Fourteenth Edition.* Revised. With Maps and Plans. *Cr. 8vo. 3s.*

ENGLISH SOCIAL REFORMERS. *Second Edition. Cr. 8vo. 2s. 6d.* See also Commercial Series and R. A. Hadfield.

Gibbon (Edward). THE DECLINE AND FALL OF THE ROMAN EMPIRE. Edited with Notes, Appendices, and Maps, by J. B. BURY, M.A., Litt.D., Regius Professor of Greek at Cambridge. *In Seven Volumes. Demy 8vo. Gilt top, 8s. 6d. each. Also, Cr. 8vo. 6s. each.*

MEMOIRS OF MY LIFE AND WRITINGS. Edited by G. BIRKBECK HILL, LL.D. *Cr. 8vo. 6s.* See also Standard Library.

Gibson (E. C. S.), D.D., Lord Bishop of Gloucester. See Westminster Commentaries, Handbooks of Theology, and Oxford Biographies.

Gilbert (A. R.). See Little Books on Art.

Gloag (M. R.) and Wyatt (Kate M.). A BOOK OF ENGLISH GARDENS. With 24 Illustrations in Colour. *Demy 8vo. 10s. 6d. net.*

Godfrey (Elizabeth). A BOOK OF REMEMBRANCE. Edited by. *Fcap. 8vo. 2s. 6d. net.*

Godley (A. D.), M.A., Fellow of Magdalen College, Oxford. LYRA FRIVOLA. *Fourth Edition. Fcap. 8vo. 2s. 6d.*

VERSES TO ORDER. *Second Edition. Fcap. 8vo. 2s. 6d.*

SECOND STRINGS. *Fcap. 8vo. 2s. 6d.*

Goldsmith (Oliver). THE VICAR OF WAKEFIELD. *Fcap. 32mo.* With 10 Plates in Photogravure by Tony Johannot. *Leather, 2s. 6d. net.* See also I.P.L. and Standard Library.

Goodrich-Freer (A.). IN A SYRIAN SADDLE. *Demy 8vo. 7s. 6d. net.* A Colonial Edition is also published.

Gorst (Rt. Hon. Sir John). THE CHILDREN OF THE NATION. *Second Edition. Demy 8vo. 7s. 6d. net.*

Goudge (H. L.), M.A., Principal of Wells Theological College. See Westminster Commentaries.

Graham (P. Anderson). THE RURAL EXODUS. *Cr. 8vo. 2s. 6d.*

Granger (F. S.), M.A., Litt.D. PSYCHOLOGY. *Third Edition. Cr. 8vo. 2s. 6d.*

THE SOUL OF A CHRISTIAN. *Cr. 8vo. 6s.*

Gray (E. M'Queen). GERMAN PASSAGES FOR UNSEEN TRANSLATION. *Cr. 8vo. 2s. 6d.*

Gray (P. L.), B.Sc. THE PRINCIPLES OF MAGNETISM AND ELECTRICITY: an Elementary Text-Book. With 181 Diagrams. *Cr. 8vo. 3s. 6d.*

Green (G. Buckland), M.A., late Fellow of St. John's College, Oxon. NOTES ON GREEK AND LATIN SYNTAX. *Second Ed. revised. Crown 8vo. 3s. 6d.*

Green (E. T.), M.A. See Churchman's Library.

Greenidge (A. H. J.), M.A. A HISTORY OF ROME: From 133-104 B.C. *Demy 8vo.* 10s. 6d. net.

Greenwell (Dora). See Miniature Library.

Gregory (R. A.). THE VAULT OF HEAVEN. A Popular Introduction to Astronomy. Illustrated. *Cr. 8vo.* 2s. 6d.

Gregory (Miss E. C.). See Library of Devotion.

Grubb (H. C.). See Textbooks of Technology.

Gwynn (M. L.). A BIRTHDAY BOOK. New and cheaper issue. *Royal 8vo.* 5s. net.

Haddon (A. C.), Sc.D., F.R.S. HEAD-HUNTERS BLACK, WHITE, AND BROWN. With many Illustrations and a Map. *Demy 8vo.* 15s.

Hadfield (R. A.) and Gibbins (H. de B.). A SHORTER WORKING DAY. *Cr. 8vo.* 2s. 6d.

Hall (R. N.) and Neal (W. G.). THE ANCIENT RUINS OF RHODESIA. Illustrated. *Second Edition, revised. Demy 8vo.* 10s. 6d. net.

Hall (R. N.). GREAT ZIMBABWE. With numerous Plans and Illustrations. *Second Edition. Royal 8vo.* 10s. 6d. net.

Hamilton (F. J.), D.D. See Byzantine Texts.

Hammond (J. L.). CHARLES JAMES FOX. *Demy 8vo.* 10s. 6d.

Hannay (D.) A SHORT HISTORY OF THE ROYAL NAVY, 1200-1688. Illustrated. *Demy 8vo.* 7s. 6d. each.

Hannay (James O.), M.A. THE SPIRIT AND ORIGIN OF CHRISTIAN MONASTICISM. *Cr. 8vo.* 6s.

THE WISDOM OF THE DESERT. *Fcap. 8vo.* 3s. 6d. net.

Hardie (Martin). See Connoisseur's Library.

Hare (A. T.), M.A. THE CONSTRUCTION OF LARGE INDUCTION COILS. With numerous Diagrams. *Demy 8vo.* 6s.

Harrison (Clifford). READING AND READERS. *Fcap. 8vo.* 2s. 6d.

Harvey (Alfred), M.B. See Ancient Cities.

Hawthorne (Nathaniel). See Little Library.

HEALTH, WEALTH AND WISDOM. *Cr. 8vo.* 1s. net.

Heath (Frank R.). See Little Guides.

Heath (Dudley). See Connoisseur's Library.

Hello (Ernest). STUDIES IN SAINTSHIP. Translated from the French by V. M. CRAWFORD. *Fcap 8vo.* 3s. 6d.

Henderson (B. W.), Fellow of Exeter College, Oxford. THE LIFE AND PRINCIPATE OF THE EMPEROR NERO. Illustrated. *New and cheaper issue. Demy 8vo.* 7s. 6d. net.

AT INTERVALS. *Fcap 8vo.* 2s. 6d. net.

Henderson (T. F.). See Little Library and Oxford Biographies.

Henderson (T. F.), and Watt (Francis). SCOTLAND OF TO-DAY. With many Illustrations, some of which are in colour. *Second Edition. Cr. 8vo.* 6s.

Henley (W. E.). ENGLISH LYRICS. *Second Edition. Cr. 8vo.* 2s. 6d. net.

Henley (W. E.) and Whibley (C.) A BOOK OF ENGLISH PROSE. *Cr. 8vo.* 2s. 6d. net.

Henson (H. H.), B.D., Canon of Westminster. APOSTOLIC CHRISTIANITY: As Illustrated by the Epistles of St. Paul to the Corinthians. *Cr. 8vo.* 6s.

LIGHT AND LEAVEN: HISTORICAL AND SOCIAL SERMONS. *Cr. 8vo.* 6s.

Herbert (George). See Library of Devotion.

Herbert of Cherbury (Lord). See Miniature Library.

Hewins (W. A. S.), B.A. ENGLISH TRADE AND FINANCE IN THE SEVENTEENTH CENTURY. *Cr. 8vo.* 2s. 6d.

Hewitt (Ethel M.) A GOLDEN DIAL. A Day Book of Prose and Verse. *Fcap. 8vo.* 2s. 6d. net.

Heywood (W.). PALIO AND PONTE: A Book of Tuscan Games. Illustrated. *Royal 8vo.* 21s. net.
See also St. Francis of Assisi.

Hill (Clare). See Textbooks of Technology.

Hill (Henry), B.A., Headmaster of the Boy's High School, Worcester, Cape Colony. A SOUTH AFRICAN ARITHMETIC. *Cr. 8vo.* 3s. 6d.

Hind (C. Lewis). DAYS IN CORNWALL. With 16 Illustrations in Colour by WILLIAM PASCOE, and 20 Photographs. *Second Edition. Cr. 8vo.* 6s.
A Colonial Edition is also published.

Hirst (F. W.) See Books on Business.

Hoare (J. Douglas). ARCTIC EXPLORATION. With 18 Illustrations and Maps. *Demy 8vo.* 7s. 6d. net.

Hobhouse (L. T.), Fellow of C.C.C., Oxford. THE THEORY OF KNOWLEDGE. *Demy 8vo.* 10s. 6d. net.

Hobson (J. A.), M.A. INTERNATIONAL TRADE: A Study of Economic Principles. *Cr. 8vo.* 2s. 6d. net.

PROBLEMS OF POVERTY. *Sixth Edition. Cr. 8vo.* 2s. 6d.

THE PROBLEM OF THE UNEMPLOYED. *Third Edition. Cr. 8vo.* 2s. 6d.

Hodgkin (T.), D.C.L. See Leaders of Religion.

Hodgson (Mrs. W.) HOW TO IDENTIFY OLD CHINESE PORCELAIN. *Second Edition. Post 8vo.* 6s.

Hogg (Thomas Jefferson). SHELLEY AT OXFORD. With an Introduction by R. A. STREATFEILD. *Fcap. 8vo.* 2s. net.

Holden-Stone (G. de). See Books on Business.

Holdich (Sir T. H.), K.C.I.E. THE INDIAN BORDERLAND: being a Personal Record of Twenty Years. Illustrated. *Demy 8vo.* 10s. 6d. net.
A Colonial Edition is also published.

Holdsworth (W. S.), M.A. A HISTORY OF ENGLISH LAW. *In Two Volumes. Vol. I. Demy 8vo. 10s. 6d. net.*

Holland (H. Scott), Canon of St. Paul's See Library of Devotion.

Holt (Emily). THE SECRET OF POPULARITY: How to Achieve Social Success. *Cr. 8vo. 3s. 6d. net.*
A Colonial Edition is also published.

Holyoake (G. J.), THE CO-OPERATIVE MOVEMENT TO-DAY. *Fourth Edition. Cr. 8vo. 2s. 6d.*

Hone (Nathaniel J.). See Antiquary's Books.

Hoppner. See Little Galleries.

Horace. See Classical Translations.

Horsburgh (E. L. S.), M.A. WATERLOO: A Narrative and Criticism. With Plans. *Second Edition. Cr. 8vo. 5s.*
See also Oxford Biographies.

Horth (A. C.). See Textbooks of Technology.

Horton (R. F.), D.D. See Leaders of Religion.

Hosie (Alexander). MANCHURIA. With Illustrations and a Map. *Second Edition. Demy 8vo. 7s. 6d. net.*
A Colonial Edition is also published.

How (F. D.). SIX GREAT SCHOOLMASTERS. With Portraits and Illustrations. *Second Edition. Demy 8vo. 7s. 6d.*

Howell (A. G. Ferrers). FRANCISCAN DAYS. Translated and arranged 1/. *Cr. 8vo. 3s. 6d. net.*

Howell (G.). TRADE UNIONISM—New AND OLD. *Fourth Edition. Cr. 8vo. 2s. 6d.*

Hudson (Robert). MEMORIALS OF A WARWICKSHIRE PARISH. Illustrated. *Demy 8vo. 15s. net.*

Huggins (Sir William), K.C.B., O.M., D.C.L., F.R.S. THE ROYAL SOCIETY; OR, SCIENCE IN THE STATE AND IN THE SCHOOLS. With 25 Illustrations. *Wide Royal 8vo. 4s. 6d. net.*

Hughes (C. E.). THE PRAISE OF SHAKESPEARE. An English Anthology. With a Preface by SIDNEY LEE. *Demy 8vo. 3s. 6d. net.*

Hughes (Thomas). TOM BROWN'S SCHOOLDAYS. With an Introduction and Notes by VERNON RENDALL. *Leather. Royal 32mo. 2s. 6d. net.*

Hutchinson (Horace G.) THE NEW FOREST. Illustrated in colour with 50 Pictures by WALTER TYNDALE and 4 by LUCY KEMP-WELCH. *Third Edition. Cr. 8vo. 6s.*

Hutton (A. W.), M.A. See Leaders of Religion and Library of Devotion.

Hutton (Edward). THE CITIES OF UMBRIA. With many Illustrations, of which 20 are in Colour, by A. PISA. *Third Edition. Cr. 8vo. 6s.*
A Colonial Edition is also published.
THE CITIES OF SPAIN. *Third Edition.* With many Illustrations, of which 24 are in Colour, by A. W. RIMINGTON. *Demy 8vo. 7s. 6d. net.*

FLORENCE AND NORTHERN TUSCANY. With Coloured Illustrations by WILLIAM PARKINSON. *Cr. 8vo. 6s.*
A Colonial Edition is also published.

ENGLISH LOVE POEMS. Edited with an Introduction. *Fcap. 8vo. 3s. 6d. net.*

Hutton (R. H.). See Leaders of Religion.

Hutton (W. H.), M.A. THE LIFE OF SIR THOMAS MORE. With Portraits. *Second Edition. Cr. 8vo. 5s.*
See also Leaders of Religion.

Hyde (A. G.) GEORGE HERBERT AND HIS TIMES. With 32 Illustrations. *Demy 8vo. 10s. 6d. net.*

Hyett (F. A.). A SHORT HISTORY OF FLORENCE. *Demy 8vo. 7s. 6d. net.*

Ibsen (Henrik). BRAND. A Drama. Translated by WILLIAM WILSON. *Third Edition. Cr. 8vo. 3s. 6d.*

Inge (W. R.), M.A., Fellow and Tutor of Hertford College, Oxford. CHRISTIAN MYSTICISM. The Bampton Lectures for 1899. *Demy 8vo. 12s. 6d. net.* See also Library of Devotion.

Innes (A. D.), M.A. A HISTORY OF THE BRITISH IN INDIA. With Maps and Plans. *Cr. 8vo. 6s.*
ENGLAND UNDER THE TUDORS. With Maps. *Second Edition. Demy 8vo. 10s. 6d. net.*

Jackson (C. E.), B.A. See Textbooks of Science.

Jackson (S.), M.A. See Commercial Series.

Jackson (F. Hamilton). See Little Guides.

Jacob (F.), M.A. See Junior Examination Series.

James (W. H. N.), A.R.C.S., A.I.E.E. See Textbooks of Technology.

Jeans (J. Stephen). TRUSTS, POOLS, AND CORNERS. *Cr. 8vo. 2s. 6d.*
See also Books on Business.

Jeffreys (D. Gwyn). DOLLY'S THEATRICALS. Described and Illustrated with 24 Coloured Pictures. *Super Royal 16mo. 2s. 6d.*

Jenks (E.), M.A., Reader of Law in the University of Oxford. ENGLISH LOCAL GOVERNMENT. *Second Edition. Cr. 8vo. 2s. 6d.*

Jenner (Mrs. H.). See Little Books on Art.

Jennings (Oscar), M.D., Member of the Bibliographical Society. EARLY WOODCUT INITIALS, containing over thirteen hundred Reproductions of Pictorial Letters of the Fifteenth and Sixteenth Centuries. *Demy 4to. 21s. net.*

Jessopp (Augustus), D.D. See Leaders of Religion.

Jevons (F. B.), M.A., Litt.D., Principal of Bishop Hatfield's Hall, Durham. RELIGION IN EVOLUTION. *Cr. 8vo. 3s. 6d. net.*
See also Churchman's Library and Handbooks of Theology.

Johnson (Mrs. Barham). WILLIAM BODHAM DONNE AND HIS FRIENDS. Illustrated. *Demy 8vo. 10s. 6d. net.*

Johnston (Sir H. H.), K.C.B. BRITISH CENTRAL AFRICA. With nearly 200 Illustrations and Six Maps. *Third Edition. Cr. 4to. 18s. net.*
A Colonial Edition is also published.

Jones (R. Crompton), M.A. POEMS OF THE INNER LIFE. Selected by. *Thirteenth Edition. Fcap. 8vo. 2s. 6d. net.*

Jones (H.). See Commercial Series.

Jones (H. F.). See Textbooks of Science.

Jones (L. A. Atherley), K.C., M.P. THE MINERS' GUIDE TO THE COAL MINES REGULATION ACTS. *Cr. 8vo. 2s. 6d. net.*
COMMERCE IN WAR. *Royal 8vo. 21s. net.*

Jonson (Ben). See Standard Library.

Juliana (Lady) of Norwich. REVELATIONS OF DIVINE LOVE. Ed. by GRACE WARRACK. *Second Edit. Cr. 8vo. 3s. 6d.*

Juvenal. See Classical Translations.

'Kappa.' LET YOUTH BUT KNOW: A Plea for Reason in Education. *Cr. 8vo. 3s. 6d. net.*

Kaufmann (M.). SOCIALISM AND MODERN THOUGHT. *Second Edition. Cr. 8vo. 2s. 6d. net.*

Keating (J. F.), D.D. THE AGAPE AND THE EUCHARIST. *Cr. 8vo. 3s. 6d.*

Keats (John). THE POEMS OF. Edited with Introduction and Notes by E. de Selincourt, M.A. *Second Edition. Demy 8vo. 7s. 6d. net.*
REALMS OF GOLD. Selections from the Works of. *Fcap. 8vo. 3s. 6d. net.*
See also Little Library and Standard Library.

Keble (John). THE CHRISTIAN YEAR. With an Introduction and Notes by W. LOCK, D.D., Warden of Keble College. Illustrated by R. ANNING BELL. *Third Edition. Fcap. 8vo. 3s. 6d.; padded morocco, 5s.*
See also Library of Devotion.

Kelynack (T. N.), M.D., M.R.C.P., Hon. Secretary of the Society for the Study of Inebriety. THE DRINK PROBLEM IN ITS MEDICO-SOCIOLOGICAL ASPECT. Edited by. With 2 Diagrams. *Demy 8vo. 7s. 6d. net.*

Kempis (Thomas à). THE IMITATION OF CHRIST. With an Introduction by DEAN FARRAR. Illustrated by C. M. GERE. *Third Edition. Fcap. 8vo. 3s. 6d.; padded morocco. 5s.*
Also Translated by C. BIGG, D.D. *Cr. 8vo. 3s. 6d.* See also Library of Devotion and Standard Library.

Kennedy (Bart.). THE GREEN SPHINX. *Cr. 8vo. 3s. 6d. net.*
A Colonial Edition is also published.

Kennedy (James Houghton), D.D., Assistant Lecturer in Divinity in the University of Dublin. ST. PAUL'S SECOND AND THIRD EPISTLES TO THE CORINTHIANS. With Introduction, Dissertations and Notes. *Cr. 8vo. 6s.*

Kimmins (C. W.), M.A. THE CHEMISTRY OF LIFE AND HEALTH. Illustrated. *Cr. 8vo. 2s. 6d.*

Kinglake (A. W.). See Little Library.

Kipling (Rudyard). BARRACK-ROOM BALLADS. *82nd Thousand. Twenty-third Edition. Cr. 8vo. 6s.*
A Colonial Edition is also published.
THE SEVEN SEAS. *65th Thousand. Eleventh Edition. Cr. 8vo. 6s.*
A Colonial Edition is also published.
THE FIVE NATIONS. *42nd Thousand. Third Edition. Cr. 8vo. 6s.*
A Colonial Edition is also published.
DEPARTMENTAL DITTIES. *Sixteenth Edition. Cr. 8vo. 6s.*
A Colonial Edition is also published.

Knight (Albert E.). THE COMPLETE CRICKETER. Illus. *Demy 8vo. 7s. 6d. net.*
A Colonial Edition is also published.

Knight (H. J. C.), M.A. See Churchman's Bible.

Knowling (R. J.), M.A., Professor of New Testament Exegesis at King's College, London. See Westminster Commentaries.

Lamb (Charles and Mary), THE WORKS OF. Edited by E. V. LUCAS. Illustrated *In Seven Volumes. Demy 8vo. 7s. 6d. each.*
See also Little Library and E. V. Lucas.

Lambert (F. A. H.). See Little Guides.

Lambros (Professor). See Byzantine Texts.

Lane-Poole (Stanley). A HISTORY OF EGYPT IN THE MIDDLE AGES. Fully Illustrated. *Cr. 8vo. 6s.*

Langbridge (F.), M.A. BALLADS OF THE BRAVE: Poems of Chivalry, Enterprise, Courage, and Constancy. *Third Edition. Cr. 8vo. 2s. 6d.*

Law (William). See Library of Devotion and Standard Library.

Leach (Henry). THE DUKE OF DEVONSHIRE. A Biography. With 12 Illustrations. *Demy 8vo. 12s. 6d. net.*
See also James Braid.
GREAT GOLFERS IN THE MAKING. With 34 Portraits. *Demy 8vo. 7s. 6d. net.*

Le Braz (Anatole). THE LAND OF PARDONS. Translated by FRANCES M. GOSTLING. Illustrated in colour. *Second Edition. Demy 8vo. 7s. 6d. net.*

Lee (Captain L. Melville). A HISTORY OF POLICE IN ENGLAND. *Cr. 8vo. 3s. 6d. net.*

Leigh (Percival), THE COMIC ENGLISH GRAMMAR. Embellished with upwards of 50 characteristic Illustrations by JOHN LEECH. *Post 16mo. 2s. 6d. net.*

Lewes (V. B.), M.A. AIR AND WATER. Illustrated. *Cr. 8vo. 2s. 6d.*

Lewis (Mrs. Gwyn). A CONCISE HANDBOOK OF GARDEN SHRUBS. Illustrated. *Fcap. 8vo. 3s. 6d. net.*

Lisle (Fortunéede). See Little Books on Art.

Littlehales (H.). See Antiquary's Books.

Lock (Walter), D.D., Warden of Keble College. ST. PAUL, THE MASTER-BUILDER. *Second Ed. Cr. 8vo. 3s. 6d.*
THE BIBLE AND CHRISTIAN LIFE. *Cr. 8vo. 6s.*
See also Leaders of Religion and Library of Devotion.

Locker (F.). See Little Library.

Lodge (Sir Oliver), F.R.S. THE SUB-STANCE OF FAITH ALLIED WITH SCIENCE: A Catechism for Parents and Teachers. *Eighth Ed. Cr. 8vo. 2s. net.*

Lofthouse (W. F.), M.A. ETHICS AND ATONEMENT. With a Frontispiece. *Demy 8vo. 5s. net.*

Longfellow (H. W.). See Little Library.

Lorimer (George Horace). LETTERS FROM A SELF-MADE MERCHANT TO HIS SON. *Sixteenth Edition. Cr. 8vo. 3s. 6d.*
A Colonial Edition is also published.

OLD GORGON GRAHAM. *Second Edition. Cr. 8vo. 6s.*
A Colonial Edition is also published.

Lover (Samuel). See I. P. L.

E. V. L. and C. L. G. ENGLAND DAY BY DAY: Or, The Englishman's Handbook to Efficiency. Illustrated by GEORGE MORROW. *Fourth Edition. Fcap. 4to. 1s. net.*

Lucas (E. V.). THE LIFE OF CHARLES LAMB. With 25 Illustrations. *Fourth Edition. Demy 8vo. 7s. 6d. net.*
A Colonial Edition is also published.

A WANDERER IN HOLLAND. With many Illustrations, of which 20 are in Colour by HERBERT MARSHALL. *Eighth Edition. Cr. 8vo. 6s.*
A Colonial Edition is also published.

A WANDERER IN LONDON. With 16 Illustrations in Colour by NELSON DAWSON, and 36 other Illustrations. *Sixth Edition. Cr. 8vo. 6s.*
A Colonial Edition is also published.

FIRESIDE AND SUNSHINE. *Third Edition. Fcap. 8vo. 5s.*

THE OPEN ROAD: a Little Book for Wayfarers. *Twelfth Edition. Fcap. 8vo. 5s.; India Paper, 7s. 6d.*

THE FRIENDLY TOWN: a Little Book for the Urbane. *Third Edition. Fcap. 8vo. 5s.; India Paper, 7s. 6d.*

CHARACTER AND COMEDY. *Third Edition.*

Lucian. See Classical Translations.

Lyde (L. W.), M.A. See Commercial Series.

Lydon (Noel S.). See Junior School Books.

Lyttelton (Hon. Mrs. A.). WOMEN AND THEIR WORK. *Cr. 8vo. 2s. 6d.*

Macaulay (Lord). CRITICAL AND HISTORICAL ESSAYS. Edited by F. C. MONTAGUE, M.A. *Three Volumes. Cr. 8vo. 18s.*
The only edition of this book completely annotated.

M'Allen (J. E. B.), M.A. See Commercial Series.

MacCulloch (J. A.). See Churchman's Library.

MacCunn (Florence A.). MARY STUART. With over 60 Illustrations, including a Frontispiece in Photogravure. *New and Cheaper Edition. Cr. 8vo. 6s.*
See also Leaders of Religion.

McDermott (E. R.). See Books on Business.

M'Dowall (A. S.). See Oxford Biographies.

Mackay (A. M.). See Churchman's Library.

Macklin (Herbert W.), M.A. See Antiquary's Books.

Mackenzie (W. Leslie), M.A., M.D., D.P.H., etc. THE HEALTH OF THE SCHOOL CHILD. *Cr. 8vo. 2s. 6d.*

Mdlle Mori (Author of). ST. CATHERINE OF SIENA AND HER TIMES. With 28 Illustrations. *Demy 8vo. 7s. 6d. net.*

Magnus (Laurie), M.A. A PRIMER OF WORDSWORTH. *Cr. 8vo. 2s. 6d.*

Mahaffy (J. P.), Litt.D. A HISTORY OF THE EGYPT OF THE PTOLEMIES. Fully Illustrated. *Cr. 8vo. 6s.*

Maitland (F. W.), LL.D., Downing Professor of the Laws of England in the University of Cambridge. CANON LAW IN ENGLAND. *Royal 8vo. 7s. 6d.*

Malden (H. E.), M.A. ENGLISH RECORDS. A Companion to the History of England. *Cr. 8vo. 3s. 6d.*

THE ENGLISH CITIZEN: HIS RIGHTS AND DUTIES. *Seventh Edition. Cr. 8vo. 1s. 6d.*
See also School Histories.

Marchant (E. C.), M.A., Fellow of Peterhouse, Cambridge. A GREEK ANTHOLOGY *Second Edition. Cr. 8vo. 3s. 6d.*
See also A. M. Cook.

Marr (J. E.), F.R.S., Fellow of St John's College, Cambridge. THE SCIENTIFIC STUDY OF SCENERY. *Second Edition.* Illustrated. *Cr. 8vo. 6s.*

AGRICULTURAL GEOLOGY. Illustrated. *Cr. 8vo. 6s.*

Marriott (J. A. R.). THE LIFE AND TIMES OF LORD FALKLAND. With 20 Illustrations. *Second Ed. Dy. 8vo. 7s. 6d. net.*
A Colonial Edition is also published.

Marvell (Andrew). See Little Library.

Masefield (John). SEA LIFE IN NELSON'S TIME. Illustrated. *Cr. 8vo. 3s. 6d. net.*

ON THE SPANISH MAIN. With 22 Illustrations and a Map. *Demy 8vo. 10s. 6d. net.*

A SAILOR'S GARLAND. Edited and Selected by. *Second Ed. Cr. 8vo. 3s. 6d. net.*

Maskell (A.). See Connoisseur's Library.

Mason (A. J.), D.D. See Leaders of Religion.

Massee (George). THE EVOLUTION OF PLANT LIFE: Lower Forms. Illustrated. *Cr. 8vo. 2s. 6d.*

Masterman (C. F. G.), M.A., M.P. TENNYSON AS A RELIGIOUS TEACHER. *Cr. 8vo. 6s.*

Matheson (Mrs. E. F.). COUNSELS OF LIFE. *Fcap. 8vo. 2s. 6d. net.*

May (Phil). THE PHIL MAY ALBUM. *Second Edition. 4to. 1s. net.*

Mellows (Emma S.). A SHORT STORY OF ENGLISH LITERATURE. *Cr. 8vo. 3s. 6d.*

Methuen (A. M. S.). THE TRAGEDY OF SOUTH AFRICA. *Cr. 8vo. 2s. net. Also Cr. 8vo. 3d. net.*
A revised and enlarged edition of the author's 'Peace or War in South Africa.'

ENGLAND'S RUIN: DISCUSSED IN SIX-
TEEN LETTERS TO THE RIGHT HON.
JOSEPH CHAMBERLAIN, M.P. *Seventh Edi-
tion. Cr. 8vo. 3d. net.*

Miles (Eustace), M.A. LIFE AFTER
LIFE, OR, THE THEORY OF REIN-
CARNATION. *Cr. 8vo. 2s. 6d. net.*

Millais (J. G.). THE LIFE AND LET-
TERS OF SIR JOHN EVERETT
MILLAIS, President of the Royal Academy.
With many Illustrations, of which 2 are in
Photogravure. *New Edition. Demy 8vo.
7s. 6d. net.*
See also Little Galleries.

Millin (G. F.). PICTORIAL GARDEN-
ING. Illustrated. *Cr. 8vo. 3s. 6d. net.*

Millis (C. T.), M.I.M.E. See Textbooks of
Technology.

Milne (J. G.), M.A. A HISTORY OF
ROMAN EGYPT. Fully Illus. *Cr. 8vo. 6s.*

Milton (John). A DAY BOOK OF.
Edited by R. F. Towndrow. *Fcap. 8vo.
3s. 6d. net.*
See also Little Library and Standard
Library.

Minchin (H. C.), M.A. See R. Peel.

Mitchell (P. Chalmers), M.A. OUTLINES
OF BIOLOGY. Illustrated. *Second Edition. Cr. 8vo. 6s.*

Mitton (G. E.). JANE AUSTEN AND
HER TIMES. With many Portraits and
Illustrations. *Second and Cheaper Edition.
Cr. 8vo. 6s.*
A Colonial Edition is also published.

Moffat (Mary M.). QUEEN LOUISA OF
PRUSSIA. With 20 Illustrations. *Fourth
Edition. Demy 8vo. 7s. 6d. net.*

'Moll (A.).' See Books on Business.

Moir (D. M.). See Little Library.

Molinos (Dr. Michael de). See Library of
Devotion.

Money (L. G. Chiozza), M.P. RICHES
AND POVERTY. *Fourth Edition. Demy
8vo. 5s. net.*

Montagu (Henry), Earl of Manchester. See
Library of Devotion.

Montaigne. A DAY BOOK OF. Edited
by C. F. Pond. *Fcap. 8vo. 3s. 6d. net.*

Montmorency (J. E. G. de), B.A., LL.B.
THOMAS À KEMPIS, HIS AGE AND
BOOK. With 22 Illustrations. *Second
Edition. Demy 8vo. 7s. 6d. net.*

Moore (H. E.). BACK TO THE LAND.
An Inquiry into Rural Depopulation. *Cr.
8vo. 2s. 6d.*

Moorhouse (E. Hallam). NELSON'S
LADY HAMILTON. With 51 Portraits.
Second Edition. Demy 8vo. 7s. 6d. net.
A Colonial Edition is also published.

Moran (Clarence G.). See Books on Business.

More (Sir Thomas). See Standard Library.

Morfill (W. R.), Oriel College, Oxford. A
HISTORY OF RUSSIA FROM PETER
THE GREAT TO ALEXANDER II.
With Maps and Plans. *Cr. 8vo. 3s. 6d.*

Morich (R. J.), late of Clifton College. See
School Examination Series.

Morris (J.). THE MAKERS OF JAPAN.
With 24 Illustrations. *Demy 8vo. 12s. 6d.
net.*
A Colonial Edition is also published.

Morris (J. E.). See Little Guides.

Morton (Miss Anderson). See Miss Brodrick.

Moule (H. C. G.), D.D., Lord Bishop of Durham. See Leaders of Religion.

Muir (M. M. Pattison), M.A. THE
CHEMISTRY OF FIRE. Illustrated.
Cr. 8vo. 2s. 6d.

Mundella (V. A.), M.A. See J. T. Dunn.

Munro (R.), LL.D. See Antiquary's Books.

Naval Officer (A). See I. P. I..

Neal (W. G.). See R. N. Hall.

Newman (Ernest). HUGO WOLF.
Demy 8vo. 6s.

Newman (George), M.D., D.P.H., F.R.S.E.,
Lecturer on Public Health at St. Bartholo-
mew's Hospital, and Medical Officer of
Health of the Metropolitan Borough of
Finsbury. INFANT MORTALITY, A
SOCIAL PROBLEM. With 16 Diagrams.
Demy 8vo. 7s. 6d. net.

Newman (J. H.) and others. See Library
of Devotion.

Nichols (J. B. B.). See Little Library.

Nicklin (T.), M.A. EXAMINATION
PAPERS IN THUCYDIDES. *Cr. 8vo. 2s.*

Nimrod. See I. P. L.

Norgate (G. Le Grys). THE LIFE OF
SIR WALTER SCOTT. Illustrated.
Demy 8vo. 7s. 6d. net.

Norregaard (B. W.). THE GREAT
SIEGE: The Investment and Fall of Port
Arthur. Illustrated. *Demy 8vo. 10s. 6d. net.*

Norway (A. H.). NAPLES. With 25 Coloured Illustrations by MAURICE GREIFFEN-
HAGEN. *Second Edition. Cr. 8vo. 6s.*

Novalis. THE DISCIPLES AT SAIS AND
OTHER FRAGMENTS. Edited by Miss
UNA BIRCH. *Fcap. 8vo. 3s. 6d.*

Oldfield (W. J.), M.A., Prebendary of
Lincoln. A PRIMER OF RELIGION.
BASED ON THE CATECHISM OF THE CHURCH
OF ENGLAND. *Fcap. 8vo. 2s. 6d.*

Oldham (F. M.), B.A. See Textbooks of
Science.

Oliphant (Mrs.). See Leaders of Religion.

Oman (C. W. C.), M.A., Fellow of All Souls',
Oxford. A HISTORY OF THE ART
OF WAR. The Middle Ages, from the
Fourth to the Fourteenth Century. Illus-
trated. *Demy 8vo. 10s. 6d. net.*

Ottley (R. L.), D.D. See Handbooks of
Theology and Leaders of Religion.

Overton (J. H.). See Leaders of Religion.

Owen (Douglas). See Books on Business.

Oxford (M. N.), of Guy's Hospital. A HAND-
BOOK OF NURSING. *Fourth Edition.
Cr. 8vo. 3s. 6d.*

Pakes (W. C. C.). THE SCIENCE OF
HYGIENE. Illustrated. *Demy 8vo. 15s.*

Parker (Gilbert). A LOVER'S DIARY.
Fcap. 8vo. 5s.

Parkes (A. K.). SMALL LESSONS ON
GREAT TRUTHS. Fcap. 8vo. 1s. 6d.

Parkinson (John). PARADISI IN SOLE
PARADISUS TERRESTRIS, OR A
GARDEN OF ALL SORTS OF PLEA-
SANT FLOWERS. Folio. £3, 3s. net.

Parmenter (John). HELIO-TROPES, OR
NEW POSIES FOR SUNDIALS, 1625.
Edited by PERCIVAL LANDON. Quarto.
3s. 6d. net.

Parmentier (Prof. Leon). See Byzantine
Texts.

Parsons (Mrs. Clement). GARRICK
AND HIS CIRCLE. With 36 Illustrations. Second Edition. Demy 8vo.
12s. 6d. net.
A Colonial Edition is also published.

Pascal. See Library of Devotion.

Paston (George). SOCIAL CARICA-
TURE IN THE EIGHTEENTH
CENTURY. With over 200 Illustrations.
Imperial Quarto. £2, 12s. 6d. net.
See also Little Books on Art and I.P.L.

LADY MARY WORTLEY MONTAGU.
With 24 Portraits and Illustrations.
Second Edition. Demy 8vo. 15s. net.
A Colonial Edition is also published.

Paterson (W. R.) (Benjamin Swift). LIFE'S
QUESTIONINGS. Cr. 8vo. 3s. 6d. net.

Patterson (A. H.). NOTES OF AN EAST
COAST NATURALIST. Illustrated in
Colour by F. SOUTHGATE. Second Edition.
Cr. 8vo. 6s.

NATURE IN EASTERN NORFOLK.
A series of observations on the Birds,
Fishes, Mammals, Reptiles, and Stalk-
eyed Crustaceans found in that neighbourhood, with a list of the species. With
12 Illustrations in colour, by FRANK
SOUTHGATE. Second Edition. Cr. 8vo.
6s.

Peacock (N.). See Little Books on Art.

Peake (C. M. A.), F.R.H.S. A CON-
CISE HANDBOOK OF GARDEN
ANNUAL AND BIENNIAL PLANTS.
With 24 Illustrations. Fcap. 8vo. 3s. 6d. net.

Peel (Robert), and Minchin (H. C.), M.A.
OXFORD. With 100 Illustrations in
Colour. Cr. 8vo. 6s.

Peel (Sidney), late Fellow of Trinity College,
Oxford, and Secretary to the Royal Com-
mission on the Licensing Laws. PRACTI-
CAL LICENSING REFORM. Second
Edition. Cr. 8vo. 1s. 6d.

Petrie (W. M. Flinders), D.C.L., LL.D., Pro-
fessor of Egyptology at University College.
A HISTORY OF EGYPT, FROM THE
EARLIEST TIMES TO THE PRESENT DAY.
Fully Illustrated. In six volumes. Cr.
8vo. 6s. each.

VOL. I. PREHISTORIC TIMES TO XVITH
DYNASTY. Sixth Edition.

VOL. II. THE XVIITH AND XVIIITH
DYNASTIES. Fourth Edition.

VOL. III. XIXTH TO XXXTH DYNASTIES.

VOL. IV. THE EGYPT OF THE PTOLEMIES.
J. P. MAHAFFY, Litt.D.

VOL. V. ROMAN EGYPT. J. G. MILNE, M.A.

VOL. VI. EGYPT IN THE MIDDLE AGES.
STANLEY LANE-POOLE, M.A.

RELIGION AND CONSCIENCE IN
ANCIENT EGYPT. Illustrated. Cr.
8vo. 2s. 6d.

SYRIA AND EGYPT, FROM THE TELL
EL AMARNA TABLETS. Cr. 8vo. 2s. 6d.

EGYPTIAN TALES. Illustrated by TRIS-
TRAM ELLIS. In Two Volumes. Cr. 8vo.
3s. 6d. each.

EGYPTIAN DECORATIVE ART. With
120 Illustrations. Cr. 8vo. 3s. 6d.

Phillips (W. A.). See Oxford Biographies.

Phillpotts (Eden). MY DEVON YEAR.
With 38 Illustrations by J. LEY PETHY-
BRIDGE. Second and Cheaper Edition.
Large Cr. 8vo. 6s.

UP ALONG AND DOWN ALONG.
Illustrated by CLAUDE SHEPPERSON.
Cr. 4to. 5s. net.
A volume of poems.

Piarr (Victor G.). See School Histories.

Plato. See Standard Library.

Plautus. THE CAPTIVI. Edited, with
an Introduction, Textual Notes, and a Commentary, by W. M. LINDSAY, Fellow of
Jesus College, Oxford. Demy 8vo. 10s. 6d. net.

Plowden-Wardlaw (J. T.), B.A., King's
College, Cambridge. See School Examination Series.

Podmore (Frank). MODERN SPIRI-
TUALISM. Two Volumes. Demy 8vo.
21s. net.
A History and a Criticism.

Poer (J. Patrick Le). A MODERN
LEGIONARY. Cr. 8vo. 6s.

Pollard (Alice). See Little Books on Art.

Pollard (A. W.). OLD PICTURE BOOKS.
Illustrated. Demy 8vo. 7s. 6d. net.

Pollard (Eliza F.). See Little Books on Art.

Pollock (David), M.I.N.A. See Books on
Business.

Potter (M. C.), M.A., F.L.S. A TEXT-
BOOK OF AGRICULTURAL BOTANY.
Illustrated. Second Edition. Cr. 8vo.
4s. 6d.

Power (J. O'Connor). THE MAKING
OF AN ORATOR. Cr. 8vo. 6s.

Prance (G.). See R. Wyon.

Prescott (O. L.). ABOUT MUSIC, AND
WHAT IT IS MADE OF. Cr. 8vo.
3s. 6d. net.

Price (L. L.), M.A., Fellow of Oriel College,
Oxon. A HISTORY OF ENGLISH
POLITICAL ECONOMY. Fifth Edi-
tion. Cr. 8vo. 2s. 6d.

Primrose (Deborah). A MODERN
BŒOTIA. Cr. 8vo. 6s.

Protheroe (Ernest). THE DOMINION
OF MAN. GEOGRAPHY IN ITS HUMAN
ASPECT. With 32 full-page Illustrations.
Cr. 8vo. 2s.

Sells (V. P.), M.A. THE MECHANICS OF DAILY LIFE. Illustrated. *Cr. 8vo.* 2s. 6d.

Selous (Edmund). TOMMY SMITH'S ANIMALS. Illustrated by G. W. ORD. *Ninth Edition. Fcap. 8vo.* 2s. 6d. *School Edition,* 1s. 6d.
TOMMY SMITH'S OTHER ANIMALS. With 12 Illustrations by AUGUSTA GUEST. *Fourth Edition. Fcap. 8vo.* 2s. 6d. *School Edition,* 1s. 6d.

Settle (J. H.). ANECDOTES OF SOLDIERS. *Cr. 8vo.* 3s. 6d. net.

Shakespeare (William).
THE FOUR FOLIOS, 1623 ; 1632 ; 1664 ; 1685. Each £4, 4s. net, or a complete set, £12, 12s. net.
Folios 3 and 4 are ready.
Folio 2 is nearly ready.
See also Arden, Standard Library and Little Quarto Shakespeare.

Sharp (A.). VICTORIAN POETS. *Cr. 8vo.* 2s. 6d.

Sharp (Cecil). See S. Baring-Gould.

Sharp (Mrs. E. A.). See Little Books on Art.

Shedlock (J. S.) THE PIANOFORTE SONATA. *Cr. 8vo.* 5s.

Shelley (Percy B.). ADONAIS; an Elegy on the death of John Keats, Author of 'Endymion,' etc. Pisa. From the types of Didot, 1821. 2s. net.

Sheppard (H. F.), M.A. See S. Baring-Gould.

Sherwell (Arthur), M.A. LIFE IN WEST LONDON. *Third Edition. Cr. 8vo.* 2s. 6d.

Shipley (Mary E.). AN ENGLISH CHURCH HISTORY FOR CHILDREN. A.D. 597-1066. With a Preface by the Bishop of Gibraltar. With Maps and Illustrations. *Cr. 8vo.* 2s. 6d. net.

Sime (J.). See Little Books on Art.

Simonson (G. A.). FRANCESCO GUARDI. With 41 Plates. *Imperial 4to.* £2, 2s. net.

Sketchley (R. E. D.). See Little Books on Art.

Skipton (H. P. K.). See Little Books on Art.

Sladen (Douglas). SICILY: The New Winter Resort. With over 200 Illustrations. *Second Edition. Cr. 8vo.* 5s. net.

Small (Evan), M.A. THE EARTH. An Introduction to Physiography. Illustrated. *Cr. 8vo.* 2s. 6d.

Smallwood (M. G.). See Little Books on Art.

Smedley (F. E.). See I.P.L.

Smith (Adam). THE WEALTH OF NATIONS. Edited with an Introduction and numerous Notes by EDWIN CANNAN, M.A. *Two volumes. Demy 8vo.* 21s. net.

Smith (Horace and James). See Little Library.

Smith (H. Bompas), M.A. A NEW JUNIOR ARITHMETIC. *Crown 8vo.* 2s. With Answers, 2s. 6d.

Smith (R. Mudie). THOUGHTS FOR THE DAY. Edited by. *Fcap. 8vo.* 3s. 6d. net.

Smith (Nowell C.). See W. Wordsworth.

Smith (John Thomas). A BOOK FOR A RAINY DAY: Or, Recollections of the Events of the Years 1766-1833. Edited by WILFRED WHITTEN. Illustrated. *Wide Demy 8vo.* 12s. 6d. net.

Snell (F. J.). A BOOK OF EXMOOR. Illustrated. *Cr. 8vo.* 6s.

Snowden (C. E.). A HANDY DIGEST OF BRITISH HISTORY. *Demy 8vo.* 4s. 6d.

Sophocles. See Classical Translations.

Sornet (L. A.). See Junior School Books.

South (E. Wilton), M.A. See Junior School Books.

Southey (R.). ENGLISH SEAMEN. Edited by DAVID HANNAY.
Vol. I. (Howard, Clifford, Hawkins, Drake, Cavendish). *Second Edition. Cr. 8vo.* 6s.
Vol. II. (Richard Hawkins, Grenville, Essex, and Raleigh). *Cr. 8vo.* 6s.
See also Standard Library.

Spence (C. H.), M.A. See School Examination Series.

Spicer (A. D.). THE PAPER TRADE. With Maps and Diagrams. *Demy 8vo.* 12s. 6d. net.

Spooner (W. A.), M.A. See Leaders of Religion.

Staley (Edgcumbe). THE GUILDS OF FLORENCE. Illustrated. *Second Edition. Royal 8vo.* 16s. net.

Stanbridge (J. W.), B.D. See Library of Devotion.

'Stancliffe.' GOLF DO'S AND DONT'S. *Second Edition. Fcap. 8vo.* 1s.

Stead (W. J.). See D. Gallaher.

Stedman (A. M. M.), M.A.
INITIA LATINA: Easy Lessons on Elementary Accidence. *Tenth Edition. Fcap. 8vo.* 1s.
FIRST LATIN LESSONS. *Tenth Edition. Cr. 8vo.* 2s.
FIRST LATIN READER. With Notes adapted to the Shorter Latin Primer and Vocabulary. *Seventh Edition.* 18mo. 1s. 6d.
EASY SELECTIONS FROM CÆSAR. The Helvetian War. *Third Edition.* 18mo. 1s.
EASY SELECTIONS FROM LIVY. The Kings of Rome. 18mo. *Second Edition.* 1s. 6d.
EASY LATIN PASSAGES FOR UNSEEN TRANSLATION. *Twelfth Ed. Fcap. 8vo.* 1s. 6d.
EXEMPLA LATINA. First Exercises in Latin Accidence. With Vocabulary. *Fourth Edition. Cr. 8vo.* 1s.

EASY LATIN EXERCISES ON THE SYNTAX OF THE SHORTER AND REVISED LATIN PRIMER. With Vocabulary. *Eleventh and Cheaper Edition, re-written. Cr. 8vo. 1s. 6d. Original Edition. 2s. 6d.* KEV, 3s. net.

THE LATIN COMPOUND SENTENCE: Rules and Exercises. *Second Edition. Cr. 8vo. 1s. 6d.* With Vocabulary. 2s.

NOTANDA QUAEDAM: Miscellaneous Latin Exercises on Common Rules and Idioms. *Fifth Edition. Fcap. 8vo. 1s. 6d.* With Vocabulary. 2s. Key, 2s. net.

LATIN VOCABULARIES FOR REPETITION: Arranged according to Subjects. *Fourteenth Edition. Fcap. 8vo. 1s. 6d.*

A VOCABULARY OF LATIN IDIOMS. *18mo. Fourth Edition. 1s.*

STEPS TO GREEK. *Third Edition, revised. 18mo. 1s.*

A SHORTER GREEK PRIMER. *Second Edition. Cr. 8vo. 1s. 6d.*

EASY GREEK PASSAGES FOR UNSEEN TRANSLATION. *Fourth Edition, revised. Fcap. 8vo. 1s. 6d.*

GREEK VOCABULARIES FOR REPETITION. Arranged according to Subjects. *Fourth Edition. Fcap. 8vo. 1s 6d.*

GREEK TESTAMENT SELECTIONS. For the use of Schools. With Introduction, Notes, and Vocabulary. *Fourth Edition. Fcap. 8vo. 2s. 6d.*

STEPS TO FRENCH. *Eighth Edition. 18mo. 8d.*

FIRST FRENCH LESSONS. *Eighth Edition, revised. Cr. 8vo. 1s.*

EASY FRENCH PASSAGES FOR UNSEEN TRANSLATION. *Sixth Edition, revised. Fcap. 8vo. 1s. 6d.*

EASY FRENCH EXERCISES ON ELEMENTARY SYNTAX. With Vocabulary. *Fourth Edition. Cr. 8vo. 2s. 6d.* KEY. 3s. net.

FRENCH VOCABULARIES FOR REPETITION: Arranged according to Subjects. *Thirteenth Edition. Fcap. 8vo. 1s.* See also School Examination Series.

Steel (R. Elliott), M.A., F.C.S. THE WORLD OF SCIENCE. With 147 Illustrations. *Second Edition. Cr. 8vo. 2s. 6d.* See also School Examination Series.

Stephenson (C.), of the Technical College, Bradford, and Suddards (F.) of the Yorkshire College, Leeds. ORNAMENTAL DESIGN FOR WOVEN FABRICS. Illustrated. *Demy 8vo. Third Edition. 7s. 6d.*

Stephenson (J.), M.A. THE CHIEF TRUTHS OF THE CHRISTIAN FAITH. *Cr. 8vo. 3s. 6d.*

Sterne (Laurence). See Little Library.

Sterry (W.), M.A. ANNALS OF ETON COLLEGE. Illustrated. *Demy 8vo. 7s. 6d.*

Stewart (Katherine). BY ALLAN WATER. *Second Edition. Cr. 8vo. 6s.*

Stevenson (R. L.) THE LETTERS OF ROBERT LOUIS STEVENSON TO HIS FAMILY AND FRIENDS. Selected and Edited by SIDNEY COLVIN. *Third Edition. Cr. 8vo. 12s.*
LIBRARY EDITION. *Demy 8vo. 2 vols. 25s. net.*
A Colonial Edition is also published.

VAILIMA LETTERS. With an Etched Portrait by WILLIAM STRANG. *Sixth Edition. Cr. 8vo. Buckram. 6s.*
A Colonial Edition is also published.

THE LIFE OF R. L. STEVENSON. See G. Balfour.

Stevenson (M. I.). FROM SARANAC TO THE MARQUESAS. Being Letters written by Mrs. M. I. STEVENSON during 1887-8. *Cr. 8vo. 6s. net.*

LETTERS FROM SAMOA, 1891-95. Edited and arranged by M. C. BALFOUR. With many Illustrations. *Second Edition Cr. 8vo. 6s. net.*

Stoddart (Anna M.). See Oxford Biographies.

Stokes (F. G.), B.A. HOURS WITH RABELAIS. From the translation of SIR T. URQUHART and P. A. MOTTEUX. With a Portrait in Photogravure. *Cr. 8vo. 3s. 6d. net.*

Stone (S. J.). POEMS AND HYMNS. With a Memoir by F. G. ELLERTON, M.A. With Portrait. *Cr. 8vo. 6s.*

Storr (Vernon F.), M.A., Lecturer in the Philosophy of Religion in Cambridge University; Examining Chaplain to the Archbishop of Canterbury; formerly Fellow of University College, Oxford. DEVELOPMENT AND DIVINE PURPOSE *Cr. 8vo. 5s. net.*

Straker (F.). See Books on Business.

Streane (A. W.), D.D. See Churchman's Bible.

Streatfeild (R. A.). MODERN MUSIC AND MUSICIANS. With 24 Illustrations. *Second Edition. Demy 8vo. 7s. 6d. net.*

Stroud (H.), D.Sc., M.A. PRACTICAL PHYSICS. With many Diagrams. *Second Edition. 3s. net.*

Strutt (Joseph). THE SPORTS AND PASTIMES OF THE PEOPLE OF ENGLAND. Illustrated by many Engravings. Revised by J. CHARLES COX, LL.D., F.S.A. *Quarto. 21s. net.*

Stuart (Capt. Donald). THE STRUGGLE FOR PERSIA With a Map. *Cr. 8vo. 6s.*

Sturch (F.), Staff Instructor to the Surrey County Council. MANUAL TRAINING DRAWING (WOODWORK). Its Principles and Application, with Solutions to Examination Questions, 1892-1905, Orthographic, Isometric and Oblique Projection. With 50 Plates and 140 Figures. *Foolscap. 5s. net.*

Suddards (F.). See C. Stephenson.

Surtees (R. S.). See I.P.L.

Symes (J. E.), M.A. THE FRENCH REVOLUTION. *Second Edition. Cr. 8vo. 2s. 6d.*

Sympson (E. M.), M.A., M.D. See Ancient Cities.

Tacitus. AGRICOLA. With Introduction Notes, Map, etc., by R. F. DAVIS, M.A., *Fcap. 8vo. 2s.*
GERMANIA. By the same Editor. *Fcap. 8vo. 2s.* See also Classical Translations.
Tallack (W.). HOWARD LETTERS AND MEMORIES. *Demy 8vo. 10s. 6d. net.*
Tauler (J.). See Library of Devotion.
Taylor (A. E.). THE ELEMENTS OF METAPHYSICS. *Demy 8vo. 10s. 6d. net.*
Taylor (F. G.), M.A. See Commercial Series.
Taylor (I. A.). See Oxford Biographies.
Taylor (John W.). THE COMING OF THE SAINTS : Imagination and Studies in Early Church History and Tradition. With 26 Illustrations. *Demy 8vo. 7s. 6d. net.*
Taylor T. M.), M.A., Fellow of Gonville and Caius College, Cambridge. A CONSTITUTIONAL AND POLITICAL HISTORY OF ROME. *Cr. 8vo. 7s. 6d.*
Teasdale-Buckell (G. T.). THE COMPLETE SHOT. Illustrated. *Second Ed.*
Tennyson (Alfred, Lord). THE EARLY POEMS OF. Edited, with Notes and an Introduction, by J. CHURTON COLLINS, M.A. *Cr. 8vo. 6s.*
IN MEMORIAM, MAUD, AND THE PRINCESS. Edited by J. CHURTON COLLINS, M.A. *Cr. 8vo. 6s.* See also Little Library.
Terry (C. S.). See Oxford Biographies.
Thackeray (W. M.). See Little Library.
Theobald (F. V.), M.A. INSECT LIFE. Illustrated. *Second Edition Revised. Cr. 8vo. 2s. 6d.*
Thompson (A. H.). See Little Guides.
Tileston (Mary W.). DAILY STRENGTH FOR DAILY NEEDS. *Fourteenth Edition. Medium 16mo. 2s. 6d. net.* Also an edition in superior binding, *6s.*
Tompkins (H. W.), F.R.H.S. See Little Guides.
Townley (Lady Susan). MY CHINESE NOTE-BOOK. With 16 Illustrations and 2 Maps. *Third Ed. Demy 8vo. 10s. 6d. net*
Toynbee (Paget), M.A., D.Litt. See Oxford Biographies.
Trench (Herbert). DEIRDRE WEDDED AND OTHER POEMS. *Cr. 8vo. 5s.*
An episode of Thirty hours delivered by the three voices. It deals with the love of Deirdre for Naris and is founded on a Gaelic Version of the Tragical Tale of the Sons of Usnach.
Trevelyan (G. M.), Fellow of Trinity College, Cambridge. ENGLAND UNDER THE STUARTS. With Maps and Plans. *Third Edition. Demy 8vo. 10s. 6d. net.*
Troutbeck (G. E.). See Little Guides.
Tyler (E. A.), B.A., F.C.S. See Junior School Books.
Tyrrell-Gill (Frances). See Little Books on Art.
Vardon (Harry). THE COMPLETE GOLFER. Illustrated. *Eighth Edition. Demy 8vo. 10s. 6d. net.*
A Colonial Edition is also published.
Vaughan (Henry). See Little Library.

Vaughan (Herbert M.), B.A. (Oxon.). THE LAST OF THE ROYAL STUARTS, HENRY STUART, CARDINAL, DUKE OF YORK. With 20 Illustrations. *Second Edition. Demy 8vo. 10s. 6d. net.*
THE NAPLES RIVIERA. With 25 Illustrations in Colour by MAURICE GREIFFENHAGEN. *Cr. 8vo. 6s.*
A Colonial Edition is also published.
Voegelin (A.), M.A. See Junior Examination Series.
Waddell (Col. L. A.), LL.D., C.B. LHASA AND ITS MYSTERIES. With a Record of the Expedition of 1903-1904. With 155 Illustrations and Maps. *Third and Cheaper Edition. Demy 8vo. 7s. 6d. net.*
Wade (G. W.), D.D. OLD TESTAMENT HISTORY. With Maps. *Fifth Edition. Cr. 8vo. 6s.*
Wagner (Richard). MUSIC DRAMAS : Interpretations, embodying Wagner's own explanations. By A. L. CLEATHER and B. CRUMP. *In Four Volumes. Fcap 8vo. 2s. 6d. each.*
　　VOL. I.—THE RING OF THE NIBELUNG. *Third Edition.*
　　VOL. II.—PARSIFAL, LOHENGRIN, and THE HOLY GRAIL.
　　VOL. III.—TRISTAN AND ISOLDE.
Wall (J. C.). DEVILS. Illustrated by the Author and from photographs. *Demy 8vo. 4s. 6d. net.* See also Antiquary's Books.
Walters (H. B.). See Little Books on Art and Classics of Art.
Walton (F. W.). See School Histories.
Walton (Izaac) and **Cotton (Charles).** See I.P.L., Standard Library, and Little Library.
Warren-Vernon (Hon. William), M.A. READINGS ON THE INFERNO OF DANTE, based on the Commentary of BENVENUTO DA IMOLA and other authorities. With an Introduction by the Rev. Dr. MOORE. In Two Volumes. *Second Edition,* entirely re-written. *Cr. 8vo. 15s. net.*
Waterhouse (Mrs. Alfred). WITH THE SIMPLE-HEARTED : Little Homilies to Women in Country Places. *Second Edition. Small Pott 8vo. 2s. net.*
See also Little Library.
Watt (Francis). See T. F. Henderson.
Weatherhead (T. C.), M.A. EXAMINATION PAPERS IN HORACE. *Cr. 8vo. 2s.* See also Junior Examination Series.
Webber (F. C.). See Textbooks of Technology.
Weir (Archibald), M.A. AN INTRODUCTION TO THE HISTORY OF MODERN EUROPE. *Cr. 8vo. 6s.*
Wells (Sidney H.) See Textbooks of Science.
Wells (J.), M.A., Fellow and Tutor of Wadham College. OXFORD AND OXFORD LIFE. *Third Edition. Cr. 8vo. 3s. 6d.*
A SHORT HISTORY OF ROME. *Eighth Edition.* With 3 Maps. *Cr. 8vo. 3s. 6d.*
See also Little Guides.
Wheldon (P. W.). A LITTLE BROTHER TO THE BIRDS. With 15 Illustrations,

7 of which are by A. H. BUCKLAND. *Large Cr. 8vo. 6s.*

Whibley (C.). See W. E. Henley.

Whibley (L.), M.A., Fellow of Pembroke College, Cambridge. GREEK OLIGAR-CHIES : THEIR ORGANISATION AND CHARACTER. *Cr. 8vo. 6s.*

Whitaker (G. H.), M.A. See Churchman's Bible.

White (Gilbert). THE NATURAL HISTORY OF SELBORNE. Edited by L. C. MIALL, F.R.S., assisted by W. WARDE FOWLER, M.A. *Cr. 8vo. 6s.*
See also Standard Library.

Whitfield (E. E.). See Commercial Series.

Whitehead (A. W.). GASPARD DE COLIGNY. Illustrated. *Demy 8vo. 12s. 6d. net.*

Whiteley (R. Lloyd), F.I.C., Principal of the Municipal Science School, West Bromwich. AN ELEMENTARY TEXT-BOOK OF INORGANIC CHEMISTRY. *Cr. 8vo. 2s. 6d.*

Whitley (Miss). See Lady Dilke.

Whitten (W.). See John Thomas Smith.

Whyte (A. G.), B.Sc. See Books on Business.

Wilberforce (Wilfrid). See Little Books on Art.

Wilde (Oscar). DE PROFUNDIS. *Eleventh Edition. Cr. 8vo. 5s. net.*
A Colonial Edition is also published.

THE DUCHESS OF PADUA. *Demy 8vo. 12s. 6d. net.*

POEMS. *Demy 8vo. 12s. 6d. net.*

INTENTIONS. *Demy 8vo. 12s. 6d. net.*

SALOME, AND OTHER PLAYS. *Demy 8vo. 12s. 6d. net.*

LADY WINDERMERE'S FAN. *Demy 8vo. 12s. 6d. net.*

A WOMAN OF NO IMPORTANCE. *Demy 8vo. 12s. 6d. net.*

AN IDEAL HUSBAND. *Demy 8vo. 12s. 6d. net.*

THE IMPORTANCE OF BEING EAR-NEST. *Demy 8vo. 12s. 6d. net.*

A HOUSE OF POMEGRANATES and THE HAPPY PRINCE. *Demy 8vo. 12s. 6d. net.*

LORD ARTHUR SAVILE'S CRIME and OTHER PROSE PIECES. *Demy 8vo. 12s. 6d. net.*

Wilkins (W. H.), B.A. THE ALIEN INVASION. *Cr. 8vo. 2s. 6d.*

Williams (A.). PETROL PETER: or Pretty Stories and Funny Pictures. Illustrated in Colour by A. W. MILLS. *Demy 4to. 3s. 6d. net.*

Williamson (M. G.). See Ancient Cities.

Williamson (W.). THE BRITISH GARDENER. Illustrated. *Demy 8vo. 10s. 6d.*

Williamson (W.), B.A. See Junior Examination Series, Junior School Books, and Beginner's Books.

Willson (Beckles). LORD STRATH-CONA: the Story of his Life. Illustrated. *Demy 8vo. 7s. 6d.*
A Colonial Edition is also published.

Wilmot-Buxton (E. M.). MAKERS OF EUROPE. *Cr. 8vo. Eighth Ed. 3s. 6d.*
A Text-book of European History for Middle Forms.

THE ANCIENT WORLD. With Maps and Illustrations. *Cr. 8vo. 3s. 6d.*
See also Beginner's Books.

Wilson (Bishop.). See Library of Devotion.

Wilson (A. J.). See Books on Business.

Wilson (H. A.). See Books on Business.

Wilson (J. A.). See Simplified French Texts.

Wilton (Richard), M.A. LYRA PAS-TORALIS : Songs of Nature, Church, and Home. *Pott 8vo. 2s. 6d.*

Winbolt (S. E.), M.A. EXERCISES IN LATIN ACCIDENCE. *Cr. 8vo. 1s. 6d.*

LATIN HEXAMETER VERSE: An Aid to Composition. *Cr. 8vo. 3s. 6d.* KEY, *5s. net.*

Windle (B. C. A.), F.R.S., F.S.A. See Antiquary's Books, Little Guides, Ancient Cities, and School Histories.

Winterbotham (Canon), M.A., B.Sc., LL.B. See Churchman's Library.

Wood (Sir Evelyn), F.M., V.C., G.C.B., G.C.M.G. FROM MIDSHIPMAN TO FIELD-MARSHAL. With 24 Illustrations and Maps. *A New and Cheaper Edition. Demy 8vo. 7s. 6d. net.*
A Colonial Edition is also published.

Wood (J. A. E.). See Textbooks of Technology.

Wood (J. Hickory). DAN LENO. Illustrated. *Third Edition. Cr. 8vo. 6s.*
A Colonial Edition is also published.

Wood (W. Birkbeck), M.A., late Scholar of Worcester College, Oxford, and Edmonds (Major J. E.), R.E., D.A.Q.-M.-G. A HISTORY OF THE CIVIL WAR IN THE UNITED STATES. With an Introduction by H. SPENSER WILKINSON. With 24 Maps and Plans. *Second Edition. Demy 8vo. 12s. 6d. net.*

Wordsworth (Christopher). See Antiquary's Books.

Wordsworth (W.). POEMS BY. Selected by STOPFORD A. BROOKE. With 40 Illustrations by EDMUND H. NEW. With a Frontispiece in Photogravure. *Demy 8vo. 7s. 6d. net.*
A Colonial Edition is also published.

Wordsworth (W.) and Coleridge (S. T.). See Little Library.

Wright (Arthur), D.D., Fellow of Queen's College, Cambridge. See Churchman's Library.

Wright (C. Gordon). See Dante.

Wright (J. C.). TO-DAY. *Demy 16mo. 1s. 6d. net.*

Wright (Sophie). GERMAN VOCABU-LARIES FOR REPETITION. *Fcap. 8vo. 1s. 6d.*

Wrong (George M.), Professor of History in the University of Toronto. THE EARL OF ELGIN. Illustrated. *Demy 8vo. 7s. 6d. net.*
A Colonial Edition is also published.

Wyatt (Kate M.). See M. R. Gloag.

Wylde (A. B.). MODERN ABYSSINIA. With a Map and a Portrait. *Demy 8vo.* 15s. net.
A Colonial Edition is also published.

Wyndham (Rt. Hon. George), M.P. THE POEMS OF WILLIAM SHAKE-SPEARE. With an Introduction and Notes. *Demy 8vo. Buckram, gilt top.* 10s. 6d.

Wyon (R.) and Prance (G.). THE LAND OF THE BLACK MOUNTAIN. Being a Description of Montenegro. With 40 Illustrations. *Cr. 8vo.* 2s. 6d. net.

Yeats (W. B.). A BOOK OF IRISH VERSE. Selected from Modern Writers.

Revised and Enlarged Edition. Cr. 8vo 3s. 6d.

Young (Filson). THE COMPLETE MOTORIST. With 138 Illustrations. *Seventh Edition, Revised and Rewritten. Demy. 8vo.* 12s. 6d. net.
A Colonial Edition is also published.
THE JOY OF THE ROAD: An Appreciation of the Motor Car. *Small Demy 8vo.* 5s. net.

Young (T. M.). THE AMERICAN COTTON INDUSTRY: A Study of Work and Workers. *Cr. 8vo. Cloth,* 2s. 6d.; *paper boards,* 1s. 6d.

Zimmern (Antonia). WHAT DO WE KNOW CONCERNING ELECTRICITY? *Fcap. 8vo.* 1s. 6d. net.

Ancient Cities

General Editor, B. C. A. WINDLE, D.Sc., F.R.S.

Cr. 8vo. 4s. 6d. net.

CHESTER. By B. C. A. Windle, D.Sc. F.R.S. Illustrated by E. H. New.
SHREWSBURY. By T. Auden, M.A., F.S.A. Illustrated.
CANTERBURY. By J. C. Cox, LL.D., F.S.A. Illustrated.
EDINBURGH. By M. G. Williamson, M.A. Illustrated by Herbert Railton.

LINCOLN. By E. Mansel Sympson, M.A., M.D. Illustrated by E. H. New.
BRISTOL. By Alfred Harvey. Illustrated by E. H. New.
DUBLIN. By S. A. O. Fitzpatrick. Illustrated by W. C. Green.

The Antiquary's Books

General Editor, J. CHARLES COX, LL.D., F.S.A.

Demy 8vo. 7s. 6d. net.

ENGLISH MONASTIC LIFE. By the Right Rev. Abbot Gasquet, O.S.B. Illustrated. *Third Edition.*
REMAINS OF THE PREHISTORIC AGE IN ENGLAND. By B. C. A. Windle, D.Sc., F.R.S. With numerous Illustrations and Plans.
OLD SERVICE BOOKS OF THE ENGLISH CHURCH. By Christopher Wordsworth, M.A., and Henry Littlehales. With Coloured and other Illustrations.
CELTIC ART. By J. Romilly Allen, F.S.A. With numerous Illustrations and Plans.
ARCHÆOLOGY AND FALSE ANTIQUITIES. By R. Munro, LL.D. Illustrated.
SHRINES OF BRITISH SAINTS. By J. C. Wall. With numerous Illustrations and Plans.

THE ROYAL FORESTS OF ENGLAND. By J. C. Cox, LL.D., F.S.A. Illustrated.
THE MANOR AND MANORIAL RECORDS. By Nathaniel J. Hone. Illustrated.
ENGLISH SEALS. By J. Harvey Bloom. Illustrated.
THE DOMESDAY INQUEST. By Adolphus Ballard, B.A., LL.B. With 27 Illustrations.
THE BRASSES OF ENGLAND. By Herbert W. Macklin, M.A. With many Illustrations. *Second Edition.*
PARISH LIFE IN MEDIÆVAL ENGLAND. By the Right Rev. Abbot Gasquet, O.S.B. With many Illustrations. *Second Edition.*
THE BELLS OF ENGLAND. By Canon J. J. Raven, D.D., F.S.A. With Illustration. *Second Edition.*

The Arden Shakespeare

Demy 8vo. 2s. 6d. net each volume.

General Editor, W. J. CRAIG.

An edition of Shakespeare in single Plays. Edited with a full Introduction, Textual Notes, and a Commentary at the foot of the page.

HAMLET. Edited by Edward Dowden.
ROMEO AND JULIET. Edited by Edward Dowden.

KING LEAR. Edited by W. J. Craig.
JULIUS CÆSAR. Edited by M. Macmillan.
THE TEMPEST. Edited by Moreton Luce.

[Continued

ARDEN SHAKESPEARE—*continued.*

OTHELLO. Edited by H. C. Hart.
TITUS ANDRONICUS. Edited by H. B. Baildon.
CYMBELINE. Edited by Edward Dowden.
THE MERRY WIVES OF WINDSOR. Edited by H. C. Hart.
A MIDSUMMER NIGHT'S DREAM. Edited by H. Cuningham.
KING HENRY V. Edited by H. A. Evans.
ALL'S WELL THAT ENDS WELL. Edited by W. O. Brigstocke.
THE TAMING OF THE SHREW. Edited by R. Warwick Bond.
TIMON OF ATHENS. Edited by K. Deighton.
MEASURE FOR MEASURE. Edited by H. C. Hart.
TWELFTH NIGHT. Edited by Moreton Luce.

THE MERCHANT OF VENICE. Edited by C. Knox Pooler.
TROILUS AND CRESSIDA. Edited by K. Deighton.
ANTONY AND CLEOPATRA. Edited by R. H. Case.
LOVE'S LABOUR'S LOST. Edited by H. C. Hart.
THE TWO GENTLEMAN OF VERONA. R, Warwick Bond.
PERICLES. Edited by K. Deighton.
THE COMEDY OF ERRORS. Edited by H. Cuningham.
KING RICHARD III. Edited by A. H. Thompson.
KING JOHN. Edited by Ivor B. John.

The Beginner's Books
Edited by W. WILLIAMSON, B.A.

EASY FRENCH RHYMES. By Henri Blouet. *Second Edition.* Illustrated. *Fcap. 8vo.* 1s.

EASY STORIES FROM ENGLISH HISTORY. By E. M. Wilmot-Buxton, Author of 'Makers of Europe.' *Third Edition.* *Cr. 8vo.* 1s.

EASY EXERCISES IN ARITHMETIC. Arranged by W. S. Beard. *Second Edition.* *Fcap.*

8vo. Without Answers, 1s. With Answers. 1s. 3d.

EASY DICTATION AND SPELLING. By W. Williamson, B.A. *Sixth Ed.* *Fcap. 8vo.* 1s.

AN EASY POETRY BOOK. Selected and arranged by W. Williamson, B.A., Author of 'Dictation Passages.' *Second Edition.* *Cr. 8vo.* 1s.

Books on Business
Cr. 8vo. 2s. 6d. net.

PORTS AND DOCKS. By Douglas Owen.
RAILWAYS. By E. R. McDermott.
THE STOCK EXCHANGE. By Chas. Duguid. *Second Edition.*
THE BUSINESS OF INSURANCE. By A. J. Wilson.
THE ELECTRICAL INDUSTRY: LIGHTING, TRACTION, AND POWER. By A. G. Whyte, B.Sc.
THE SHIPBUILDING INDUSTRY: Its History, Science, Practice, and Finance. By David Pollock, M.I.N.A.
THE MONEY MARKET. By F. Straker.
THE BUSINESS SIDE OF AGRICULTURE. By A. G. L. Rogers, M.A.
LAW IN BUSINESS. By H. A. Wilson.
THE BREWING INDUSTRY. By Julian L. Baker, F.I.C., F.C.S.

THE AUTOMOBILE INDUSTRY. By G. de H. Stone.
MINING AND MINING INVESTMENTS. By 'A. Moil.'
THE BUSINESS OF ADVERTISING. By Clarence G. Moran, Barrister-at-Law. Illustrated.
TRADE UNIONS. By G. Drage.
CIVIL ENGINEERING. By T. Claxton Fidler, M.Inst. C.E. Illustrated.
THE IRON TRADE OF GREAT BRITAIN. By J. Stephen Jeans. Illustrated.
MONOPOLIES, TRUSTS, AND KARTELLS. By F. W. Hirst.
THE COTTON INDUSTRY AND TRADE. By Prof. S. J. Chapman, Dean of the Faculty of Commerce in the University of Manchester. Illustrated.

Byzantine Texts
Edited by J. B. BURY, M.A., Litt.D.

A series of texts of Byzantine Historians, edited by English and foreign scholars.

ZACHARIAH OF MITYLENE. Translated by F. J. Hamilton, D.D., and E. W. Brooks. *Demy 8vo.* 12s. 6d. net.

EVAGRIUS. Edited by Léon Parmentier and M. Bidez. *Demy 8vo.* 10s. 6d. net.

THE HISTORY OF PSELLUS. Edited by C. Sathas. *Demy 8vo.* 15s. net.
ECTHESIS CHRONICA. Edited by Professor Lambros. *Demy 8vo.* 7s. 6d. net.
THE CHRONICLE OF MOREA. Edited by John Schmitt. *Demy 8vo.* 15s. net.

The Churchman's Bible

General Editor, J. H. BURN, B.D., F.R.S.E.

Fcap. 8vo.   1s. 6d. net each.

A series of Expositions on the Books of the Bible, which will be of service to the general reader in the practical and devotional study of the Sacred Text.

Each Book is provided with a full and clear Introductory Section, in which is stated what is known or conjectured respecting the date and occasion of the composition of the Book, and any other particulars that may help to elucidate its meaning as a whole.   The Exposition is divided into sections of a convenient length, corresponding as far as possible with the divisions of the Church Lectionary.   The Translation of the Authorised Version is printed in full, such corrections as are deemed necessary being placed in footnotes.

THE EPISTLE OF ST. PAUL THE APOSTLE TO THE GALATIANS. Edited by A. W. Robinson, M.A. *Second Edition.*

ECCLESIASTES. Edited by A. W. Streane, D.D.

THE EPISTLE OF ST. PAUL THE APOSTLE TO THE PHILIPPIANS. Edited by C. R. D. Biggs, D.D. *Second Edition.*

THE EPISTLE OF ST. JAMES. Edited by H. W. Fulford M.A.

ISAIAH. Edited by W. E. Barnes, D.D. *Two Volumes.* With Map. 2s. *net each.*

THE EPISTLE OF ST. PAUL THE APOSTLE TO THE EPHESIANS. Edited by G. H. Whitaker, M.A.

THE GOSPEL ACCORDING TO ST. MARK. Edited by J. C. Du Buisson, M.A. 2s. 6d. net.

ST. PAUL'S EPISTLES TO THE COLOSSIANS AND PHILEMON. Edited by H. J. C. Knight, M.A. 2s. net.

The Churchman's Library

General Editor, J. H. BURN, B.D., F.R.S.E.

Crown 8vo.   3s. 6d. each.

THE BEGINNINGS OF ENGLISH CHRISTIANITY. By W. E. Collins, M.A. With Map.

THE KINGDOM OF HEAVEN HERE AND HEREAFTER. By Canon Winterbotham, M.A., B.Sc., LL.B.

THE WORKMANSHIP OF THE PRAYER BOOK: Its Literary and Liturgical Aspects. By J. Dowden, D.D. *Second Edition.*

EVOLUTION. By F. B. Jevons, M.A., Litt.D.

SOME NEW TESTAMENT PROBLEMS. By Arthur Wright, D.D. 6s.

THE CHURCHMAN'S INTRODUCTION TO THE OLD TESTAMENT. By A. M. Mackay, B.A. *Second Edition.*

THE CHURCH OF CHRIST. By E. T. Green, M.A. 6s.

COMPARATIVE THEOLOGY. By J. A. MacCulloch. 6s.

Classical Translations

Edited by H. F. FOX, M.A., Fellow and Tutor of Brasenose College, Oxford.

Crown 8vo.

A series of Translations from the Greek and Latin Classics, distinguished by literary excellence as well as by scholarly accuracy.

ÆSCHYLUS—Agamemnon Choephoroe, Eumenides. Translated by Lewis Campbell, LL.D. 5s.

CICERO—De Oratore I. Translated by E. N. P. Moor, M.A. 3s. 6d.

CICERO—Select Orations (Pro Milone, Pro Mureno, Philippic II., in Catilinam). Translated by H. E. D. Blakiston, M.A. 5s.

CICERO—De Natura Deorum. Translated by F. Brooks, M.A. 3s. 6d.

CICERO—De Officiis. Translated by G. B. Gardiner, M.A. 2s. 6d.

HORACE—The Odes and Epodes. Translated by A. D. Godley, M.A. 2s.

LUCIAN—Six Dialogues (Nigrinus, Icaro-Menippus, The Cock, The Ship, The Parasite, The Lover of Falsehood) Translated by S. T. Irwin, M.A. 3s. 6d.

SOPHOCLES—Electra and Ajax. Translated by E. D. A. Morshead, M.A. 2s. 6d.

TACITUS—Agricola and Germania. Translated by R. B. Townshend. 2s. 6d.

THE SATIRES OF JUVENAL. Translated by S. G. Owen. 2s. 6d.

Classics of Art

Edited by DR. J. H. W. LAING

THE ART OF THE GREEKS. By H. B. Walters. With 112 Plates and 18 Illustrations in the Text. *Wide Royal 8vo.* 12s. 6d. net.

VELAZQUEZ. By A. de Beruete. With 94 Plates. *Wide Royal 8vo.* 10s. 6d. net.

Commercial Series

Edited by H. DE B. GIBBINS, Litt.D., M.A.

Crown 8vo.

COMMERCIAL EDUCATION IN THEORY AND PRACTICE. By E. E. Whitfield, M.A. 5s.
An introduction to Methuen's Commercial Series treating the question of Commercial Education fully from both the point of view of the teacher and of the parent.

BRITISH COMMERCE AND COLONIES FROM ELIZABETH TO VICTORIA. By H. de B. Gibbins, Litt.D., M.A. *Third Edition.* 2s.

COMMERCIAL EXAMINATION PAPERS. By H. de B. Gibbins, Litt.D., M.A. 1s. 6d.

THE ECONOMICS OF COMMERCE. By H. de B. Gibbins, Litt.D., M.A. *Second Edition.* 1s. 6d.

A GERMAN COMMERCIAL READER. By S. E. Bally. With Vocabulary. 2s.

A COMMERCIAL GEOGRAPHY OF THE BRITISH EMPIRE. By L. W. Lyde, M.A. *Sixth Edition.* 2s.

A COMMERCIAL GEOGRAPHY OF FOREIGN NATIONS. By F. C. Boon, B.A. 2s.

A PRIMER OF BUSINESS. By S. Jackson, M.A. *Third Edition.* 1s. 6d.

COMMERCIAL ARITHMETIC. By F. G. Taylor, M.A. *Fourth Edition.* 1s. 6d.

FRENCH COMMERCIAL CORRESPONDENCE. By S. E. Bally. With Vocabulary. *Third Edition.* 2s.

GERMAN COMMERCIAL CORRESPONDENCE. By S. E. Bally. With Vocabulary. *Second Edition.* 2s. 6d.

A FRENCH COMMERCIAL READER. By S. E. Bally. With Vocabulary. *Second Edition.* 2s.

PRECIS WRITING AND OFFICE CORRESPONDENCE. By E. E. Whitfield, M.A. *Second Edition.* 2s.

A GUIDE TO PROFESSIONS AND BUSINESS. By H. Jones. 1s. 6d.

THE PRINCIPLES OF BOOK-KEEPING BY DOUBLE ENTRY. By J. E. B. M'Allen, M.A. 2s.

COMMERCIAL LAW. By W. Douglas Edwards. *Second Edition.* 2s.

The Connoisseur's Library

Wide Royal 8vo. 25s. net.

A sumptuous series of 20 books on art, written by experts for collectors, superbly illustrated in photogravure, collotype, and colour. The technical side of the art is duly treated. The first volumes are—

MEZZOTINTS. By Cyril Davenport. With 40 Plates in Photogravure.

PORCELAIN. By Edward Dillon. With 19 Plates in Colour, 20 in Collotype, and 5 in Photogravure.

MINIATURES. By Dudley Heath. With 9 Plates in Colour, 15 in Collotype, and 15 in Photogravure.

IVORIES. By A. Maskell. With 80 Plates in Collotype and Photogravure.

ENGLISH FURNITURE. By F. S. Robinson. With 160 Plates in Collotype and one in Photogravure. *Second Edition.*

EUROPEAN ENAMELS. By Henry H. Cunynghame, C.B. With 54 Plates in Collotype and Half-tone and 4 Plates in Colour.

GOLDSMITHS' AND SILVERSMITHS' WORK. By Nelson Dawson. With many Plates in Collotype and a Frontispiece in Photogravure. *Second Edition.*

ENGLISH COLOURED BOOKS. By Martin Hardie. With 28 Illustrations in Colour and Collotype.

GLASS. By Edward Dillon. With 37 Illustrations in Collotype and 12 in Colour.

The Library of Devotion

With Introductions and (where necessary) Notes.

Small Pott 8vo, cloth, 2s. ; *leather,* 2s. 6d. net.

THE CONFESSIONS OF ST. AUGUSTINE. Edited by C. Bigg, D.D. *Sixth Edition.*

THE CHRISTIAN YEAR. Edited by Walter Lock, D.D. *Fourth Edition.*

THE IMITATION OF CHRIST. Edited by C. Bigg, D.D. *Fourth Edition.*

A BOOK OF DEVOTIONS. Edited by J. W. Stanbridge. B.D. *Second Edition.*

[Continued.

THE LIBRARY OF DEVOTION—*continued.*

LYRA INNOCENTIUM. Edited by Walter Lock, D.D. *Second Edition.*

A SERIOUS CALL TO A DEVOUT AND HOLY LIFE. Edited by C. Bigg, D.D. *Fourth Edition.*

THE TEMPLE. Edited by E. C. S. Gibson, D.D. *Second Edition.*

A GUIDE TO ETERNITY. Edited by J. W. Stanbridge, B.D.

THE PSALMS OF DAVID. Edited by B. W. Randolph, D.D.

LYRA APOSTOLICA. By Cardinal Newman and others. Edited by Canon Scott Holland and Canon H. C. Beeching, M.A.

THE INNER WAY. By J. Tauler. Edited by A. W. Hutton, M.A.

THE THOUGHTS OF PASCAL. Edited by C. S. Jerram, M.A.

ON THE LOVE OF GOD. By St. Francis de Sales. Edited by W. J. Knox-Little, M.A.

A MANUAL OF CONSOLATION FROM THE SAINTS AND FATHERS. Edited by J. H. Burn, B.D.

THE SONG OF SONGS. Edited by B. Blaxland, M.A.

THE DEVOTIONS OF ST. ANSELM. Edited by C. C. J. Webb, M.A.

GRACE ABOUNDING. By John Bunyan. Edited by S. C. Freer, M.A.

BISHOP WILSON'S SACRA PRIVATA. Edited by A. E. Burn, B.D.

LYRA SACRA: A Book of Sacred Verse. Edited by H. C. Beeching, M.A., Canon of Westminster. *Second Edition, revised.*

A DAY BOOK FROM THE SAINTS AND FATHERS. Edited by J. H. Burn, B.D.

HEAVENLY WISDOM. A Selection from the English Mystics. Edited by E. C. Gregory.

LIGHT, LIFE, and LOVE. A Selection from the German Mystics. Edited by W. R. Inge, M.A.

AN INTRODUCTION TO THE DEVOUT LIFE. By St. Francis de Sales. Translated and Edited by T. Barns, M.A.

MANCHESTER AL MONDO: a Contemplation of Death and Immortality. By Henry Montagu, Earl of Manchester. With an Introduction by Elizabeth Waterhouse, Editor of 'A Little Book of Life and Death.'

THE LITTLE FLOWERS OF THE GLORIOUS MESSER ST. FRANCIS AND OF HIS FRIARS. Done into English by W. Heywood. With an Introduction by A. G. Ferrers Howell.

THE SPIRITUAL GUIDE, which Disentangles the Soul and brings it by the Inward Way to the Fruition of Perfect Contemplation, and the Rich Treasure of Internal Peace. Written by Dr. Michael de Molinos, Priest. Translated from the Italian copy, printed at Venice, 1685. Edited with an Introduction by Kathleen Lyttelton. With a Preface by Canon Scott Holland.

The Illustrated Pocket Library of Plain and Coloured Books

Fcap 8vo.   3s. 6d. net each volume.

A series, in small form, of some of the famous illustrated books of fiction and general literature. These are faithfully reprinted from the first or best editions without introduction or notes. The Illustrations are chiefly in colour.

COLOURED BOOKS

OLD COLOURED BOOKS. By George Paston. With 16 Coloured Plates. *Fcap. 8vo. 2s. net.*

THE LIFE AND DEATH OF JOHN MYTTON, ESQ. By Nimrod. With 18 Coloured Plates by Henry Alken and T. J. Rawlins. *Fourth Edition.*

THE LIFE OF A SPORTSMAN. By Nimrod. With 35 Coloured Plates by Henry Alken.

HANDLEY CROSS. By R. S. Surtees. With 17 Coloured Plates and 100 Woodcuts in the Text by John Leech. *Second Edition.*

MR. SPONGE'S SPORTING TOUR. By R. S. Surtees. With 13 Coloured Plates and 90 Woodcuts in the Text by John Leech.

JORROCKS' JAUNTS AND JOLLITIES. By R. S. Surtees. With 15 Coloured Plates by H. Alken. *Second Edition.*
This volume is reprinted from the extremely rare and costly edition of 1843, which contains Alken's very fine illustrations instead of the usual ones by Phiz.

ASK MAMMA. By R. S. Surtees. With 13 Coloured Plates and 70 Woodcuts in the Text by John Leech.

THE ANALYSIS OF THE HUNTING FIELD. By R. S. Surtees. With 7 Coloured Plates by Henry Alken, and 43 Illustrations on Wood.

THE TOUR OF DR. SYNTAX IN SEARCH OF THE PICTURESQUE. By William Combe. With 30 Coloured Plates by T. Rowlandson.

THE TOUR OF DOCTOR SYNTAX IN SEARCH OF CONSOLATION. By William Combe. With 24 Coloured Plates by T. Rowlandson.

THE THIRD TOUR OF DOCTOR SYNTAX IN SEARCH OF A WIFE. By William Combe. With 24 Coloured Plates by T. Rowlandson.

THE HISTORY OF JOHNNY QUAE GENUS: the Little Foundling of the late Dr. Syntax. By the Author of 'The Three Tours.' With 24 Coloured Plates by Rowlandson.

THE ENGLISH DANCE OF DEATH, from the Designs of T. Rowlandson, with Metrical Illustrations by the Author of 'Doctor Syntax.' *Two Volumes.*
This book contains 76 Coloured Plates.

THE DANCE OF LIFE: A Poem. By the Author of 'Doctor Syntax.' Illustrated with 26 Coloured Engravings by T. Rowlandson.

[*Continued.*

ILLUSTRATED POCKET LIBRARY OF PLAIN AND COLOURED BOOKS—*continued.*

LIFE IN LONDON: or, the Day and Night Scenes of Jerry Hawthorn, Esq., and his Elegant Friend, Corinthian Tom. By Pierce Egan. With 36 Coloured Plates by I. R. and G. Cruikshank. With numerous Designs on Wood.

REAL LIFE IN LONDON: or, the Rambles and Adventures of Bob Tallyho, Esq., and his Cousin, The Hon. Tom Dashall. By an Amateur (Pierce Egan). With 31 Coloured Plates by Alken and Rowlandson, etc. *Two Volumes.*

THE LIFE OF AN ACTOR. By Pierce Egan. With 27 Coloured Plates by Theodore Lane, and several Designs on Wood.

THE VICAR OF WAKEFIELD. By Oliver Goldsmith. With 24 Coloured Plates by T. Rowlandson.

THE MILITARY ADVENTURES OF JOHNNY NEWCOME. By an Officer. With 15 Coloured Plates by T. Rowlandson.

THE NATIONAL SPORTS OF GREAT BRITAIN. With Descriptions and 51 Coloured Plates by Henry Alken.

This book is completely different from the large folio edition of 'National Sports' by the same artist, and none of the plates are similar.

THE ADVENTURES OF A POST CAPTAIN. By A Naval Officer. With 24 Coloured Plates by Mr. Williams.

GAMONIA : or, the Art of Preserving Game ; and an Improved Method of making Plantations and Covers, explained and illustrated by Lawrence Rawstorne, Esq. With 15 Coloured Plates by T. Rawlins.

AN ACADEMY FOR GROWN HORSEMEN : Containing the completest Instructions for Walking, Trotting, Cantering, Galloping, Stumbling, and Tumbling. Illustrated with 27 Coloured Plates, and adorned with a Portrait of the Author. By Geoffrey Gambado, Esq.

REAL LIFE IN IRELAND, or, the Day and Night Scenes of Brian Boru, Esq., and his Elegant Friend, Sir Shawn O'Dogherty. By a Real Paddy. With 19 Coloured Plates by Heath, Marks, etc.

THE ADVENTURES OF JOHNNY NEWCOME IN THE NAVY. By Alfred Burton. With 16 Coloured Plates by T. Rowlandson.

THE OLD ENGLISH SQUIRE : A Poem. By John Careless, Esq. With 20 Coloured Plates after the style of T. Rowlandson.

PLAIN BOOKS

THE GRAVE : A Poem. By Robert Blair. Illustrated by 12 Etchings executed by Louis Schiavonetti from the original Inventions of William Blake. With an Engraved Title Page and a Portrait of Blake by T. Phillips, R.A.

The illustrations are reproduced in photogravure.

ILLUSTRATIONS OF THE BOOK OF JOB. Invented and engraved by William Blake.

These famous Illustrations—21 in number—are reproduced in photogravure.

ÆSOP'S FABLES. With 380 Woodcuts by Thomas Bewick.

WINDSOR CASTLE. By W. Harrison Ainsworth. With 22 Plates and 87 Woodcuts in the Text by George Cruikshank.

THE TOWER OF LONDON. By W. Harrison Ainsworth. With 40 Plates and 58 Woodcuts in the Text by George Cruikshank.

FRANK FAIRLEGH. By F. E. Smedley. With 30 Plates by George Cruikshank.

HANDY ANDY. By Samuel Lover. With 24 Illustrations by the Author.

THE COMPLEAT ANGLER. By Izaak Walton and Charles Cotton. With 14 Plates and 77 Woodcuts in the Text.

This volume is reproduced from the beautiful edition of John Major of 1824.

THE PICKWICK PAPERS. By Charles Dickens. With the 43 Illustrations by Seymour and Phiz, the two Buss Plates, and the 32 Contemporary Onwhyn Plates.

Junior Examination Series

Edited by A. M. M. STEDMAN, M.A. *Fcap. 8vo.* 1s.

JUNIOR FRENCH EXAMINATION PAPERS. By F. Jacob, M.A. *Second Edition.*

JUNIOR LATIN EXAMINATION PAPERS. By C. G. Botting, B.A. *Fourth Edition.*

JUNIOR ENGLISH EXAMINATION PAPERS. By W. Williamson, B.A.

JUNIOR ARITHMETIC EXAMINATION PAPERS. By W. S. Beard. *Fourth Edition.*

JUNIOR ALGEBRA EXAMINATION PAPERS. By S. W. Finn, M.A.

JUNIOR GREEK EXAMINATION PAPERS. By T. C. Weatherhead, M.A.

JUNIOR GENERAL INFORMATION EXAMINATION PAPERS. By W. S. Beard.

A KEY TO THE ABOVE. 3s. 6d. *net.*

JUNIOR GEOGRAPHY EXAMINATION PAPERS. By W. G. Baker, M.A.

JUNIOR GERMAN EXAMINATION PAPERS. By A. Voegelin, M.A.

Junior School-Books

Edited by O. D. INSKIP, LL.D., and W. WILLIAMSON, B.A.

A CLASS-BOOK OF DICTATION PASSAGES. By W. Williamson, B.A. *Thirteenth Edition.* Cr. 8vo. 1s. 6d.

THE GOSPEL ACCORDING TO ST. MATTHEW. Edited by E. Wilton South, M.A. With Three Maps. Cr. 8vo. 1s. 6d.

THE GOSPEL ACCORDING TO ST. MARK. Edited by A. E. Rubie, D.D. With Three Maps. Cr. 8vo. 1s. 6d.

A JUNIOR ENGLISH GRAMMAR. By W. Williamson, B.A. With numerous passages for parsing and analysis, and a chapter on Essay Writing. *Fourth Edition.* Cr. 8vo. 2s.

A JUNIOR CHEMISTRY. By E. A. Tyler, B.A., F.C.S. With 78 Illustrations. *Fourth Edition.* Cr. 8vo. 2s. 6d.

THE ACTS OF THE APOSTLES. Edited by A. E. Rubie, D.D. Cr. 8vo. 2s.

A JUNIOR FRENCH GRAMMAR. By L. A. Sornet and M. J. Acatos. *Second Edition.* Cr. 8vo. 2s.

ELEMENTARY EXPERIMENTAL SCIENCE. PHYSICS by W. T. Clough, A.R.C.S. CHEMISTRY by A. E. Dunstan, B.Sc. With 2 Plates and 154 Diagrams. *Fifth Edition.* Cr. 8vo. 2s. 6d.

A JUNIOR GEOMETRY. By Noel S. Lydon. With 276 Diagrams. *Sixth Edition.* Cr. 8vo. 2s.

ELEMENTARY EXPERIMENTAL CHEMISTRY. By A. E. Dunstan, B.Sc. With 4 Plates and 109 Diagrams. *Second Edition revised.* Cr. 8vo. 2s.

A JUNIOR FRENCH PROSE. By R. R. N. Baron, M.A. *Third Edition.* Cr. 8vo. 2s.

THE GOSPEL ACCORDING TO ST. LUKE. With an Introduction and Notes by William Williamson, B.A. With Three Maps. Cr. 8vo. 2s.

THE FIRST BOOK OF KINGS. Edited by A. E. RUBIE, D.D. With Maps. Cr. 8vo. 2s.

Leaders of Religion

Edited by H. C. BEECHING, M.A., Canon of Westminster. *With Portraits.*

Cr. 8vo. 2s. net.

CARDINAL NEWMAN. By R. H. Hutton.

JOHN WESLEY. By J. H. Overton, M.A.

BISHOP WILBERFORCE. By G. W. Daniell, M.A.

CARDINAL MANNING. By A. W. Hutton, M.A.

CHARLES SIMEON. By H. C. G. Moule, D.D.

JOHN KEBLE. By Walter Lock, D.D.

THOMAS CHALMERS. By Mrs. Oliphant.

LANCELOT ANDREWES. By R. L. Ottley, D.D. *Second Edition.*

AUGUSTINE OF CANTERBURY. By E. L. Cutts, D.D.

WILLIAM LAUD. By W. H. Hutton, M.A. *Third Edition.*

JOHN KNOX. By F. MacCunn. *Second Edition.*

JOHN HOWE. By R. F. Horton, D.D.

BISHOP KEN. By F. A. Clarke, M.A.

GEORGE FOX, THE QUAKER. By T. Hodgkin, D.C.L. *Third Edition.*

JOHN DONNE. By Augustus Jessopp, D.D.

THOMAS CRANMER. By A. J. Mason, D.D.

BISHOP LATIMER. By R. M. Carlyle and A. J. Carlyle, M.A.

BISHOP BUTLER. By W. A. Spooner, M.A.

Little Books on Art

With many Illustrations. Demy 16mo. 2s. 6d. net.

A series of monographs in miniature, containing the complete outline of the subject under treatment and rejecting minute details. These books are produced with the greatest care. Each volume consists of about 200 pages, and contains from 30 to 40 illustrations, including a frontispiece in photogravure.

GREEK ART. H. B. Walters. *Third Edition.*

BOOKPLATES. E. Almack.

REYNOLDS. J. Sime. *Second Edition.*

ROMNEY. George Paston.

GREUZE AND BOUCHER. Eliza F. Pollard.

VANDYCK. M. G. Smallwood.

TURNER. Frances Tyrrell-Gill.

DÜRER. Jessie Allen.

HOPPNER. H. P. K. Skipton.

HOLBEIN. Mrs. G. Fortescue.

WATTS. R. E. D. Sketchley.

LEIGHTON. Alice Corkran.

VELASQUEZ. Wilfrid Wilberforce and A. R. Gilbert.

COROT. Alice Pollard and Ethel Birnstingl.

RAPHAEL. A. R. Dryhurst.

MILLET. Netta Peacock.

ILLUMINATED MSS. J. W. Bradley.

CHRIST IN ART. Mrs. Henry Jenner.

JEWELLERY. Cyril Davenport.

[Continued.

LITTLE BOOKS ON ART—*continued*.

BURNE-JONES. Fortunée de Lisle. *Third* | CLAUDE. Edward Dillon.
Edition. | THE ARTS OF JAPAN. Edward Dillon.
REMBRANDT. Mrs. E. A. Sharp. | ENAMELS. Mrs. Nelson Dawson.

The Little Galleries

Demy 16mo. 2s. 6d. net.

A series of little books containing examples of the best work of the great painters. Each volume contains 20 plates in photogravure, together with a short outline of the life and work of the master to whom the book is devoted.

A LITTLE GALLERY OF REYNOLDS. | A LITTLE GALLERY OF MILLAIS.
A LITTLE GALLERY OF ROMNEY. | A LITTLE GALLERY OF ENGLISH POETS.
A LITTLE GALLERY OF HOPPNER. |

The Little Guides

With many Illustrations by E. H. NEW and other artists, and from photographs.

Small Pott 8vo, cloth, 2s. 6d. net.; leather, 3s. 6d. net.

Messrs. METHUEN are publishing a small series of books under the general title of THE LITTLE GUIDES. The main features of these books are (1) a handy and charming form, (2) artistic Illustrations by E. H. NEW and others, (3) good plans and maps, (4) an adequate but compact presentation of everything that is interesting in the natural features, history, archæology, and architecture of the town or district treated.

CAMBRIDGE AND ITS COLLEGES. By A. Hamilton Thompson. *Second Edition.*
OXFORD AND ITS COLLEGES. By J. Wells, M.A. *Seventh Edition.*
ST. PAUL'S CATHEDRAL. By George Clinch.
WESTMINSTER ABBEY. By G. E. Troutbeck.

THE ENGLISH LAKES. By F. G. Brabant, M.A.
THE MALVERN COUNTRY. By B. C. A. Windle, D.Sc., F.R.S.
SHAKESPEARE'S COUNTRY. By B. C. A. Windle, D.Sc., F.R.S. *Third Edition.*

BUCKINGHAMSHIRE. By E. S. Roscoe.
CHESHIRE. By W. M. Gallichan.
CORNWALL. By A. L. Salmon.
DERBYSHIRE. By J. Charles Cox, LL.D., F.S.A.
DEVON. By S. Baring-Gould.
DORSET. By Frank R. Heath.
HAMPSHIRE. By J. Charles Cox, LL.D., F.S.A.

HERTFORDSHIRE. By H. W. Tompkins, F.R.H.S.
THE ISLE OF WIGHT. By G. Clinch.
KENT. By G. Clinch.
KERRY. By C. P. Crane.
MIDDLESEX. By John B. Firth.
NORTHAMPTONSHIRE. By Wakeling Dry.
NORFOLK. By W. A. Dutt.
OXFORDSHIRE. By F. G. Brabant, M.A.
SUFFOLK. By W. A. Dutt.
SURREY. By F. A. H. Lambert.
SUSSEX. By F. G. Brabant, M.A. *Second Edition.*
THE EAST RIDING OF YORKSHIRE. By J. E. Morris.
THE NORTH RIDING OF YORKSHIRE. By J. E. Morris.

BRITTANY. By S. Baring-Gould.
NORMANDY. By C. Scudamore.
ROME By C. G. Ellaby.
SICILY. By F. Hamilton Jackson.

The Little Library

With Introductions, Notes, and Photogravure Frontispieces.

Small Pott 8vo. Each Volume, cloth, 1s. 6d. net; leather, 2s. 6d. net.

Anon. ENGLISH LYRICS, A LITTLE BOOK OF.
Austen (Jane). PRIDE AND PREJUDICE. Edited by E. V. LUCAS. *Two Vols.*

NORTHANGER ABBEY. Edited by E. V. LUCAS.
Bacon (Francis). THE ESSAYS OF LORD BACON. Edited by EDWARD WRIGHT.

[*Continued.*

THE LITTLE LIBRARY—*continued.*

Barham (R. H.). THE INGOLDSBY LEGENDS. Edited by J. B. ATLAY. *Two Volumes.*

Barnett (Mrs. P. A.). A LITTLE BOOK OF ENGLISH PROSE. *Second Edition.*

Beckford (William). THE HISTORY OF THE CALIPH VATHEK. Edited by E. DENISON ROSS.

Blake (William). SELECTIONS FROM WILLIAM BLAKE. Edited by M. PERUGINI.

Borrow (George). LAVENGRO. Edited by F. HINDES GROOME. *Two Volumes.*

THE ROMANY RYE. Edited by JOHN SAMPSON.

Browning (Robert). SELECTIONS FROM THE EARLY POEMS OF ROBERT BROWNING. Edited by W. HALL GRIFFIN, M.A.

Canning (George). SELECTIONS FROM THE ANTI-JACOBIN: with GEORGE CANNING's additional Poems. Edited by LLOYD SANDERS.

Cowley (Abraham). THE ESSAYS OF ABRAHAM COWLEY. Edited by H. C. MINCHIN.

Crabbe (George). SELECTIONS FROM GEORGE CRABBE. Edited by A. C. DEANE.

Craik (Mrs.). JOHN HALIFAX, GENTLEMAN. Edited by ANNE MATHESON. *Two Volumes.*

Crashaw (Richard). THE ENGLISH POEMS OF RICHARD CRASHAW. Edited by EDWARD HUTTON.

Dante (Alighieri). THE INFERNO OF DANTE. Translated by H. F. CARY. Edited by PAGET TOYNBEE, M.A., D.Litt.

THE PURGATORIO OF DANTE. Translated by H. F. CARY. Edited by PAGET TOYNBEE, M.A., D.Litt.

THE PARADISO OF DANTE. Translated by H. F. CARY. Edited by PAGET TOYNBEE, M.A., D.Litt.

Darley (George). SELECTIONS FROM THE POEMS OF GEORGE DARLEY. Edited by R. A. STREATFEILD.

Deane (A. C.). A LITTLE BOOK OF LIGHT VERSE.

Dickens (Charles). CHRISTMAS BOOKS. *Two Volumes.*

Ferrier (Susan). MARRIAGE. Edited by A. GOODRICH - FREER and LORD IDDESLEIGH. *Two Volumes.*

THE INHERITANCE. *Two Volumes.*

Gaskell (Mrs.). CRANFORD. Edited by E. V. LUCAS. *Second Edition.*

Hawthorne (Nathaniel). THE SCARLET LETTER. Edited by PERCY DEARMER.

Henderson (T. F.). A LITTLE BOOK OF SCOTTISH VERSE.

Keats (John). POEMS. With an Introduction by L. BINYON, and Notes by J. MASEFIELD.

Kinglake (A. W.). EOTHEN. With an Introduction and Notes. *Second Edition.*

Lamb (Charles). ELIA, AND THE LAST ESSAYS OF ELIA. Edited by E. V. LUCAS.

Locker (F.). LONDON LYRICS. Edited by A. D. GODLEY, M.A. A reprint of the First Edition.

Longfellow (H. W.). SELECTIONS FROM LONGFELLOW. Edited by L. M. FAITHFULL.

Marvell (Andrew). THE POEMS OF ANDREW MARVELL. Edited by E. WRIGHT.

Milton (John). THE MINOR POEMS OF JOHN MILTON. Edited by H. C. BEECHING, M.A., Canon of Westminster.

Moir (D. M.). MANSIE WAUCH. Edited by T. F. HENDERSON.

Nichols (J. B. B.). A LITTLE BOOK OF ENGLISH SONNETS.

Rochefoucauld (La). THE MAXIMS OF LA ROCHEFOUCAULD. Translated by Dean STANHOPE. Edited by G. H. POWELL.

Smith (Horace and James). REJECTED ADDRESSES. Edited by A. D. GODLEY, M.A.

Sterne (Laurence). A SENTIMENTAL JOURNEY. Edited by H. W. PAUL.

Tennyson (Alfred, Lord). THE EARLY POEMS OF ALFRED, LORD TENNYSON. Edited by J. CHURTON COLLINS, M.A.

IN MEMORIAM. Edited by H. C. BEECHING, M.A.

THE PRINCESS. Edited by ELIZABETH WORDSWORTH.

MAUD. Edited by ELIZABETH WORDSWORTH.

Thackeray (W. M.). VANITY FAIR. Edited by S. GWYNN. *Three Volumes.*

PENDENNIS. Edited by S. GWYNN. *Three Volumes.*

ESMOND. Edited by S. GWYNN.

CHRISTMAS BOOKS. Edited by S. GWYNN.

Vaughan (Henry). THE POEMS OF HENRY VAUGHAN. Edited by EDWARD HUTTON.

Walton (Izaak). THE COMPLEAT ANGLER. Edited by J. BUCHAN.

Waterhouse (Mrs. Alfred). A LITTLE BOOK OF LIFE AND DEATH. Edited by. *Tenth Edition.*

Wordsworth (W.). SELECTIONS FROM WORDSWORTH. Edited by NOWELL C. SMITH.

Wordsworth (W.) and Coleridge (S. T.). LYRICAL BALLADS. Edited by GEORGE SAMPSON.

The Little Quarto Shakespeare

Edited by W. J. CRAIG. With Introductions and Notes

Pott 16mo. In 40 Volumes. Leather, price 1s. net each volume.
Mahogany Revolving Book Case. 10s. net.

Miniature Library

Reprints in miniature of a few interesting books which have qualities of
humanity, devotion, or literary genius.

EUPHRANOR: A Dialogue on Youth. By Edward FitzGerald. From the edition published by W. Pickering in 1851. *Demy 32mo. Leather, 2s. net.*

POLONIUS: or Wise Saws and Modern Instances. By Edward FitzGerald. From the edition published by W. Pickering in 1852. *Demy 32mo. Leather, 2s. net.*

THE RUBÁIYÁT OF OMAR KHAYYÁM. By Edward FitzGerald. From the 1st edition of 1859, *Fourth Edition. Leather, 1s. net.*

THE LIFE OF EDWARD, LORD HERBERT OF CHERBURY. Written by himself. From the edition printed at Strawberry Hill in the year 1764. *Demy 32mo. Leather, 2s. net.*

THE VISIONS OF DOM FRANCISCO QUEVEDO VILLEGAS, Knight of the Order of St. James. Made English by R. L. From the edition printed for H. Herringman, 1668. *Leather, 2s. net.*

POEMS. By Dora Greenwell. From the edition of 1848. *Leather, 2s. net.*

Oxford Biographies

Fcap. 8vo. Each volume, cloth, 2s. 6d. net; leather, 3s. 6d. net.

DANTE ALIGHIERI. By Paget Toynbee, M.A., D.Litt. With 12 Illustrations. *Second Edition.*

SAVONAROLA. By E. L. S. Horsburgh, M.A. With 12 Illustrations. *Second Edition.*

JOHN HOWARD. By E. C. S. Gibson, D.D., Bishop of Gloucester. With 12 Illustrations.

TENNYSON. By A. C. Benson, M.A. With 9 Illustrations.

WALTER RALEIGH. By I. A. Taylor. With 12 Illustrations.

ERASMUS. By E. F. H. Capey. With 12 Illustrations.

THE YOUNG PRETENDER. By C. S. Terry. With 12 Illustrations.

ROBERT BURNS. By T. F. Henderson. With 12 Illustrations.

CHATHAM. By A. S. M'Dowall. With 12 Illustrations.

ST. FRANCIS OF ASSISI. By Anna M. Stoddart. With 16 Illustrations.

CANNING. By W. Alison Phillips. With 12 Illustrations.

BEACONSFIELD. By Walter Sichel. With 12 Illustrations.

GOETHE. By H. G. Atkins. With 12 Illustrations.

FENELON. By Viscount St Cyres. With 12 Illustrations.

School Examination Series

Edited by A. M. M. STEDMAN, M.A. *Cr. 8vo. 2s. 6d.*

FRENCH EXAMINATION PAPERS. By A. M. M. Stedman, M.A. *Fourteenth Edition.*
A KEY, issued to Tutors and Private Students only to be had on application to the Publishers. *Fifth Edition. Crown 8vo. 6s. net.*

LATIN EXAMINATION PAPERS. By A. M. M. Stedman, M.A. *Thirteenth Edition.*
KEY (*Sixth Edition*) issued as above. 6s. net.

GREEK EXAMINATION PAPERS. By A. M. M. Stedman, M.A. *Ninth Edition.*
KEY (*Fourth Edition*) issued as above. 6s. net.

GERMAN EXAMINATION PAPERS. By R. J. Morich *Seventh Edition.*

KEY (*Third Edition*) issued as above 6s. net.

HISTORY AND GEOGRAPHY EXAMINATION PAPERS. By C. H. Spence, M.A. *Third Edition.*

PHYSICS EXAMINATION PAPERS. By R. E. Steel, M.A., F.C.S.

GENERAL KNOWLEDGE EXAMINATION PAPERS. By A. M. M. Stedman, M.A. *Sixth Edition.*
KEY (*Fourth Edition*) issued as above. 7s. net.

EXAMINATION PAPERS IN ENGLISH HISTORY. By J. Tait Plowden-Wardlaw, B.A.

School Histories

Illustrated.   Crown 8vo.   1s. 6d.

A SCHOOL HISTORY OF WARWICKSHIRE.   By
B. C. A. Windle, D.Sc., F.R.S.

A SCHOOL HISTORY OF SOMERSET.   By
Walter Raymond.   *Second Edition.*

A SCHOOL HISTORY OF LANCASHIRE.   by
W. E. Rhodes.

A SCHOOL HISTORY OF SURREY.   By H. E.
Malden, M.A.

A SCHOOL HISTORY OF MIDDLESEX.   By V.
G. Plarr and F. W. Walton.

Textbooks of Science

Edited by G. F. GOODCHILD, M.A., B.Sc., and G. R. MILLS, M.A.

PRACTICAL MECHANICS.   By Sidney H. Wells.
Fourth Edition. Cr. 8vo.   3s. 6d.

PRACTICAL CHEMISTRY.   Part I.   By W.
French, M.A.   *Cr. 8vo.   Fourth Edition.*
1s. 6d.   Part II.   By W. French, M.A., and
T. H. Boardman, M.A.   *Cr. 8vo.   1s. 6d.*

TECHNICAL ARITHMETIC AND GEOMETRY.
By C. T. Millis, M.I.M.E.   *Cr. 8vo.*
3s. 6d.

EXAMPLES IN PHYSICS.   By C. E. Jackson,
B.A.   *Cr. 8vo.   2s. 6d.*

PLANT LIFE, Studies in Garden and School.
By Horace F. Jones, F.C.S.   With 320
Diagrams. *Cr. 8vo.   3s. 6d.*

THE COMPLETE SCHOOL CHEMISTRY.   By F.
M. Oldham, B.A.   With 126 Illustrations.
Cr. 8vo.

AN ORGANIC CHEMISTRY FOR SCHOOLS AND
TECHNICAL INSTITUTES. By A. E. Dunstan,
B.Sc.   (Lond.),   F.C.S.   Illustrated.
Cr. 8vo.

ELEMENTARY SCIENCE FOR PUPIL TEACHERS.
PHYSICS SECTION.   By W. T. Clough,
A.R.C.S. (Lond.), F.C.S.   CHEMISTRY
SECTION. By A. E. Dunstan, B.Sc. (Lond.).
F.C.S.   With 2 Plates and 10 Diagrams.
Cr. 8vo.   2s.

Methuen's Simplified French Texts

Edited by T. R. N. CROFTS, M.A.

One Shilling each.

L'HISTOIRE D'UNE TULIPE. Adapted by T. R.
N.Crofts, M.A.   *Second Edition.*

ABDALLAH.   Adapted by J. A. Wilson.

LA CHANSON DE ROLAND.   Adapted by H.
Rieu, M.A.   *Second Edition.*

MÉMOIRES DE CADICHON.   Adapted by J. F.
Rhoades.

Methuen's Standard Library

In Sixpenny Volumes.

THE STANDARD LIBRARY is a new series of volumes containing the great classics of the
world, and particularly the finest works of English literature. All the great masters will be
represented, either in complete works or in selections.   It is the ambition of the publishers to
place the best books of the Anglo-Saxon race within the reach of every reader, so that the
series may represent something of the diversity and splendour of our English tongue.   The
characteristics of THE STANDARD LIBRARY are four :—1. SOUNDNESS OF TEXT. 2. CHEAPNESS.
3. CLEARNESS OF TYPE.   4. SIMPLICITY.   The books are well printed on good paper at a
price which on the whole is without parallel in the history of publishing.   Each volume contains from 100 to 250 pages, and is issued in paper covers, Crown 8vo, at Sixpence net, or in
cloth gilt at One Shilling net.   In a few cases long books are issued as Double Volumes
or as Treble Volumes.

THE MEDITATIONS OF MARCUS AURELIUS.
The translation is by R. Graves.

SENSE AND SENSIBILITY.   By Jane Austen.

ESSAYS AND COUNSELS and THE NEW
ATLANTIS.   By Francis Bacon, Lord
Verulam.

RELIGIO MEDICI and URN BURIAL.   By
Sir Thomas Browne. The text has been
collated by A. R. Waller.

THE PILGRIM'S PROGRESS.   By John Bunyan.

REFLECTIONS ON THE FRENCH REVOLUTION.
By Edmund Burke.

THE POEMS AND SONGS OF ROBERT BURNS.
Double Volume.

THE ANALOGY OF RELIGION, NATURAL AND
REVEALED.   By Joseph Butler, D.D.

THE POEMS OF THOMAS CHATTERTON.   In 2
volumes.
Vol. I.—Miscellaneous Poems.

[Continued.

METHUEN'S STANDARD LIBRARY—*continued*.

Vol. II.—The Rowley Poems.

THE NEW LIFE AND SONNETS. By Dante. Translated into English by D. G. Rossetti.

TOM JONES. By Henry Fielding. Treble Vol.

CRANFORD. By Mrs. Gaskell.

THE HISTORY OF THE DECLINE AND FALL OF THE ROMAN EMPIRE. By Edward Gibbon. In 7 double volumes.

The Text and Notes have been revised by J. B. Bury, Litt. D., but the Appendices of the more expensive edition are not given.

THE VICAR OF WAKEFIELD. By Oliver Goldsmith.

THE POEMS AND PLAYS OF OLIVER GOLDSMITH.

THE WORKS OF BEN JONSON.

Vol. I.—The Case is Altered. Every Man in His Humour. Every Man out of His Humour.

Vol. II.—Cynthia's Revels; The Poetaster. The text has been collated by H. C. Hart.

THE POEMS OF JOHN KEATS. Double volume. The Text has been collated by E. de Selincourt.

ON THE IMITATION OF CHRIST. By Thomas à Kempis.

The translation is by C. Bigg, DD., Canon of Christ Church.

A SERIOUS CALL TO A DEVOUT AND HOLY LIFE. By William Law.

PARADISE LOST. By John Milton.

EIKONOKLASTES AND THE TENURE OF KINGS AND MAGISTRATES. By John Milton.

UTOPIA AND POEMS. By Sir Thomas More.

THE REPUBLIC OF PLATO. Translated by Sydenham and Taylor. Double Volume. The translation has been revised by W. H. D. Rouse.

THE LITTLE FLOWERS OF ST. FRANCIS. Translated by W. Heywood.

THE WORKS OF WILLIAM SHAKESPEARE. In 10 volumes.

Vol. I.—The Tempest; The Two Gentlemen of Verona; The Merry Wives of Windsor; Measure for Measure; The Comedy of Errors.

Vol. II.—Much Ado About Nothing; Love's Labour's Lost; A Midsummer Night's Dream; The Merchant of Venice; As You Like It.

Vol. III.—The Taming of the Shrew; All's Well that Ends Well; Twelfth Night; The Winter's Tale.

Vol. IV.—The Life and Death of King John; The Tragedy of King Richard the Second; The First Part of King Henry IV.; The Second Part of King Henry IV.

Vol. V.—The Life of King Henry V.; The First Part of King Henry VI.; The Second Part of King Henry VI.

Vol. VI.—The Third Part of King Henry VI.; The Tragedy of King Richard III.; The Famous History of the Life of King Henry VIII.

THE POEMS OF PERCY BYSSHE SHELLEY. In 4 volumes.

Vol. I.—Alastor; The Dæmon of the World; The Revolt of Islam, etc.

The Text has been revised by C. D. Locock.

THE LIFE OF NELSON. By Robert Southey.

THE NATURAL HISTORY AND ANTIQUITIES OF SELBORNE. By Gilbert White.

Textbooks of Technology

Edited by G. F. GOODCHILD, M.A., B.Sc., and G. R. MILLS, M.A.

Fully Illustrated.

HOW TO MAKE A DRESS. By J. A. E. Wood. *Fourth Edition. Cr. 8vo.* 1s. 6d.

CARPENTRY AND JOINERY. By F. C. Webber. *Fifth Edition. Cr. 8vo.* 3s. 6d.

MILLINERY, THEORETICAL AND PRACTICAL. By Clare Hill. *Fourth Edition. Cr. 8vo.* 2s.

AN INTRODUCTION TO THE STUDY OF TEXTILE DESIGN. By Aldred F. Barker. *Demy 8vo.* 7s. 6d.

BUILDERS' QUANTITIES. By H. C. Grubb. *Cr. 8vo.* 4s. 6d.

RÉPOUSSÉ METAL WORK. By A. C. Horth. *Cr. 8vo.* 2s. 6d.

ELECTRIC LIGHT AND POWER: An Introduction to the Study of Electrical Engineering. By E. E. Brooks, B.Sc. (Lond.) Second Master and Instructor of Physics and Electrical Engineering, Leicester Technical School, and W. H. N. James, A.R.C.S., A.I.E.E., Assistant Instructor of Electrical Engineering, Manchester Municipal Technical School. *Cr. 8vo.* 4s. 6d.

ENGINEERING WORKSHOP PRACTICE. By C. C. Allen, Lecturer on Engineering, Municipal Technical Institute, Coventry. With many Diagrams. *Cr. 8vo.* 2s.

Handbooks of Theology

Edited by R. L. OTTLEY, D.D., Professor of Pastoral Theology at Oxford, and Canon of Christ Church, Oxford.

The series is intended, in part, to furnish the clergy and teachers or students of Theology with trustworthy Textbooks, adequately representing the present position of the questions dealt with; in part, to make accessible to the reading public an accurate and concise statement of facts and principles in all questions bearing on Theology and Religion.

THE XXXIX. ARTICLES OF THE CHURCH OF ENGLAND. Edited by E. C. S. Gibson, D.D. *Fifth Edition. Demy 8vo.* 12s. 6d.

AN INTRODUCTION TO THE HISTORY OF RELIGION. By F. B. Jevons, M.A., Litt.D. *Third Edition. Demy 8vo.* 10s. 6d.

THE DOCTRINE OF THE INCARNATION. By R. L. Ottley, D.D. *Third Edition revised. Demy 8vo.* 12s. 6d.

AN INTRODUCTION TO THE HISTORY OF THE CREEDS. By A. E. Burn, D.D. *Demy 8vo.* 10s. 6d.

THE PHILOSOPHY OF RELIGION IN ENGLAND AND AMERICA. By Alfred Caldecott, D.D. *Demy 8vo.* 10s. 6d.

A HISTORY OF EARLY CHRISTIAN DOCTRINE. By J. F. Bethune-Baker, M.A. *Demy 8vo.* 10s. 6d.

The Westminster Commentaries

General Editor, WALTER LOCK, D.D., Warden of Keble College, Dean Ireland's Professor of Exegesis in the University of Oxford.

The object of each commentary is primarily exegetical, to interpret the author's meaning to the present generation. The editors will not deal, except very subordinately, with questions of textual criticism or philology; but, taking the English text in the Revised Version as their basis, they will try to combine a hearty acceptance of critical principles with loyalty to the Catholic Faith.

THE BOOK OF GENESIS. Edited with Introduction and Notes by S. R. Driver, D.D. *Sixth Edition Demy 8vo.* 10s. 6d.

THE BOOK OF JOB. Edited by E. C. S. Gibson, D.D. *Second Edition. Demy 8vo.* 6s.

THE ACTS OF THE APOSTLES. Edited by R. B. Rackham, M.A. *Demy 8vo. Third Edition.* 10s. 6d.

THE FIRST EPISTLE OF PAUL THE APOSTLE TO THE CORINTHIANS. Edited by H. L. Goudge, M.A. *Demy 8vo.* 6s.

THE EPISTLE OF ST. JAMES. Edited with Introduction and Notes by R. J. Knowling, D.D. *Demy 8vo.* 6s.

THE BOOK OF EZEKIEL. Edited H. A. Redpath, M.A., D.Litt. *Demy 8vo.* 10s. 6d.

PART II.—FICTION

Adderley (Hon. and Rev. James), Author of 'Stephen Remarx.' BEHOLD THE DAYS COME. *Second Edition. Cr. 8vo.* 3s. 6d.

Albanesi (E. Maria). SUSANNAH AND ONE OTHER. *Fourth Edition. Cr. 8vo.* 6s.

THE BLUNDER OF AN INNOCENT. *Second Edition. Cr. 8vo.* 6s.

CAPRICIOUS CAROLINE. *Second Edition. Cr. 8vo.* 6s.

LOVE AND LOUISA. *Second Edition. Cr. 8vo.* 6s.

PETER, A PARASITE. *Cr. 8vo.* 6s.

THE BROWN EYES OF MARY. *Third Edition. Cr. 8vo.* 6s.

I KNOW A MAIDEN. *Third Edition. Cr. 8vo.* 6s.

Baget (Richard). A ROMAN MYSTERY. *Third Edition. Cr. 8vo.* 6s.

THE PASSPORT. *Fourth Edition. Cr. 8vo.* 6s.

TEMPTATION. *Fifth Edition. Cr. 8vo.* 6s.

CASTING OF NETS. *Twelfth Edition. Cr. 8vo.* 6s.

DONNA DIANA. *Second Edition. Cr. 8vo.* 6s.

LOVE'S PROXY. *A New Edition. Cr. 8vo.* 6s.

Baring-Gould (S.). ARMINELL. *Fifth Edition. Cr. 8vo.* 6s.

URITH. *Fifth Edition. Cr. 8vo.* 6s.

IN THE ROAR OF THE SEA. *Seventh Edition. Cr. 8vo.* 6s.

CHEAP JACK ZITA. *Fourth Edition. Cr. 8vo.* 6s.

MARGERY OF QUETHER. *Third Edition. Cr. 8vo.* 6s.

THE QUEEN OF LOVE. *Fifth Edition. Cr. 8vo.* 6s.

JACQUETTA. *Third Edition. Cr. 8vo.* 6s.

KITTY ALONE. *Fifth Edition. Cr. 8vo.* 6s.

NOÉMI. Illustrated. *Fourth Edition. Cr. 8vo.* 6s.

THE BROOM-SQUIRE. Illustrated. *Fifth Edition. Cr. 8vo.* 6s.

DARTMOOR IDYLLS. *Cr. 8vo.* 6s.

THE PENNYCOMEQUICKS. *Third Edition. Cr. 8vo.* 6s.

GUAVAS THE TINNER. Illustrated. *Second Edition. Cr. 8vo.* 6s.

DOMITIA. Illustrated. *Cr. 8vo. 6s.*
BLADYS OF THE STEWPONEY. Illustrated. *Second Edition. Cr. 8vo. 6s.*
PABO THE PRIEST. *Cr. 8vo. 6s.*
WINEFRED. Illustrated. *Second Edition. Cr. 8vo. 6s.*
ROYAL GEORGIE. Illustrated. *Cr. 8vo. 6s.*
CHRIS OF ALL SORTS. *Cr. 8vo. 6s.*
IN DEWISLAND. *Second Ed. Cr. 8vo. 6s.*
LITTLE TU'PENNY. *A New Edition. 6d.*
See also Shilling Novels.
Barnett (Edith A.). A WILDERNESS WINNER. *Second Edition. Cr. 8vo. 6s.*
Barr (James). LAUGHING THROUGH A WILDERNESS. *Cr. 8vo. 6s.*
Barr (Robert). IN THE MIDST OF ALARMS. *Third Edition. Cr. 8vo. 6s.*
THE STRONG ARM. *Second Edition. Cr. 8vo. 6s.*
THE MUTABLE MANY. *Third Edition. Cr. 8vo. 6s.*
THE COUNTESS TEKLA. *Fourth Edition. Cr. 8vo. 6s.*
THE LADY ELECTRA. *Second Edition. Cr. 8vo. 6s.*
THE TEMPESTUOUS PETTICOAT. Illustrated. *Third Edition. Cr. 8vo. 6s.*
See also Shilling Novels and S. Crane.
Begbie (Harold). THE ADVENTURES OF SIR JOHN SPARROW. *Cr. 8vo. 6s.*
Belloc (Hilaire). EMMANUEL BURDEN, MERCHANT. With 36 Illustrations by G. K. CHESTERTON. *Second Ed. Cr. 8vo. 6s.*
Benson (E. F.) DODO. *Fifteenth Edition. Cr. 8vo. 6s.*
See also Shilling Novels.
Benson (Margaret). SUBJECT TO VANITY. *Cr. 8vo. 3s. 6d.*
Bretherton (Ralph). THE MILL. *Cr. 8vo. 6s.*
Burke (Barbara). BARBARA GOES TO OXFORD. *Third Edition.*
Burton (J. Bloundelle). THE FATE OF VALSEC. *Cr. 8vo. 6s.*
See also Shilling Novels.
Capes (Bernard), Author of 'The Lake of Wine.' THE EXTRAORDINARY CONFESSIONS OF DIANA PLEASE. *Third Edition. Cr. 8vo. 6s.*
A JAY OF ITALY. *Fourth Ed. Cr. 8vo. 6s.*
LOAVES AND FISHES. *Second Edition. Cr. 8vo. 6s.*
A ROGUE'S TRAGEDY. *Second Edition. Cr. 8vo. 6s.*
THE GREAT SKENE MYSTERY. *Second Edition. Cr. 8vo. 6s.*
Charlton (Randall). MAVE. *Second Edition. Cr. 8vo. 6s.*
Carey (Wymond). LOVE THE JUDGE. *Second Edition. Cr. 8vo. 6s.*
Chesney (Weatherby). THE TRAGEDY OF THE GREAT EMERALD *Cr. 8vo. 6s.*
THE MYSTERY OF A BUNGALOW. *Second Edition. Cr. 8vo. 6s.*
See also Shilling Novels.
Conrad (Joseph). THE SECRET AGENT. *Fourth Edition. Cr. 8vo. 6s.*

Corelli (Marie). A ROMANCE OF TWO WORLDS. *Twenty-Eighth Ed. Cr. 8vo. 6s.*
VENDETTA. *Twenty-Fifth Edition. Cr. 8vo. 6s.*
THELMA. *Thirty-Seventh Ed. Cr. 8vo. 6s.*
ARDATH : THE STORY OF A DEAD SELF. *Eighteenth Edition. Cr. 8vo. 6s.*
THE SOUL OF LILITH. *Fifteenth Edition. Cr. 8vo. 6s.*
WORMWOOD. *Fifteenth Ed. Cr. 8vo. 6s.*
BARABBAS: A DREAM OF THE WORLD'S TRAGEDY. *Forty-second Edition. Cr. 8vo. 6s.*
THE SORROWS OF SATAN. *Fifty-third Edition. Cr. 8vo. 6s.*
THE MASTER CHRISTIAN. *Eleventh Edition. Cr. 8vo. 6s.*
TEMPORAL POWER: A STUDY IN SUPREMACY. *150th Thousand. Cr. 8vo. 6s.*
GOD'S GOOD MAN: A SIMPLE LOVE STORY. *Twelfth Edition.* 144th Thousand. *Cr. 8vo. 6s.*
THE MIGHTY ATOM. *Twenty-sixth Edition. Cr. 8vo. 6s.*
BOY : a Sketch. *Tenth Edition. Cr. 8vo. 6s.*
CAMEOS *Twelfth Edition. Cr. 8vo. 6s.*
Cotes (Mrs. Everard). See Sara Jeannette Duncan.
Cotterell (Constance). THE VIRGIN AND THE SCALES. Illustrated. *Second Edition. Cr. 8vo. 6s.*
Crane (Stephen) and **Barr (Robert).** THE O'RUDDY. *Third Edition. Crown 8vo. 6s.*
Crockett (S. R.), Author of 'The Raiders,' etc. LOCHINVAR. Illustrated. *Third Edition. Cr. 8vo. 6s.*
THE STANDARD BEARER. *Cr. 8vo. 6s.*
Croker (B. M.). THE OLD CANTONMENT. *Cr. 8vo. 6s.*
JOHANNA. *Second Edition. Cr. 8vo. 6s.*
THE HAPPY VALLEY. *Third Edition. Cr. 8vo. 6s.*
A NINE DAYS' WONDER. *Third Edition. Cr. 8vo. 6s.*
PEGGY OF THE BARTONS. *Sixth Edition. Cr. 8vo. 6s.*
ANGEL. *Fourth Edition. Cr. 8vo. 6s.*
A STATE SECRET. *Third Edition. Cr. 8vo. 3s. 6d.*
Crosbie (Mary). DISCIPLES. *Second Ed. Cr. 8vo. 6s.*
Dawson (A. J.). DANIEL WHYTE. *Cr. 8vo. 3s. 6d.*
Deane (Mary). THE OTHER PAWN. *Cr. 8vo. 6s.*
Doyle (A. Conan), Author of 'Sherlock Holmes,' 'The White Company,' etc. ROUND THE RED LAMP. *Tenth Edition. Cr. 8vo. 6s.*
Duncan (Sara Jeannette) (Mrs. Everard Cotes). THOSE DELIGHTFUL AMERICANS. Illustrated. *Third Edition. Cr. 8vo. 6s.* See also Shilling Novels.
Findlater (J. H.). THE GREEN GRAVES OF BALGOWRIE. *Fifth Edition. Cr. 8vo. 6s.*

THE LADDER TO THE STARS. *Second Edition. Cr. 8vo. 6s.*
   See also Shilling Novels.

Findlater (Mary). A NARROW WAY. *Third Edition. Cr. 8vo.. 6s.*
THE ROSE OF JOY. *Third Edition. Cr. 8vo.*
A BLIND BIRD'S NEST. With 8 Illustrations. *Second Edition. Cr. 8vo. 6s.*
   See also Shilling Novels.

Fitzpatrick (K.) THE WEANS AT ROWALLAN. Illustrated. *Second Edition. Cr. 8vo. 6s.*

Francis (M. E.). STEPPING WESTWARD. *Second Edition. Cr. 8vo. 6s.*
MARGERY O' THE MILL. *Third Edition. Cr. 8vo. 6s.*

Fraser (Mrs. Hugh), Author of 'The Stolen Emperor.' THE SLAKING OF THE SWORD. *Second Edition. Cr. 8vo. 6s.*
IN THE SHADOW OF THE LORD. *Third Edition. Crown 8vo. 6s.*

Fry (B. and C. B.). A MOTHER'S SON. *Fifth Edition. Cr. 8vo. 6s.*

Fuller-Maitland (Ella), Author of ' The Day Book of Bethia Hardacre.' BLANCHE ESMEAD. *Second Edition. Cr. 8vo. 6s.*

Gates (Eleanor), Author of 'The Biography of a Prairie Girl.' THE PLOW-WOMAN. *Cr. 8vo. 6s.*

Gerard (Dorothea), Author of ' Lady Baby.' HOLY MATRIMONY. *Second Edition. Cr. 8vo. 6s.*
MADE OF MONEY. *Cr. 8vo. 6s.*
THE BRIDGE OF LIFE. *Cr. 8vo. 6s.*
THE IMPROBABLE IDYL. *Third Edition. Cr. 8vo. 6s.*
   See also Shilling Novels.

Gissing (George), Author of 'Demos,' 'In the Year of Jubilee,' etc. THE TOWN TRAVELLER. *Second Ed. Cr. 8vo. 6s.*
THE CROWN OF LIFE. *Cr. 8vo. 6s.*

Gleig (Charles). BUNTER'S CRUISE. Illustrated. *Cr. 8vo. 3s. 6d.*

Hamilton (M.), Author of 'Cut Laurels.' THE FIRST CLAIM. *Second Edition. Cr. 8vo. 6s.*

Harraden (Beatrice). IN VARYING MOODS. *Fourteenth Edition. Cr. 8vo. 6s.*
HILDA STRAFFORD and THE REMITTANCE MAN. *Twelfth Ed. Cr. 8vo. 6s.*
THE SCHOLAR'S DAUGHTER. *Fourth Edition. Cr. 8vo. 6s.*

Harrod (F.) (Frances Forbes Robertson). THE TAMING OF THE BRUTE. *Cr. 8vo. 6s.*

Herbertson (Agnes G.). PATIENCE DEAN. *Cr. 8vo. 6s.*

Hichens (Robert). THE PROPHET OF BERKELEY SQUARE. *Second Edition. Cr. 8vo. 6s.*
TONGUES OF CONSCIENCE. *Third Edition. Cr. 8vo. 6s.*
FELIX. *Fifth Edition. Cr. 8vo. 6s.*
THE WOMAN WITH THE FAN. *Sixth Edition. Cr. 8vo. 6s.*
BYEWAYS. *Cr. 8vo. 6s.*

THE GARDEN OF ALLAH. *Sixteenth Edition. Cr. 8vo. 6s.*
THE BLACK SPANIEL. *Cr. 8vo. 6s.*
THE CALL OF THE BLOOD. *Seventh Edition. Cr. 8vo. 6s.*

Hope (Anthony). THE GOD IN THE CAR. *Tenth Edition. Cr. 8vo. 6s.*
A CHANGE OF AIR. *Sixth Ed. Cr. 8vo. 6s.*
A MAN OF MARK. *Fifth Ed. Cr. 8vo. 6s.*
THE CHRONICLES OF COUNT ANTONIO. *Sixth Edition. Cr. 8vo. 6s.*
PHROSO. Illustrated by H. R. MILLAR. *Sixth Edition. Cr. 8vo. 6s.*
SIMON DALE. Illustrated. *Seventh Edition. Cr. 8vo. 6s.*
THE KING'S MIRROR. *Fourth Edition. Cr. 8vo. 6s.*
QUISANTE. *Fourth Edition. Cr. 8vo. 6s.*
THE DOLLY DIALOGUES. *Cr. 8vo. 6s.*
A SERVANT OF THE PUBLIC. Illustrated. *Fourth Edition. Cr 8vo. 6s.*
TALES OF TWO PEOPLE. *Third Ed. Cr. 8vo. 6s.*

Hope (Graham), Author of ' A Cardinal and his Conscience,' etc., etc. THE LADY OF LYTE. *Second Edition. Cr. 8vo. 6s.*

Housman (Clemence). THE LIFE OF SIR AGLOVALE DE GALIS. *Cr. 8vo. 6s.*

Hueffer (Ford Madox). AN ENGLISH GIRL. *Second Edition. Cr. 8vo. 6s.*

Hyne (C. J. Cutcliffe), Author of 'Captain Kettle.' MR. HORROCKS, PURSER. *Fourth Edition. Cr. 8vo. 6s.*
PRINCE RUPERT, THE BUCCANEER. Illustrated. *Third Edition. Cr. 8vo. 6s.*

Jacobs (W. W.). MANY CARGOES. *Thirtieth Edition. Cr. 8vo. 3s. 6d.*
SEA URCHINS. *Fourteenth Edition.. Cr. 8vo. 3s. 6d.*
A MASTER OF CRAFT. Illustrated. *Eighth Edition. Cr. 8vo. 3s. 6d.*
LIGHT FREIGHTS. Illustrated. *Seventh Edition. Cr. 8vo. 3s. 6d.*
THE SKIPPER'S WOOING. *Eighth Edition. Cr. 8vo. 3s. 6d.*
DIALSTONE LANE. Illustrated. *Seventh Edition. Cr. 8vo. 3s. 6d.*
ODD CRAFT. Illustrated. *Seventh Edition. Cr. 8vo. 3s. 6d.*
AT SUNWICH PORT. Illustrated. *Eighth Edition. Cr. 8vo. 3s. 6d.*

James (Henry). THE SOFT SIDE. *Second Edition. Cr. 8vo. 6s.*
THE BETTER SORT. *Cr. 8vo. 6s.*
THE AMBASSADORS. *Second Edition. Cr. 8vo. 6s.*
THE GOLDEN BOWL. *Third Edition. Cr. 8vo. 6s.*

Keays (H. A. Mitchell). HE THAT EATETH BREAD WITH ME. *Cr. 8vo. 6s.*

Kester (Vaughan). THE FORTUNES OF THE LANDRAYS. *Cr. 8vo. 6s.*

Lawless (Hon. Emily). WITH ESSEX IN IRELAND. *Cr. 8vo. 6s.*
   See also Shilling Novels.

Le Queux (W.). THE HUNCHBACK OF WESTMINSTER. *Third Ed. Cr. 8vo. 6s.*
THE CLOSED BOOK. *Third Ed. Cr. 8vo. 6s.*

THE VALLEY OF THE SHADOW. Illustrated. *Third Edition. Cr. 8vo. 6s.*

BEHIND THE THRONE *Third Edition. Cr. 8vo. 6s.*

Levett-Yeats (S.). ORRAIN. *Second Edition. Cr. 8vo. 6s.*

London (Jack), Author of 'The Call of the Wild,' 'The Sea Wolf,' etc. WHITE FANG. *Sixth Edition. Cr. 8vo. 6s.*

Lucas (E. V.). LISTENER'S LURE: An Oblique Narration. *Crown 8vo. Fourth Edition. Cr. 8vo. 6s.*

Lyall (Edna). DERRICK VAUGHAN, NOVELIST. *42nd Thousand. Cr. 8vo. 3s. 6d.*

M'Carthy (Justin H.), Author of 'If I were King.' THE LADY OF LOYALTY HOUSE. Illustrated. *Third Edition. Cr. 8vo. 6s.*

THE DRYAD. *Second Edition. Cr. 8vo. 6s.*

Macdonald (Ronald). A HUMAN TRINITY. *Second Edition. Cr. 8vo. 6s.*

Macnaughtan (S.). THE FORTUNE OF CHRISTINA MACNAB. *Fourth Edition. Cr. 8vo. 6s.*

Malet (Lucas). COLONEL ENDERBY'S WIFE. *Fourth Edition. Cr. 8vo. 6s.*

A COUNSEL OF PERFECTION. *New Edition. Cr. 8vo. 6s.*

THE WAGES OF SIN. *Fifteenth Edition. Cr. 8vo. 6s.*

THE CARISSIMA. *Fifth Ed. Cr. 8vo. 6s.*

THE GATELESS BARRIER. *Fourth Edition. Cr. 8vo. 6s.*

THE HISTORY OF SIR RICHARD CALMADY. *Seventh Edition. Cr. 8vo. 6s.* See also Books for Boys and Girls.

Mann (Mrs. M. E.). OLIVIA'S SUMMER. *Second Edition. Cr. 8vo. 6s.*

A LOST ESTATE. *A New Ed. Cr. 8vo. 6s.*

THE PARISH OF HILBY. *A New Edition. Cr. 8vo. 6s.*

THE PARISH NURSE. *Fourth Edition. Cr. 8vo. 6s.*

GRAN'MA'S JANE. *Cr. 8vo. 6s.*

MRS. PETER HOWARD. *Cr. 8vo. 6s.*

A WINTER'S TALE. *A New Edition. Cr. 8vo. 6s.*

ONE ANOTHER'S BURDENS. *A New Edition. Cr. 8vo. 6s.*

ROSE AT HONEYPOT. *Third Ed. Cr. 8vo. 6s.* See also Books for Boys and Girls.

THE MEMORIES OF RONALD LOVE. *Cr. 8vo. 6s.*

THE EGLAMORE PORTRAITS. *Third Edition. Cr. 8vo. 6s.*

THE SHEEP AND THE GOATS. *Third Edition. Cr. 8vo. 6s.*

Marriott (Charles), Author of 'The Column.' GENEVRA. *Second Edition. Cr. 8vo. 6s.*

Marsh (Richard). THE TWICKENHAM PEERAGE. *Second Edition. Cr. 8vo. 6s.*

THE MARQUIS OF PUTNEY. *Second Edition. Cr. 8vo. 6s.*

A DUEL. *Cr. 8vo. 6s.*

IN THE SERVICE OF LOVE. *Third Edition. Cr. 8vo. 6s.*

THE GIRL AND THE MIRACLE. *Third Edition. Cr. 8vo. 6s.* See also Shilling Novels.

Mason (A. E. W.), Author of 'The Four Feathers,' etc. CLEMENTINA. Illustrated. *Second Edition. Cr. 8vo. 6s.*

Mathers (Helen), Author of 'Comin' thro' the Rye.' HONEY. *Fourth Ed. Cr. 8vo. 6s.*

GRIFF OF GRIFFITHSCOURT. *Cr. 8vo. 6s.*

THE FERRYMAN. *Second Edition. Cr. 8vo. 6s.*

TALLY-HO! *Fourth Edition. Cr. 8vo. 6s.*

Maxwell (W. B.), Author of 'The Ragged Messenger.' VIVIEN. *Ninth Edition. Cr. 8vo. 6s.*

THE RAGGED MESSENGER. *Third Edition. Cr. 8vo. 6s.*

FABULOUS FANCIES. *Cr. 8vo. 6s.*

THE GUARDED FLAME. *Seventh Edition. Cr. 8vo. 6s.*

THE COUNTESS OF MAYBURY. *Fourth Edition. Cr. 8vo. 6s.*

ODD LENGTHS. *Second Ed. Cr. 8vo. 6s.*

Meade (L. T.). DRIFT. *Second Edition. Cr. 8vo. 6s.*

RESURGAM. *Cr. 8vo. 6s.*

VICTORY. *Cr. 8vo. 6s.* See also Books for Boys and Girls.

Melton (R.). CÆSAR'S WIFE. *Second Edition. Cr. 8vo. 6s.*

Meredith (Ellis). HEART OF MY HEART. *Cr. 8vo. 6s.*

Miller (Esther). LIVING LIES. *Third Edition. Cr. 8vo. 6s.*

'Miss Molly' (The Author of). THE GREAT RECONCILER. *Cr. 8vo. 6s.*

Mitford (Bertram). THE SIGN OF THE SPIDER. Illustrated. *Sixth Edition. Cr. 8vo. 3s. 6d.*

IN THE WHIRL OF THE RISING. *Third Edition. Cr. 8vo. 6s.*

THE RED DERELICT. *Second Edition. Cr. 8vo. 6s.*

Montresor (F. F.), Author of 'Into the Highways and Hedges.' THE ALIEN. *Third Edition. Cr. 8vo. 6s.*

Morrison (Arthur). TALES OF MEAN STREETS. *Seventh Edition. Cr. 8vo. 6s.*

A CHILD OF THE JAGO. *Fifth Edition. Cr. 8vo. 6s.*

CUNNING MURRELL. *Cr. 8vo. 6s.*

THE HOLE IN THE WALL. *Fourth Edition. Cr. 8vo. 6s.*

DIVERS VANITIES. *Cr. 8vo. 6s.*

Nesbit (E.). (Mrs. E. Bland). THE RED HOUSE. Illustrated. *Fourth Edition. Cr. 8vo. 6s.* See also Shilling Novels.

Norris (W. E.). HARRY AND URSULA. *Second Edition. Cr. 8vo. 6s.*

Ollivant (Alfred). OWD BOB, THE GREY DOG OF KENMUIR. *Tenth Edition. Cr. 8vo. 6s.*

Oppenheim (E. Phillips). MASTER OF MEN. *Fourth Edition. Cr. 8vo. 6s.*

Oxenham (John), Author of 'Barbe of Grand Bayou.' A WEAVER OF WEBS. *Second Edition. Cr. 8vo. 6s.*

THE GATE OF THE DESERT. *Fifth Edition. Cr. 8vo. 6s.*

PROFIT AND LOSS. With a Frontispiece in photogravure by HAROLD COPPING. *Fourth Edition. Cr. 8vo. 6s.*

THE LONG ROAD. With a Frontispiece by HAROLD COPPING. *Fourth Edition. Cr. 8vo. 6s.*

Pain (Barry). LINDLEY KAYS. *Third Edition. Cr. 8vo. 6s.*

Parker (Gilbert). PIERRE AND HIS PEOPLE. *Sixth Edition. Cr. 8vo. 6s.*

MRS. FALCHION. *Fifth Edition. Cr. 8vo. 6s.*

THE TRANSLATION OF A SAVAGE. *Third Edition. Cr. 8vo. 6s.*

THE TRAIL OF THE SWORD. Illustrated. *Ninth Edition. Cr. 8vo. 6s.*

WHEN VALMOND CAME TO PONTIAC: The Story of a Lost Napoleon. *Sixth Edition. Cr. 8vo. 6s.*

AN ADVENTURER OF THE NORTH. The Last Adventures of 'Pretty Pierre.' *Third Edition. Cr. 8vo. 6s.*

THE SEATS OF THE MIGHTY. Illustrated. *Fifteenth Edition. Cr. 8vo. 6s.*

THE BATTLE OF THE STRONG: a Romance of Two Kingdoms. Illustrated. *Sixth Edition. Cr. 8vo. 6s.*

THE POMP OF THE LAVILETTES. *Third Edition. Cr. 8vo. 3s. 6d.*

Pemberton (Max). THE FOOTSTEPS OF A THRONE. Illustrated. *Third Edition. Cr. 8vo. 6s.*

I CROWN THEE KING. With Illustrations by Frank Dadd and A. Forrestier. *Cr. 8vo. 6s.*

Phillpotts (Eden). LYING PROPHETS. *Third Edition. Cr. 8vo. 6s.*

CHILDREN OF THE MIST. *Fifth Edition. Cr. 8vo. 6s.*

THE HUMAN BOY. With a Frontispiece. *Fourth Edition. Cr. 8vo. 6s.*

SONS OF THE MORNING. *Second Edition. Cr. 8vo. 6s.*

THE RIVER. *Third Edition. Cr. 8vo. 6s.*

THE AMERICAN PRISONER. *Fourth Edition. Cr. 8vo. 6s.*

THE SECRET WOMAN. *Fourth Edition. Cr. 8vo. 6s.*

KNOCK AT A VENTURE. With a Frontispiece. *Third Edition. Cr. 8vo. 6s.*

THE PORTREEVE. *Fourth Ed. Cr. 8vo. 6s.*

THE POACHER'S WIFE. *Second Edition. Cr. 8vo. 6s.*

See also Shilling Novels.

Pickthall (Marmaduke). SAID THE FISHERMAN. *Sixth Ed. Cr. 8vo. 6s.*

BRENDLE. *Second Edition. Cr. 8vo. 6s.*

THE HOUSE OF ISLAM. *Third Edition. Cr. 8vo. 6s.*

'Q,' Author of 'Dead Man's Rock.' THE WHITE WOLF. *Second Ed. Cr. 8vo. 6s.*

THE MAYOR OF TROY. *Fourth Edition. Cr. 8vo. 6s.*

MERRY GARDEN AND OTHER STORIES. *Cr. 8vo. 6s.*

MAJOR VIGOUREUX. *Third Edition. Cr. 8vo. 6s.*

Rawson (Maud Stepney), Author of 'A Lady of the Regency.' 'The Labourer's Comedy,' etc. THE ENCHANTED GARDEN. *Fourth Edition. Cr. 8vo. 6s.*

Rhys (Grace). THE WOOING OF SHEILA. *Second Edition. Cr. 8vo. 6s.*

Ridge (W. Pett). LOST PROPERTY. *Second Edition. Cr. 8vo. 6s.*

ERB. *Second Edition. Cr. 8vo. 6s.*

A SON OF THE STATE. *Second Edition. Cr. 8vo. 3s. 6d.*

A BREAKER OF LAWS. *A New Edition. Cr. 8vo. 3s. 6d.*

MRS. GALER'S BUSINESS. Illustrated. *Second Edition. Cr. 8vo. 6s.*

SECRETARY TO BAYNE, M.P. *Cr. 8vo. 3s. 6d.*

THE WICKHAMSES. *Fourth Edition. Cr. 8vo. 6s.*

NAME OF GARLAND. *Third Edition. Cr. 8vo. 6s.*

Roberts (C. G. D.). THE HEART OF THE ANCIENT WOOD. *Cr. 8vo. 3s. 6d.*

Russell (W. Clark). MY DANISH SWEETHEART. Illustrated. *Fifth Edition. Cr. 8vo. 6s.*

HIS ISLAND PRINCESS. Illustrated. *Second Edition. Cr. 6vo. 6s.*

ABANDONED. *Second Edition. Cr. 8vo. 6s.*

See also Books for Boys and Girls.

Sergeant (Adeline). BARBARA'S MONEY. *Cr. 8vo. 6s.*

THE PROGRESS OF RACHAEL. *Cr. 8vo. 6s.*

THE MYSTERY OF THE MOAT. *Second Edition. Cr. 8vo. 6s.*

THE COMING OF THE RANDOLPHS. *Cr. 8vo. 6s.*

See also Shilling Novels.

Shannon. (W. F. THE MESS DECK. *Cr. 8vo. 3s. 6d.*

See also Shilling Novels.

Shelley (Bertha). ENDERBY. *Third Ed. Cr. 8vo. 6s.*

Sidgwick (Mrs. Alfred), Author of 'Cynthia's Way.' THE KINSMAN. With 8 Illustrations by C. E. BROCK. *Third Ed. Cr. 8vo. 6s.*

Sonnichsen (Albert). DEEP-SEA VAGABONDS. *Cr. 8vo. 6s.*

Sunbury (George). THE HA'PENNY MILLIONAIRE. *Cr. 8vo. 3s. 6d.*

Urquhart (M.), A TRAGEDY IN COMMONPLACE. *Second Ed. Cr. 8vo. 6s.*

Waineman (Paul). THE SONG OF THE FOREST. *Cr. 8vo. 6s.*

THE BAY OF LILACS. *Second Edition. Cr. 8vo. 6s.*

See also Shilling Novels.

Waltz (E. C.). THE ANCIENT LANDMARK: A Kentucky Romance. *Cr. 8vo. 6s.*

Watson (H. B. Marriott). ALARUMS AND EXCURSIONS. *Cr. 8vo. 6s.*
CAPTAIN FORTUNE. *Third Edition. Cr. 8vo. 6s.*
TWISTED EGLANTINE. With 8 Illustrations by FRANK CRAIG. *Third Edition. Cr. 8vo. 6s.*
THE HIGH TOBY. With a Frontispiece. *Third Edition. Cr. 8vo. 6s.*
A MIDSUMMER DAY'S DREAM. *Third Edition. Crown 8vo. 6s.* See also Shilling Novels.
Wells (H. G.). THE SEA LADY. *Cr. 8vo. 6s.*
Weyman (Stanley), Author of 'A Gentleman of France.' UNDER THE RED ROBE. With Illustrations by R. C. WOODVILLE. *Twenty-First Edition. Cr. 8vo. 6s.*
White (Stewart E.), Author of 'The Blazed Trail.' CONJUROR'S HOUSE. A Romance of the Free Trail. *Second Edition. Cr. 8vo. 6s.*
White (Percy). THE SYSTEM. *Third Edition. Cr. 8vo. 6s.*
Williams (Margery). THE BAR. *Cr. 8vo. 6s.*

Williamson (Mrs. C. N.), Author of 'The Barnstormers.' THE ADVENTURE OF PRINCESS SYLVIA. *Second Edition. Cr. 8vo. 6s.*
THE WOMAN WHO DARED. *Cr. 8vo. 6s.*
THE SEA COULD TELL. *Second Edition. Cr. 8vo. 6s.*
THE CASTLE OF THE SHADOWS. *Third Edition. Cr. 8vo. 6s.*
PAPA. *Cr. 8vo. 6s.*
Williamson (C. N. and A. M.). THE LIGHTNING CONDUCTOR: Being the Romance of a Motor Car. Illustrated. *Seventeenth Edition. Cr. 8vo. 6s.*
THE PRINCESS PASSES. Illustrated. *Ninth Edition. Cr. 8vo. 6s.*
MY FRIEND THE CHAUFFEUR. With 16 Illustrations. *Ninth Edit. Cr. 8vo. 6s.*
THE CAR OF DESTINY AND ITS ERRAND IN SPAIN. *Fourth Edition.* Illustrated.
LADY BETTY ACROSS THE WATER. *Ninth Edition. Cr. 8vo. 6s.*
THE BOTOR CHAPERON *Fourth Ed. Cr. 8vo. 6s.*
Wyllarde (Dolf), Author of 'Uriah the Hittite.' THE PATHWAY OF THE PIONEER (Nous Autres). *Fourth Edition. Cr. 8vo. 6s.*

Methuen's Shilling Novels

Cr. 8vo. Cloth, 1s. net.

Author of 'Miss Molly.' THE GREAT RECONCILER.
Balfour (Andrew). VENGEANCE IS MINE.
TO ARMS.
Baring-Gould (S.). MRS. CURGENVEN OF CURGENVEN.
DOMITIA.
THE FROBISHERS.
CHRIS OF ALL SORTS.
DARTMOOR IDYLLS.
Barlow (Jane), Author of 'Irish Idylls.' FROM THE EAST UNTO THE WEST.
A CREEL OF IRISH STORIES.
THE FOUNDING OF FORTUNES.
THE LAND OF THE SHAMROCK.
Barr (Robert). THE VICTORS.
Bartram (George). THIRTEEN EVENINGS.
Benson (E. F.), Author of 'Dodo.' THE CAPSINA.
Bowles (G. Stewart). A STRETCH OFF THE LAND.
Brooke (Emma). THE POET'S CHILD.
Bullock (Shan F.). THE BARRYS.
THE CHARMER.
THE SQUIREEN.
THE RED LEAGUERS.
Burton (J. Bloundelle). THE CLASH OF ARMS.
DENOUNCED.
FORTUNE'S MY FOE.
A BRANDED NAME.

Capes (Bernard). AT A WINTER'S FIRE.
Chesney (Weatherby). THE BAPTIST RING.
THE BRANDED PRINCE.
THE FOUNDERED GALLEON.
JOHN TOPP.
THE MYSTERY OF A BUNGALOW.
Clifford (Mrs. W. K.). A FLASH OF SUMMER.
Cobb, Thomas. A CHANGE OF FACE.
Collingwood (Harry). THE DOCTOR OF THE 'JULIET.'
Cornford (L. Cope). SONS OF ADVERSITY.
Cotterell (Constance). THE VIRGIN AND THE SCALES.
Crane (Stephen). WOUNDS IN THE RAIN.
Denny (C. E.). THE ROMANCE OF UPFOLD MANOR.
Dickinson (Evelyn). THE SIN OF ANGELS.
Dickson (Harris). THE BLACK WOLF'S BREED.
Duncan (Sara J.). THE POOL IN THE DESERT.
A VOYAGE OF CONSOLATION. Illustrated.
Embree (C. F.). A HEART OF FLAME. Illustrated.
Fenn (G. Manville). AN ELECTRIC SPARK.
A DOUBLE KNOT.

Findlater (Jane H.).   A DAUGHTER OF STRIFE.

Fitzstephen (G.).   MORE KIN THAN KIND.

Fletcher (J. S.).   DAVID MARCH.
LUCIAN THE DREAMER.

Forrest (R. E.).   THE SWORD OF AZRAEL.

Francis (M. E.).   MISS ERIN.

Gallon (Tom).   RICKERBY'S FOLLY.

Gerard (Dorothea).   THINGS THAT HAVE HAPPENED.
THE CONQUEST OF LONDON.
THE SUPREME CRIME.

Gilchrist (R. Murray).   WILLOWBRAKE.

Glanville (Ernest).   THE DESPATCH RIDER.
THE KLOOF BRIDE.
THE INCA'S TREASURE.

Gordon (Julien).   MRS. CLYDE.
WORLD'S PEOPLE.

Goss (C. F.).   THE REDEMPTION OF DAVID CORSON.

Gray (E. M'Queen).   MY STEWARD-SHIP.

Hales (A. G.).   JAIR THE APOSTATE.

Hamilton (Lord Ernest).   MARY HAMILTON.

Harrison (Mrs. Burton).   A PRINCESS OF THE HILLS.   Illustrated.

Hooper (I.).   THE SINGER OF MARLY.

Hough (Emerson).   THE MISSISSIPPI BUBBLE.

'Iota' (Mrs. Caffyn).   ANNE MAULE-VERER.

Jepson (Edgar).   THE KEEPERS OF THE PEOPLE.

Keary (C. F.).   THE JOURNALIST.

Kelly (Florence Finch).   WITH HOOPS OF STEEL.

Langbridge (V.) and Bourne (C. H.).
THE VALLEY OF INHERITANCE.

Linden (Annie).   A WOMAN OF SENTIMENT.

Lorimer (Norma).   JOSIAH'S WIFE.

Lush (Charles K.).   THE AUTOCRATS.

Macdonell (Anne).   THE STORY OF TERESA.

Macgrath (Harold).   THE PUPPET CROWN.

Mackie (Pauline Bradford).   THE VOICE IN THE DESERT.

Marsh (Richard).   THE SEEN AND THE UNSEEN.
GARNERED.
A METAMORPHOSIS.
MARVELS AND MYSTERIES.
BOTH SIDES OF THE VEIL.

Mayall (J. W.).   THE CYNIC AND THE SYREN.

Meade (L. T.).   RESURGAM.

Monkhouse (Allan).   LOVE IN A LIFE.

Moore (Arthur).   THE KNIGHT PUNCTILIOUS.

Nesbit, E. (Mrs. Blan ARY SENSE.

Norris (W. E.).   AN C MATTHEW AUSTIN.
THE DESPOTIC LAI

Oliphant (Mrs.).   THI SIR ROBERT'S FORT
THE TWO MARY'S.

Pendered (M. L.).   Al

Penny (Mrs. Frank).   AGE.

Phillpotts (Eden).   HOURS.
FANCY FREE.

Pryce (Richard).   T WOMAN.

Randall (John).   J BUTTON.

Raymond (Walter).   LING.

Rayner (Olive Pratt).

Rhys (Grace).   THE LAGE.

Rickert (Edith).   OUT SWAMP.

Roberton (M. H.).   A GA

Russell, (W. Clark).

Saunders (Marshall).   LITTE.

Sergeant (Adeline).   ACCUSER.
BARBARA'S MONEY.
THE ENTHUSIAST.
A GREAT LADY.
THE LOVE THAT O'
THE MASTER OF Bl
UNDER SUSPICION.
THE YELLOW DIAM
THE MYSTERY OF '

Shannon (W. F.).   JI

Stephens (R. N.).   AN KING.

Strain (E. H.).   ELMSl

Stringer (Arthur).   TH

Stuart (Esmè).   CHR:
A WOMAN OF FORT

Sutherland (Duchess AND THE NEXT.

Swan (Annie).   LOVE

Swift (Benjamin).   SC SIREN CITY.

Tanqueray (Mrs. B. N QUAKER.

Thompson (Vance).   S LIFE.

Trafford-Taunton (Mr DOMINION.

Upward (Allen).   ATH

Walneman (Paul).   A FINLAND.
BY A FINNISH LAK

Watson (H. B. Marrio OF HAPPY CHANC

'Zack.'   TALES OF DU

Books for Boys and Girls
Illustrated. Crown 8vo. 3s. 6d.

THE GETTING WELL OF DOROTHY. By Mrs. W. K. Clifford. *Second Edition.*

ONLY A GUARD-ROOM DOG. By Edith E. Cuthell.

THE DOCTOR OF THE JULIET. By Harry Collingwood.

LITTLE PETER. By Lucas Malet. *Second Edition.*

MASTER ROCKAFELLAR'S VOYAGE. By W. Clark Russell. *Third Edition.*

THE SECRET OF MADAME DE MONLUC. By the Author of "Mdlle. Mori."

SYD BELTON : Or, the Boy who would not go to Sea. By G. Manville Fenn.

THE RED GRANGE. By Mrs. Molesworth.

A GIRL OF THE PEOPLE. By L. T. Meade. *Second Edition.*

HEPSY GIPSY. By L. T. Meade. 2s. 6d.

THE HONOURABLE MISS. By L. T. Meade. *Second Edition.*

THREE WAS ONCE A PRINCE. By Mrs. M. E. Mann.

WHEN ARNOLD COMES HOME. By Mrs. M. E. Mann.

The Novels of Alexandre Dumas
Price 6d. Double Volumes, 1s.

ACTÉ.

THE ADVENTURES OF CAPTAIN PAMPHILE.

AMAURY.

THE BIRD OF FATE.

THE BLACK TULIP.

THE CASTLE OF EPPSTEIN.

CATHERINE BLUM.

CÉCILE.

THE CHEVALIER D'HARMENTAL. Double volume.

CHICOT THE JESTER. Being the first part of The Lady of Monsoreau.

CONSCIENCE.

THE CONVICT'S SON.

THE CORSICAN BROTHERS ; and OTHO THE ARCHER.

CROP-EARED JACQUOT.

THE FENCING MASTER.

FERNANDE.

GABRIEL LAMBERT.

GEORGES.

THE GREAT MASSACRE. Being the first part of Queen Margot.

HENRI DE NAVARRE. Being the second part of Queen Margot.

HÉLÈNE DE CHAVERNY. Being the first part of the Regent's Daughter.

LOUISE DE LA VALLIÈRE. Being the first part of THE VICOMTE DE BRAGELONNE. Double Volume.

MAITRE ADAM.

THE MAN IN THE IRON MASK. Being the second part of THE VICOMTE DE BRAGELONNE. Double volume.

THE MOUTH OF HELL.

NANON. Double volume.

PAULINE ; PASCAL BRUNO ; and BONTEKOE.

PÈRE LA RUINE.

THE PRINCE OF THIEVES.

THE REMINISCENCES OF ANTONY.

ROBIN HOOD.

THE SNOWBALL and SULTANETTA.

SYLVANDIRE.

TALES OF THE SUPERNATURAL.

THE THREE MUSKETEERS. With a long Introduction by Andrew Lang. Double volume.

TWENTY YEARS AFTER. Double volume.

THE WILD DUCK SHOOTER.

THE WOLF-LEADER.

Methuen's Sixpenny Books

Albanesi (E. M.). LOVE AND LOUISA.

Austen (Jane). PRIDE AND PRE-JUDICE.

Bagot (Richard). A ROMAN MYSTERY.

Balfour (Andrew). BY STROKE OF SWORD.

Baring-Gould (S.). FURZE BLOOM.

CHEAP JACK ZITA.

KITTY ALONE.

URITH.

THE BROOM SQUIRE.

IN THE ROAR OF THE SEA.

NOÉMI.

A BOOK OF FAIRY TALES. Illustrated.

LITTLE TU'PENNY.

THE FROBISHERS.

WINEFRED.

Barr (Robert). JENNIE BAXTER, JOURNALIST.

IN THE MIDST OF ALARMS.

THE COUNTESS TEKLA.

THE MUTABLE MANY.

Benson (E. F.). DODO.

Brontë (Charlotte). SHIRLEY.

Brownell (C. L.). THE HEART OF JAPAN.

Burton (J. Bloundelle). ACROSS THE SALT SEAS.

Caffyn (Mrs.), ('Iota'). ANNE MAULE-VERER.

Capes (Bernard). THE LAKE OF WINE.

Clifford (Mrs. W. K.). A FLASH OF SUMMER.

MRS. KEITH'S CRIME.

Corbett (Julian). A BUSINESS IN GREAT WATERS.

Croker (Mrs. B. M.). PEGGY OF THE HARTONS.

A STATE SECRET.

ANGEL.
JOHANNA.
Dante (Alighieri). THE VISION OF DANTE (Cary).
Doyle (A. Conan). ROUND THE RED LAMP.
Duncan (Sara Jeannette). A VOYAGE OF CONSOLATION.
THOSE DELIGHTFUL AMERICANS.
Eliot (George). THE MILL ON THE FLOSS.
Findlater (Jane H.). THE GREEN GRAVES OF BALGOWRIE.
Gallon (Tom). RICKERBY'S FOLLY.
Gaskell (Mrs.). CRANFORD.
MARY BARTON.
NORTH AND SOUTH.
Gerard (Dorothea). HOLY MATRI-MONY.
THE CONQUEST OF LONDON.
MADE OF MONEY.
Gissing (George). THE TOWN TRAVEL-LER.
THE CROWN OF LIFE.
Glanville (Ernest). THE INCA'S TREASURE.
THE KLOOF BRIDE.
Gleig (Charles). BUNTER'S CRUISE.
Grimm (The Brothers). GRIMM'S FAIRY TALES. Illustrated.
Hope (Anthony). A MAN OF MARK.
A CHANGE OF AIR.
THE CHRONICLES OF COUNT ANTONIO.
PHROSO.
THE DOLLY DIALOGUES.
Hornung (E. W.). DEAD MEN TELL NO TALES.
Ingraham (J. H.). THE THRONE OF DAVID.
Le Queux (W.). THE HUNCHBACK OF WESTMINSTER.
Levett-Yeats (S. K.). THE TRAITOR'S WAY.
Linton (E. Lynn). THE TRUE HIS-TORY OF JOSHUA DAVIDSON.
Lyall (Edna). DERRICK VAUGHAN.
Malet (Lucas). THE CARISSIMA.
A COUNSEL OF PERFECTION.
Mann (Mrs. M. E.). MRS. PETER HOWARD.
A LOST ESTATE.
THE CEDAR STAR.
ONE ANOTHER'S BURDENS.
Marchmont (A. W.). MISER HOAD-LEY'S SECRET.
A MOMENT'S ERROR.
Marryat (Captain). PETER SIMPLE.
JACOB FAITHFUL.
Marsh (Richard). THE TWICKENHAM PEERAGE.
THE GODDESS.

THE JOSS.
A METAMORPHOSIS.
Mason (A. E. W.). CLEMENTINA.
Mathers (Helen). HONEY.
GRIFF OF GRIFFITHSCOURT.
SAM'S SWEETHEART.
Meade (Mrs. L. T.). DRIFT.
Mitford (Bertram). THE SIGN OF THE SPIDER.
Montresor (F. F.). THE ALIEN.
Morrison (Arthur). THE HOLE IN THE WALL.
Nesbit (E.). THE RED HOUSE.
Norris (W. E.). HIS GRACE.
GILES INGILBY.
THE CREDIT OF THE COUNTY.
LORD LEONARD.
MATTHEW AUSTIN.
CLARISSA FURIOSA.
Oliphant (Mrs.). THE LADY'S WALK.
SIR ROBERT'S FORTUNE.
THE PRODIGALS.
Oppenheim (E. Phillips). MASTER OF MEN.
Parker (Gilbert). THE POMP OF THE LAVILETTES.
WHEN VALMOND CAME TO PONTIAC.
THE TRAIL OF THE SWORD.
Pemberton (Max). THE FOOTSTEPS OF A THRONE.
I CROWN THEE KING.
Phillpotts (Eden). THE HUMAN BOY.
CHILDREN OF THE MIST.
'Q.' THE WHITE WOLF.
Ridge (W. Pett). A SON OF THE STATE.
LOST PROPERTY.
GEORGE AND THE GENERAL.
Russell (W. Clark). A MARRIAGE AT SEA.
ABANDONED.
MY DANISH SWEETHEART.
HIS ISLAND PRINCESS.
Sergeant (Adeline). THE MASTER OF BEECHWOOD.
BARBARA'S MONEY.
THE YELLOW DIAMOND.
THE LOVE THAT OVERCAME.
Surtees (R. S.). HANDLEY CROSS. Illustrated.
MR. SPONGE'S SPORTING TOUR. Illustrated.
ASK MAMMA. Illustrated.
Walford (Mrs. L. B.). MR. SMITH.
COUSINS.
THE BABY'S GRANDMOTHER.
Wallace (General Lew). BEN-HUR.
THE FAIR GOD.
Watson (H. B. Marriot). THE ADVEN-TURERS.
Weekes (A. B.). PRISONERS OF WAR.
White (Percy). A PASSIONATE PILGRIM.

www.ingramcontent.com/pod-product-compliance
Lightning Source LLC
Chambersburg PA
CBHW021437020726
47499CB00006BA/2032